LEAGUE OF GALLIZE SHIFTERS

GRAY WOLF MATE

DIANNA LOVE

GRAY WOLF MATE
League of Gallize Shifters series

Shifters came out to the public eight years ago and, since then, the world has never been the same for many.

Tess Janver and Cole Cavanaugh fell deeply in love in college ... then he disappeared without a word. She feared the worst, or so she'd thought. After seven years, he returns as a beefed up version of his former self. That's not the only thing different. As someone working in a preternatural criminal investigation unit and the daughter of a senator determined to rid the world of dangerous shifters, Tess is caught between performing her duty to humans, protecting the only family she has left and risking her heart to a man who once destroyed it.

Cole had no choice in becoming a Gallize shifter and now faces a deadline from a fatal mating curse he can't stop. The only woman he's ever loved is human and wouldn't survive bonding with him. He never planned on Tess finding out he was a wolf shifter, but she's in danger from a rogue pack. He's not leaving until she's safe ... and he has a chance to redeem himself in her eyes before his time is up.

Dedication

This book is for Joyce Ann McLaughlin who is generous of soul and always willing to help authors and readers everywhere.
I appreciate you so much.

League of Gallize Shifters:
GRAY WOLF MATE
MATING A GRIZZLY (2018)

CHAPTER 1

Cole Cavanaugh tuned his sensitive wolf hearing to every sound along this southeast corner area of metropolitan Spartanburg. Quiet for a Monday night, but this wasn't exactly a party area and he was not here for social activity.

He couldn't risk being caught off guard and blow this mission.

Time was short. For him, anyhow.

Steady rain had started coming down hours ago, before dark. Just a sign of spring showing up. It reminded him of a sweet female voice telling him spring showers would bring May flowers.

That had been back when he was human and in love with a human woman.

Not the time to dial up that memory, Cavanaugh.

Ignoring the rain, he kept scouting for other predators stalking the night who might pick up his scent in spite of the weather.

As a Gallize wolf shifter, he included himself in the category of predators. Not all Gallize were wolves, but every one was just as dangerous as Cole.

Sure, he fought with the good guys, protecting humans, law-abiding shifters and his Gallize teammates, but he was no choirboy. He'd been trained to kill from the moment he finally took control of his raging wolf.

That had been the month he turned twenty, nine months after discovering he no longer belonged to the human race.

At twenty-six, he accepted what he couldn't change.

A sharp pain drove through his chest. He stopped short and hissed under his breath at Gray Wolf, "Back down, dammit."

Wasted words. The beast who shared his body wanted out to prowl and hated being denied. He could hear Cole speak, out loud or silently, but generally ignored him unless they were working as one, with the same goal.

That hadn't happened in more than two weeks and might not ever again.

Catching his breath, Cole yanked back control, gritted his teeth and continued. It would be over for him and Gray Wolf soon, but right now they had a mission to complete.

He wasn't sure which one would be more relieved when the end came.

Water dripped off the bill of the black Carolina Panthers ball cap he'd worn for tonight. The constant drizzle muffled sound for humans, but not so much for someone like him. He wouldn't be the only shifter walking these streets in human form this late in the evening.

Things had changed drastically in the human world from eight years ago, when an undercover reporter—a jackal shifter—exposed the preternatural community to the world. Cole had felt the same shock as every other citizen and could admit he'd experienced a primal fear when battles broke out across the US, then in other countries. Frightened humans hunted the shifters, even those who had threatened no one. Angry shifters retaliated.

Nine bloody weeks later, a ceasefire was called and parties from each group met to create a tentative agreement.

Then the Power Barons showed up.

They were five legendary mages who'd made a pact early in the game, forming political alliances with humans before *their* kind ended up exposed and attacked, too. The Power Barons negotiated deals with heads of the major human governments, eventually proving there could be something worse than a person who grew claws and fur.

Some days the US reminded Cole of the old west, where towns lived through a roller coaster ride of peaceful days and bloody battles.

Did the jackal shifters care that one of theirs had exposed the preternatural world, putting everyone at risk?

No. They had no conscience when it came to making a dollar, which was why most of them were mercs.

Cole hoped that jackal bastard who started this mess had enjoyed his money for the three days he'd lived after earning it before an alpha lion shifter hunted down the jackal.

Were the Power Barons all *really* mages? Cole had no idea, but that was the story floated through the media. Those five now formed a ruling body, which governed any non-shifter being with extraordinary powers.

The US and other national governments echoed a common message that they considered the Power Barons an ally.

Politicians would join with the devil if they thought he could guarantee they remained in office.

Humans had no idea just who could do what in Cole's world, much less the extent of terror the Power Barons were capable of committing under the guise of playing protectors.

He and Tess had sat staring at the carnage when the first images of confirmed shifters were televised. His initial concern had been finding a way to protect the woman who was his world.

Those college days belonged to another man.

A human man.

Cole swallowed and grunted at another push from Gray Wolf.

Our mate, rumbled from the beast.

"No." He didn't want Gray Wolf getting worked up, so he pushed him back on track. "Pay attention or we'll get killed."

The beast calmed again, but for how long?

He shook off the morose direction of his thoughts and kept his head down, eyes up and alert.

If one of the Black River wolf pack caught Cole before he found the rogue pack's meet point tonight, he'd pay the price for being a lone wolf in the wrong place at the wrong time.

As a Gallize shifter, he could handle three or four on his own.

But that was in a fair fight.

Black River pack members used the drugs they peddled, some of which supposedly enhanced strength for any type of shifter. Rumors flew that they had concoctions capable of taking down a shifter elephant, if there was such a thing. Also, the Black River pack generally operated in large groups.

Cole had two additional Gallize team members in the area, but they would be well hidden.

For now, he just needed to make the most of the tip their boss had received ninety minutes ago. He and his two teammates had been sent here to be on site and ready if the call came.

Hunching his shoulders so he appeared nonthreatening to any eyes on him, he plodded across the dark street to the next corner.

He'd like to be excited about gaining a break in this case and at the chance to find his missing teammate, Sammy Dubois, but concern clawed across Cole's neck over one small detail of the tip.

Their resource claimed Sammy had been fingered for a recent double homicide—the murder of a honeymooning couple.

Cole had known Sammy for seven years. They'd fought side by side for six of those years, putting their lives on the line for humans.

Sammy had been his Gallize mentor and was a deadly bear shifter.

Now Sammy supposedly had turned into a murderer overnight and joined up with the Black River wolf pack that made and sold dangerous synthetic drugs in the US.

Neither of those two things fit the man Cole knew. Plus, wolf packs didn't take in other animals.

But Sammy had gone missing four days ago, right before a young couple hiking in the Nantahala National Park was found ripped to pieces by a grizzly, based on forensic evidence. Justin "Herc" Labeau, another grizzly shifter on their team, had confirmed the scent on the bodies as Sammy's. But Justin quickly pointed out that the scent hadn't been as strong as he'd expect.

As Gallize bear shifters, Justin and Sammy had been friends a long time, which had to make this just as hard for him as for Cole.

Had the Black River pack set up Sammy for the killing?

Just one more in a long line of questions Cole had about Sammy joining a wolf pack.

A voice coming through Cole's comm unit broke into his thoughts. *"Smokey in place and eyes on the picnic."*

That would be Justin letting Cole know he was in a high point position where he could watch the roof of the warehouse being used as a food bank.

Cole replied, "Copy that." He kept strolling slowly, waiting for his other team member, Rory Wallace, to check in.

"Hobbes on site and eyes on the porch."

That meant Rory was set up on the backside of the building, but as a jaguar shifter, the only thing he had in common with the cartoon tiger was claws and a tail.

If they were in animal form, they could communicate telepathically. For team communication while in human forms, their Gallize tech department had developed unique radio systems that transmitted their words mixed with a loud, irritating noise intended to damage an eavesdropping shifter's hearing.

Cole and his team wore headgear that filtered out everything but their words.

Just before the next corner, he paused at the sight of a homeless man tucked into the narrow doorway of a closed business. The balled up human shivered in spite of the moderate temperature. The skinny old guy's threadbare shirt and pants were no defense against a bone-chilling rain. His baggy pants were soaked all the way up his thighs.

One sleeve had ripped half off, exposing the tattoo of an eagle, a world globe and an anchor on that bicep.

US Marine Corp.

It didn't matter which division of the military this guy had come from. He'd served his country and deserved better.

Seeing the poor soul in this condition gutted Cole. He'd fought alongside soldiers who hadn't known the special unit supporting them had been made up of shifters with a better chance of surviving if someone had to take a bullet.

Many times he'd wanted to inform them, but the military leaders who knew about shifters did not want their identities known.

Terrorists were better accepted than shifters.

Those human soldiers had raced into danger, knowing it might be their last day on earth.

Shit. Cole couldn't stay to get this guy help right now, like so many others he'd gotten off the streets, but neither could he leave him in this condition. He dug out cash from his jeans and shoved it into the pocket of his custom-designed windbreaker, then shrugged out of the garment.

The boss would dock his pay for it and chew his ass for taking it off.

Fine.

Cole draped the temporary cover over the old guy and whispered, "I'll be back later."

He hadn't expected a reply and didn't get one.

Rain quickly saturated his dark T-shirt and jeans, but his body ran hot thanks to Gray Wolf. To be honest, he welcomed the cool relief on his skin. He'd been ordered to wear the windbreaker because it had an inner liner similar to Microlattice, a synthetic, high-tech material constructed of very small, interconnected, hollow tubes. The lightest metal developed, supposedly, and impervious to a tactical blade.

Created in a similar fashion, the middle layer of his windbreaker was intended to prevent sharp claws from slicing open the arms and chest of a human body.

That wouldn't be a problem as long as Cole didn't actually engage with shifters while in human form.

If he did, well, he wasn't just a shifter and Gray Wolf wasn't just a wolf. Gallize shifters came with a few extra bells and whistles. In Cole's case, he had the ability to push his preternatural power to an even higher level for a short period when needed for battle.

You can still die if the enemy rips out your heart.

Sammy's words bounced around in Cole's head, reminding him that while the Gallize were harder to kill than most shifters, they were not immortal.

A harder downpour slapped the street and sidewalk by the time he reached the last block leading up to the building. Pathetic light from streetlamps managed to poke through the weather.

Keeping his voice soft when he spoke into his comm, Cole said, "Big Bad with eyes on the cottage," letting his team know he was in place. From this side of the street, he could observe the overhead door used for truck access.

Rory confirmed then said, *"No lights on the porch."*

Justin followed up with, *"Quiet here, too. That hobo better not be playing games."*

Justin had voiced concerns about the snitch, Sonic, who was human. If Sonic had fed them good information, they'd have action in the next ten minutes.

Cole respected Justin's opinion, but Sonic had not given them a reason to doubt him. Yet. Sonic wore a silver skull earring and sported skull tattoos all over his body. He talked a big game, which Cole attributed to Sonic's need to hold his own with a brother who shifted into a mountain lion.

Couldn't be easy for a human sibling.

Sonic wasn't a bad sort and he'd come through for them more than once, especially in this area.

But no one on Cole's team had liked Sonic's news about Sammy.

As someone familiar with the dark underbelly of the human and shifter worlds in this city, Sonic had been the only person to discover intel about the Black River pack possibly infiltrating a local food bank. If that turned out to be true, that pack was using this food distribution point as a cover for trafficking Jugo Loco.

"You think someone's cookin' in there?" Justin asked.

"Maybe," Cole allowed.

Justin was questioning whether the drug was being made here. Jugo Loco had been developed from the powerful hallucinogenic derivative of Ayahuasca, a plant grown in South America. For many years, humans had touted how a simple tea made from the plant produced shamanistic experiences.

Then a pack of enterprising wolf shifters with no morals had taken the flowering vine into a lab and developed a synthetic drug capable of jacking up a nonhuman.

That's when it earned the street name Jugo Loco.

Crazy Juice.

As if shifters needed one more reason for humans to hate them?

Sixteen deaths had been attributed to the substance in the past eight months. Nine shifters overdosed and seven humans had been attacked by some of those shifters who had lost their minds on the drug. The Black River pack was building a powerful reputation for having a state-of-the-art medical facility somewhere in South America.

They maintained it was dedicated to shifter enhancement and healing.

That might impress some in Cole's world, but not him.

His people believed it was an experimental lab capable of doing worse to his kind than the human scientists who were anxious to cut open shifters for study.

Moving further along the broken sidewalk, Cole found a dark cubbyhole that offered a decent view of the loading area.

He could also watch the walk-in entrance to the left of the overhead door.

Three minutes had passed when a figure stumbled along the sidewalk on the food bank side of the street.

Wearing rags wrapped around his head and more hanging from his body, he hunched against the rain. It was hard to determine much about the stranger until he paused to down a slug from a whiskey bottle.

Cole growled under his breath.

Not a good time for a civilian to step into this operation.

The homeless guy had made it to the corner near the door entrance when he sat down beside a large trashcan and practically disappeared into the night. He leaned back against the wall where the short roof overhang for the delivery entrance shielded him from the rain.

Sighing, Cole couldn't begrudge a homeless person shelter of any sort.

A pair of large headlights pierced the rain two blocks away on Cole's right and headed in his direction.

The truck turned out to be a food bank delivery vehicle.

Cole pulled back tight, waiting.

In thirty seconds, he would have to make a decision.

As it passed between Cole and the food bank across the street, gears groaned and squealed as the metal overhead door rolled up.

Evidently the driver had a remote control.

Or he'd called someone to tell them he was approaching. That would mean two people inside once the truck was parked.

The vagrant turned toward the noise and scurried toward the opening as the truck pulled inside. Amazingly, the shrunken guy moved fast in a stooped run and managed to get inside the building just before the big metal door would have squashed him.

Cole couldn't believe his eyes.

First rule of a mission was if something could get fucked up, it would.

Tonight's mission guidelines were simple. Gather intel and evidence while leaving no DNA or trail.

Their boss would then hand the information over to the specific US authorities who would make the bust.

Cole had no issue with being a shadow operator that no one knew existed. He preferred it, but sometimes things just did not work out as planned.

He couldn't stand by while an innocent walked into danger.

The truck driver could be a Black River pack member. There could be another inside.

That vagrant might be another veteran on the streets.

Veteran or civilian, one of those wolf shifters would scent him at some point and kill the guy in the most heinous way.

The Guardian would not approve Cole's new plan.

Their boss was not entirely like Cole and his fellow Gallize shifters, but for over three hundred years their leader had owned the title *Väktare*, which meant guardian.

Cole held their Guardian in the highest respect, but he had no intention of informing the boss of his plan, since doing so could not bring help in the next minute. Besides, no one on Cole's team tonight would be in danger except him.

Rory and Justin were not putting their lives, and futures, at risk when this was Cole's call alone to make.

His days were numbered.

That made him expendable.

They weren't. They had a chance at mating and beating the curse.

If he didn't survive this, he knew in his heart that his team would continue trying to locate and save Sammy.

Easing from the shadow, Cole took a step forward, decision made.

CHAPTER 2

Cole strode quietly into the empty street and veered toward the walk-in door on the food bank building. He kept his senses open for any other monkey wrenches flying toward the mission.

Speaking softly into his comm unit, he said, "Got a hiccup. Clueless night crawler just entered the lion's den."

That informed his team he was referencing an innocent homeless person getting in the way.

Justin came back with a reminder. *"Interfering will change the transcript."*

"Copy that." Cole knew the mission parameters. At this point he was supposed to cross the street, wait for the truck to leave and tag a tracking device to it. If the truck departed before regular food bank workers showed up around daylight, he would enter the building to hunt for hard evidence of Jugo Loco, then leave unnoticed.

Going in now would risk engaging the perpetrators.

Cole added, "I'm catching the night crawler and bugging out. Maintain status quo until you hear from me."

He heard cursing in stereo.

Rory and Justin could be pissed, but they'd be alive to complain.

If he was unable to get out with the homeless guy, it would be because the wolves had killed them both.

If he found the evidence and couldn't exit the building, he'd break protocol and send word for his men to alert headquarters.

Every shifter on the Gallize teams knew the importance of leaving a scene clean in this type of operation.

Cole wouldn't have to worry about leaving any evidence of his presence if he were caught by the Black River pack, because they fed prisoners to their pack.

Disgusting cannibals.

The one upshot of getting killed and eaten if he had to engage? He wouldn't have to face an ass-chewing.

Cole stepped onto the pavement and crossed the street at a slow pace to avoid drawing attention, but adrenaline spiked through him.

Sensing a hunt, Gray Wolf nudged Cole. *Me first.*

Not going to happen. Cole didn't need one more headache right now and Gray Wolf had become increasingly difficult to manage every day over the past two weeks. At one time, his wolf would go dark and stay quiet for twenty to thirty hours, which would worry Cole back during the early days.

Now, he'd welcome any respite from Gray Wolf's constant pushing to be released.

Cole would have to face the Guardian soon and admit he was close to losing control due to the mating curse, just not right now.

When questioned by other members on the team, the Guardian confirmed that he'd witnessed one case more than a hundred years ago when a Gallize wolf shifter failed to bond with a mate within ten years of his first shift.

That first shift usually happened when a Gallize was in his early twenties.

Not like Cole, who'd met his wolf at nineteen.

Once the curse took effect on that shifter long ago, he'd lost control of his animal within three weeks. The Guardian had put him down, explaining it was the only humane treatment for both the human and the animal.

Over the years, Cole and his teammates had joked about it, making bets on who would bite the bullet and take a mate first.

That was before Cole witnessed the powerful Sammy struggling to manage his animal.

Gray Wolf snarled at being ignored.

Cole paused on the food bank side of the street and clenched his muscles at the internal struggle he fought constantly now. He curled his fingers, feeling the tips of his claws release. His neck muscles tightened. Gritting his teeth, he forced the claws back out of sight and flexed his hands.

When he had control again, he continued toward the food bank door. Rain failed to subdue the noxious smells of urine, rotted food and just plain trash.

He reached the walk-in access to the building and put his ear against the metal door, listening.

No voices or other sounds came through.

Maybe there weren't any wolves here, since it didn't sound like they'd found the human yet.

He didn't have that kind of luck these days.

Using skills he'd gained after joining the Gallize teams, he made quick work with his lockpick tools, then slowly turned the knob.

He pulled the door open an inch.

Pitch dark greeted him.

He sniffed, taking in the odor of multiple humans who probably worked here.

Acceptable.

His night vision took over as he entered slowly, sniffing for any shifter scent. Nothing stood out to him besides mildew-laden air, but it had a weird acidic tinge.

What the hell could that smell be?

No scent of Sammy, either.

Cole wanted to feel relief at that, but Sonic had heard that the Black River pack was taking in shifters for experimental treatments. Word was, a mountain lion shifter had offered big money if the Black River pack could make him *normal*.

Rumors circulated that the pack had a doctor performing successful transformations, turning shifters into human only.

Cole rolled his eyes every time someone mentioned the ridiculous idea.

Did people really believe you could pry the animal from a shifter's body? That would be as realistic as infusing an animal into the complex makeup of a normal human.

Magic played a role, but even that didn't fully explain the transformation for some shifters.

A new thought sent chills through Cole.

Could Sammy have believed that offer and gone looking for help for the mating curse?

Sammy had been on edge and showing more signs, but ...

No. Surely Sammy wouldn't have bought into that load of crap. He'd been the one to teach Cole the difference between truth and myth in their world.

Claws broke through Cole's fingertips. Again.

Gray Wolf banged back and forth, agitated. *I protect us.*

Cole forced his breathing to stay calm when his skin rippled with the need to change his shape.

Clenching his jaw, he wrangled power back into his own hands and locked down his shaking body. Gray Wolf was getting worse.

Staring at the half claws, Cole couldn't deny the seduction of a possible cure. At the same time, he could not fathom that the Black River pack had one for any shifter, especially a Gallize-specific problem.

He would accept his fate when the time came.

Not yet. Not as long as he had a chance of finding Sammy.

When the claw tips finally retracted, Cole let out a breath and dismissed all thought of cures. He focused on locating the homeless guy inside. Once he did, he had to get them both out without drawing attention. With a deep inhale, he stepped into the area the truck had entered and caught the scent of a human who hadn't bathed in a while.

The scent trailed around the rear of the delivery truck to the driver's side.

No sounds of a human being killed and no scent of a wolf shifter. Maybe a human had delivered the truck and was in the office doing paperwork or drinking coffee.

Getting that kind of break would be nice, and it would allow a minute or two to investigate.

Cole took note of food stacked on pallets in untidy rows and on shelving closer to the door. Stepping carefully, he searched until he spotted cases of pre-made sweet and unsweetened tea in gallon jugs.

Jugo Loco had been discovered shipped as plain old tea more than once, because it was extremely difficult for anyone to determine if a jug had tainted product by smell alone.

Even for the sensitive nose of a wolf shifter.

Taste would work, but Cole didn't trust touching the liquid with his tongue. Apparently one sip was all it took, since any shifter accidentally getting ahold of the drug would taste the taint immediately and stop drinking. The reports of vicious attacks by out-of-control shifters had been graphic, and his wolf stayed on the edge of crazy as it was these days.

Digging into his back pocket, Cole pulled out a plastic baggie containing a set of test strips coated with a reactive chemical which would turn blue if any of the drug was present in the gallon units.

The first two jugs tested negative, but the strip changed color to blue on the third jug.

Gotcha.

Now to find the civilian before any wolves showed up and detected a human—or Cole—on site. He had to attach a satellite transmitter to the truck for tracking, get the homeless guy in hand, then exit as quietly as he'd entered.

When he neared the back of the truck, he peeked into the bed area where cases of tea were stacked.

Sonic had come through.

Based on what Cole had just found in the storage area, this load could very possibly hold more Jugo Loco.

Cole sent a series of taps on his comm unit, letting his men know he was inside and all quiet.

What he didn't have a code for was how something felt off about all of this.

No sign of life stirred.

But the human's scent increased the closer he got to the driver's side.

So did that sharp, stinging smell.

Closing his eyes for a second, Cole struggled to pull out a single scent and processed ... the strong scent of death.

Shit.

But what was that pungent smell overriding everything else?

Where were the people to unload the truck? He moved silently along the truck toward the driver's door, breathing through his mouth.

A tiny scuff of noise jerked his head around to the left.

Cole found his homeless guy trying to hide behind a stack of empty pallets.

Sniffing in spite of how the tart smell burned his nostrils, Cole picked up the human's scent again. What the hell was in that cab that smelled so bad?

Please don't let it be Sammy.

Cole would have to be closer to scent even Sammy over that stench.

With one more look at the human hiding on his left, their eyes met.

It wasn't a man, but an elderly woman who looked to be seventy going on two hundred. Her pale, wrinkled face told the story of a hard life. The sickly gaze she held on him said she had one foot in the grave.

He lifted a finger to his lips and she became very still, watching Cole with the attention of prey facing predator. But she didn't make a sound. That worked for him.

Easing forward again, he swept a look through the dark and too-quiet room. On the next breath, he finally picked up a mild scent of shifter that was no longer in the room. The putrid smell from the cab overwhelmed Cole's olfactory senses.

He sucked in a deep breath and fought not to cough, but this time he picked up the smell of fresh blood.

Hell. He moved forward quickly.

A worn out yellow ball cap snagged his attention first.

He knew that cap.

Then a skull earring flickered into view.

No. He leaped to stand on the running board and gagged at the mix of bitter odor, blood and body fluids. Sonic stared straight ahead with wide-open, dead eyes. His throat had been cut from side to side. His hands were taped to the steering wheel and a note was pinned to his chest. The message was written below the Black River snarling wolf logo that every member wore as a tattoo, and read:

Surprise, Cavanaugh. Tick. Tock.

Cole's mind revolted against the words and image.

His heart banged viciously.

A loud click sounded, then ticking started. Cole's gaze shot to Sonic's feet where a bomb had been strapped between his legs.

Nine seconds ... eight ...

Cole might get out in time if he ran straight for the door, but he couldn't leave the woman.

He wheeled around and launched off the truck, landing in front of her. His claws extended and his face tried to change shape.

She backed away and froze.

Cole could hear each tick. *Five ... four...*

In one scoop, he slung her over his shoulder and raced for the door while shouting in his comm, *"Bomb! Retreat, retreat!"*

Justin and Rory's voices blurred with the roar in Cole's ears.

Gray Wolf howled to be released to save them.

Sirens screeched from multiple emergency units advancing. Were they coming here? How could anyone know already?

Cole kicked the door open.

The last second ticked in his mind.

In one move, he yanked the woman down, wrapped his body around her and leaped forward.

The explosion blasted him higher off his feet and threw him across the street.

Time slowed and heat wrapped his body in a scalding blanket, burning clothes and skin.

He hit a brick surface, snapping bones in the arm and hand he'd shoved out to protect the woman from being crushed.

Blood spewed from his mouth. His momentum held him in place for two slow seconds. Then he slid to the ground.

Sirens faded until he heard nothing.

CHAPTER 3

Sounds rumbled around Cole, noises lifting and dropping like a warped wave.

He struggled, trying to wake up, but couldn't reach the surface of consciousness. His eyelids felt made of lead. His body was one big ball of pain, especially on the left side from his face to his feet.

Gray Wolf rumbled inside of him. *Hurt. Must shift.*

Cole agreed. Why hadn't he shifted to heal? What was ...

Drowning in agony, he went under again, releasing his fragile hold on consciousness.

Time ceased to exist.

He floated through darkness until light appeared far away. As the light became brighter, he realized he was running for pleasure in a forest with Gray Wolf running at his side.

Had he died?

That was the only way he could be running *with* Gray Wolf. There was no end to forest or sky. Cole's body was perfect. No pain. Everything was vibrant from the green trees and undergrowth to the bright blue sky peeking through the leaves. Up ahead, an energy began to grow. It emitted a vibrant joy that called to him like a starving man drawn to an endless feast.

Cole wanted to let go of everything and just be.

No, Cole, a gentle voice said in his mind. *It's not your time.*

Why not? He knew he'd find peace in that light.

Go back, Cole. Your journey is not finished. You must mate first.

Who are you?

I am Vercane, the Gallizenae druidess who gifted your ancestor with the powers you possess. I will be here for you when it is time, but your time has not yet come. I refuse to lose another Gallize to the mating curse. You are strong. Go back and take your place with a mate.

Words of anguish screamed in his head. *I have no mate.*

Yes, you do. Go to her. The light faded to a tiny dot that blinked out of existence.

Darkness swallowed him and Gray Wolf until nothing remained but misery.

Cole's mind drifted along, unable to latch onto any one thought until someone interrupted his respite from agony.

Light flashed in his right eye.

He squinted hard to block it out. Who would do that to a shifter with sensitive vision?

The irritating glow went away.

Maybe that hadn't been intentional. Maybe he'd just opened his eye at the wrong time. What about his other eye? He couldn't open it or move either arm to lift his hands and feel his face. He couldn't move his legs either.

What had happened?

His mind threw jumbled visions at him. He swam through the confusion, hunting for something he could grasp.

Slowly, it started coming back to him. The warehouse. Sonic. The bomb.

Damn. He might be too fucked up physically to fix.

How long had it been since the explosion?

Where was Gray Wolf?

Cole's head pounded and his damn skin was on fire. His claws extended. Maybe he *could* shift.

Sharp points pricked his skin and he was hit with a load of electrical power. Pain shot through every part of him. He howled, then drifted into oblivion again.

The next time Cole surfaced, agony and aches shuddered through his body with every beat of his heart.

He'd been taught how to endure pain. Where?

The military. Back when he ran missions with his team.

He sucked in a deep breath.

Oh, fuck, that hurt. Stick to shallow breaths.

Gray Wolf came alive inside him. Making sounds, but not

making sense. Still, Cole could tell Gray Wolf was worried and wanted to heal him. That was a welcome change from his beast's constant battling against him of late.

Cole didn't have the ability to fight his animal in this condition. He needed to shift and heal, but he didn't want Gray Wolf running free with no way to pull his wolf back from harming someone. So Cole just lay there like a corpse and waited for the change to come over him once Gray Wolf realized he could force it. Cole hoped he'd regain consciousness quickly once he shifted and had a chance to prevent Gray Wolf from tearing into someone.

Seconds passed.

Nothing happened.

His wolf gave a little push, then gave a mournful howl when he couldn't break out, then just stopped trying.

Why wasn't his wolf mad with rage and taking advantage of Cole's inability to stop the shift?

Back during the first year with Gray Wolf, Cole had no chance of preventing the change when he'd been badly injured in training. Gray Wolf might be difficult, but he had never failed to take over and heal Cole in dire circumstances.

This definitely qualified as dire.

With the unstable condition his wolf had been in right up to the explosion, Gray Wolf wouldn't be slumbering now.

Cole waited, fighting to stay present and breathe softly.

His wolf ... was subdued.

Gray Wolf had never been what anyone would call *calm* from the moment Cole had first shifted, but now? His beast had settled down significantly.

This was monumental, but was it a good thing or a bad thing?

Could the explosion have altered Cole's mating curse?

That didn't make sense at all, but he wouldn't complain about the pain if getting a grip on his wolf again was a side effect of almost dying.

He could figure it out once his head stopped feeling like someone was using a pile driver on it. Worse than that was the searing pain in his face that had him wanting to claw the skin off.

Yeah, that would convince everyone he was stable. *Suck it up. Mind-over-matter exercises, Cavanaugh.* He'd been taught how to focus through pain in the early days of training to control his wolf.

He should concentrate on his chest and shoulder injuries first. They weren't as demanding of his attention as the pain in his face and left side. He tried to curl his fingers and call up his wolf to heal, but his hands were wrapped.

Bandaged?

Now that he took inventory of his body, his head was wrapped up, too. Left eye had been completely covered. The other felt too swollen to open.

Why would anyone wrap up a shifter?

He could heal faster with no bandages.

Couldn't he?

Was he so close to death he couldn't shift or heal?

Gray Wolf, Cole silently called to his animal.

His wolf began vibrating inside of him and Cole finally realized the wolf was not in a normal state, but ... stressed about Cole. Had Cole's inability to shift frightened his animal?

Or ... *shit* ... had he forced his wolf to stay inside for so long he'd damaged both of them severely?

The Guardian had warned all the Gallize shifters about making time for their animals to run free. That hadn't been a possibility for Cole in the past two weeks, because he'd feared Gray Wolf breaking free of Cole's control and attacking anything he perceived a threat.

He forced his breathing to smooth, focusing on how he *wanted* to feel, instead of the fact that he hurt all over. After a bit, his headache dropped from DEFCON One to DEFCON Four.

Better.

Now he could force his mind to work on other issues like his surroundings. He started listening and searching out scents beyond the antiseptic odor of an infirmary. It actually smelled as if all the scents had been wiped away. Even so, if he could get down and sniff closely, he could still pick up the scent of anything living that had passed through here.

Hold everything. An infirmary?

Hot damn. He had to be in one of the Guardian's facilities, which also meant Cole's team had gotten him away from the scene.

His heart took a badly needed break at that realization. If the Guardian thought Cole needed bandages, then so be it, since the

Guardian was the pinnacle of shifter knowledge for the team.

As a massive, sea eagle shifter who had flown over the world for three centuries, the Guardian guided all of them through the ups and downs of being Gallize shifters.

At the sound of a door swishing open, Cole jerked back to the present. Damn. Fighting the pain must be wearing him out, because he'd been drifting again.

Gray Wolf came to sharp attention, but with no hint of wanting out. Curious.

If Cole couldn't shift, his wolf couldn't harm anyone. He wanted to give in to the heaviness weighing on him and the need for sleep, but a scent tickled his nose.

A sweet smell he recognized.

His mind gave up on sleep, because this scent had belonged to a human. Someone from long ago. Pain of a completely different kind seared him now.

At one time, he'd associated the smell with good times, great sex and plans for his future.

Mate. Gray Wolf had the same visceral reaction to the scent, but his wolf was wrong. Cole had thought of Tess many times while learning how to shift. When the word 'mate' was tossed around, he'd immediately think of her and spreading her favorite lotion across her amazing skin and making love to her.

Gray Wolf persisted. *Mate.*

Cole couldn't explain why that wasn't possible to his animal. The wolf associated that scent with the woman Cole had obsessed over during his early days with Gray Wolf. That had been back when Cole first met the Guardian, their powerful leader who'd called up Cole's wolf, then proceeded to teach him how to be a shifter.

That was also when Cole realized the woman he'd loved in college could never be in his life.

Not a human woman.

That particular woman wouldn't be anywhere around the Guardian, which meant the scent did not belong to her. His boss did have some humans in the operation, but they'd been with the Guardian for decades before Cole showed up. This person was probably a female medical specialist who liked the same lotion. Not an easy product to find, because it was made in France and sold in the US by a small cosmetics group.

His throat ached when he swallowed, remembering how he'd tracked it down and wrapped the pretty bottle as a birthday gift. The memory threatened to drag him away from consciousness again, back to a time when he'd been happier than any man deserved. In college with her.

He'd never smelled that fragrance on another woman.

His heart twisted at the memories.

He could deal with the physical pain and healing, but one deep breath of that scent and he suffered an emotional pain that drilled deep into his chest.

Gray Wolf moaned a sorrowful sound.

More than ever, Cole needed to shift and run hard.

Go anywhere to get away from the reminder of all he'd had at one time and lost forever.

Mind over matter.

Screw this. He pulled inside himself and let the darkness suck him into a deep sleep again. He went to a place of peace where he was alone without his wolf.

The place he'd been taught to access when suffering the most excruciating pain.

No physical injury had ever equaled losing her.

CHAPTER 4

Tess Janver should be home in bed this late at night. Or rather, early in the morning, since it was now after midnight. She'd thought by this time Wednesday morning, their patient would be awake.

She'd sat with him all Monday night until she had to go home and shower. Exhaustion had hit by lunch yesterday. She'd locked her office door and asked her assistant to not allow anyone to interrupt. She'd managed an hour of sleep that way, enough to keep her on her feet through the past evening, but she had to go home soon.

This visit would have to be short. She wouldn't be able to function without a night of decent sleep, but she had so many questions for this shifter.

Standing next to unconscious John Doe, she studied the partially disfigured body retrieved from the failed food bank bust on Monday.

How could anyone, human or not, have survived being so close to that explosion?

John Doe was a wolf shifter, based on what the jackal shifters on staff said. After the initial intake, Tess had kept those jackals away from John Doe.

Some of the jackals working on staff for SCIS, Shifter Criminal Investigation Service, had been known to lose control around an injured shifter. They'd change shape and attack. Sometimes the agency's powerful tranquilizer dart guns didn't work quickly enough. That meant using deadly force to protect the wounded shifter, who was defenseless.

Even if they maintained control, she didn't trust the jackal shifters on the SCIS payroll.

They treated her with respect, but instinct warned her not to end up alone with any of them. She'd researched all forms of shifters while gaining her master's degree on the topic. One of the first to complete a program formed when mainstream universities scrambled to form viable think tanks, Tess had been in on the earliest stages of studying shifters. Once shifters were revealed as undeniably real, professors and institutions of higher learning reached out to available resources they would once have shunned as non-science.

Combining her existing law degree, her unusual credentials, and a buttload of hard work and determination, Tess earned her reputation as a top legal expert on shifters. That was how she'd landed this position investigating Black River Wolf Pack crimes committed in the southeastern district of SCIS.

She'd become the liaison between SCIS and all human law enforcement agencies.

Jackals working for SCIS weren't her responsibility.

But John Doe was.

This guy was her best lead on finding the grizzly bear shifter responsible for the Nantahala Honeymoon Massacre, as that case had been nicknamed in the press. She still hadn't figured out why the Black River wolf pack had a bear with them. Wolves particularly did not like other animals in their packs, but the Black River wolf pack's calling card had been found near the murder scene.

Literally, a card, but oddly ... there was no scent.

She'd fought for this SCIS position so she could take down the Black River pack for their many crimes over the past seven years, including her mother's death. Now that SCIS had captured one of their wolves, she had a real chance at making some headway.

Six years ago, SCIS had not existed as such. But the initial investigating agency, which later morphed into SCIS, was the one that handled her mother's death.

Tess felt the sharp pang that accompanied any memory of her mom, a sweet, innocent human who had been caught in the middle of an early shifter battle over territory.

Already reeling from the disappearance of the man she'd

expected to marry after college, Tess had gone numb when her mother died, barely managing to get through the days by simply going through the motions expected of a grieving daughter. But two weeks after burying her mom, Tess changed her career direction from focusing only on human law. She became a woman with a mission, determined to find answers once she had the background to go looking for them. That had taken longer than she'd thought. When she landed this position five months back, she'd started quietly digging.

And run into one wall after another.

The court case, with all its files, had been sealed and her powerful father refused to help, demanding she leave it be. That stung more than she'd like to admit, given that she'd followed him into law and would like to think he had some respect for what she'd accomplished..

She swung her attention back to the only case she could control right now.

John Doe, wolf shifter.

She took a step closer to the foot of his stretcher and her insides buzzed sharply with a sudden lurch of energy.

She knew that energy. She'd grown up accidentally disabling watch batteries and frying small electronics just by touching them. As a child, she'd found it amusing until she realized it was truly strange. Something that marked her a freak until she'd learned to hide it.

The buzzing energy hadn't been this noticeable since she was nineteen, or more specifically, the night the man she loved abandoned her.

Gritting her teeth, she silently reprimanded herself for thinking about *him.*

He has no place in your life anymore, Tess.

Got it. Get John Doe healed so he can be interrogated.

Her gaze traveled over the still form of her burned captive. Yes, he *was* a captive and suspected to be part of the Black River pack, but it was hard to look at anyone burned and battered that way. She hoped the medicine they were giving him eased his pain.

Based on her background in shifter studies, she contended this man needed to shift to promote his own healing.

The medic working on this case had warned that would be a

mistake. He claimed he'd never seen a shifter in such bad shape. He pointed out they had no idea how damaged John Doe's wolf might be. If they used medicines to force this man to shift too soon and his wolf wasn't up to the task, John Doe might end up stuck halfway through a shift.

If that happened, they'd have to perform a mercy killing.

She shuddered at the thought.

Even as a shifter, how had this man survived such a catastrophic injury? She'd reviewed cases of others who had died from far less damage. As preternatural humans, these people were practically bulletproof, but based on how close the bomb techs estimated he'd been to the detonation, it was mind-boggling that he still breathed.

She lifted John Doe's medical chart and read it again. The list of injuries made her wince. She should have no sympathy for shifters who killed humans, especially after what happened to her mother.

But her mother had been the one to teach Tess respect for all forms of nature.

Her father preached the opposite. He believed shifters belonged in cages.

Sighing at the internal conflict she suffered every time she had that conversation with her father, she continued reviewing Mr. Doe.

She snorted. That sounded ridiculous.

Like he was a gender-confused deer.

Burns covered half of his body along the left side.

Her gaze ran down to where a narrow band of sheet hid his hips and private area. She blushed at the memory of medics checking his naked body for injuries, but at that moment they'd been trying to determine if he was alive or dead.

He hadn't spoken a word.

She'd expected him to wake up by now, confused and shouting at everyone to explain what happened to him. Maybe start checking for body parts.

Some men would worry about their penis before a leg or arm.

John Doe would be glad to find his intact.

Not that she'd been checking him out. God, no. The sad fact was that she'd only ever been interested in ogling one man and he'd loved it. That had been a long time ago when she'd let an attractive face and sexy smile steal her heart.

That bastard had taught her how to guard against allowing anyone else in. He'd taught her not to trust men who professed to care about her and only her. Lies.

Tough lesson at nineteen, but one that had served her well.

Besides, this man was a shifter.

In spite of suffering so much physical damage, once he shifted and healed, he'd have a fit body with carved up muscle. All shifters seemed to be built like gorgeous Spartan warriors.

Not being very clinical, Tess.

With her professional mask back in place, she replayed what she knew for the tenth time. The more she turned the details over in her mind, the less sensational these events would become, and then she could pick out inconsistencies.

The explosion had launched John Doe across the street into a brick building. His right hand and arm had more broken bones than his left, the side that had been burned the worst.

So he'd shoved out a hand to prevent hitting the wall?

Why? It seemed that if he'd taken the hit against his whole body, he probably would have come out better.

He'd landed on a terrified homeless woman who had been frantic, speaking gibberish for two minutes before she passed out.

Poor thing. Tess had gotten her medical aid on site, then sent her to a hospital where the staff reported she'd fallen into a coma from light head trauma. Tess couldn't question that witness yet.

John Doe groaned all of a sudden, as if in deep pain.

Tess jumped at the unexpected sound.

She'd been told John Doe had howled earlier while being treated, but that he'd still been unconscious. Since then he'd remained silent. Had he howled because he'd been trying to shift before her medics had loaded him with one of their heavy-duty tranqs for shifters?

She stepped over to his side, where wires ran from his body to monitoring equipment. She didn't touch any of it with her bare hands for fear of screwing up the electronics.

This was not the place to make that mistake.

She hated the thin, white gloves she wore to protect the sensitive electrical equipment. She should probably have them on now, but she didn't plan to touch any of the gear. The gloves were stuffed in her pocket for handy access in case someone else on staff came in and she needed to help in some way.

Some people claimed they couldn't wear a wristwatch due to electrical current in their body killing the battery. What Tess had experienced as a child had been similar, but her watches had actually stopped, then run backwards.

Some of those watches had not used batteries.

Over the past seven years, since the night Cole-Asshole-Cavanaugh vanished, the problem had gotten continually worse. She'd lost countless phones, computers, kitchen appliances, clocks and more when the electronics had fried.

Was she admitting *that* to anyone?

Not a chance. The staff would look at her as if she were stranger than a shifter.

She'd kept it hidden from her dad for years, especially the details of what happened the day her mother died.

The weird energy inside her had intensified the very night Cole disappeared, which made no sense to her back then. Through trial and error, she'd figured out that gloves would dull the effect and had finally started wearing them almost constantly while at law school. She'd explained them away with the excuse that she was highly allergic.

If someone asked her specifically what bothered her skin, she shook her head and said there were too many things to list.

In recent years, high-end phone cases offered a layer of protection as well as the stylus she used on her cell phone and laptop. But other electronics still got toasted if she grew careless.

This new intensity to her energy wasn't about MIA Cole, though. The buzzing had felt stronger in general over the past two weeks, interrupting her sleep and distracting her.

Right now it droned in her ears and her skin actually vibrated. Between that and erotic dreams of the bastard who had broken her heart, the last two weeks had been hellish.

Why dream about Cole at all? He'd left.

Stupid mind.

John Doe grunted.

She watched the part of his face she could see for signs of pain. The medical log hadn't indicated any significant change since yesterday.

Shifters often responded to SCIS drugs, but not absolutely. Not like they did with Jugo Loco.

She gritted her teeth over the sting operation that had gone badly. She wanted to rail at this shifter for his role in putting humans—and other shifters—in such danger just for personal gain. Oh, and money always played a role.

Her conscience argued, *what if he isn't part of the Black River pack?*

What was he doing there when the bomb exploded? she countered.

No answer. Just as she thought. This guy was guilty of something even her conscience couldn't argue.

Still, she believed in due process. Innocent until proven guilty even for nonhumans.

Glancing at the clock, she frowned. It was time to get some rest. When she turned away, though, she couldn't take a step. Her body still functioned like normal, but the energy inside her stopped her cold. It didn't want to move away.

She knew that, but didn't understand *why* she knew.

The buzzing inside her cranked up even higher.

"Don't leave," a voice implored.

Tess jerked around, looking everywhere around her, because it had sounded like the whisper filled the room.

Looking down, she stared at John Doe.

He couldn't have said anything. He was still out cold and that had sounded ... *ethereal.*

She was losing her marbles.

Then again, a few years ago she would have said the same thing at the idea of shifters being real. Could that have been some sort of telepathy?

She'd never read about shifters speaking telepathically in human form. Nothing in her studies had shown evidence of actual telepathic communication, but a jackal on staff who'd once had a mate said he had been able to communicate with her when they were both in animal form.

She'd never heard of *any* shifter using telepathy with a human. But if anything ever fit the ideal definition of telepathy, that desperate cry in her mind hit dead-on.

That couldn't happen, right?

Lack of sleep was screwing with her. Had to be.

But that didn't explain why her heart raced and her skin felt hot. What was going on?

She had no idea, but she was loath to leave this man alone for some reason. The longer she stared at him, the more his suffering bothered her.

He was a shifter.

A Black River wolf shifter, almost certainly. One who had no thought for the well-being of anyone other than himself. She should be standing far away.

But when she looked at John Doe, she saw only a man in pain. Logic said that made her a candidate for some serious therapy.

When would he open his eyes?

She had the sudden urge to put a hand on his forehead and check that he was okay.

As if her touch could determine that?

"Touch me," whispered through the air, reaching her ears past the soft sounds of humming and whirring equipment.

She froze and looked down at his mouth.

Had he really spoken this time? She battled a mix of fear and excitement. Curiosity and a sense of purpose had driven her to take on the study of shifters. That same curiosity took over now.

He was restrained. If not incapacitated, he was injured and she had a stun weapon designed specifically for shifters.

She gently ran her fingers down the length of his broken forearm.

Something moved under the skin.

She snatched her fingers back, watching as the bones in his forearm appeared to mend.

But only that arm.

The one she'd touched.

Could that mean ... that her energy could heal?

Right. If that was the case, why hadn't she healed anyone else in all these years?

"More touch."

His masculine voice was hardly more than a croak, but she understood the words.

Was he dreaming?

Had she actually made him feel better with her touch?

Afraid to touch anywhere else, she slipped her fingers over his newly mended arm and down to his hand. His fingers lifted in tiny increments and wove through hers as she watched, dumbfounded. According to the X-rays, that hand was broken in at least eight places. He should not be able to move those fingers.

He sighed, a deep sound of peace.

She couldn't speak. Her throat clogged with an unnamed emotion. His hand was warm and strong.

Energy inside her churned all of a sudden and heat flushed down her arm, brushing along her skin until it reached her hand that still held his.

She started to pull away, but her fingers refused to do what she told them.

He wasn't holding her. She just wouldn't—*couldn't*—let go of him.

Panic rushed up her spine and her heart rate jumped. Her whole body trembled. She had to get a grip or she'd start hyperventilating any minute now.

His thumb barely moved, brushing slowly across the skin on the hand he held.

A strange sense of peace settled over her as she realized *he* was touching her now, soothing her.

She didn't want to let go.

Her heart thumped hard, then slower with every second, until she could swear she felt the rhythmic pumping of *his* heart ... in sync with hers.

What was happening to her? Was he causing it? Or was she?

This was foolish.

And dangerous. He was a shifter.

Never forget that.

She flexed her fingers, relieved to have muscle control, and started to withdraw her hand again.

His fingers tightened around hers, not the crushing grip that a shifter was capable of, but one that begged her not to let go.

She turned into a statue. Her brain short-circuited.

What other reason would explain this feeling that he was trying to let her know he needed her to stay?

He needed her close to him.

How could she know what he was feeling or needing?

The energy reversed course and raced back up her arm, then

spread into her chest, warm and comforting. She could definitely hear the double thump of two heartbeats in her ear, beating in time.

Nothing like this had even happened with her internal energy.

But something bizarre was going on with John Doe. The last time something really crazy happened with her energy, she'd exploded her phone and never received the last call from her mother.

A call that might have saved her mother's life.

Tess couldn't catch her breath.

She'd never passed out, but she felt clammy and light headed.

Mangled words slipped from John Doe's lips. "Won't ... hurt you. Not ... you."

What?

He moaned a sad sound, then his grip relaxed and his hand fell loose.

She grabbed her chest where her heart now beat like it auditioned for a heavy metal band.

The unburned, but badly bruised, right side of his face relaxed and his breathing evened out. He mumbled something else that came out garbled.

She rolled her eyes at herself for thinking it was all about her.

You're an idiot. John Doe had been caught in a dream and her energy was playing tricks on her mind.

She whispered, "Enjoy your dreams. Reality won't be nearly as nice once you wake up."

Thinking about his upcoming interrogation made her sad, which was ridiculous since being present to witness shifter interrogations was part of her job.

He murmured again.

She couldn't stop herself from leaning close to his lips to hear him. She whispered, "What?"

On the next exhale, he said, "Need ... you."

Tess stood up and backed away, pulling the gloves from her pocket. She left before she started seeing ghosts or faeries or mice turning into pumpkins.

He was screwing with her somehow even though all his vitals showed him deeply under the tranq's influence.

She had to keep a certain distance between them. She couldn't have John Doe exposing her weird energy.

If that happened, she'd lose her job and her father would find out. He'd look at her like she was a freak.

No one, not a shifter or human, was going to cost her the job she'd fought so hard to earn.

CHAPTER 5

Cole moved his jaw. *So* thirsty.

A nasty creature had crawled around in his mouth and died there. He licked his lips.

"Ready for a drink?" an angel's voice asked.

He forced his eyes open.

Correction. He slowly pried open his right eye, the one that was not covered with a bandage. He squinted to focus, but all he got was a blur of sun-kissed skin and black hair. At least, the black was where he'd assume a head would be.

What the hell had they given him and why hadn't he been encouraged to shift yet?

His mind tripped back over a memory of being hit with a stun gun while he was injured. That couldn't be right.

He tried to talk, but got a croak for his effort.

The bed moved up slowly until he was halfway to a sitting position. He inhaled the sweet smell of her lotion. He'd dreamed about that scent. The fragrance woke up parts of his body he hadn't been sure survived the blast.

Now he recalled. This was the woman who had the same lotion as Tess.

Gray Wolf was there, Cole could feel him, but the wolf was being strangely silent.

Cole was glad for the drugs that had quieted Gray Wolf, because this was not the time to think about ... *her*.

"Open your mouth," the angel said softly.

When he did, she slipped a straw in and he sucked down the best tasting water he'd ever drunk.

Then the straw went away.

"Hey." That should have sounded forceful, not whiny.

"You can't have a lot yet, but you can have sips more often for the first hour."

His angel was right. He knew that, but it didn't change the fact that he wanted to drink a lake dry.

His brain jumped from thirst to her voice.

He'd heard it before. Sort of.

She almost sounded familiar. Where would he have heard her? He hadn't been in the infirmary at headquarters for years. Maybe that was a voice from a television broadcast.

That made zero sense.

The drugs must still be screwing with his head.

No one who worked close enough with the Guardian to treat a Gallize shifter would ever show their face on television. He should just stop trying to figure things out on his own and get someone in here who could update him.

Licking his lips again, but with success this time, he asked in his rough voice, "Where is everyone?"

He sensed her hesitation before she replied, "Who do you want to see?"

Warning bells rang loud in his head.

The Guardian would have already been in here and made it clear he was to be notified the minute Cole could speak.

Rory and Justin would have been taking turns staying here.

Damn it, Toto, we're not in Kansas or anywhere friendly.

Who Toto? Gray Wolf grumbled.

Cole silently hushed him. *We're captured. Let me think.*

His wolf hadn't seemed drugged. Odd, but okay.

He had to answer his angel in a way that sounded normal for someone in his position. "The doctor. Where is he?" Cole quickly amended, "Or she? You just smell too good to be a doctor."

"Wasting your time. I'm allergic to bad boys."

She sounded insulted, but that wasn't what snapped Cole to attention.

His heart rate clicked up.

He *did* know that voice. Intimately.

It couldn't be her.

His heart rolled in his chest.

The first time he'd met Tess, she told him, "Wasting your time. I'm allergic to bad boys," in that same cocky tone.

Add that to the lotion and ... damn. This had to be some twisted nightmare.

That couldn't be Tess. Not his Tess.

What the hell would she be doing here?

"That all you got?" she said with just a hint of tease in her voice.

Oh, hell. That sounded just like Miss High and Mighty Tessella Janver when she'd ranted about laws and how when she was an attorney she wouldn't stand for this or that. Her father had been an up and coming politician back then.

Now a highly respected Senator, Janver led the congressional charge against shifters, trying to eradicate Cole's kind like a bad disease.

Cole had to find out just how deep a pile of shit he was in.

Keeping the conversation light, he avoided admitting he knew her and explained in his scratchy voice, "Not flirting. Doctors reek of blood and medicine." When in trouble, bluff and flatter in spite of claiming he wasn't a flirt. "You smell like a rose garden in full bloom."

She didn't say anything.

Not too encouraging.

Maybe she'd fill in a few holes in his memory, but he had to be careful with his questions.

He must look really bad for her not to recognize him.

On the other hand, he was seven years older and he'd beefed up quite a bit once he joined the shifter teams. He'd had the slender, but muscular, frame of a runner when he was taken to the Guardian at nineteen. The day he'd had to say goodbye to his human life when he discovered that he was a Gallize descendant who was shifting earlier than anticipated.

They normally didn't come into their powers and meet their animal until well after they turned twenty-one.

That's me. Overachiever in everything.

Shifting into his wolf early had not been a good thing, though.

It had taken a year for Cole to learn how to control the massive wolf. After that, his world narrowed to the Guardian's missions.

Save people and avoid thinking about no longer being a human.

Now he was inches from the woman he could never forget.

For now, he needed to stick with the basic dialogue anyone would expect. "How long have I been here?"

"Two days. It's Wednesday evening."

He hadn't shifted or healed in two days? What the hell was wrong?

Or maybe what the hell drug were they giving him?

At a loss for where to go next, he started with a more direct question. "Are you my doctor?"

"No. I'm not a part of the medical team."

At least that jived with her plan to go into law. Still, what was she doing here? Hmm. Would she tell him her true identity? "Who are you then?"

The blob shape he was now convinced belonged to Tess moved closer and dropped down, probably into a chair. "Let's focus on you."

He drew in a deep breath that didn't punish him quite so much this time. He smelled the mix of her favorite skin cream and her unique scent that he had never before catalogued as human.

He'd never had the chance to sniff her as a shifter.

Now, he longed for her scent with every breath.

The last time they'd been together, he'd been human and had thought his future looked too bright to stare into directly. The night he vanished, he'd possessed a ring that would fit her finger perfectly. They had already made plans for after college for him, and law school for her. They hadn't specifically said so, but they both knew she was going to have his children and they would grow old together.

His future had vanished in one night.

That loss hit him so hard, he hissed.

"Are you okay?" she said, concern wafting through her voice.

"I'm fine," he lied. He wanted to break free and get out of here. For weeks, he'd kept his wolf locked down, fighting it for control.

But now? He'd like nothing better than to unleash the beast. *If* he was anywhere but near her.

He would cut his own throat before he allowed the wolf to force a shift and harm her.

"I can call someone," she offered, sounding unsure. Nothing like the woman who had taken his heart by storm and been prepared to marry him in spite of her father expecting her to strive for a man who could match her social background.

"I'm good, really," he said, then killed his firm answer with a moment of coughing.

"I wish I knew more about shifter medicine. Here, sip more water."

He did, then laid back when she took the cup away.

What was Tess doing here? She'd been terrified of shifters when they came out, and her father hated them.

He'd been gone for a long time, supporting the military overseas and had stayed busy enough not to pay attention to the life he'd left.

But he had heard about her mother dying and a shifter being at fault.

Once again, he wondered how Tess could be sitting next to him at this moment.

When shifters first came out, he and Tess had debated about what that meant to everyone's future. Being her father's daughter, she'd agreed shifters should be put on the equivalent of a reservation.

Even as he'd worried about keeping her safe and how life as he'd known it had changed, he felt everyone born to this world deserved the chance to live free.

But her father had feared shifters, spouting that they were only mindless killing machines who should be captured and locked away.

When Senator Janver failed to get a bill through legislation to have shifters captured and put into one big compound, he changed his course and started a campaign to brand their human forms.

That bill was catching support.

Once Cole had been taken to the Guardian, he was put through a year of intense training and allowed to contact no one. He'd never returned to find Tess after that for one simple reason. He couldn't face her, knowing they now stood on opposite sides of an invisible line. He couldn't face the heartbreaking disappointment he knew he'd see.

But when the mating curse kicked in, he'd decided to make one last stop before he turned himself in to the Guardian, so that he could tell her what happened. He'd give her an edited version that would protect his Gallize family, but as much of the truth as he could. She deserved the truth, even if he had to hear her tell him she would never forgive him.

The day he'd accepted that he and Tess had no future had been the hardest moment in his life. To survive in his new world, he'd had to convince the Guardian and the team that he had let go of his past.

Until this minute, he'd believed he had.

But all he could think of right now was how much he wanted to touch Tess. Just brush his hand over her hair and feel its silky softness again. His brain took note of every tiny fraction of the scent he captured from her.

She said, "Do you need a pain med—"

"I don't. No drugs, please." He just needed to catch a breath and clear that crap out of his system. He didn't know why he hadn't healed, but drugs were never good for shifters.

Her sigh took him back to when she'd lose patience with him when they disagreed on something. He'd hear that sound and fold like a house of cards for whatever he'd done.

The next thing she knew, he'd have her up against a wall, forgetting their silly argument.

For all that was holy, he couldn't take being this close to her.

Not again.

"Okay, then," she went on. "Let's start with you telling me who *you* are."

Dream on, angel. But he kept that to himself. If he admitted to being a shifter, then he'd have to identify a pack or clan where he lived.

What was he thinking?

She'd already insinuated he was a shifter. This group had to know that much already. As a minimum, they knew he wasn't human.

How many humans could have survived being slammed into a brick wall by that explosion? None.

To tell the truth, he hadn't thought even a Gallize shifter could.

Had his little old homeless woman lived? She should have, but if he asked he'd have to admit knowing more than he wanted to right now. Surely, someone would have taken care of her.

If she hadn't survived, he hoped her passing was peaceful.

Playing dumb might not benefit him.

If he had to make an educated guess, this was some division of SCIS. That agency took the lead in any incident involving a shifter. He wished now that he was a tech geek like Rory, who probably knew the names of the most significant SCIS personnel.

Cole had never cared who did what. The Guardian handled politics and agency dealings since so few even knew about the Gallize.

The last thing Cole expected was to find Tess working at SCIS.

If this was SCIS, they could throw him in a titanium-reinforced hole in the ground to heal. Once that happened, he'd never find a way out. His people had to be searching for him right now, which begged the question—exactly where was he located? He needed information for any hope of getting out or giving his team time to locate him.

She said, "Being evasive will not help you."

That sounded all legal and serious, which fit her perfectly.

Tess had been studying law, but she'd planned to specialize in ... hell, he couldn't remember. She wanted to protect national forests and help Native Americans. Something like that.

Her father had hated the idea.

Cole had loved her rebellious side.

She sighed again.

Even if he had it in him to shove her up against a wall and kiss the daylights out of her, he doubted it would end happily.

Where to start?

Remember me, Tess? I'm now a wolf shifter, the one being you've been conditioned to think of as a monster.

To be fair, that wasn't far from the truth, especially now that his wolf and he were turning into two beings.

Cole forced his mind back on how to get out of here, which wouldn't happen until he unearthed more information. He searched mentally for everything he could recall from that night and what her group, whoever she worked with, might have figured out.

He cleared his throat. "Here's what I remember. I was walking by a building in downtown Spartanburg and the thing blew up. Have no idea what was going on or who did it, only that I was in the wrong place when everything went kaboom."

"So you weren't inside when it happened?"

"No. Why would you think that?"

"Lock pick tools were found on what was left of your clothes."

Damn. That little detail had slipped his mind. "I've had them for a long time. They were a gift. No law against owning them." He wanted that last comment back the minute it left his lips. It was definitely illegal in some states even if there was no intent to commit a crime. *So sue me for not being able to think clearly.*

"That's partially true ... for humans. However, a law has just been passed that prevents shifters from owning any lock picking tools."

Of course there was, and he'd bet her father had been behind it.

Cole had been on back-to-back missions for the last three months. He hadn't been in places where he could keep up with news that didn't involve national security.

She knew he was a shifter, but she'd soon know his full identity the minute his face healed.

He argued in a voice so rough it hurt his own ears. "That's a ridiculous law. Why shouldn't a shifter be able to apply for a locksmith job? It's tough out there for shifters. The only person who wants to hire us is another shifter, which means the business owner is limited to a small pool of applicants, or ... some human who just wants a pet around."

Yeah, his voice rolled out ripe with disgust, but that was the truth for many shifters without the network of support he enjoyed as a Gallize.

She had been tapping her finger on the rail bordering his bed, another habit from her past that he noted, but she suddenly ceased making any noise.

Silence filled the air, expanded and locked them in a stalemate.

He waited her out. People tended to talk when things got quiet, but he'd been trained to sit still for days when necessary. His patience paid off.

She said, "I don't believe you were there by accident."

Her blurry shape sat back.

He tried to squint her into focus. The image got a little better. He could make out the shape of her hair now. That black mass used to fall down to her waist, but it now seemed to be piled up on her head. Back in school, she'd chop it off, but that silky mane would grow right back before she turned around. She'd complain about having to make cut appointments as often as brushing her teeth. One time, she'd grabbed her hair in a fist and threatened to whack it off herself.

He cajoled her out of that insane action by pulling her shirt over her head and leaving her that way as he yanked her panties down and gave her something new to worry about.

"Did you hear me?" she asked.

"I did." Unfortunately she'd snapped him back to the present, which sucked, because he'd been enjoying that little moment. He kept his voice as gravelly as he could to prevent her from discovering his identity until there was no choice. "I'm not sure what you want me to say. I had nothing to do with that explosion. If you're just looking for a shifter to hang it on, then I guess I'm your guy."

She gasped before she could quell the sound.

Bull's-eye.

Tess had a streak of fairness that ran through her core. She hated to be considered unfair and dealing with shifters must be challenging that personal doctrine.

Under normal circumstances, he would never take advantage of knowledge about her, but this could be the difference between life and death.

His.

Why would she think he was involved in the explosion?

Unless ... she, or her people, knew the Black River pack were distributing through that warehouse. If so, why had SCIS shown up right then?

He pressed his advantage. "Were you just hanging around the area, waiting on some unsuspecting shifter to step into a bomb scene or was that staged?"

"Of course it wasn't staged."

"I heard sirens at the same moment the bomb detonated. How could you know to be there that quickly?"

"I'm not the one who has to answer questions. What's your name?"

"Colin. Your lack of answer means it was staged." He'd helped her practice cross examinations back in first year law school, because she'd wanted to be so ready for when she had to start trial classes. He remembered something similar she'd said during a heated exchange with him as the witness.

His agency had taught him to never share more than necessary. He'd known a boy called Colin in the children's home and the Guardian had used the name Colin O'Donnell to create an identity if he ever needed one.

He needed it.

She said, "Just to clear up any confusion about our part in this, SCIS received a tip that shifters had infiltrated the food bank. We were a half mile away when the building exploded."

SCIS? Just as he'd guessed. He'd caught snippets of news that SCIS were under threat of losing their funding if they didn't hand over someone from the Black River pack soon.

They definitely needed a shifter scapegoat.

Well, shit, even if he could expose his true identity, he couldn't prove it since there were no records of him anywhere. Talk about being the perfect fall guy.

"Do I get an attorney? Any representation?" he asked, wondering if that would tweak her belief in fairness.

"No. Due to being part of an investigation that affects national security—"

"What?"

"—you can see no one until SCIS approves it and that isn't going to happen even though I would allow it."

Yep, he'd dinged her conscience with that one. "You have nothing that ties me to that bomb other than being in the wrong place at the wrong time."

She didn't acknowledge that, instead whispering, "I can only keep you here until you're able to survive in lockup." She sounded apologetic. "If you know anything about that explosion or something that was going on in that building, you should tell me now."

He didn't want to hurt Tess, no matter what.

The sooner he got out of here, and preferably before she recognized him, the sooner she'd be safe.

The Black River pack had known he was going to be close to the building. They killed Sonic and set up that bomb. Hell, they probably paid the old woman to sneak inside. He wouldn't hold it against a homeless person trying to survive on the streets.

They also had someone inside SCIS. Emergency vehicles had

arrived within seconds after the bomb detonated.

That took coordination.

Screw this shit. He needed a plan and couldn't come up with one with Tess so close. Not when any plan included unleashing Gray Wolf.

CHAPTER 6

Cole kept his breathing calm while he raced to come up with a way to escape this facility. But he had one more question for Tess. "Why haven't I shifted?"

"The medics weren't sure you'd survive shifting in the condition you were in. They feared you might become stuck in mid-shift. You're being given a special tranquilizer mix. A full dose would stop an elephant in its tracks, but you're on a drip that is just enough to keep you from going under completely. I backed it off when I came in to see if you were ready to wake up and talk."

That explained why his wolf hadn't taken over.

He should have known better than to think the explosion might have done something positive to his wolf.

What a joke.

This crap going in his system only delayed the inevitable, and he had a bad feeling his wolf would be in even worse shape once he got off the juice.

Speaking of his wolf ... the beast had been quiet since Cole opened his eyes this time. Too quiet, even with the super-Valium cocktail. That worried him more than all he faced, which was saying something with the mess he was in between being framed for the explosion and suffering the mating curse.

Shit. The only woman he would ever take as a mate was sitting inches away and he couldn't touch her, much less claim her.

Angry now, Cole pointed out, "The only way I'd be too injured to shift was if I'd died." Not necessarily true, but while she might have knowledge of shifters, she knew nothing about the Gallize variety. He added, "Not allowing me to shift is preventing me from healing."

"I know. I mean, you *are* healing, but slowly."

"Technically, this is torture," he snapped. Okay, that was a low blow since he knew she'd never torture or harm anything. She couldn't kill a damn bug back when she'd found one in their apartment.

"Your medical treatment is not up to me and I'm not the one who blew up a building," she defended with no small amount of irritation.

Attagirl. Give me shit.

That eased his conscience. He had to get her out of here and without her turning on the drip again.

It hurt to push her away and he hated lying to her, but he said, "I'll be honest with you. I don't know how I ended up near that building just as a bomb exploded. I've had that lock pick set since I was a kid. Got it when I was captured as a runaway teen and put in a home with some sick fucks. They ... " He paused for effect. "Did things to the kids that I won't describe. All I remember before the explosion was working in that area as day labor. I went to get some dinner and ... I just don't ... know what happened. You're not going to believe me. No one will. I'm screwed." He tried to grab his head, but his bad arm hurt too much to move and his good arm was stuck. Restraints. "Oh, shit, just do whatever you're gonna do."

Tess moved forward, putting her hand next to him on the bed. "Okay, take it easy. Maybe more details will come back to you."

Hallelujah. She took the bait. Hook, line and ten-pound sinker.

"I don't understand ... who would ... " He blinked his one eye, intending to sell it some more to get her on his side, but she touched his face.

One touch and he forgot about anything except her fingers on his skin.

His body knew her.

His skin begged for her hands anywhere she could put them.

His heart cried out for the woman he loved.

She stroked his face on the side that wasn't burned and smoothed her hand over his hair that might be an inch long by now. He shook with the need to put his arm around her and feel her body next to his.

To taste her skin. He'd spent hours loving her any chance they got. She liked to have her nipples sucked when he teased her to an orgasm. If she got that wild glint in her eyes, she'd shove him back and ride him.

"I'm sorry," she apologized, misunderstanding a hard shudder that ran through his body as a reaction to pain.

Oh hell, he was definitely in pain.

He had a boner working.

If she saw that, she might up his tranq dosage.

Now *this* was torture. He wanted her to stroke him like she used to or allow him to reach down and do it himself. Neither was going to happen.

That surge of life inside him must have been enough to wake the beast.

His wolf lunged and clawed in a wild effort to break free.

"Oh, hell!" Cole ground out at the sudden pain. That killed the boner.

Tess jumped back. "What'd I do?"

"Nothing. Not ... your fault." He was half sitting up. "I just had a cramp."

Fucking wolf snarled to get out.

You're not getting near her, he silently told Gray Wolf.

His wolf howled.

Tough shit. Cole felt just as frustrated, but for a different reason. He had to get Tess out of here and shift to heal. That would be tricky. What if there was a video feed transmitting to a monitor?

He challenged her again. "Are people staring at me like a bug in a box? I heard that's what happens to shifters used in experiments."

"No, SCIS is a law enforcement arm. We do not hand anyone over for experiments. No one is watching you due to the necessity of you being naked for treatments. You have rights, unless you're convicted of killing humans. We don't want shifter lawsuits over lack of privacy while you're a suspect."

"It's okay to hold me without solid evidence, and without representation, but not to film me naked? I'd trade being filmed in exchange for being treated as innocent until proven guilty."

There came her sigh again. "I'm trying to ensure you have a fair opportunity, but apparently you're not with a pack. If you were, we'd be involving your alpha. As it is, you're rogue and fall under different rules. As for watching you, no one has time to watch every inmate. You're in a titanium-reinforced room so it's not necessary to observe you. We all check the window in the door before entering." She took a breath. "In case you think to overpower anyone once you're healthy again, we all carry a specially designed stun gun that is set to disable a shifter. You wouldn't like it. Please don't try."

He remembered being hit with a load of electrical power when he was incapacitated. Had he been shifting or had someone just taken advantage of his condition?

Based on what she said, this group had no worries about anyone breaking in to extract him or of Cole breaking out.

SCIS had probably airlifted him from the bomb scene to keep their prisoner alive. Without someone like the Guardian, who could shift into a giant sea eagle, no one else on his team that night could have followed.

Cole accepted the depressing truth.

He had no cavalry coming to the rescue. He was on his own with no tools or weapons. His only hope was in healing as quickly as he could and taking his chances at fighting his way out of here.

Tess said, "Now that you're conscious, the medics will want to be alerted. I'll switch your drip to the next stage, which is loaded with protein and a mix of something they claim will help you shift."

She wanted to do that now?

She might not get out the door before Gray Wolf exploded on the scene.

Cole debated a half second. It would be so much easier for her to make the IV switch, but he wanted her out of here and gone before that happened.

She moved her hand an inch on the bed and he snagged her wrist. His fingers were wrapped around her wrist, but not too firmly. A buzzing energy ran between them like a crazy current. She once said she couldn't wear watches, but he'd never felt this with her in the past.

She went perfectly still and stank of fear. "What are you doing?"

Yes, he could snap her bones like twigs, but he'd cut his own throat first.

Could he not get a break?

He worked to speak in a more even tone to convince her he was not dangerous, but his rough voice still sounded like an axe murderer. "I won't ever harm you. Please don't start the new concoction yet. My insides are a mess. You can't tell from the outside what's going on in there, but I can feel it. I've got organs to rebuild and bones to mend. Now that I've thought about it, your medic was right to wait. I'm at least another day from being able to shift without ripping everything apart. Shifting is part magic and part physiological. There are limits to what we do."

He wasn't being entirely honest, but if he could just get her to leave the narcotic drip off, he'd flip the valve for the protein stimulus mix once she left.

When she didn't reply, he added, "I admit I was surprised I hadn't changed on my own, but I'm glad someone had enough forethought to put me under until my body was ready." There was a speck of truth in that. He had a better chance of managing his wolf now than he would have had a few days ago.

Tess had seemed to be debating what to do during the long pause, but that had always been a positive sign with her in the past. She'd see reason if someone presented a logical argument.

To help push her in the right direction, he eased his grip and rubbed his thumb over her wrist.

He could feel her pulse race.

But not from fear this time.

That was interesting.

"Uhm, I guess I could leave that for the medics to decide when they come by to check on your progress," she offered.

That was a start. "You said it was evening now, right?"

"Yes."

"When will they come by?" Damn. That sounded suspicious even to him. He added, "I'm thinking in an hour or two, my insides might be healed enough for me to eat solid food. That's why I asked."

"Oh. Probably two hours unless I tell them to come now."

"Please don't. I'd like to catch a little more rest without the drugs so my body is better prepared for the kick of the shift."

"Very well. I'll leave you to rest."

Tension eased from his chest. That would have to do, because he could shift and heal significantly in an hour.

"Thank you." He meant it and loosened his grip.

She pulled her arm away and he wanted to think she'd been reluctant, but that had probably been him projecting emotions he wanted her to feel. He took one last inhale just to have something from her in his chest, close to his heart.

Talk about torment. He was killing himself with wanting to tell her the truth and break out of these bonds to be with her. He'd like one vision of her fully in focus, but if he was successful, he wouldn't be here long enough for that to happen.

He'd still talk to her before he met with the Guardian for the last time, but he didn't want her to know he'd been here.

She walked across the room and paused at the door. "Working with us will help you when it's time to determine where you go next. The more information you can provide, the better chance you have of ending up in an aboveground location. Maybe with a pack, if one will accept you. But if you attack someone in human or animal form, you'll be taken straight to a subterranean holding facility."

Subterranean holding facility was a fancy name for a ten-foot-square by ten-foot-deep hole in the ground, completely encased in titanium. That metal wouldn't kill a shifter unless inserted into their bodies and left there. Then it would prevent them from healing or shifting, which would result in death. Their claws wouldn't even scratch that metal.

Expensive, but money flowed when fear opened the gates.

A cage by any other name was still a cage.

If he shifted and regained all his Gallize power, he had a chance at escaping. If not, he'd just have to play it by ear. "I understand. Thank you again." He yawned intentionally. "Think I'm ready to sleep some more."

"You're welcome. I hope your wolf rests." The door swished shut behind her.

He stared at the door.

He hadn't told her his animal was a wolf.

Just how much did she know? Probably one of the jackal shifters on staff, which SCIS was known for hiring, had clued them in.

Now wasn't the time to waste on unanswerable questions when reaching that IV drip was going to take an acrobatic move.

Cole stared one last time at the door, cursing his life and accepting that this might be the last conversation he had with her. If he failed to escape or died trying, he'd never get to explain what happened when he disappeared.

Taking a deep breath, he mentally prepared for what he was about to try. This group thought he wouldn't be able to use his burned hand and they would be correct for a normal shifter.

That didn't mean this would be a cakewalk.

He lifted his burned arm. It did not want to work.

Closing his mind to the pain he was going to cause, he forced his hand up and over his head.

The pain was immediate.

He clenched his teeth and held his breath, straining to reach the drip. Pain like nothing he'd ever felt hit his hand when he pressed the button to shut off the drip from the multi-line IV pump. A series of beeps signaled the pump shutting down.

Cole dropped his arm and fell back against the pillow, taking in fast breaths and waiting for the excruciating pain to ease.

His wolf growled and snarled.

"Stop it, dammit," Cole murmured low. The searing ache streaked down his arm and along his side. He hissed at irritating his burned skin. Perspiration bubbled on his forehead, dampening the bandages. Chugging a couple of fast breaths, he dropped his head back to lock his one-eyed gaze on the second IV line.

What would that kick-him-in-the-ass potion do to his wolf?

Cole had no idea, but he was determined to take his chances.

The trigger for letting Gray Wolf out was on the other side of the pump, six inches past his reach.

Time to try again. Holding his good side as still as he could, he inched his bandaged fingers toward that button.

Unhealed skin tore and muscles pulled. Tears poured from his eyes, the salty liquid excruciating on the burned skin of his face under the bandages.

His body shook from self-induced shock and bile ran up his throat. When stars floated through his vision, he focused on that tiny button marked "C." If he didn't get to it now, he would have no other chance to be strong before the medics, or anyone else, entered.

He needed the advantage of a surprise attack.

The smell of his blood leaking from fractured skin permeated the air.

His fingers trembled as he stretched within a half inch of the IV feed.

Then he heard voices in the hallway.

CHAPTER 7

Tess closed the door and walked down the long hallway with occasional doors on each side, which led to rooms holding other shifter detainees from unrelated crimes.

She kept expecting her thundering heart to slow down. What was going on with her body?

Colin was a suspect in her Black River Wolf Pack case.

One of the jackal shifters had identified him as a wolf shifter, which had made Colin look even guiltier when no wolf pack in the general vicinity had a missing male.

Rogues didn't last long without support.

Something about the man felt familiar, which made no sense.

Or maybe it was the weird way her energy had come to life around him.

Like that was a positive sign?

If anything, it was extremely bizarre since she had minimal association with shifters beyond research projects and the consultants hired to work with SCIS. She stayed on her toes around those jackal shifters and felt guilty about it, because they wanted to be treated like staff.

That meant everyone shared the staff lounge and sometimes she was in there alone with the jackals.

But the wolf shifter in the room she'd just left hadn't made her feel anxious like the jackals. Tense, yes, but not fear. In fact it was just the opposite. She'd wanted to stay by his side.

She didn't want to admit she'd felt attracted to Colin.

The man was half burned to death. Between the swelling and the burst blood vessels under his cornea, she couldn't even see his one good eye well enough to make out its true color.

Physical appearance had never been the first thing to attract Tess.

A smile could catch her eye, but it was her ability to nail the genuine person in a first meeting that had always piqued her interest.

Colin sounded genuine, but he also hid secrets.

Rubbing her arms, she couldn't push off the insane urge to go back to Colin and spend more time with him. She'd been drawn to him and when he'd touched her ...

She'd felt it in her womb.

That was another thing she wouldn't admit to anyone. She wanted to know more about him, and she couldn't honestly call it a professional interest.

More than ever, she wanted to see him healthy just to find out what he looked like.

Was he telling the truth about his presence at the bomb scene?

If so, how could she allow them to put an innocent shifter in a death pit? That was her term for the subterranean holding facilities. Shifters might not be entirely human, but ... they weren't entirely animal either.

Her father would lose his mind if he heard her utter that sentiment.

She'd come a long way from the young college woman who cringed at the first televised images of the shifter-on-shifter bloodbaths. The same woman who had agreed with her father's rage over innocent humans being killed by these anomalies of nature.

Knowledge made the difference.

She still got her back up when an innocent was harmed, but she could now admit being open-minded enough to consider all innocent people, human or not.

The bottom line for her was right and wrong when intelligence was involved. Shifters who walked the earth in human form had human intelligence and had to be held accountable ... but so did regular humans.

Stopping short of the elevators thirty feet away, she leaned against a wall, in no hurry to see her SCIS boss until she got her body and mind in line. It had been tough getting selected for this position, but she'd found her calling and was determined to become the first female to reach the level of director at SCIS national headquarters. To do that, she had to prove herself at every turn, which meant not hesitating to be decisive when dealing with shifters. It also meant never showing a weak front, but at the same time knowing when to fight a battle she believed in.

She'd been raised by a strong woman and would not fold in the face of conflict, but ...

Colin had her in a mental and emotional flux.

Why?

She couldn't be sidetracked from gaining justice.

Tess struggled to find a balance in all of this because of what had happened with her mom. No shifter had attacked her mother, but one had tried to mug her, then another had stepped into the fray and they'd had a territorial battle.

Being caught in the midst of a violent battle with two men shifting into animals, fighting over who got the human, had been too much for her mom's heart.

Her mom had died because of out-of-control shifters.

That should clear up any confusion Tess had, even if she did hold herself just as responsible for not being with her mom that night.

Tess kept waiting for that moment of clarity.

It didn't come and she knew why.

For one brief moment, she'd been intimidated by Colin. He'd grabbed her wrist and she'd just shut down in panic, at a loss for what to do or say. What had he done? Relaxed his grip and stroked his thumb over her skin.

His gentle touch had felt as if someone reached inside and stroked her heart.

No man had drawn that kind of reaction from her since, well, since college.

Damn Daniel Cole Cavanaugh's soul.

The first time she'd had a feminine reaction to a man in forever and it had to be with a rogue shifter?

This was entirely Cole's fault.

Do you realize how insane that would sound out loud, Tess?

Yes, which was why she kept it to herself. She never talked about this kind of thing, mainly because she had no girlfriends.

Unless she counted the obstinate, contract shifter investigator on the SCIS team. Tess had met the woman after hours for drinks just one time since coming to take this position in the Spartanburg office.

Not share-your-secrets girlfriend material, definitely, but networking was networking, Tess would keep engaging for sake of their professional relationship.

Turning toward the elevator, she pulled out her mobile phone and started scrolling through messages.

"Tess? Wait up," Theo Brantley called to her from where he'd just exited the elevator on this floor.

Brantley had that clean-cut Fed look, which made sense. SCIS had recruited him from the FBI division that originally dealt with shifters when they first came out to humans. Brantley had been one of the few to step forward and take control of a chaotic situation.

Then he'd put in for a position with SCIS as head of security at the Spartanburg branch, and had accepted the assignment working with Tess like a gentleman even though she had been designated as lead agent on the Black River Pack case.

For the right woman, Brantley would be a catch with his dark-blond hair cut in the latest style for a mover and shaker in their world. His eyes had always seemed an odd shade of light brown to her, but sharp as a hawk's, and attractive enough to go with a perfect nose and mouth. Moving all of that around in a lean, fit body meant a commitment to working out.

Yep, he had all the right packaging for the perfect boyfriend.

He'd even asked her out. Twice.

She'd politely turned him down, finally citing that she never dated anyone where she worked, which was far nicer than saying she wasn't at ease around him.

Her problem.

She didn't feel comfortable with any of the men at this SCIS office, and she wasn't entirely sure why. It didn't matter. She knew better than to date anyone from her business life.

Sure, she'd had a few flings since college, but she never let anyone get close. Who could blame her? She'd opened herself up once and that relationship had destroyed her faith in love.

When Brantley walked up to her, his gaze jumped past her face and in the direction of the room where Colin slept, then back to her. "What are you doing here?"

He was her partner on this assignment at SCIS, and protocol demanded that she inform him of all her trips to see John Doe, aka Colin, but that would have been a problem. She'd been making more visits than normal over the past two days.

Nothing he needed to know.

Brantley was sharp, and he would latch onto anything that hinted of failure to maintain clinical objectivity about shifters at all times. He'd made it clear that he had little regard for any shifter, other than the jackals he oversaw for SCIS. She could have pushed to be involved with managing the jackals, but she'd been relieved when he volunteered to take the lead on jackal relations.

One less headache, which freed her up to focus on areas she considered more important.

Shrugging, she explained, "Just checking on our suspect from the explosion. We need to know as soon as he's ready to talk."

"Time to wake him up."

That was not Brantley's call to make, but she didn't argue. "He's awake."

Brantley's eyes bulged. "You went in there *alone*? You should have contacted me."

Tess bristled at the insinuation that she needed an escort, since that was *not* agency protocol for someone in her position. Brantley wouldn't need backup, but he clearly thought a woman would.

His subtle innuendo always pointed in that direction, but like any good ladder climber, he was careful with his words. Still, she'd caught on to his attitude and had no intention of giving him an opening to make a case that would cast her as a poor choice for director at some point.

She held her temper and calmly stated, "He's still weak from the tranq, so I don't need an escort. Besides, I have a stun gun, just like everyone else."

But she hadn't considered reaching for the weapon under her jacket.

If she had, she couldn't have used it. Not while he was touching her.

The security professional who'd instructed her on the specially made weapon had never expected her to willingly be in contact with someone she might have to drop. There'd been no training for that scenario.

Brantley scowled. "I know you're capable of using a defensive weapon, but you can't assume you're safe just because you have it."

She'd never told anyone that she carried the weapon and was prepared to use it at any moment mainly because of the jackal shifters who worked for SCIS. That would go over like a vat of boiling oil dropped on this man's head.

Brantley gave her a put-upon look. "Don't give me that look of indignation. I'm only saying we have no information on this shifter. He might have changed shape and attacked you."

"He's still half dead and has straps on an arm and a thigh. He isn't a threat yet." In fact, she kept thinking he needed her, but she had no reason to stay when he was clearly too exhausted to talk any more.

"You can't know he's not a threat, Tessella," Brantley argued.

Someone without her background, or sincere interest in all things shifters, was not qualified to tell her what she could know or not know.

But she had to be a team player, so she nicely explained, "I'm here because I *do* understand who and what I'm dealing with when it comes to shifters, as much as anybody in today's world can know. In fact, I probably own the most extensive library in existence on this topic, since professionals around the world contact *me* for advice and information."

She stopped short of reminding Brantley that it was her research, sometimes groundbreaking, on individual shifter animal traits, habitat, psychology and interaction that had landed her this position with SCIS.

He knew.

She waited for the obvious to sink in.

He held up his hands. "Hey, don't bite my head off. I'm just saying I'm concerned about you taking risks, that's all. No one is questioning your expertise. I didn't mean to upset you."

Argh. She hated to be dealt with as if she were an emotional female. "I'm not upset. But I am tired and ready to crack this case."

"I'm right there with you, hon."

She started to say, "Don't call me hon," something she had not tolerated while in school, but this was one of those battles that would not be worth the damage. He rarely used that term. If she chastised him for the slipup, word would get back to the staff, which was primarily male, and they'd start treating her like she had perpetual PMS.

She spun Brantley's original question on him. "What are *you* doing here this time of night?"

"Checking on John Doe. How lucid is he?"

Something told her to be careful with what she said. "He remembers before the explosion, but says he was not involved with it. He claims to be an innocent bystander."

Brantley made a snorting sound. "You didn't believe him, did you?"

Part of her wanted to speak up for Colin, to be his voice, to ensure he was treated fairly.

That was a big leap from the Tess who had wanted to put all shifters into holes after her mother's death.

The years of studying and boosting her education on shifters had given her some distance. She'd needed it to be able to approach this work with clinical professionalism and not wear her heart on her sleeve.

It still hurt, but her mother had once told her to never allow an obstacle to get in the way of her goal.

Not even grief.

With regard to his pointedly asking if she believed their captive, Tess shook her head rather than give voice to words that might not sound sincere. "Let's not jump to unsubstantiated conclusions. Everyone deserves a fair investigation. I'm heading home. I'll be back early. We can interrogate him together. If the protein doesn't kick in and our shifter doesn't shift tonight, I think he'll be ready to shift tomorrow. Maybe then he won't be so distracted by his injuries."

"That works for me."

But Brantley remained in place after saying that.

When she lifted her eyebrows in question, he said, "I'm waiting on the medical team to check his vitals. Have to give the chief an update."

He meant Southeastern SCIS Chief of Local Operations Marlin Fender, who answered directly to the national SCIS headquarters in DC. Fender was also a friend of her father. Their friendship had developed through Fender's reporting to her father's congressional committee on shifter issues.

That was fine. Fender had never shown her any preferential treatment, which was just the way she wanted it.

In fact, he'd been on her back for weeks to get results.

"I'm on my way there now to brief the chief," she told Brantley.

He smiled. "Great. I'll just take a look at John Doe and call it a night."

Nodding at Brantley, she walked away. The weight of worry on her shoulders grew heavier with every step, pushing her to go back and be present when the medics went in.

Wouldn't Brantley love her hovering?

He'd never owned up to wanting the director's position, but he did and she was his top competition.

She'd bring the roof down on her head if she went back to observe Colin now, because the worst mistake she could make was showing a bias for mercy toward any shifter. Brantley would report that in a nanosecond, then Fender would no doubt let it slip around her father.

She had worked her backside off for years to cut through the steel apron strings her father held and had no intention of answering to him for her actions in this job.

Her father had wanted her to throw in the towel and join a law firm one of his buddies ran.

Never going to happen.

But to succeed here, she couldn't show any compassion when it came time to interrogate their prisoner.

He had one chance at convincing her and Brantley of his true identity tomorrow and that he was not a Black River pack member. If he hesitated and made her feel like a fool for being sympathetic, all her good will would fly out the window.

Her gut said that wolf shifter was telling the truth, but she'd been fooled once in the past when her emotions got involved, and she couldn't dismiss the possibility that he had been playing her.

If he had, he'd find out that while she would be fair to a fault, she was the last woman any man should ever cross.

CHAPTER 8

Cole had paused to sharpen his hearing and listen to the conversation between Tess and someone else.

Who the hell was that guy?

Gray Wolf had been acting half decent while Tess was around, but he became agitated the minute she left.

When some strange man spoke to Tess, his wolf had practically chewed its way out.

That hampered Cole's efforts to reach the IV to force the special protein stimulant into his system.

If that was a medic talking to Tess, Cole might have to wait for them to come take his vitals. If so, maybe he could convince them to open the valve for his new IV flow on their way out.

Hell yes. This could work.

Protect mate. Gray Wolf was working himself into a lather.

Cole hissed, "Stop it. She is not our mate."

Wrong. More snarling.

Dropping his head back, Cole tried to calm his wolf so he could act normal around the medics. Maybe this would be the last visit for the night.

Cole worked to focus his only uncovered eye. Slowly, he made out a design on the ceiling.

The door opened and a guy with a toothpaste smile walked in. He'd dressed up his image to fool everyone, but Cole saw something unnatural when the light struck his eyes.

That was no human.

Nor was he a shifter.

Could he be a Cadell? Cole's gut instinct made his muscles tense, but he could only identify a Cadell's magic for sure while in animal form.

A Cadell working with SCIS?

Of course, because it would give Cadells, the Gallize enemy for many generations, access to all shifters.

I'm so fucked.

But ... maybe not. Cole's eagle tattoo, which marked him as Gallize, had been on the left shoulder. Getting burned would have destroyed the tattoo, right?

For now, he'd be thankful for the charring on that side of his body since it protected his identity. Otherwise, if this guy was definitely Cadell, he'd know immediately that he had a Gallize shifter in his possession.

A badly wounded Gallize.

Cadells hated Gallize shifters. The magic that spawned the first Gallize in the sixth century had been denied to Cadellus, a dangerous witch. She bred Cadells for the sole purpose of killing Gallize shifters and taking their mates.

"I'm Theo Brantley, in charge of security for the southeastern division of SCIS. I partner with Tessella on investigating extreme shifter activity, in particular the Black River pack crimes."

Cole clenched his jaw at this being speaking Tess's name, but he said nothing. Brantley must not know that Cole was a Gallize, because Cole was still alive.

All Cole could do for the moment was study the guy through his swollen eye. His vision was starting to focus better every second, now that the tranq drip had been shut off. He could definitely see an unnatural look to the man's eyes. Based on the weathered skin and slight lines at the corners of his eyes, Cole put this guy around forty ... if this Brantley were human, which Cole seriously doubted. He'd go with his first gut reaction until someone proved him wrong.

"What's your name?" Brantley asked.

"Colin."

"Last name?"

"O'Donnell."

"That's a start. Tessella indicated you don't recall anything about the explosion."

"I don't."

Brantley leaned against the wall with his arms crossed, looking casual, but Cole's ears perked at the sense he was being hunted. His wolf had quieted again for some reason. When the two of them were in sync, his wolf would become very still with Cole when they were in enemy territory.

Evidently Cole wasn't the only one who smelled an enemy in the room.

The corner of Brantley's lips tipped in a smile meant to disturb his prey. "I'm not as gullible as my associate. You have until tomorrow morning to pull your story together. If there are any holes, there are no second chances."

The door opened again and two men in hospital scrubs walked in.

Cole revised that assessment. Two *shifters* wearing medical clothing walked in. One had dirty fingernails.

These weren't medics.

What the hell did they plan to do?

In an effort to stop them from adjusting his IV feed just yet, Cole said, "I'll tell you everything I know tomorrow. I should be ready to shift and heal by then. Once I do, I'm hoping the rest of my memory returns. I'm getting bits and pieces. Not surprising considering the damage my body has suffered, but ... I'll be better tomorrow."

He hoped to be much improved in about an hour if he could convince the so-called medics to lower his bed just a few inches. He'd claim a headache and see if they bought it. Two more inches and he could definitely get his fingers on the IV.

Brantley released his full grin. "I'm certain you'll be much better in the morning. These fine men are going to help you shift. They've brought a special mix we use for shifters who can't call up their animal. They tell me yours is a wolf, which is quite a coincidence when you think about being at a scene where we were told we'd find a Black River pack member. But let's save that for tomorrow. In the meantime, your animal will be released and these men will ensure you don't hurt yourself."

Hell no. If they forced his wolf to the surface, Cole wouldn't be healed enough to defend himself against two healthy shifters. Jackals at that.

He tried to keep his heart rate from spiking, but his wolf hadn't liked this any more than he had. The beast went wild with the urge to attack, ramping up the pain Cole had just gotten to the point of managing.

Cole gritted his teeth and argued, "That's a bad idea. My wolf is injured and will come out fighting."

The jackals snickered.

Brantley had turned away as if ignoring Cole. Opening the door, Brantley paused and said, "I'm betting on it."

One of the jackal shifters moved like lightning to inject a yellow fluid into the IV feed.

Cole lunged at him with his bad arm, but the other shifter slammed the arm with a fist.

Bones snapped in Cole's restrained hand.

Gray Wolf went wild, banging like crazy to get out.

The rush of new meds shot into Cole's chest and boiled with the adrenaline already rushing through him.

He lunged up against the restraints, lashing out with his burned arm at the laughing pair.

The bigger of the two shifters grabbed the damaged arm and shoved it down.

Cole's vision distorted, his back twisted.

Gray Wolf came charging forward.

CHAPTER 9

Tess had just paid for a coffee, which she needed on the way in the next morning. She hadn't slept much and had to be to be sharp for the interrogation.

Too many dreams about a man she'd sworn not to think about again. Seven years should be long enough to forget him.

Her phone buzzed. Finding a place to drop her purse and drink, she took the call. "I'm on my way in, Brantley."

"We've got a problem. Our wolf shifter changed into his animal and went wild. He attacked two of our staff."

All her sympathy for that shifter went right out the window. She would not tolerate an out-of-control animal, be it natural or part human.

She pushed speed limits, hurrying to the facility located outside of the metro area, not stopping until she reached Colin's door. When she looked through the glass observation panel, she gasped.

The stretcher had been wrecked along with all of the IV set up, but it was the walls that raised her horror.

Deep claw marks gouged the cosmetic wood panels layered over the titanium reinforcement, and blood splatters covered everything as if a crazed artist had created macabre abstract art.

Her phone buzzed with a text.

Brantley's message said the wolf had been sedated and moved to their secure shifter cell.

She looked back at the room.

How long had that massacre gone on?

Any compassion belonged to those who had been harmed.

Turning around, she got her second workout of the morning,

hurrying to the elevator to take it to the basement floor. Good thing she'd worn jeans and sneakers. She called them running shoes to give the impression she exercised, which would only happen when ... never.

She couldn't equate the man who had touched her so gently with one who shifted into a monster, but that was clearly the reality.

At the bottom level, she walked out of the elevator and turned left at the first corridor. The ones on the right were for minimal threats.

The left wing had two holding cells where the most dangerous beings were held.

After seeing Colin's infirmary room, she had no doubt where he'd been taken.

Was that even his real name?

Fishing out her access card, she swiped it over the security panel next to a steel door with a titanium core. When the door clicked open, she hurried in and quickly found Brantley standing on an observation deck in front of six narrow vertical windows protected by a four-inch thick, acrylic-type material that had been fabricated with fine titanium wires woven through the panels. Even if a shifter managed to break these windows, the openings were only a foot wide by four feet tall.

Glancing over his shoulder, Brantley waved her over.

She had a moment of hesitation.

Would Colin finally reveal his face or look like some werewolf creature from a B movie?

Not that any shifter had looked like that yet, but her imagination had been running freely since she got the call half an hour ago.

Crossing the room, she eased up to the observation window as if looking into a snake pit. She hated snakes, especially the idea of seeing more than one.

But when she leaned forward, she didn't see a snake ... or a wolf.

Standing defiantly on the opposite wall from them was a naked male wearing a full iron head mask. She'd forgotten about those, having never seen one used until now. A thick, six-inch chain at the back of the full-face head cover was bolted a foot into the titanium wall. No room to maneuver, and shifting while wearing the mask would very likely cause death.

A space in the mask had been left open for his eyes. One slit under his nose plus another oval opening at his mouth allowed a prisoner to speak.

She felt like a voyeur, but turning away to protect Colin's privacy would play into Brantley's hand. He'd love to point out that, as a woman, she wasn't cut out to do this type of work. He was too smart to voice it out loud and make himself a target for a sexual discrimination complaint. But the wrong reaction would provide him a reason to suggest in a closed-door meeting that she couldn't handle the job.

If she were honest, she couldn't move her gaze from the most magnificent male body she'd ever seen.

She didn't know any woman who could objectively look at Colin's fit body and turn away. He surpassed any model she'd ever seen in an underwear ad. Speaking of underwear, nothing even slightly snug could hide how well he was endowed.

Damn, this was so not professional.

Eyes above the waist, Tess.

Like that downplayed his body one bit? Look at the guns on that man.

If she didn't get a grip and keep her face completely void of any reaction, Brantley would have some serious ammunition to use against her.

She would not give him that. She'd just do her best to pretend she wasn't looking at some Adonis. Could she help that she hadn't been up close and personal with many men in the last few years?

Witnessing shifters turn into naked men came with the territory of studying them, but this was the first time she'd had such a primitive reaction to one.

And she'd certainly never had this tingling in her core—the same tingling she'd felt last night at Colin's side—but the freaking buzzing was also back in a serious way.

Determined to put on her future-SCIS-director face, she asked her partner, "Has he spoken?"

"Not yet."

"When did he shift?"

"Around two this morning. Maybe a little after."

She'd gone home close to nine. "What happened between when

I left and then? Did the medics do anything?"

"I entered with them right after I saw you and took a minute to ask his name. He said he's Colin O'Donnell."

She fought a moment of disappointment over Colin giving Brantley his full name, but had to pay attention to what her partner was saying.

"The shifters on the medic staff came in to take his vitals. They said Colin's body was healed enough to shift, in fact the bones in his right arm had mended, which was a surprise."

She didn't say a word about touching Colin, just kept giving Brantley her undivided attention.

He said, "The jackals said at that point he would just be suffering the longer he was held back from shifting. O'Donnell said he wanted to sleep some more, so I told the jackals to check back after midnight."

That fit what Colin had told Tess about wanting to sleep more and that her people were basically torturing him. She asked, "What happened next?"

"Two of our shifters returned just after midnight. One of them texted me that they planned to give Colin the protein stimulus and they would stay long enough to see that he was able to shift fully into his wolf. Standard Operating Procedure."

True, but she still had a hard time understanding how Colin, who had sounded so calm and in control, would have done this when he knew he couldn't escape. He had to know that attacking the jackals would pretty much condemn him to imprisonment.

She asked, "Are there any videos of what happened?" There were no observation cameras that ran continually, but those rooms were outfitted with equipment to film interactions with patients or prisoners.

"No. I didn't think we'd need it filmed. Did you?"

She shook her head.

He huffed a tired sigh. "All I know other than that is I got a call around two this morning that the jackals had failed to check in on their hourly rounds. That's when staff looked in Colin's room and saw the walls painted in blood. A giant gray wolf stood in the middle of the massacre, baring his fangs at everyone."

"Didn't either shifter use a stun gun?"

"Yes, one of the stun guns had been discharged. It was set on a full takedown blast. Evidently, that didn't work. Our sniper on staff was called. He opened a panel in the door and the wolf lunged at him, but our guy shot the wolf with our strongest shifter tranq. Even that didn't take effect as quickly as expected. Both of our jackal shifters were taken to ICU. I transferred them to their pack house as per their contract if they were badly injured. They don't trust being around any shifters when they can't defend themselves."

She clutched her throat, envisioning the attack and the bloodbath. Colin, or whoever this guy was, would not walk free after harming those two.

Brantley hadn't taken his eyes off of the naked man as he continued. "I didn't want to call you sooner since I figured it would take time for O'Donnell to begin waking from the tranq and shift back, if he was going to return to human form. I let you know as soon as he woke and our staff got the mask in place."

"Liar."

Colin's voice boomed even inside the enclosed room.

She flinched and cursed silently, then lifted the microphone. "What?"

Silence answered her.

She cut her gaze at Brantley, who gave her the look he did every time he reminded her that these shifters were barely a step above wild beasts. She didn't agree when it came to the entire population, but now was not the time for that conversation, especially if this shifter was listening in.

Returning to the microphone, she said, "You clearly heard everything said, so my question is, why did you attack our people, *Colin?*"

The iron mask lifted to face her. When it did, piercing blue eyes studied her so hard she had the urge to back away.

Not happening.

No one, not even a shifter, was going to make her run.

His skin was still pink along the left side where he'd been burned, and his right arm that had healed last night now appeared swollen. None of that stopped him from curling both hands into fists, which indicated he had use of them.

The gouges in the walls of his room had been enough to show he was physically fit to fight.

Colin spoke in a smoother voice now that he'd healed significantly, but it had an odd quality from being filtered through the speakers. "I have no control over what my wolf does when I'm given drugs I didn't request or approve."

She heard something familiar in his voice but couldn't put her finger on it. How many people had she met over the years? Thousands, especially during her research days. His voice must remind her of someone else.

Brantley snorted at Colin's comment and muttered, "Typical."

Colin's gaze hardened to a frightening intensity and turned to Brantley. "What's the point in asking me questions when you're going to lie to her?"

Tess looked over for Brantley's reaction, but there was none. Her partner sighed and lifted the microphone, "You clearly don't need me to use a mic, but this ensures that everything we say is on record so no one can claim you weren't given a fair chance. I've run a background check on Colin O'Donnell, which shows that you were a child of the state in Dublin, Ireland. Then you fell off the map for a few years before surfacing three months ago. You don't even have an Irish accent."

Colin crossed his arms which only accentuated his guns. He was clearly comfortable in his own skin. If not for the situation, she'd call him sexy as hell, and so dangerous ...

Tess swallowed and forced herself to watch his arms, shoulders and head.

Nothing below the arms. Nothing.

Think about that wrecked room and ripped-up shifters.

That threw a load of ice water on her crazy hormones.

With only a slight pause, Brantley continued. "The thing about that kind of background is that it's a little too perfect, because we find nothing during the missing years. Where were you?"

A slight smirk lifted Colin's lips. "Not that you'll believe me, but I was living on the streets."

"You're right. I don't believe you, so let's get down to business now that you're healthy enough to answer questions and no longer taking drugs."

"More like having them forced on me."

Tess wanted to have what Brantley said verified.

What if someone had loaded Colin's IV with too much

medication? Why would anyone on staff do that without authorization, though? She hated that her gut was yapping at her to consider Colin's side of this, that he might not have had control of his wolf due to the drugs.

Brantley shrugged. "We could have let you die."

"And give up a golden opportunity for a scapegoat? No, that wouldn't happen."

Ignoring that comment, Brantley asked, "What were you doing at the food bank building Monday night?"

"Told you I was walking by."

Even Tess thought that answer came too quickly.

Sighing, she spoke into the mic. "Don't you understand the trouble you're in? Being obstinate is not working in your favor," she said with a hard voice she hoped got through.

All she received in return was a sad pair of eyes shifting to meet hers.

Tapping an index finger against the throat of the microphone, Brantley said, "Just tell us what you know about the Black River pack and we'll go easy on you. That's a fair offer."

When Colin replied, his voice packed sarcasm. "There's not a damn thing fair about your operation. You're using jackal shifters as staff. They're mercs who kill for money. You have no reason to hold me, just circumstantial evidence. But you're still going to lock me away forever. I've got nothing to say to you."

Tess crossed her arms to hide her own fingers curled into fists. Why couldn't Colin just give them a straight answer?

Brantley turned to her. "It's your call. You're the lead on this."

Oh, so *now* she was the lead?

She lifted her head and found Colin staring at her now with a look of concern.

Never leaving his gaze, she told Brantley, "Call in the transport."

Colin's eyes seemed disheartened, as if he'd expected more from her. He didn't even know her. How could he make her feel guilty when he was the one who had mauled two shifters?

For now, they had to move him to a better holding cell, much as she hated it. But no one would agree to keeping him in this facility. While he was gone, she'd do a thorough investigation of what happened last night and withhold any judgment until then. But for now, she had injured staff to worry about.

Colin said, "Don't do this."

She didn't even pick up the mic. "Not putting you into a holding cell to begin with was my decision and now two shifters are paying the price for my trying to allow you to heal. I have a duty to protect everyone in this facility, which includes any contract SCIS staff regardless of your assessment of our shifters. I will not allow another person I know to be harmed by an out-of-control shifter."

Turning away, she led Brantley out of the room.

A mournful howl rose from the room behind her.

Her chest ached as if someone had reached in and gripped her heart.

What the devil was going on with her?

She didn't know, but the farther she moved from Colin, the more pain settled in her chest. Not enough to prevent her from functioning, but real enough to make her hurry to put distance between that wolf shifter and her.

After today, she wouldn't see him again unless he decided to tell the truth about the bombing, which she seriously doubted.

CHAPTER 10

Cole wore a thin gray jumpsuit he'd been given before leaving the SCIS facility. His beard itched under the metal mask, which they'd welded shut when he was detached from the wall. His ankle chains jingled as he walked out the front door into blinding sunlight. His wrists were cuffed behind him and the mask made it hard to turn his head, but the scenery reminded him of northern South Carolina.

But there was nothing here but an old farmhouse and barn, the guards and a transport truck.

The Guardian's human in the US government kept him informed of SCIS operations, so this place would be on the Guardian's list. But if they'd marked it as a research facility, Cole's team would have no reason to hunt him here.

They'd be looking at holding facilities first.

Way to think positive, Cole.

Just keeping it real.

An armored truck had been parked in front of the house the staff used for access to the underground rooms. The truck had a South Carolina tag, possibly confirming his guess even if it wouldn't help him.

Of all the things that surprised him, Gray Wolf actually behaving for the moment topped that list.

Maybe because his wolf's rampage last night had been a pressure release, allowing his animal to run free even if it had been contained in that room.

Gray Wolf had let Cole know just how little control he maintained anymore.

Cole blamed that bastard Brantley for overdosing him with something that was not a protein compound.

Gray Wolf huffed softly, just letting Cole know he was there. That one gesture reminded Cole of the many times over the years he'd been as one with his wolf. Maybe Gray Wolf realized they were heading toward the end and it would come in a cage.

Brantley would get what he wanted.

Cole would like to know for sure Brantley was Cadell, but some of them were gifted at hiding their identities and acting as humans.

Something was going on between Tess and her so-called partner.

If Cole were to guess, he'd say Brantley wanted her out of the picture completely. He'd said that sending Cole away was her decision, meaning Tess was higher on the totem pole than Brantley. For now.

She hadn't wanted to send for transport.

That much had been clear.

If she knew the suspicion Cole harbored—that Brantley was not human—she'd be running to get away from the guy, but she couldn't know.

Even most shifters wouldn't have recognized what Brantley really was.

Gallize shifters could pick up on Cadell magic, but only in their animal forms. This guy hadn't used magic yet, so Cole *might* be wrong.

But he would bet his next breath that he was right.

If Brantley *was* Cadell, he'd wrangled a position that allowed him access to jackal shifters for his dirty work. Having those shifters inserted as SCIS staff now made even more sense.

Gray Wolf wouldn't have stopped bleeding those two jackal shifters if Cole hadn't pleaded with him. That had been the last resort when his wolf had ignored Cole's orders. It had taken shouting telepathically at Gray Wolf that he was going to get Tess in trouble.

Those two jackals had been no match for Gray Wolf even after they'd shifted, and they had Tess to thank for being alive.

Brantley and Tess stood near the box bed for the truck.

Cole swept a look around, as much as the hot, iron mask would allow. No help in sight.

A guard shoved him in the back.

He stumbled, but gained his footing.

The closer Cole got to Tess, the more alert his wolf became until it was pawing hard by the time Cole was marched up to the rear of the truck.

Brantley stepped aside to hand papers to a new pair of jackal shifters and said, "Here are your delivery forms. Let me know if you have any trouble." He stepped several feet away and lifted his phone to scroll through it.

Tess moved over to where Cole stood between two guards armed with stun guns. He didn't want to experience those hits if possible. But that didn't stop him from constantly assessing a possible escape route.

He took in her sad gaze.

Did she feel guilty for sending him to a hole in the ground? She would at some point, because eventually someone would show her his face and she'd realized what she'd done. But it might not be until they brought her the report of his death.

This wasn't her fault.

He knew she was doing her best at her job. This woman was the most honorable person he'd ever met.

Gray Wolf howled to get out.

Even if Cole didn't have this mask on, he wouldn't unleash his monster on any of these people.

I will kill them all.

No, Cole told Gray Wolf. *You can't do that.*

Well, maybe Brantley, Cole amended to himself.

They will kill us.

Gray Wolf had a point, but Cole still couldn't condone unleashing his beast on anyone. He told his wolf, *I'm trying to keep us alive right now. Don't fight me.*

His wolf had nothing to say, but then his wolf had always been about teeth and claws, not reason. Cole cut his gaze at the jackals, who were having a hard time hiding their glee at his future.

Fuck them.

If he had the chance, he'd let Gray Wolf deal with those paid murderers.

Would Tess believe him if Cole told her she was paying shifters who lived to bleed others?

Probably not.

Tess told the shifters, "I want a minute." She'd spoken with a stern edge that meant she expected to be obeyed.

The jackals moved back, eyeing her with disrespect that had a growl climbing up his throat.

Tess distracted him from his lethal thoughts when she spoke. "I don't want to do this," she whispered with that same core of iron in her voice. "Just tell us what you know and I can revoke the order until I have time to do a full investigation on what happened last night."

Her soft voice climbed inside of Cole and warmed him. But he couldn't tell her the truth without exposing that he was Gallize, which would expose the Guardian's teams. Between the shifters and the Cadells, it was getting damned hard to function in this country without exposing their Gallize league.

But he would die to protect the people he considered family.

They would do the same for him.

Before he left, Cole had to do one thing for Tess, to spare her conscience once she discovered that she'd sent the man she loved in college to his death. He had to say it in a way that she would not figure out that he knew who she was until later. "You lost someone important to a shifter, didn't you?"

His words brought a chilly change to her disposition.

She said, "That has nothing to do with this."

"Yes, it does. What happened in your past is driving you to right wrongs between shifters and humans, isn't it?" His guess? Her mother's death pushed Tess to this point.

Her heart strummed a fast beat. He could hear the pounding and scented something new. Anger. Her face pulled down shutters over her emotions, but she'd already exposed herself.

He'd been right, so he pushed once more. "You seem like you genuinely want to understand shifters. I'm asking because I'd like to know why you're so interested. Call it a dying man's last request."

Whatever tart comment had been about to launch off her tongue got pulled back at the suggestion that he wouldn't survive this.

If Cole was right about Brantley, he wouldn't see another day in this world.

She tapped her fingers on her hip in a state of thinking. "I lost a family member years ago in a shifter attack, yes. So what's your point?"

He hated to be in this position, but he hated it just as much for Tess. Maybe more. He'd been yanked into this world by dormant genes that came to life prematurely, based on what the Guardian had told him, but Tess was human.

An innocent.

Brantley headed toward them.

Cole's seconds with Tess were coming to an end. This time, he'd never see her again. He had so many things he wanted to tell her, so many things he had to explain, but he couldn't do it here and now.

What he *could* do was ease her burden. "I forgive you, Tess. I understand what you're doing and that you would never intentionally hurt someone. You're too sweet, too honorable and too decent for this world."

Her eyes widened with shock. "What did—"

Cole barely moved his head from side to side, telling her not to say another word.

"Time to go," Brantley ordered. "Load him up."

The jackal with curly, carrot-colored hair yanked Cole up the steps. The other shifter followed along behind, holding the chain around Cole's waist.

When they had him in the center of the cargo area, they positioned him spread-eagle. They hooked three-inch-wide titanium manacles around his wrists that had chains running to opposite upper corners of the box structure. Those chains ran through thick steel guides and down the corners to a unit that reminded Cole of a small motor with low gears.

That would probably cinch the chains tight.

Similar cuffs were put on each ankle before releasing his leg containments. Those cuffs had chains running to opposing corners of the cargo box, which they tightened until he stood with his feet far apart.

What the hell?

Cole could shift and drop out of any of those manacles. He perked up. Transporting him this way could provide a chance to escape.

Hadn't they tried this with other shifters?

Brantley grinned. "Like our new transport vehicle?"

Oh, so it was a first time. He'd break it in for them. Cole ignored the snide comment.

With a nod from Brantley, one of the jackals hit a button near the back door.

The grind of a winch motor hummed and chains began slowly tightening, pulling his arms straight out. Then the chains hooked to his legs slid away from him as a second motor started, forcing his legs wide. Too wide.

The motors stopped.

Cole drew short breaths and fought to stifle a groan over how taut his body was being drawn in four directions.

He clenched his jaw shut, refusing to let even a grunt slip out.

"A word to the wise," Brantley went on in his superior tone that Cole was looking forward to shoving down his throat. "It's more than a tensioning system. If you get the wise idea to change to your wolf, this has been designed with a shifter in mind. Your arms and legs draw up before the muscles and bone change, which means you'll tug on the chains at that point. One slight pull and the chains tighten a half-inch snugger ... all four. From what I'm told, once you start shifting, it's hard to stop. That would really suck, because continuing to activate it will result in at least one limb being ripped out."

Fuck.

Cole couldn't look at Tess when she gasped. He could smell her anxiety. He doubted anyone had told her about this new mode of transporting prisoners.

The rear door slammed shut and he held every muscle as still as he could to keep from activating a motor. He'd trained to endure the worst torture imaginable, but with no idea how long this trip would be, he wasn't sure he'd arrive in one piece.

CHAPTER 11

You're too sweet, too honorable and too decent for this world.
Tess couldn't breathe.

Cole Cavanaugh had once said that to her.

How would this Colin know that? She refused to believe in coincidences. If not for Colin being a shifter, she'd think that was Cole, but it couldn't be. Cole was human.

That shifter was screwing with her mind. Maybe he could read minds and found that in her thoughts.

Why?

She had no use for people jerking her chain. With that in mind, she rounded on Brantley.

"Why didn't you tell me about that transport?" Tess asked, not hiding her anger from anyone. She'd probably regret it later when she received sideways looks from the staff, but they needed to know she would not tolerate being unpleasantly surprised when dealing with a prisoner's life.

Brantley sliced a look around to where staff stood listening and opened his mouth as if to issue an order.

Oh, hell no.

Tess turned to the group and calmly announced, "Everyone, please go back to your jobs."

They glanced at Brantley, then Tess, and headed back to the house where they could access the elevator to their underground facility.

In ten seconds, it was only the two of them under a blazing sun and gentle breeze that would normally lift her spirits.

Not today.

Swatting a blunt look of irritation at her, he said, "I go along with pretty much everything you say even when I don't agree. I do that out of respect for our working together. You have your duties and I have mine, which include developing better security standards at every opportunity. That new armored vehicle is a step toward protecting our people who have to transport dangerous shifters. What's your problem with it?"

She couldn't face Colin ending up ripped into pieces.

Admitting that about a shifter who had almost killed two jackals would reach the chief before dark, for starters.

Anyone she worked with going forward would judge her as unable to make the hard choices when it came to shifters.

Would they be right?

She'd never had a problem following through with any other shifter, but she'd also not had to send a man to his death. Colin believed he was not going to survive this.

Something inside her agreed.

What had happened from the moment they'd brought him in?

She was almost getting used to the damn buzzing her internal energy was causing.

She needed to take the time off that everyone kept trying to push on her, including Brantley. Was she being unfair to criticize him when he was clearly doing his job?

"I'm sorry, Brantley, I just ... want to be fair to everyone and I guess that isn't always possible."

His face softened and his tone carried understanding. "You are fair. You're what gives this program balance, but we offered that man a chance to tell his side. He clammed up. No, he tried to play us against each other. I'm never going to allow a prisoner to do that. I trust your decisions and hope you trust mine."

"I do." She wished that had been the truth, but it was what Brantley needed to hear right now.

"Thank you. Here's what you don't realize. That shifter will be very still the entire way to SNR-4."

That would be the Southeastern Nonhuman Rehabilitation facility two hours away.

Brantley continued explaining, "The ride alone will exhaust a shifter, which will allow the guards to put him into his cell without him or anyone else getting injured. In the past, we've had shifters rested during a drive and they attacked once they were pulled out. This also starts O'Donnell toward rethinking his position sooner. By the time he spends a week in a hole, he'll be willing to negotiate a deal. That's when we'll gain intel on the bombing and the Black River pack." He smiled, Mr. Charming coming out to play.

He added in a joking, self-deprecating tone, "There is a method to my madness."

She suffered a moment of guilt over her lack of faith in a man who had been at her side during the Black River pack investigation for months, even if he was vying for the same position she wanted.

Forcing a smile she didn't feel, she nodded in agreement. "Good points. Maybe next time, give me a tour of your new security so I won't be surprised."

He looked chagrined. "You're right. I should have thought to do that, but so much has been going on that it didn't dawn on me. Consider me chastised."

She rolled her eyes. "As if."

"Now, let's go grab lunch and look over our case files."

Her stomach had no interest in food. A group of carnival performers were doing nonstop stunts that had started the minute the truck pulled away.

She had the unreasonable urge to get in her car and follow.

But she didn't.

Walking inside with Brantley, she decided to put in for time off. She had to get her head on straight before the upcoming congressional meeting. She had to be spot-on during the questioning.

Any hint of weakness and someone who opposed SCIS would go for blood, regardless of how much pull her father had.

He would not be at this meeting, and to be honest, she was glad for that since they did not agree on anything to do with shifters. Still, she could not walk into the meeting unprepared.

If Brantley was right and Colin O'Donnell decided to play ball once he got a look at his new home, then she'd have something really strong to share at the meeting.

That didn't appease the sick churning in her stomach.

Colin still hadn't been proven guilty of belonging to the Black River pack.

She'd give Colin a couple of days, then she'd make a trip to the SNR facility and push him for answers. That would help her with the committee and put her in a position to get him out of that hole, as long as Brantley didn't buck her.

They had to look united when she gave her report since he'd be sitting next to her.

All these years she'd worked toward the moment where she could turn SCIS from a law enforcement support agency to a bigger operation. One capable of managing shifter investigations and human-shifter relations.

That might be what it took to find answers she needed on her mother's case. Her father refused to even discuss her mother's death and if Tess guessed right, he'd been instrumental in getting that case sealed.

But Tess had her own resources now.

As she walked into the farmhouse, she opened the door to the elevator that would take her back underground.

Colin's words still echoed in her mind.

You're too sweet, too honorable and too decent for this world.

CHAPTER 12

Cole kept doing deep breathing exercises to maintain his imitation of a twisted statue, talking to himself so he didn't so much as sneeze.

Thursday was as good a day to die as any, but he preferred a different day—one much later than today.

The road had been smooth for the last forty or fifty minutes. If that continued, he could hold out for hours.

The truck slowed and made a right.

It felt as if they were on an interstate, which would mean he was being transported to SNR-4, a maximum-security shifter prison. They called it a rehab center as if someone was going to teach shifters how to not be predators.

No fences or concertina wire.

All the cells were below ground with concrete walls two feet thick and inch-thick titanium inner walls. Not even a Gallize shifter could get through that structure. His people believed a Cadell had been involved in designing those pits.

That level of security wasn't necessary for standard shifters.

A few minutes later, the truck slowed again and turned to the left onto a bumpy road.

"Whoa." Cole tightened the muscles in his body to keep his balance steady so that he didn't move his arms or legs. "What the fuck?"

The jackal shifters up front could hear him, just like he heard them chuckle. He had to work harder to maintain his balance or he would lose a limb.

Where were they taking him?

The road into the prison should be a two-lane highway through flat terrain. They couldn't be anywhere close to it yet. He knew because he'd scouted the prison when it was under construction in hopes of catching a Cadell on site.

Another bump had him sucking in his abs and arching to hold his arms in place. He might have managed to reach the prison in one piece if the driver had stayed on the interstate, but he wouldn't survive an unpaved road.

Was the point to force him to succumb to this chain system and rip his body apart?

That way, Brantley could point at what was left of his body and say, "This is the reason we need a barbarian transportation plan to deal with mindless beasts."

Cole wobbled and rolled his hips, adjusting to the rough road. He wouldn't give in, no matter what they did. If he thought the jackals would stop to check on him, he'd twist a wrist until the manacle cut his skin and call for help.

But these two would howl with laughter if he asked for anything.

If he managed to avoid literally being drawn and quartered by the tension system, the jackal shifters would have to go to Plan B. Take him out of the cargo space and use his head for target practice.

That would be a mistake he'd capitalize on if they gave him an opening.

His wolf hadn't pushed to get out since they left, but now Gray Wolf had gotten agitated again.

Not crazy agitated this time. Stressed.

His wolf probably sensed that they were facing death, but Cole was saying nothing to clue him in. Better to have Gray Wolf in curious mode than crazy mode, which Cole couldn't handle in this position.

The truck hit a dip that bounced the entire frame.

Cole lost his balance.

Four chains cinched tighter.

His muscles stretched. Tendons strained. Shit, he wasn't going to make it. One more bump and an arm might tear at the shoulder.

Now Gray Wolf knew they were in trouble.

He snarled to be released.

Cole had learned early on that ordering his wolf to do anything was a mistake and last night was a reminder. Gray Wolf had been working with him during some of the captivity so Cole pleaded, *Please don't fight me or we'll die faster.*

His wolf howled at him.

Cole understood. He'd managed to let them both down. On top of that, he was pretty sure he'd left Tess exposed to a Cadell with no idea what kind of being she had as a partner.

How much more miserable could this day get?

Two thumps landed on the roof of the cargo area.

Shit. Who would that be? His mind wanted to convince him it was his team, but they had no way to track him.

Not unless they'd followed him to the SCIS facility. If that had been the case, the Guardian would have come up with a way to extract Cole before now.

The sound of glass crashing came next. Someone screamed. Might be a jackal ... might be whoever had attacked them.

Then the van rocked from one side to another, giving Cole's abs a lethal workout to maintain his balance.

Damn. This could be an attack by the Black River pack who wanted Cole. This supported the suspicion of a leak in SCIS.

Someone might have alerted the local Black River wolf pack that Cole was being transported. The note stuck to Sonic had been specifically for Cole. He still couldn't figure out how they knew he'd been the one leading teams to bust their balls.

They probably tortured Sonic to get what he knew, but Sonic wouldn't have had that information. The next possibility was a mole inside Gallize, which was ... beyond something Cole would even consider.

He'd like to feel encouraged by an attack on the jackals, because he could take on three or four Black River pack shifters in a straight up battle.

But tied up like a hog for roasting, he had no chance.

Gray Wolf shoved and pushed.

Cole told him, *If I have no other hope, I'll try to shift and let you loose, but we'll lose body parts.*

That didn't calm his wolf, but it made Cole feel better to give that promise.

The truck slowed and bumped to a stop as if the driver just took his foot off the brake.

Releasing a breath he'd held too long, Cole became very still. His shoulder and hip joints were strained beyond belief. His abs were shot.

Every muscle trembled from doing its best to keep his body from being yanked apart.

He heard the sound of a helicopter's whomp, whomp, whomp approaching and landing close enough to hear the rotors slow down.

That would be his next ride, but to where?

That's when he realized his wolf had quieted. Really? Now, when it was time to rise up and kick ass?

Had he ever been in a more vulnerable position while conscious? None that he could recall.

A shirring sound started at the rear. He saw sparks coming through from a blowtorch being used. That wouldn't be the jackal shifters, but did that mean his questionable rescuers hadn't found the key to unlock the doors?

Could this be his team?

No. His team would have called out and let him know they were breaking into the cargo area.

Just another reason to prepare himself for the Black River pack. Had they wanted to kill him in the bombing? If so, this would be quick, but if that wasn't today's mission, he could be facing worst than the pit.

The torch sound ceased. Water splashed on the metal, then the doors opened slowly.

Cole squinted against the sun backlighting them and blinding him.

CHAPTER 13

"Hey man, this looks like a bad S and M scene. You shouldn't have any clothes on."

Cole almost sagged with relief at hearing Justin's voice, but he caught himself before he ruined a great rescue. "If I move, this setup will rip my arms off."

A string of cursing came from behind Justin. That would be Rory who then asked, "Think we can cut it with the torch?"

"No. Any movement pulls all the chains another half inch tighter."

"Another, as in it's already done it once?"

"Yep," Cole grunted, all of a sudden tired. His wolf was active, but not acting like the roaring asshole Gray Wolf could be.

Rory said, "I got an idea. Don't move."

"Not funny, dickhead," Cole muttered.

"It will be when I get you out of there." Rory stepped up into the cargo bay with a portable torch. He pointed at Cole's right arm and told Justin, "Grab that chain right where it goes into the tubing and don't let it move."

Sweat beaded on Cole's neck, but he trusted these two with his life.

Justin clamped one hand next to the other at the last links of the chain before they disappeared down the corner tubing. Being a grizzly bear and a Gallize, he was the strongest of the three.

Rory fired up the torch and started cutting.

Cole held both arms dead still, wanting this to work.

When the chain broke, Cole almost fell toward the opposite side, but Rory immediately clamped onto the manacle on his wrist, holding him in place.

Minutes later, Cole walked out of the cargo bay to find the SCIS transport truck inches from the edge of what had to be a five-hundred-foot drop-off.

That would have been a Super Bowl finish of sudden death.

Not the kind he'd have cheered for either.

"Thanks, guys. Why didn't you call out before cutting through?"

"We didn't know if this thing was rigged with any kind of transmitter that would pick up voices. Figured we'd wait until we got the door open to confirm there were no bugs inside."

"Good thinking. I got questions, but they'll wait until you get this fucking helmet off me."

"It's welded on."

"I know." Cole would find Brantley and make him pay for every second of misery he'd been put through. "Cut it off."

"I'll end up burning you."

"Can't be any worse than what I just went through."

The usually jovial Justin looked miserable. "We had no idea what had happened to you until we got around the building after the explosion. By the time we figured out who had you, they'd vamoosed. Guardian told us to follow and extract you. That would have been possible if they hadn't airlifted you."

Just as Cole had thought. He lifted his hand with the chain still dangling. "You're here now. That's all that matters. Let's cut this thing off me."

The back of his head took a beating again. Cole was tired of asking his body to keep taking so much abuse. Water leaked through holes in the helmet as Justin doused the metal, trying to cool it to lessen the burns. When the welds finally loosened, Cole reached up and grasped around the back next to his neck and ripped it apart.

He threw it into the cargo area.

The sound of a helicopter approaching pulled all three heads around to the east. Cole yelled, "We got incoming. Who's flying our chopper?"

"Hawk," Rory answered, grabbing the torch and turning toward their bird.

Justin was right behind him, then Cole.

Hawk was indeed a big hawk when he shifted, but he was also a lunatic chopper pilot they'd met in the military. Not a Gallize shifter, but one of the Guardian's men now.

"Got a bird coming in hot from the east. Those jackals might have had a panic button or your captors had a tracking system on the truck," Justin was calling back over his shoulder as the rotor blades spun up to full power.

Cole dove in as Hawk lifted off. That pilot would make you hang from a skid if you didn't get your ass inside when he was ready to go.

Pulling on a set of headphones so he could communicate with everyone, Cole snagged a pair of binoculars to look out the open door. Hawk whipped the craft around in one of his gut churning maneuvers.

Cole shouted, "Are the jackal shifters still alive?"

"No," Justin and Rory replied as one.

Cole warned, "We shouldn't leave any trace of you two—"

The business end of an M-32 grenade launcher shoved past Cole's face.

Rory sighted in on the van and shot two 40mm, high-energy rounds.

The approaching helicopter bore down on the truck just as the armor-piercing grenades blew it to pieces.

Justin shoved over next to Cole. "Damn I love that shit."

When the smoke cleared, the other helicopter had spun away from the billowing fire. Dialing in the lens of a high-powered spotting scope, Cole caught the gold-and-black SCIS scales-of-justice insignia on the side of the chopper.

Brantley would not be happy about losing his captive.

Cole had no doubt that the Cadell had been behind the detour to this cliff road, but that left a bigger concern. How would Brantley react at losing Cole? Tess had no idea she was working in the middle of a viper nest.

Justin shouted, "The Guardian wants us in for debriefing."

Cole wanted to head back to SCIS and yank his mate away from danger, but he couldn't do that without explaining where he'd gone years ago, and how he knew she was in danger.

Mate? What was he thinking?

Gray Wolf vibrated with anger. *She is our mate.*

Like Cole could tell her that?

Trying to explain to Gray Wolf that she could never be their mate was impossible. The wolf only knew they had to protect her no matter what.

For once, Cole was in complete agreement with his wolf.

CHAPTER 14

Tess waited for Brantley to get over his rant. She wanted to shove him out of her office so she wouldn't show a crack in her armor in front of him.

She was doing a hell of a job just by not throwing up.

He complained, "This is going to cost us our funding."

She didn't snap back at Brantley, but this was his fault. He was the one who'd ordered the truck and sent the two shifters to deliver Colin.

Now Colin was dead.

Even he couldn't have survived the burned truck. The brutal containment system in the cargo area would have ripped him apart as soon as he tried to escape.

All of this was Brantley's doing.

He'd been so excited to send Colin off in his new toy that it made Tess sick.

She faced Brantley's anger and unleashed some of her own. "You have yet to tell me what your driver and guard were doing on an unmarked road in the mountains, going in the wrong direction."

"What?"

"Did I mince any words?" she snapped. "I want to know what that truck was doing so far off track." To avoid wasting time arguing whether the information was accurate, she added, "I received a report that firefighters and police were sent to a burning truck in the mountains north of here. They traced the vehicle VIN to SCIS."

Brantley glared at her. "How should I know what happened? You were standing there with me when I sent them off. Someone clearly sabotaged the transport. My best guess is that we have a mole, someone sympathetic to shifters. I'm thinking the Black River pack hijacked the truck and it went bad when our people fought back." He paused with a thoughtful expression. "Or maybe that freaking wolf shifter tried to escape and somehow caused the truck to wreck."

"Colin? You think *he* did all that while he was stretched like a guitar string?"

Cocking his head to look at her hard, Brantley said, "Don't tell me you're defending him?"

Careful, she warned herself, but she was not backing down. "I'm not even going to acknowledge that ridiculous comment. This is huge. We *will* lose funding if they think we can't maintain custody of someone that important. I'll be facing the congressional committee to convince them SCIS is making progress. O'Donnell was the closest we've come to anyone who might be able to tell us about the Black River pack—"

"No, *we'll* be facing that committee and O'Donnell *was* with the Black River pack even if he didn't admit it," Brantley said, cutting her off. "I know you think that tensioning system in the truck was an inhumane way to transport him, but it was the best plan my security team had come up with to manage someone like Colin. I hadn't planned on using it yet, but seeing what he did to our two jackals when he shifted changed my mind. I agree that he couldn't have gotten himself out on his own, but that leaves the Black River pack behind this. If that's the case, we have a hole in our security. There's no telling what happened until I get a team out there to investigate."

She understood the words coming out of Brantley's mouth, but her gut screamed that he had edited out a few significant things.

He was hiding more than he was telling.

Only a few people had known about this transport and they were all security.

Who on Brantley's team would undermine him?

Or had he set *her* up to take the fall for losing Colin? All failure for today would fall on her head. Because while she believed in sharing success with everyone, even giving Brantley credit at times he hadn't exactly earned it, the responsibility for failure belonged to her. That's how she operated as a leader, plain and simple.

That driver and guard had been in on it, but she'd get no answers from them. Why had they gone into the mountains if the Black River pack was behind all of this?

If none of that was true, then who had ordered Colin's death?

She looked hard at Brantley.

Would he actually go to the extreme of killing people to force her to step down so he could take over her position as lead on this investigation?

Okay, she was starting to sound paranoid even to herself.

She'd known, as a woman entering a primarily male work arena, that she'd be up against prejudice. She'd been prepared for those challenges, and always wanted to believe that working with professionals meant a level playing field once she'd proven her worth.

She agreed with Brantley on one point.

They had a mole. She had to figure out who it was and follow that trail to whoever was pulling the strings.

Killing to get ahead was cold-blooded murder, even if some thought less of a shifter's death than a human's. During the past months of working with Brantley, she'd seen his true colors about women in his field, but otherwise, he'd been professional, if annoying, with his innuendos. When she'd rebuffed his attentions though, he'd been pleasant about it and never acted as if he intended to make her pay for rejecting him.

She couldn't equate that man with one who would kill just for professional advancement.

He stopped his pacing and huffed out a deep breath. "Sorry if I'm ranting at you when this is not your fault. I'm just sick over losing a major prisoner, two of our staff and that new truck, which I'd hoped would prevent deaths. I feel like we're losing ground with the Black River pack."

Now she felt like a slug for being so suspicious of him, but she actually hurt over the thought of what had happened to Colin. She couldn't explain the odd connection she'd made with the wolf shifter, but right now she had a difficult time holding back her emotions.

She would not crack. Not here.

Colin had died a horrible death and it was as much her fault as it was Brantley's.

She had final say. She could have refused to send Colin to the holding facility chained that way, but a sense of duty had forced her into what she'd thought had been the right decision.

Then Colin had said he forgave her even before all this happened.

How could he forgive someone who had sent him to his death? He'd predicted it, in fact. Had known he was going to die.

Her head felt like the ball at a national ping-pong match with so many conflicted thoughts slamming back and forth. She'd figure it out later. For now, she still had an investigation to see finished.

Feeling as if she had to extend an olive branch to Brantley, she said, "I share your frustration and we'll keep pressing harder on the Black River pack."

So much for taking time off.

She mentally ripped up the form she'd been planning to submit today for a four-day weekend. She needed to know more on Colin for any hope of putting this behind her.

Ready to forge ahead, she said, "I sent Colin's DNA to be matched in the shifter database, but it could take days or weeks. In the meantime, let's offer a reward for anyone who might have recent information on a rogue wolf in the area. Did we get any facial shots?"

"Nope. The team who put the mask on him didn't waste a second after seeing what he did to the jackals."

"I understand."

Brantley perked up. "We *should* offer a reward, though. Those people will sell out their own mother with enough incentive."

She cringed at the 'those people' shifter reference for now, but she'd have a conversation with him soon about the need for everyone on their team to at least show a modicum of respect for all people ... and sub-species ... once things settled down. This conflict had to end or she'd need a new supply of aspirin.

Her assistant knocked on the door, then opened it to say, "We just got an initial police report about the destroyed truck."

Tess steeled herself for the news. She'd been prepared to accept that she'd never see Colin again, not alive, but hearing someone verify his death would carve up her insides.

Brantley asked, "What'd they say?"

"The bodies of our driver and second guard are being sent to the coroner, but there's no sign of the prisoner's body."

Tess stared in shock.

Brantley snarled, "What? How'd he get out?"

"They didn't say. The only detail they gave me was that the chains in the back appeared to have been cut with a torch."

Regaining her composure quickly, Tess fought to keep her relief from showing, but it wasn't easy. She wouldn't wish death on the two jackal shifters, but Colin ... might be alive.

Her relief took a swift nosedive when she realized she would have been better off facing the committee with his death than with his escape.

CHAPTER 15

Five hours after his harrowing escape from death, Cole entered the elevator with Justin and Rory, all of them headed to the penthouse to see the Guardian. Cole kept his hands in the pockets of his cargo pants to hide the claws that kept poking out of his fingers.

He had to keep this from the Guardian for a little longer.

This had been the longest day of his life since becoming a shifter, but he'd survived Brantley's death-by-transport-truck plan.

He should have known this morning that bastard Brantley wasn't sending him to any SNR location.

Gray Wolf had been anxious since Cole's rescue and angry about their not going to claim Tess, but somewhat manageable. Cole didn't know what had taken the worst of the edge off his wolf, but the ongoing battle to keep his claws retracted and his head from changing shape meant he still had to face the mating curse.

He'd expected his wolf to choose a mate at some point, since that's how it apparently worked for some Gallize, but he now realized that had never happened because Cole had chosen Tess first.

He didn't understand Gray Wolf's interest in her when she wasn't a wolf shifter or a Gallize female.

Tess was human.

If Cole took even a non-Gallize shifter mate and bonded with her, he'd share telepathic communication in wolf form, plus the supernatural powers they each possessed would grow stronger. As he understood it, only a shifter female or a Gallize female could handle bonding with his power.

Ideally she would be a Gallize female shifter, but finding a unicorn would be easier. The Gallize women had not been as fortunate as the males, who had a guardian watching over them. Their female guardian had vanished along the way and not been replaced, which was why Cole and his Gallize brothers had no clue where to find a woman who could handle their power.

In the past, a Gallize shifter who bonded with a human had killed his mate the minute the power rushed inside her.

Even if it had happened only once, Cole would not risk it with Tess. Nor would he trust his wolf around her. Gray Wolf might think he could change Tess into a wolf with a bite, but that wasn't going to happen.

Cole would protect Tess, even from himself.

Gray Wolf snarled at him. *Our mate.*

Cole silently snarled right back. *Tough shit.*

When the elevator stopped, the doors opened into a living area. He followed Rory and Justin through a tastefully decorated room designed to be minimal and efficient, then out to the balcony atop a forty-three-story building in Baltimore.

The apartment would be impressive enough without adding in the fact that their boss owned the entire building, plus a few others that Cole knew about. There could be more real estate, considering the man had lived so many centuries.

After Justin sent word that Cole needed a safe place to shift due to the drugs forced on him and Gray Wolf, the Guardian had authorized the team to take Cole to a private reserve to shift so he could heal completely before coming into Baltimore to meet. Between that shift being uneventful and a hot shower, Cole had a new burst of energy.

Gray Wolf did too, but Cole had regained the ability to keep his beast in line. For now.

Stepping outside, the air cooled significantly from when he'd stood on the busy street way below. The moderate wind buffeting the building was noticeable at this height.

Neither Rory nor Justin had any news to share on the Guardian's reaction to Cole being inside the food bank building when the bomb detonated.

Their boss had issued one order. *Do whatever it takes to find*

Cole and bring him back.

That's why everyone on the Gallize team would do anything asked of them. It was understood that they took care of their own.

The Guardian stood at the far end of the wide balcony with his back to them. He appeared to be nothing more than a physically fit, well-groomed businessman staring at the city, preparing for his next major venture. Cole had never seen him in anything except suits, which might be from having lived through eras when men of substance dressed accordingly.

But when the man turned around, his eyes bore the shape of a sea eagle's. He was centuries older than the mid-forties suggested by a touch of gray hair at his temples. His skin belonged to someone more like thirty and the rest of his dark brown hair could be mistaken for black at first glance.

Rumors floated around about a few Gallize who lived beyond the expected one hundred and fifty years, give or take a few, but their boss, though Gallize, was more than just a shifter. Cole had heard that the ancient guardians who watched over the Gallize joined so closely with their animals that at some point, their eyes changed from human to those of an eagle.

All the Gallize guardians were some type of eagle.

Their Guardian had the ability to speak mind-to-mind in human form when in close proximity to any of the Gallize shifters.

Cole and his buddies could use mind talk only in animal form.

He'd been to this penthouse often over the years, the last time being when Sammy and his eight-man team, which included Cole, Rory and Justin, were called back to operate in the US. Cole had been Sammy's right hand, which is why he refused to give up on his friend.

Cole, Justin and Rory each said, "Hello, Väktare."

Cole took a seat in one of the cushy outdoor chairs placed in a half circle across from the matching sofa where the Guardian lowered himself to sit.

Just like last time, the minute he was in the Guardian's presence, Gray Wolf settled down as if docile.

That would not last long with an apex predator, but his wolf recognized their alpha, the greater predator in the room.

With Rory on one side and Justin on the other, Cole prepared to answer for his actions. He launched straight to the topic of his insubordination.

"The decision to enter the food bank building was mine, Väktare. Rory and Justin warned me to not change the plan, but I ... felt it was my duty to protect a human who had only been looking for a place to shelter from the rain. I will be honest. In hindsight, I would do it again, but I also understand I will be disciplined and accept whatever you decide with no argument."

Rory breathed in and out slowly, as though bored, but Cole had been around him a long time and knew it was hiding his concern.

Justin, on the other hand, never missed an opportunity to piss off someone. "It wasn't as if Cole knew someone wanted to blow up the building."

Cole murmured, "Not helping, Justin."

"Just sayin'."

The Guardian gave a nod for him to continue.

During the flight back, Cole had filled Justin and Rory in on some details, which they'd passed on to the Guardian in an update, but Cole had been waiting until now to explain everything fully, so he could go through it just one time. "I observed a truck entering the building. While that was happening, the homeless woman slipped inside, probably thinking she was safe in there. The more I've thought on it, I would almost bet they set her up to sneak in as soon as the door opened, but I have no way to say for sure."

"They did," the Guardian confirmed. "We located the woman and found someone who could understand her ramblings. She hid in the back of the building on occasion."

"Is she okay?" Cole had worried about her surviving. "Did I break any of her bones when we hit the building across the street?"

"She had a fractured wrist and light head trauma. She was in a coma for two days, but she's being cared for now and will not return to the streets. Neither will she be interrogated by anyone from SCIS."

"Good, and thank you." One positive had come out of that night.

"Has my mark returned to your shoulder, Cole?"

"Yes, it did slowly today. It surprised me. I thought I'd have to ask you to do it again."

"That should never be necessary. Few things will remove my mark from the shifters I protect."

Cole exchanged looks with Justin and Rory that told him they were as surprised as he was.

"You were correct in thinking the homeless lady was positioned intentionally," the Guardian continued. "Someone bribed her to sneak into the building as soon as the truck went inside. That person promised food, alcohol and that she could spend the night there any time she wanted. The group responsible for the truck and bomb evidently expected someone connected to law enforcement to be watching the building. The question is whether they knew it was you, since that was perfect bait, given your background, or was that bomb meant for someone else?"

"It was for the Gallize, and the trap was set specifically for *me*, but ..." Cole shook his head at how well someone had played him. "Everyone got played. Sonic gave us the intel and he was the one in the driver's seat, but he was already dead when I found him. Whoever drove it in parked the truck, slid the body in place, then taped his hands to the steering wheel. His throat was slit. I'm thinking the shifter escaped over the roofs since none of the team saw him exit. By the time I entered the building, the trap had been set, including a note pinned to Sonic's chest that said, 'Surprise, Cavanaugh.' It had the Black River pack gang sign on it."

Justin growled.

"Do you think they expected you to escape that bomb?" Rory asked, incredulous.

"Not sure. If so, our reputations as Gallize shifters who can jump higher than the tallest buildings and outrun speeding bullets precedes us," Cole joked, then turned serious.

Justin offered, "If Cole hadn't lived, I'll bet they would have found a way to send a second message to us just to brag."

The Guardian said, "I agree. We have another question that needs to be answered. Whether the Black River pack knows you survived, Cole, which I would say is a very strong possibility."

Cole had something else to point out. "I think there's a leak in SCIS. They had the same information we had about the food bank. That opens the possibility that Sonic sold us out to someone in that group or they tortured the information out of him, which would explain how they knew who was coming."

"That's the problem with scumbags," Justin grumbled. "They got no business ethics. Like a damn jackal. If Sonic did try to play both sides, then he got what was coming to him."

Rory noted, "The Black River pack could have set up Sonic, too."

That was a better possibility. Cole had one more thing to drop on this group. "Also, I think there's a Cadell working inside SCIS."

Tension spiked at that announcement.

Justin sat forward. "What the hell?"

Rory pointed out, "It's not like SCIS can screen for Cadells. Even we can't recognize them in human form." His gaze flashed to the Guardian when he amended, "With the exception of you, Guardian. How would humans know about Cadells when we never tell them about the enemy, or that we even exist, and we're the ones who know the most?"

The Guardian spoke. "What's his name?"

"Theo Brantley."

After a moment of silence, the Guardian said, "If it's a Cadell, it's not his real name. They've gotten better about hiding among humans in recent years."

"I was never around him as a wolf, so I'm not positive, but my gut says I'm right."

"I would trust your gut," the Guardian said. "Your capture is another reason why I'm considering going public with our Gallize shifters."

"*What?*" Cole, Justin and Rory said as one voice.

"Think about what happened to Cole. If we had a public front known among the human intel agencies, Cole could have called for a Gallize representative. Times are changing with technology better than ever, and we have to change as well. The world has gone through an initial reaction to shifters and power manipulators. I think we can do more good by being known. That doesn't mean we'll expose all of the operatives, but enough to claim one of ours when need be. With the Black River pack constantly developing new synthetic drugs to use against all shifters, we need to protect our own from being given drugs involuntarily somewhere like SCIS or sent to titanium holding facilities without full authorization."

Scratching his head, Justin said, "I see your point, Väktare."

The Guardian clarified, "It's not happening today, but after this incident I'm moving up my timeline. I'll inform all of you before any changes occur. My first priority is locating the head of the Black River wolves."

Cole wanted that bunch more than ever, but he switched gears to a topic that hadn't been broached. "Any word on Sammy?"

No one volunteered a thing until the Guardian said, "We may have to accept that Sammy is beyond our help."

Cole knew better, but he still argued, "We don't know how Sammy is doing. We haven't seen him since he disappeared."

"Exactly," the Guardian confirmed. "I called him home and he hasn't come in."

Justin muttered, "Fuck," which pretty much covered Cole's thought on that.

When the Guardian called anyone home, that shifter would have an overwhelming desire to do just that. The only reason the Guardian hadn't called Cole was because they all knew Cole would have returned on his own. Calling him would only have put him in more danger.

Rory asked the question that hung in the back of every Gallize shifter's mind. "Are we all facing death by the mating curse?"

No point tiptoeing around that elephant in the room.

Cole was thankful his wolf had calmed around the Guardian, but he'd had to hide his claw issue from Rory and Justin. At one point, he'd dashed into a men's room when he felt his jaw beginning to stretch.

He would do the right thing and submit to the Guardian before the mating curse took over completely. Until then, he wanted to find Sammy and ensure that Tess was safe.

After hesitating a moment to answer, the Guardian said, "I take responsibility for Sammy succumbing to the mating curse, because I failed to realize he was suffering from it already."

Cole felt just as responsible. He'd been closest to Sammy.

"Up to this point, Gallize shifters have had approximately ten years after their animal was called up to bond with a mate before the curse set in. Since most had their animals called up around the age of twenty-one or two, we worked on the logic of mating by thirty, to be safe. It's hard to say for sure, because we haven't had enough cases to study. At one time, mating before the age of thirty was not a problem, because most people made that decision early in life. Now, not so much."

Rory offered, "Sammy won't be thirty for another two years."

The Guardian gave a solemn nod. "That's what makes his situation all the more disturbing. It might mean the curse is accelerating faster than expected." The Guardian looked away for a moment, out toward the sea, then turned to them before he spoke again.

"Even three hundred years ago, the age for me to call up the animal in a Gallize was around twenty-two or twenty-three. But Sammy lost his entire family in a shifter attack. When he was brought to me at barely twenty, I had to call up his bear in order to save Sammy's life. I've never known of a Gallize suffering the mating curse as young as he has, only eight years into being a shifter. I have to find a way to make certain it doesn't happen to the rest of you."

Eight years.

Cole managed to not let his breathing change with the panic he was fighting inside. He was only twenty-six. He'd been a shifter for seven years. He should have had at least one more year even if he used Sammy's situation as a benchmark, but Cole couldn't deny the physical issues he was having.

Justin popped off, "You gonna find us women, Väktare?"

When the Guardian leveled his eagle-eyed gaze on Justin, the joker turned into a mime, sans movement.

That intense gaze shifted to Cole, who had the unusual urge to squirm.

What could the Guardian see? Cole had shielded the first signs of the mating curse from everyone. He knew the signs only because he'd witnessed the effects when it began on Sammy during a hike the two of them made through the Smoky Mountains. Sammy had come clean, telling Cole to keep an eye on himself, since Cole, like Sammy, had started prematurely as a Gallize.

Regarding Sammy, Cole asked the Guardian, "Have you found anything on Katelyn? She could give Sammy a fighting chance."

"That girlfriend who *broke up* with Sammy and sent him into a downward spiral?" Justin interjected, sounding appalled. "You want to find *her*?"

The Guardian watched all three of them, as if curious to hear them all out before giving his input.

With the Guardian sounding close to accepting Sammy's demise, Cole felt justified in what he said next.

"Sammy didn't want the team to know about Katelyn, because he was concerned about what a bunch of black ops friends would do to save him. He would give his life for any of us and knows we'd do the same, but he wouldn't have any of us pushing her around to step up for him or trying to influence her. That's why he didn't tell the rest of you that Katelyn had agreed to marry him." Cole watched eyebrows shoot up on all but the Guardian.

Then Cole added, "Sammy had hidden the fact that he was a shifter from Katelyn."

Rory groaned. "He can't do that."

"I know," Cole said, sighing. "But Sammy had never been in love and his bear wanted her for a mate. He said he was terrified to tell her the truth." Cole could appreciate that feeling. "He gave it a couple of days to be sure she was serious about marrying him, then he told her he was a shifter and tried to explain that he didn't expect her to change from human. He said she was almost on board until he told her they might have baby grizzlies. She panicked at that point and ran."

Sammy admitted that he had suffered his first physical impairment from the curse the following day. He didn't blame Katelyn, because he hadn't really believed it was possible or that something would trigger it to start early.

Sammy wouldn't risk killing Katelyn, just as Cole wouldn't risk killing Tess. But if Sammy only had days left, he wanted his friend to spend them with Katelyn if she would agree. That might at least slow Sammy's deterioration.

Probably wishful thinking, but Cole was not quitting on his friend.

Justin grabbed his head. "Fuck. No one could handle having his mate ripped away. Man, that totally screwed Sammy."

Cole explained, "Actually, Sammy wasn't going to bond his power with her."

"Why would he go through all that and not complete the mating?"

The Guardian answered for everyone. "Very few humans have survived the mating bond with a Gallize due to the level of our powers."

"I know, but ... " Justin sat back in a huff of frustration. "We should be able to help him."

Thinking about the agony Sammy was going through without his mate dropped a rock in Cole's chest. He'd found Tess again and knew he'd never want another woman as his mate, but Cole wouldn't risk her life even if she lost her mind and agreed to become the mate of a shifter.

Cole had a better chance of becoming entirely human again than Tess voluntarily getting involved with someone who shifted into a wolf.

Rory calmly offered, "Then we find Katelyn, because she might be key to helping us get Sammy back." He held up his hand to stop Cole from arguing and said, "We'll see if she's willing to talk to us. Sometimes people get scared and hide because they think a problem is too big for them. I've talked to shifter females who were terrified of their first labor and delivery, and they had been raised in our world. Maybe Katelyn just needs some answers and to know we'll all protect her no matter what happens. If she agrees, then at least ... Sammy will have that time with her."

"That's a good idea," Cole allowed, since Rory was thinking along the same lines as Cole for giving Sammy some peace before the end. "But we still need to find her." His last words were for the Guardian.

In measured words, the Guardian said, "I have someone looking for her and he sent word just before you arrived that he had news he wouldn't share over the phone."

The Guardian had probably told him not to, because while this man was the baddest shifter around, he still didn't fully trust technology.

"I was hoping to have something by the time we found Cole," the Guardian explained. "Having been so close to Sammy, Cole will probably have the best chance at convincing her to talk to him. If my man has found her and we scare her off, we might not find her any time soon again because he did say the person he spoke to indicated Katelyn thinks she's being hunted."

That might sound encouraging if it was Sammy hunting her, because it would solve a lot of problems. But Sammy would have found her if he was on her trail.

Was she just feeling paranoid or had someone been stalking

her?

"What's our plan?" Cole asked calmly, when what he wanted was to demand the number and leave now to find this woman.

"I'll give you the number," the Guardian told Cole, easing his concern. He also said, "But I want you to take backup if you go to meet her. Understood?"

"Yes, sir." Cole would prefer to go solo, but he knew better than to cross the Guardian right now.

"Back to the original problem at hand," the Guardian said, moving the conversation to the Black River pack. "We have no credible intel on that pack right now. We destroyed their operation in Nicaragua. In return, they've made a shot over our bow by trying to kill Cole. It's time we made it clear they must never touch one of ours."

Justin smiled like he did any time they were going on offense. "How we gonna do that?"

"They want Cole. We'll wave him under their noses, but with a full contingent of support."

That was going to screw Cole's plans for tonight. He could not have company for what he had in mind.

With a few more directions, the Guardian dismissed Justin and Rory, stating Cole would join them downstairs in fifteen minutes.

Does Väktare want to chew me out in private?

Cole should be thankful for small favors.

When the doors on the private elevator closed behind Rory and Justin, Cole waited for the Guardian to have his say.

"Did you think I wouldn't know, Cole?"

Oh, shit. "What are you talking about?" Cole bluffed.

"The mating curse. You are only a year younger than Sammy, and you shifted even earlier. You're different than the rest. I've never known a Gallize to shift at nineteen."

"I didn't exactly shift on my own," Cole said, pointing out that the Guardian had called up his wolf. Cole had never understood all of the Guardian's powers, but this man kept track of those descended from the original five Gallize families. Cole's mother had run away from her abusive husband when she was pregnant. She gave birth, and died two weeks later from malnutrition.

Cole had ended up in a group home.

The Guardian explained later that Cole's mother had eluded the person he'd tasked with following that branch of the Gallize family bloodline. Just like the majority of Gallize shifters, Cole had been born to a human. He and his Gallize brethren only popped up every few generations since they lived so long. They sometimes became fathers of another Gallize, but not often.

Years passed as the Guardian searched all over the world for Cole after he'd fallen off the radar. The Guardian had located Cole while he was in college and set a three-man task force on keeping track of him.

Gallize descendants who carried the shifter DNA had a lavender aura until their animal was called up the first time, then the aura turned a vibrant blue.

The night Cole's beast decided it wanted out, evidently Cole's aura became bright enough to call in backup.

He thought back seven years to the night he'd been kidnapped. That might not be a fair description, knowing what he did now, but what else was he to think when a black ops team snatched him from the woods where he'd been running. They'd shoved his head into a black bag, then carted him up to this penthouse.

He'd been out of his mind, shouting and howling.

The howling should have been a clue.

He'd imagined a hundred bad scenarios while that team manhandled him, but nothing he imagined ended with this man telling him he was a wolf shifter, then proving it by using his Gallize guardian power to force Cole to shift.

The Guardian had grown quiet. He watched Cole with the stoic patience of an eagle eyeing the world below him. "To have your wolf surface at only nineteen was extremely unusual, Cole. I've pondered it often. I had hoped you wouldn't face the mating curse younger than you should, but we both know that is exactly what's happening. Right?"

Cornered, he admitted, "I have a few issues. Nothing major."

"Has it ever occurred to you why you shifted so early?"

Shrugging, Cole said, "Thought you said it was the dominance of my wolf."

"I did say that and your wolf is a brute, but that's not the entire reason. You found your mate before you knew you were a shifter. You chose her and were ready to ask her to marry you the night you ran into the woods unsure of what was happening to you."

"You think my wolf surfaced because of ..." Cole stopped short, not wanting to bring Tess into this.

"I think you falling in love with that young woman at college triggered the change. You were willing to bond your life to hers even as a human."

Shit. Cole leaned forward and dropped his head into his hands. He'd suspected that recently, but he would not blame her for this. Looking up, he said, "It's not her fault."

"I realize that. You're determined to fix Sammy's problem, but what about yours?"

Cole gave a sad laugh. "I'll have a better chance of convincing Katelyn to go back to Sammy than getting the *human* daughter of a senator who hates shifters and lost her mother in a shifter attack to consider being my mate. Also, this woman is in a position of authority at SCIS. I have to bond with a mate who can accept my powers to stop the curse. To say it would be impossible with Tess is a severe understatement."

"Only if you believe it is."

Leave it to the Guardian to quote the *Mad Hatter* from *Alice in Wonderland* as words of wisdom.

Cole's hackles lifted when the words sank in. "Are you saying I should risk her death to bond?"

"No. We do not risk anyone for our own well-being. I'm only pointing out that we've solved many seemingly impossible mission problems by tackling them from every direction. Are you sure you've looked at this every possible way? Have you researched her history?"

Sitting back, Cole nodded. "I see what you're saying. You want to know if she could possibly be a Gallize."

"If she is, she has her own core power even if she hasn't discovered it. Some females displayed very unusual gifts many years ago. We'd have a better chance of determining whether a woman possessed Gallize blood if the females had not lost their guardian more than two hundred years back. For you to be so strongly drawn to Tess even before your wolf manifested, it leads me to think she could be one. If so, that would allow her to bond with you."

Tess was special in so many ways, but not that one. Cole admitted, "Guess I should confess that I thought about it often in my early days as a shifter, more like fantasized about it. I did try to match her to the requirements for being a Gallize female. She doesn't possess an important one."

"I see."

So did Cole. He saw his future, a dead end coming at him at light speed.

CHAPTER 16

Glad to finally be home, even if it was after dark and this apartment in downtown Spartanburg was only home for while, Tess peeled out of the business suit she'd worn to face her SCIS chief. That had been the low point of her day and it had gone downhill from there. He didn't blow his stack often, but losing a potential Black River pack member had pushed him over the edge.

One more day until Friday, the official end of a normal workweek.

Not for her.

Friday used to mean something special, but these days it was just the start of her work weekend.

She tossed her suit on top of her ruined black dress from the night of the bombing.

Could the drycleaner get the smell of smoke out of the material? It wasn't as though she dressed up much, but she'd worn that dress to please her father who had asked her to join him Monday night at a fundraiser in Charlotte, North Carolina.

He'd been so happy she was attending, until she called to cancel a minute before she went tearing out to meet up with her SCIS team.

Stepping into a hot shower, she started soaping her body, thinking about Colin. Had he actually survived? Was he a pawn in some game being orchestrated by unknown players or just as guilty as Brantley thought?

Where was Colin tonight?

She brushed her nipples with the washrag and hissed at the sensitive buds. Her body had felt odd for days. Like it had a mind of its own and wanted something.

What? A man?

Well, duh. She hadn't been with anyone in ...

Trying to calculate how long was too depressing. This crazy, over-sensitive state was Colin's fault.

Had to be.

It had started the minute he'd touched her wrist. That was all. It wasn't as if the man had stroked between her legs.

Oh, crap. Just thinking about that sent heat pooling down there. She locked her legs together and stood in the rush of water, thinking about changing it to a cold blast. Damn her traitorous hormones because they were begging for a better way to be wet and hot ... with a wet and hot man.

Not Colin. How could she be reacting to him this way? He was a shifter, not exactly dating material in her little world.

And even if she were willing to go there, he wasn't around and the chances of her ever seeing him again were slim to none.

This was just her twisted heart trying to confuse that shifter with Cole because of what Collin had said right before he was put in the transport. Those last words had raised the hair on her neck as well as a memory she'd fought years to get past. She kept those moments shoved down deep, out of her daily life.

But Colin's voice had sounded so much like Cole's in that one moment. Everything she'd loved about Cole had come rushing back at her in a tidal wave of emotion.

Shaking her head, she scoffed at her weakness. She was only worked up by the ghost of sex past. She missed the touch of the man she'd given her heart to. The one who had stomped on it when he disappeared.

Hadn't she sworn to never let Cole Cavanaugh take another day from her after all that he'd destroyed?

Blaming Colin for stirring up these emotions was unfair. Words were just words. Beyond that, the shifter had only touched her wrist.

And stroked his thumb across her skin.

And made her feel as if she were being pulled to him, inside him. She'd struggled to leave his side every time she'd been in his room.

Had he somehow ... infected her with a shifter cootie?

She slapped her forehead, laughing at the silly thought. "Good grief, Tess, you moron. It isn't like he can turn you into a werewolf or a sex nymph with one touch," she muttered. "I just need someone to scratch an itch. Isn't that what a man would say?"

But she didn't want that.

She wanted more than just great sex. She wanted to look into a man's eyes and see her happiness reflected.

More than a quickie with a stranger.

Irritated for a lot of reasons, unwanted arousal being just one, she scrubbed her aching breasts then finished washing with brisk efficiency. Lingering could end with her satisfying herself, but to be honest, she hadn't been very happy dealing with her love life single-handed.

Stepping out, she dried quickly.

Blast it. Even the towel brushing over her skin bothered her. She might just have to take matters into her own hands tonight after all.

Too many days working with no playtime demanded a price.

Evidently it was her sanity.

She pulled on silk boxers and a thin knit top that would cause the least abrasion, then smoothed lotion on her skin on the way to her bed. Even her king-size bed was a perpetual workspace covered in paperwork.

If not for her laptop, the other half of the bed would be empty.

Sitting down with her legs crossed, she opened an email and had started scanning it when her skin pricked with an innate awareness that she was not alone.

The freaky energy in her body revved up.

She couldn't say how, but she knew for sure someone was inside her apartment.

Her building had top security and she lived on the seventh floor. Who could make it past the front doorman and a key-carded elevator?

She covertly checked around the room.

Her walk-in closet was open to view. No one there.

She'd just been in the bathroom. No one there.

Her gaze moved to the door leading to her living room and kitchen. Hadn't she left that open all the way? It was almost closed now.

Next to that doorway, the alarm panel display still showed as ready to arm. She hadn't set it yet, but she normally didn't until she was ready for sleep.

But wouldn't she have heard the normal ding if the door had opened?

That did nothing to instill confidence in her or quiet the fast beating of her heart.

Having spent many years alone, she wasn't rattled easily, but dammit, this was bugging her.

She had to think. No fast movements.

Picking up the closest work papers as if she planned to read them, she casually reached to her left where a writing pen sat next to her Glock 17 on the nightstand.

In one move, she snatched up the loaded 9mm and dropped the papers to wrap both hands around the grip.

She ordered in a loud voice, "Show yourself or I'll shoot through the door." Not really. She'd never risk the bullet going through a wall to hit an innocent.

When no one admitted to being inside, she started feeling like a fool, but she was going to clear the rooms herself, then call security to ask if any nonresident had traveled to her floor in the last half hour.

Before she could make a move, the door to the living room opened slowly, as if given a little shove.

Her heart tried to climb up into her throat. Was she ready to shoot someone? Oh, she'd trained and could nail a headshot at twenty-five yards, but she had never faced actually shooting a real person.

There was a first time for everything. If she saw a weapon, she was shooting.

Hands raised, a man stepped into view.

It can't be.

Cole.

Her eyes rushed up and down, taking in every bit of him. All of it was far bigger than it had been in college. As a cross-country runner, he'd been sexy as they came back then, but the man standing in front of her had a beefed-up body and a dangerous edge about him.

One part remained the same.

That searing blue gaze. The last time she recalled seeing those eyes and that face up close, he'd been leaning over her as he drove deep inside ...

Damn. That was not the visual she needed in the middle of this moment.

Her mind raced with questions. Her heart jumped into panic gear, beating as fast as the wings of a hummingbird on crack.

What the hell was he doing here?

For that matter, where had he disappeared to all those years ago? He'd been hot as the devil back then, but he was off the charts now.

"Hello, Tess." He lowered his arms slowly and crossed those drool-worthy forearms.

His voice had deepened. In fact, it sounded like Colin.

Now she was projecting Colin's attributes onto Cole, but if she put the two side by side, they'd match up in size.

Cole took his time reviewing her during the silence then said, "Long time no see."

She needed to slap herself. Drool worthy?

No. This man had vanished without a word, then just showed up now? Had broken into her apartment? He wanted to chat as if nothing had transpired between them?

Anger shoved aside the ball of hurt growing in her chest at seeing him again.

Anger she could manage much better than the emotions crashing around inside her.

"What are you doing here?" she asked, glad to hear the brusque professionalism drown out her quaking heart.

"I just want to talk." He took another step forward. "I'm not armed."

"Stop right there." She raised the gun a notch higher. "Armed or not, you can't just break into my apartment after being gone *sev-en* years and expect me to offer you coffee."

"I don't expect anything. But I do need to talk to you."

She quickly sorted through her options and came up with holding the gun on him while she called security.

She couldn't do that. They would call the police.

Even if she wanted to suffer the potential news that would leak out, which would be inevitable since her father was a US senator,

Cole wouldn't be willing to answer questions if she had him arrested.

Those years of wondering what had happened tipped in favor of allowing him to stay.

She kept the gun pointed at his chest. "So talk."

"Your arms are going to get tired."

When she said nothing, he shrugged. "You have a leak in your SCIS division. Someone is undermining everything you do."

Not what she expected him to say. "How can you possibly know anything about what I do or my agency?"

His eyes finally dropped away, but before they did, she saw a flood of disappointment. Why?

When he looked back up, he said, "Because I just spent three days in your facility and barely survived your jackals trying to kill me."

Blood rushed from her head.

He was saying ... no, that ... the room spun. Her arms felt heavy, dropping.

"Tess?" He stepped toward her.

She snapped the gun back into place fast and shook off the dizzy wave. "What the hell are you saying?"

"I didn't want to tell you this way, baby."

"Don't you fucking call me baby!" Tears sprang from her eyes, but she could see just fine to hit center of body mass four yards away. She tried to swallow and coughed, choking on what she couldn't believe.

Her voice came out broken. "You can't be ... you aren't ... Colin."

"Colin is a cover name."

"Don't play with me, Cole. You know what I'm saying."

He moved his jaw around as if trying to form words. "I am a wolf shifter, but I'm not with the Black River pack. I'm hunting them."

A wolf shifter. Her heart had tried to tell her, but her mind hadn't gotten on board. In fact, her mind still wasn't accepting it. "I don't believe you, Cole. Get out."

He jerked as if from a phantom slap.

She didn't care. He'd destroyed her once and was doing it all over again.

"Tess, please. I want to explain what happened."

"Why? To convince me not to turn you over to the police, or if you want to maintain you're a shifter, maybe SCIS security?"

"If you don't believe what I have to tell you, then I'll understand whatever action you choose to take."

Why was he being so damn nice?

She bent her legs so she could prop her arms on her knees.

He lifted an eyebrow, reminding her he'd said the gun would get heavy.

That pissed her off all over again. She gave him an evil smile. "If I empty out a few rounds, the gun will feel lighter."

His face fell.

Oh, he didn't find that amusing?

He muttered, "You were nicer when I was burned half to death."

He could only know that if ... he was actually the person who had called himself Colin.

No wonder she kept mixing together Cole and Colin, but the strange feeling she'd been having was not natural. Like that weird energy stirring up havoc in her chest. What was causing that to get stronger?

She asked, "Are you really a ... shifter?"

"Yes, but it's not like I've turned into a zombie or something like that."

She didn't say anything that could be construed as agreeing with him. "Did you do anything to me when you touched me yesterday?"

Frowning with disbelief, he said, "Like what? I'd never harm you."

Colin's voice kept echoing in her head. He'd also said he wouldn't harm her, but both men were the same, and Colin had not tried to hurt her.

Was she really going to tell Cole her sexual appetite had quadrupled since his touch? Only if she were an idiot. "Never mind. I just wanted to know if you passed along anything."

Now he looked insulted. "Like a germ or a disease? No. Human diseases can't touch us. Anything you might have gotten came from a human."

"I didn't say I had anything."

"Good." That one word had been full of relief.

"I don't understand any of this, Cole."

He nodded. "Hear me out. I couldn't tell you any of this when you held me captive."

She flinched at that, because he said it as if she'd put him a cage, which she'd never do.

Not true.

Oh, wait. She *had* agreed to send him to a hole in the ground. Flinching internally, she held quiet so he could explain.

"I was inside the food bank building the night of the bombing. I work for a national security agency—"

She interrupted. "Which one?"

"I can't tell you. There are a lot of things I'm not supposed to be telling you, but I'm going to share as much as I can and trust that you still have the same core of integrity you had back when I first met you."

"I can't promise I won't share what you say if I think it needs to be passed along for national security."

"I knew that coming in here and I'm willing to take my chances. I trust you, even though you may never trust me again."

How did he do that?

One minute she was ready to fill him full of holes and the next he was saying he would give her information that could come back on him.

Her silence must have convinced him to continue. "I wasn't supposed to enter the building. We'd been told Jugo Loco was being distributed out of that building. My team was there to observe and place a tracking device on the Black River pack's truck, then one of our people would have sent information through channels that would reach SCIS."

"Why would your people do that?"

"Because we don't make the law enforcement collars."

Tess took a mental step back at the law enforcement term.

Cole went on. "We work similarly to military covert operations. We go in, perform a mission or gather intel, and leave with no one knowing we were there."

"You screwed that up," she said in a flat voice.

"I did," he admitted.

She'd meant his team, but Cole seemed to be taking all the

blame. "Why were you in the warehouse?"

"When the truck arrived and entered the building, an elderly homeless woman ducked inside before the overhead door closed. I knew if shifters were there, they would definitely scent a human. The Black River pack would kill her for sport."

Tess thought back over the bombing scene. "The woman you were lying on top of when we found you unconscious."

"Probably."

"She wasn't burned."

"Good." There was that one word, which said nothing and a lot at the same time. "Our people have taken care of her."

Tess hadn't heard anything about the woman being moved from the hospital. She would be looking into that tomorrow to find out who had taken her and why Tess had not been informed.

Had Brantley known? Probably. She'd finally hit her limit with him and spent all day doing her own internal investigations. They'd exposed how he'd been working behind her back while professing his trust and support of her.

As soon as she got through that damned meeting next week, things were going to change at SCIS, starting with Brantley.

This had been the longest Thursday of her life.

She gave Cole a nod. "Go on."

"Our intel came from a snitch called Sonic. When I got inside the building, there were no shifters, just a mild residue of at least one having been there. I saw the woman hiding near the truck parked inside and gave a hand sign to stay quiet. I'm not sure she understood anything much that was going on. We know now that someone offered her food and shelter to slip inside. That's all she knew. I found Sonic with his hands taped to a steering wheel and a bomb strapped around his ankles. The best we can figure, someone had to be watching via camera and triggered the timer remotely, leaving me ten seconds to get out."

Goosebumps pebbled over her skin at hearing Cole walk through the pre-explosion scene. The attorney in her noted that he did so with the dispassionate analytical ability of a professional, even though he'd been in the middle of the explosion.

And he'd been burned. Badly.

Her stupid heart clenched.

He said, "A note with the Black River icon had been pinned to

Sonic's shirt. I believe the entire scene had been set up for m ... someone in my organization."

She'd read his lips. He'd been about to say the bomb had been set for him. Now her heart was off to the races. She could have lost Cole a second time, but would she have known it was him even after a complete forensics workup?

Maintaining her calm voice, she asked, "So someone died in that bombing?"

"No. Sonic was already dead. His throat had been slit."

She shifted the gun in her grip, but she wasn't ready to put it down.

Could she use it on him?

No. She wasn't stupid enough to believe she could, and her finger would go nowhere near the trigger. But it was a barrier. A divide between what they were and what they had to be now. She needed it.

"What else did you find?"

"Jugo Loco. That and the note on Sonic confirmed our intel, which indicated that was one of the Black River pack distribution points."

Speaking of intelligence, he'd just shared something no one at SCIS knew. "Are you sure you found Jugo Loco in there?"

"Yes. I used a test strip, but it burned in the fire so it's only my word at this point. Not admissible evidence."

"You're right, *if* I believe you. Why would I?"

He shifted his legs in place. Regardless of how he stood, he was imposing, standing above her like a towering force.

Cole said, "This is definitely something I'm not supposed to share, but I want you to believe me. The three anonymous tips SCIS has received over the last nine weeks are a result of my team discovering fingers of the Jugo Loco distribution network." He rattled off the exact dates, locations and times SCIS had received, plus additional information that convinced her he might just be telling the truth.

She recalled that information coming through their intelligence network.

Still, that wasn't as big a deal as staring at the man she had once loved who was now a wolf shifter.

She deserved to indulge in a serious breakdown as soon as she could fit it into her schedule.

Cole angled his head, studying her in a way that made her think he'd climbed inside of her screwed-up head and caught some of that.

To cover the secret crazy she had going on, she gave him a surly, "What now?"

"I can tell by the surprise on your face that you know I'm telling the truth."

She forced a blank expression into place. "I'm not confirming or denying anything."

"Tess, I'm trying to get you to realize that I work with the good guys who have been helping you."

"Again, no way to prove it and I have no reason to trust what you say." Okay, that was just tired, bitchy noise.

He raked a hand over his short hair.

She jerked the gun up.

"Whoa," he said, hands back up. "Would you please put that thing down?"

"No." One question had churned over and over until she couldn't keep it in any longer. She might never get a better chance to ask it. "Did you know you were a ... uh ... "

"Shifter," he filled in.

"Right. A shifter. Did you know when we were ... together?"

"No."

She wanted to believe him. "When did you find out?"

"The last night I saw you. Remember how I said I needed to go for a run?"

"As if I could forget the last time I saw you?" The pain rushed through her chest again. He'd made love to her and whispered, "Mine." She thought she'd found heaven.

She'd waited and waited while he was gone.

Then she'd gone out looking. Worrying, she'd called around. When she went to the police, they took her seriously until they checked with the school. The administrative office at their college informed her Cole had contacted them to say he was joining the military.

Tess had called them liars. Not her best moment.

The school representative calmly explained that he answered all the security questions on file correctly and asked that no one contact him.

She'd turned into a zombie. Empty inside.

Cole had vanished.

She'd spent days crying and walking the empty apartment.

"I'm so sorry, Tess."

Sucking it up, she said, "Just finish. What happened that night?"

His eyes darkened with sadness. "It's hard to explain, but something inside drove me to go to the woods for my run. I didn't know why I felt the need to run at night. I'd never run after dark in the woods because of the chance of hitting a hole. I ran like someone was chasing me, but I was alone. At the time, I really don't think I even realized what was happening to me, and I eventually lost consciousness. When I came to, I had two men standing over me. I thought they were going to kill me. I was shaking, making weird noises and unable to defend myself."

She swallowed hard, imagining the threat he'd felt.

"They took me to a man in charge of a special unit of shifters he trained specifically for aiding the military. He has, well, let's just call them *unusual* abilities. He knew what I was and said it was not normal for me to be shifting at nineteen."

"Wait a minute. I've studied shifters extensively. They're raised knowing they're shifters. Many shift anywhere from right after birth to somewhere during the first year."

"I'm not like them."

"Why? What's different about you?"

"I'm trying to tell you as much as I can, but let's just say that my kind needs to have their animal called up."

This was the first she'd ever heard of that and she was considered an authority. "I don't understand."

"Basically, my wolf was ready to make an appearance and my body wasn't prepared for it. Unlike other shifters who are known to the public, no one had ever told me I was anything other than human, so I had no background for understanding what was happening."

The academic side of her that had spent years studying their species wanted to know it all. "What did you do?"

"Nothing on my part. Like I said, my superior called up my wolf."

"You're serious about that," she stated in disbelief.

"Yes."

She couldn't wrap her head around it. "Are you saying this man can just do ... whatever..." she sputtered. "And make someone a shifter?"

He chuckled at her outburst and her heart curled around the sound. That was the sound of Cole, the man she'd thought she'd be spending her life with forever.

"My boss can't make anyone a shifter if the animal is not already part of his or her being. He can only order the animal to the surface. If he was standing here and told me to shift, I couldn't deny him. He's that powerful."

"He's an alpha. I know about them."

"It's a bit bigger than just being under an alpha."

Good grief. Cole was saying things that skewed everything she knew about shifters. She mused out loud, "You're special."

"I think of us as just ... different."

She bent her arms to prop her elbows against her stomach. This damn gun was getting heavier by the second.

"You got any coffee, Tess?"

"Huh?"

"Coffee? I've had almost no sleep in the last two days. I'd like a cup."

"Are you mental?" she asked, dead serious.

"No. Think about it. I could have waited until you went to sleep and pinned you down to make you listen."

Her mind went to the image of him draped over her, holding her to the bed and ...

She shook that ridiculous thought off. Man, was she tired.

Cole wasn't through. "Put the gun down."

"No."

"I need to tell you something and you're not going to like it."

CHAPTER 17

Cole couldn't get enough of staring at Tess.

He hadn't minded standing here under her barrage of questions, because he could finally see her clearly and smell her sweet scent.

Even Gray Wolf was behaving. He'd been calm around the Guardian, but now his wolf was downright ... happy.

Mate.

Cole wanted to role his eyes at Gray Wolf's persistence.

Before breaking into her apartment, Cole had paced around like a schoolboy afraid to walk up to the girl he wanted to ask out.

But he'd had to insert into her apartment ahead of her arrival.

Plus, he hadn't been able to get rid of Rory and Justin, who were determined to watch his six. But when he asked for help without questions, they did their part to get past Tess's building security, so he couldn't complain too much.

Well, except that pair would demand he tell everything in exchange for their assistance. Especially Justin, the nosy bastard.

The moment Cole stepped inside this room, his body had come alive at the overload of her scent.

The only thing better than smelling Tess everywhere would be to taste her now, from head to toe in all her sexy places, which was pretty much anywhere on that luscious body.

Standing this close and holding himself back from going to her tested his ability to maintain his distance, especially after she'd just walked out of the shower all fresh and ready.

Oh, yes, definitely ready. Her sweet arousal still swirled through the air.

His wolf had been growling until Cole entered this domain.

Gray Wolf wanted Cole to claim her, to make her their mate forever.

In my dreams, Cole mused silently.

Mate. Now.

Not happening, wolf.

Gray Wolf snarled.

Cole hadn't felt this much control in two weeks. He silently told his wolf, "Go to sleep and we'll run later."

Amazingly, after a few seconds, Gray Wolf receded.

"Okay," Tess grumbled, waving that gun around again. "What else can you possibly say that's going to make me any angrier?"

"There's no firing pin in the gun. You might as well put it down."

She looked at the weapon as if the thing had betrayed her, then cursed and slapped it down on the mattress. Watching her climb off the bed threatened to give Cole a heart attack.

He sucked in a sharp breath at the sight of her wearing nothing but a short top of thin, white material that failed to hide her dark nipples, and silky red boxers he'd like to tear off of her with his teeth.

She must have sensed something and looked up.

In that moment energy pulsed between them.

He felt it even if she didn't recognize the mating bond trying to make a connection. That wouldn't happen unless she opened her heart and body to his bond, which he'd made sure would never happen when he'd told her he was a shifter.

But that didn't stop her electric blue gaze from sizzling with a familiar heat he'd seen the last time they'd been together.

The tips of her nipples promptly turned into hard beads, which that flimsy top failed to hide.

His jeans were doing no better job at shielding how much he wanted her.

She must have caught herself staring at that very place where his jeans strained, because she jerked her head up. She fumbled around to grab a kimono off the foot of her bed, mumbling in an irritated tone.

Didn't like it that she still reacted to him?

He exhaled a little relief at that one sign that she didn't hate him. In fact, her reacting to him as a woman made him downright happy.

She worked with shifters and had to know that he could hear her heart pounding and smell the tipoff of her arousal.

Tying the sash with a sharp jerk, she strode past him, slowing only to slash an evil look at the smile curving his lips.

She warned, "Don't even think about it."

"Too late," he murmured behind her.

In the kitchen, she put on a pot of coffee and he could tell by the way she was shaking her head every so often that she was deep in a conversation with herself.

He'd missed that she talked to an empty room when she was sorting out her thoughts.

Missed so damn much about her.

She was probably listing all the reasons why just talking to him fell under the heading of insanity.

When she turned her back to the coffee maker and faced him, she drew up short.

Cole had moved to only four feet away.

Close enough to be suffering his own level of insanity for thinking he could come here and walk away without looking back. Had he really thought he could simply explain everything that had happened in the past to clear his conscience, expect her to get on board with his plan for the Black River pack, and then leave as he would on any other assignment?

Guess so, because here he was.

Gray Wolf wasn't happy with Cole, but his wolf was definitely content being so close to Tess.

The woman who thought he'd walked away without looking back.

Cole had looked back so many times his head should be facing the other way.

She asked, "Are you healed?"

"Yes."

"Good." Then more silence.

"I didn't have a choice," Cole blurted out, then cursed himself for just throwing it out there. Smooth, he was not.

"Choice in what?"

"In leaving you without a word. I was basically taken away that night. By the time I was able to contact you it was more than a year later and by then I ... figured you never wanted to hear from me again."

He kept waiting for her to yell at him. That little bit of ranting earlier was nothing more than her being caught off guard. She'd had time to process some of what he'd told her by now.

All he could see in her face was hurt, and that cut him deeper than any claw had slashed him in shifter battles.

"You're right and wrong," she finally admitted. "Part of me wants to scream at you that you don't matter to me and act as if I'm living just fine without you, but that would be unfair to the woman who mourned losing you. She's still here and not sure what to think about you showing up again."

Shit. He was dying listening to her and sensing just how deeply he'd damaged her even if it had been out of his control.

She came from a shifter-hating household. Once he'd finished training and learned about her mom's death, all he could think was how much she'd despise him and he couldn't face her disgust.

He'd taken the coward's way out because he couldn't tell her the truth, nor could he lie to her and say he left because he didn't love her any more.

In retrospect, he now realized he should have done more, but he'd been shipped overseas with his team. He'd been young, confused, and angry at losing his life and his woman, and had spent most of the first two years just trying to keep his wolf from killing everyone in sight.

Eventually, his head finally acknowledged his new life and forced his heart to buck up and take it like a man.

The coffee beeped and she jumped, turning to pull down two mugs. She filled them and placed one for him three feet from hers.

She wanted boundaries.

He could respect that, but being in the same room with her and not touching her would haunt him when he left.

Sitting down, she took a sip. "You were telling me how you're a different kind of shifter."

He'd hoped to bypass that with the coffee interruption, but if a change of subject was better for her it was good by him.

"There are shifters, then there are apex predators, which are not part of a clan, pride or pack. An apex predator is at the top of the shifter food chain."

She narrowed it down for him. "You're more dangerous than a plain old shifter?"

There was no such thing as a plain old shifter, but he said, "Yes."

She dragged a hand through her half-dry mane of black hair.

He longed to be her fingers.

Giving him a wary glance, she said, "You're not giving me a reason to feel warm and fuzzy right now."

No one should feel comfortable with an apex predator. All Gallize faced dealing with an unruly beast that required an unnaturally powerful force to control.

Cole's beast was a step worse than the others.

It had been out of control from the minute he shifted the first time and freed Gray Wolf. The Guardian had claimed he'd never seen anything like it, which was hard to imagine coming from a man who had been around as long as he had.

Telling Tess that much about his wolf would not ease her tension, so he appealed to her logical brain. "There's a flip side to how dangerous we are. We're the ultimate enforcement when it comes to shifter law, which is much more severe than human laws for shifters."

"I know their laws," she spat at him.

"Point taken, but there are laws within the shifter society that you *don't* know if you're not part of a pack or a shifter yourself," he said, trying to nicely let her know that if she'd gained her knowledge through academia, it was not the same as a hands-on education. "I was taken away and trained so that when I was ordered to deal with dangerous shifters who had become a threat to humans and to their own kind, I became a killing machine. Once I was deemed ready for the field, I was sent overseas with a special unit created to support US Special Forces. I'm on the right side of the law. I'm on your side."

Sounding more interested than wary this time, she asked, "What's the name of your group?"

"I can't share that or anything about my group with you or anyone else. I've told you more than I've been authorized to say already, but I felt you deserved an explanation. We work behind the scenes, supporting human *and* shifter law enforcement. As I mentioned, the Black River pack knew my team was going to be at that building the other night." He had sidestepped this before, but he had to give her all he could for any hope of gaining some trust. "In fact, it appeared that their pack was specifically tracking ... me, but I don't want you to worry about me being here because no one knows I am. I would never lead danger to your door."

She clearly struggled with what he was telling her, but Tess was brilliant and reasonable. She'd figure out where to stand in all this. He only hoped she could see past all the hurt and realize he'd been thrown into a situation not of his own doing.

After staring at the floor while mulling over her thoughts, she raised her chin and declared, "You should be in a safe house somewhere right now."

He hadn't expected her to say that. His heart flipped over in his chest at the worry in her voice.

She still cared.

His team would always watch his back, but he'd forgotten how much he liked when she used to make him call her when he traveled just so she'd know he was safe.

"We protect those who go to safe houses. We don't hide from anyone or anything," he explained, trying not to give in and pull her into his arms. She'd probably freak at a shifter doing that, but damn he wanted to just hold her one more time.

Tess hugged herself. Her brow crinkled with confusion. She rubbed her arms, trembling. When her gaze shot to him, she accused, "What are you doing to me, Cole?"

CHAPTER 18

Tess started to worry about the vibration running through her body, increasing now to the point it felt ready to come through her skin. Okay, weird didn't begin to describe that thought.

Could her energy hurt Cole?

Logic said she was looking at it the wrong way. She'd felt an increase in the intense buzzing every time she'd been around Colin, aka Cole, when he'd touched her.

Cole looked at her, obviously bewildered. "I'm not doing anything to you, Tess. I swear it."

When she stood, he did too. She moved across the small apartment kitchen toward his side of the table. Her body kept wanting to move closer to him.

Okay, yes, she'd been aroused constantly since touching Colin, but this was jacking up sexual frustration to a whole new level she couldn't just accept.

"What's wrong, Tess? What do you need?"

He looked and sounded sincere, but answering that truthfully would get her into true trouble.

She couldn't very well say she needed him out of those jeans and down on the floor where she could have her way with him. Could she?

Wow, that just went over the edge of crazy and into needing a straightjacket.

She had to get him out of here.

They'd always burned hot and wild as a couple, but this was not happening. Not again.

Her skin felt flush and her insides were molten heat. She

couldn't take another minute and yelled, *"Stop whatever you're doing to make me vibrate!"*

His eyes widened.

Then his expression showed guilty as charged.

Cole said nothing else, just stood there looking like sex on a stick, but slowly the tension in her eased.

She still struggled between wanting to touch him again and being angry at how they'd been ripped apart. Oh, and that he was a shifter.

Nothing like a new way to screw with her head and emotions.

Her heart argued, *he said he'd been sort of kidnapped.*

More like an intervention by strange beings.

Her head chimed in.

Don't make excuses for him, Tess.

She'd gone through every stage of grief and had spent months depressed that he'd just pulled up stakes and left without a word. As if their relationship had been that easy to walk away from when she'd thought they were on the verge of planning their future together.

"This wasn't what I wanted either, Tess."

And now it sounded like he knew what she'd been thinking.

Her body slowly came back under control, even if her lady parts were humming with anticipation. Stupid parts.

The constant rollercoaster of changes and emotions had depleted her bank of patience. She wanted to feel strong now, not fall apart like she had in college after he'd left.

Sucking it up, she said in an offhanded tone, "Hey, no big deal, Cole. I figured you'd found someone new and moved on."

Instead of sounding strong, her words came out angry and flippant.

Worse, she regretted them the minute they left her mouth.

She'd never thought that for one minute. Even if she had, she hated sounding flippant when the pain, even after all these years, was still raw.

Embarrassed, she turned away to hide the lie her face would reveal.

Cole moved faster than she'd thought possible, hooking her arm and turning her back to him. She slapped her hands on his hard chest to hold her balance. His heart pounded beneath her fingers and heat rolled off his body.

She couldn't meet his eyes.

"You really thought I could walk away from you that easily?" he asked in a tight voice.

A hurt voice.

She did not buy that he was that good a liar.

He hurt, too.

Her heart caught on a beat. But she could not fold so easily and excuse him for never contacting her.

"What'd you expect me to think, Cole?"

"Damn it, Tess. I get that you didn't know for all these years and you're angry. I would be too, in your shoes, but I told you what happened. What you don't realize is that leaving you was like ripping a hole in my chest. If there was any way I could have come back on my knees to ask for forgiveness in the beginning, I would have, even though being a shifter hadn't been by choice. I ... I was lost for a long time and I didn't want to hurt you even more."

Her head hurt from trying to figure out where her heart had to stand in all of this. "But you never lifted the phone or sent a letter in seven years. Nothing."

Her hands moved with his deep breaths. She finally looked up, expecting to see anger.

Guilt spread across Cole's face like a slow moving storm. "I didn't know how you'd react. I died a thousand deaths the minute I found out what I was and realized that even if I ever saw you again, that you'd hate me. I'm sorry ... I was angry for a long time, drowning in self-pity and battling to accept my future. When I finally got my head out of my ass, I accepted that no one had done this to me. To us. But all the excuses I came up with doesn't change the fact that you deserved answers before now. I should have manned up and faced you sooner with the truth. You're right to not forgive me. I'll never forgive myself."

She clinched her fingers, fisting a wad of his shirt in each hand. Honestly, back at nineteen she *would* have lost it at learning he was a shifter.

Seven years had changed a lot.

She'd had time to deal with the pain and the loss, and now she could accept that Cole losing his humanity was a loss for everyone.

She'd also had time to become familiar with shifters.

Some were definitely monsters, but she'd met some decent ones she wouldn't put in that category.

Cole kept talking in a low voice that gave away no emotion, but his eyes failed to shield how much it had hurt for him to think she hated him.

He said, "I've never been so sorry to be alive as I was then, but day after day of battling to learn how to control my wolf and training for my future beat me into a kind of submission. When I finally accepted what I couldn't change, I put my head down to get through it. I can never say I'm sorry enough to make up for what happened."

He swallowed and drew a breath. She knew he had more to say and waited to hear him out.

"When I was finally at a point that I was allowed to send you a letter, I couldn't tell you the truth about what I'd been through. I couldn't tell you who I worked with or what my future involved." His finger was gently stroking her cheek. "That left me with one option. Sending a letter saying I left you because I wasn't ready to settle down and didn't love you. There was no way I'd write those lies even if someone had held a gun to my head. I thought about having my boss report news of my death to give you closure."

Her heart ached at the agony he had been through. She couldn't fathom telling her father or the man she loved that she'd become a shifter overnight.

After hearing his heart-wrenching story, she wanted to hold him and make all that pain go away.

Her lip trembled and she broke. "I'm sorry for what happened to both of us."

Cole was so close he could kiss her, but he was clearly holding back, being careful with her.

Did she want him to kiss her?

Yes.

She waited to feel guilt for wanting to kiss a shifter.

Not feeling it.

Her father would lose his mind if he saw her right now, but this wasn't her father's life.

Or was this just her admitting to a curiosity that had started when she was around Colin?

Cole.

Damn, she had to get her head together.

Make a decision.

Kissing him wouldn't change the world, but it felt like a monumental decision. Touching Cole's lips, tasting him again, seemed so simple, but where would that leave her after this? How would that change *her*?

And what about Cole?

He hadn't said one thing that sounded as if he planned to stick around. Would she take this risk only to be left alone once he vanished again?

He couldn't even tell her who he worked for.

She drew a deep breath that caused her robe to fall open slightly.

His eyes flicked down, then back up. No apology in that gaze. He'd clearly take whatever she'd give him.

The question was, how much would she give him?

He lifted his hand and stroked her hair, reminding her of how she used to wake up to him leaning over her, brushing her hair off her face.

Her stomach quivered. Her body longed for his touch.

That frustrating energy buzzed in her chest.

He whispered, "I'm so damned sorry for not coming back sooner to say something. I would cut off an arm if it would make your pain vanish. I would never intentionally hurt you."

She closed her eyes, struggling between backing away and jumping into his arms.

Why did making one decision have to be so blasted hard?

Why couldn't she ...

"You're killin' me," he muttered and pulled her into his arms. His lips met hers and he kissed her with a fierceness she'd never felt from him. His hungry mouth wiped her mind free of any thought except kissing him back.

She knew if she gave one squeak or push he'd let her go.

The last thing she wanted right now was for him to stop.

His lips moved to her throat as he lifted her up. She arched into him, feeling the thick ridge of his erection. She made a noise, something foreign and needy, so unlike her.

"What do you want, baby? It's yours."

She fought to keep her lips closed and lost the battle. "Touch me, please touch me."

He made a sound that matched the way she was feeling.

His lips were kissing her the way they had long ago. As he whispered to her, his hand pushed inside her robe, which suddenly had a major tie failure and draped all the way open. When his fingers touched her breast, she lost her mind, gripping him to her.

He lifted her to the counter and returned his attention to the other breast, teasing her nipples until she cried out.

He shoved the band of her silk shorts down and stroked his fingers between her legs.

"You're so damn wet. I love it. Love everything about you."

She could barely hear him through the roar in her ears. She clutched his neck, pulling his mouth to hers. He gave her everything she demanded without her ever having to utter a word.

No more talking. She just wanted to feel, to let go of all the burdens weighing her down and feel him everywhere.

Her inner energy hummed now as it spread through her body and into her womb where it coiled with the heat building there.

His finger slid inside her and he kissed her harder. His tongue swept across her lips and into her mouth, mimicking his finger play that pushed her closer to oblivion.

She arched back as far as she could, shaking with the need to let go.

His head moved down and he sucked her breast.

Stars danced in her vision. So close. "Don't stop."

He didn't answer, but neither did he pause. His fingers knew her better than she knew herself. He stroked her to a feverish point, then brushed his thumb over the sensitive nub ... pushing her until she fractured.

Energy like she'd never experienced burst through her and spun her orgasm beyond belief. She rode his hand and gripped his shoulders, hanging on for her life.

When the sizzle slowed back to a hum, Cole pulled her to him. He kissed her gently and continued stroking her slowly until the last shock waves stopped.

Holy mother of orgasms. She could hardly talk. "That ... that was not like ... "

His lips swallowed her next words and she didn't care, but what had that been? They'd had an incredible sex life before, but this had been ... a new level.

And she'd been the only one to enjoy it.

Selfish guilt landed on her shoulders. "You, uhm, didn't ..."

"Don't," he whispered.

"Don't what?"

"Don't feel bad, please."

Was he reading her mind? Before she could ask, he said, "I loved sharing that with you. Loved holding you again and touching you. That was a gift I never expected to have again. Don't take that away by saying you regret it."

She heard something she'd never heard in his voice.

Vulnerability. She could so easily take this opening and hurt him back, but she'd rather gouge out her eyes than hurt him when he'd shown her how he had suffered, too.

Squeezing him in a bear hug, which was not easy now that he'd grown up as big as one, she said, "I don't regret it, though I will admit I'm not sure how I'll feel later once I have time to process this."

He chuckled and it made her smile.

She asked, "What's so funny?"

"You. I always enjoyed the way you turned something around and around in your mind until you wore the corners off and forced it into a hole. Then you'd know exactly what to do."

She dropped her head onto his shoulder.

For the first time in seven years, she smiled at a memory from that time.

Sure, this would all feel different the minute she pulled back and had to face everything he'd shared with her, but right here, right now, she was at peace.

When was the last time a man had held her as if that was just as important as having sex with her? No name came to mind and there'd been so few that it was a sad commentary on the men she'd dated.

"This isn't going to be easy, is it?" she asked.

He gave a deep sigh. "No."

She appreciated his honesty. Pushing up to face him, she brushed her palm down one side of his face.

He closed his eyes and leaned into her hand.

She'd spent years shoring up her defenses and now the man

she'd never forgotten had shown up. On top of everything else, he was a shifter.

Damn. Just damn.

There was no way forward for the two of them that didn't end up with them standing on opposing sides of a line in the sand. She was a key player in SCIS and he was a rogue shifter.

He'd admitted as much. Maybe not rogue, technically, but not part of a pack.

If only he'd tell her the name of his organization so she could stand on his side.

Her mind was churning with the need to get back on level footing, which wouldn't happen if she didn't put some space between them.

She cleared her throat and said, "I need to go to the bathroom."

When she moved to jump down, he caught her around the waist, lifting her off the counter as if she weighed no more than the magazine sitting on the corner.

He slowly lowered her to the floor and her body voted for round two with him.

She wasn't considering it.

Really.

She was just a little unstable and slow to move.

Getting a second load of that strange energy in the middle of another orgasm might just stop her heart. As if worry about dying from too many orgasms had ever been a concern?

Oh, hell. She was going to fold.

Cole straightened her robe, tying the sash. He dropped a kiss on her forehead. "You wanted to go to the bathroom. We still need to talk."

Her mind had been mush, but the tone of his voice woke up her professional side, which she dragged back on deck.

Sidestepping, she said, "Right. Go ahead and get some more coffee. I'll be back."

Then she did an award-winning job of not running from the room, but when she closed the bathroom door she leaned on the vanity. Lifting her gaze, she stared at her tousled hair, which was now completely dry.

Had she really just let Cole give her an orgasm?

"I am so screwed." She wanted Cole to stay, but couldn't ask him. She could not get involved with a shifter, not even him. Realizing that made her sick.

She would lose him all over again.

After a quick cleanup, she brushed her hair back over her shoulders then put on jeans and a T-shirt.

The buzz had settled into a hum of happiness.

She and this funky energy needed a new plan if it expected a mind-blowing orgasm to calm it down.

But her body felt human again.

Now to challenge her hormones not to do an about face the minute she walked out there. If she lost the challenge, she and Cole would be on the floor finishing what he'd started.

Not happening. She had to get her head screwed back on right.

He wanted to talk.

What do you talk about after the best orgasm you've ever had? And the ones she'd had with him in college had topped the charts back then.

Back to a game plan. After what they'd just done, it felt wrong to talk about SCIS and Cole's role in the Black River pack case, but talking shop had always been her safe zone.

What if he hadn't meant talking about that, but wanted to discuss *them*? He'd be insulted if she treated what they just did so lightly, right?

She'd find out soon enough, but she was not acting as if she wouldn't have taken him to her bed. Still would.

Argh. If she faced him in court, she'd lose the minute he looked at her.

But he hadn't said he wanted to continue what he'd started just now. Did that mean he had reservations?

Why?

Time to find out.

Plus, she still needed to know what he knew about the Black River pack. Finally, her brain began functioning again.

In the kitchen, her mug had been refilled with steaming coffee. She lifted it and pushed her chair around, putting more distance between them since she didn't want to sit right now.

His expression said he knew what she was doing, but he didn't argue.

Wrapping an arm around her waist, she propped her elbow on it and sipped her coffee. "You wanted to talk, so I'm guessing we're back to what we were discussing before, uh ... "

Crap. Her mouth was determined to walk her back into non-professional territory.

Cole came to her rescue, saying, "We were talking about the Black River pack problem."

Always a gentleman, Cole was helping her out. She said, "Right, but I have other questions first. If what you say is true about you and your people being an enforcement arm for shifters, why doesn't SCIS know about you?"

"A person very high in human government knows our leader, but they both keep it secret. They decided it was the best way to help each other and protect national security. That may change at some point in the near future, but I can't share more until I'm given authority."

"You were explaining how you were different than other shifters. Why weren't you born into a shifter colony of some sort?"

He ran a hand over his forehead and started explaining. "I belong to a line of an ancient group of shifters that has been in existence since the sixth century. Shifters such as the ones you know about were around then, but so far from human villages they rarely crossed paths with humans. When they did, werewolf stories developed, which are more myth than truth. But you know what they say about every myth being rooted in some truth. If I'm ever allowed to tell you the full history of my group, I will, but let's just say we carry power originally bestowed from a druidess long ago."

This just got stranger by the moment, but strange had become her norm once she focused on studying shifters. "Are there any other differences?"

Cole drank his coffee slowly, never moving his gaze from her. He seemed to consider what he was going to say, then put the mug down. "As I mentioned before, most shifters need a clan of some sort to survive and function. That's because of the power hierarchy in packs and the necessity of being under the protection of an alpha."

"I know that."

"I have to keep reminding myself that you know some of this since you're with SCIS."

She scoffed. "That's not why I know about shifters. Most

humans read a little and assume a lot. I changed directions after law school and got my masters in the very new study of shifters. She cocked her head at him when he couldn't hide his surprise. "You're wondering why?"

"Yes, I am."

"Shifters had been out for a year when you ... left. Two more years later, I finished my law degree."

"That doesn't surprise me after you started college when you turned sixteen. You were always going to steamroll your way to wherever you were going."

She never liked bragging about jumping classes from the time she was in sixth grade. Cole hadn't seemed to mind that she was two years ahead of him at the same age in college.

"I didn't mean to interrupt," he said.

She wanted him to understand that she knew how their world treated shifters and where she stood. "As part of a class exercise for one of my law professors, we each had to choose a role to be played in one of three mock trials involving shifters. I waited too long and got stuck with being the defense attorney for a cougar shifter charged with first-degree murder of a human. It was just bizarre enough to push me out of the ... mental lull I'd been in."

He didn't react beyond a muscle jumping in his neck, a tiny physical tell at the peek into the way her life had been wrecked after he left.

She wasn't trying to make him feel bad, just explain what caused her to dive into a field that practically gave her father a stroke.

Moving ahead, she explained, "I guess I needed to think about anything but the normal world while I was trying to finish college. I prepared and presented a case for the shifter. My so-called client, a student in my class, found the whole thing amusing and told me he wouldn't hold losing against me. The person playing the DA presented a totally bullshit case with crappy evidence. At worst, a human would get off with involuntary manslaughter for an accident that happened during inclement weather. Watching the unfair judgment bothered me, but I also struggled with a shifter's place in society. I managed a hung jury and turned everyone in the room against me, even my pseudo client, but that's not what pushed me over the edge."

"Your mother?"

"Yes. How ... "

He gave her an apologetic look. "Another confession. When I was about to board the truck, I asked if you had lost someone close, because I was trying to leave without you knowing it was me."

When she'd thought he was Colin, Cole had been protecting her even then and had told her he forgave her for what would happen. "You knew about my mother?"

"I was overseas at the time it happened, and didn't keep up with a lot of news from back home, but I saw that because your dad is so high profile in the world of shifters."

Understatement.

Taking a sip of her coffee, she said, "Yes, losing my mother had a huge influence on my thinking and career direction. Then there was another incident the first year I had my law degree and was taking on any pro bono case I could fit in that was shifter-related. I figured I'd gain experience while I pushed through my master's degree. I'd submitted my application to SCIS with the idea that starting there would put me one step closer to becoming a district attorney. I had this idea I could help humans prove cases against shifters."

Cole flinched at her admitted one-sided thinking, but said nothing while she continued.

"I'd seen first-hand how prejudice would eventually end up working against those who failed to present a believable case. A woman I'd met the last year of law school had become a close friend. She was attacked and killed on a hiking trip. I had a personal interest from day one and decided to study that case as it unfolded. Maybe even offer some help if it was needed. First, I reviewed the body. The attack had been ... gruesome. Less than twenty-four hours after the killing, the police captured a shifter and accused him of the crime."

Sighing, Cole said, "It had to be a very lucky shifter, or a foolish, trusting one, or more likely, it was the wrong shifter."

Curious, she asked, "Why would you say he was lucky?"

"Under our law, a shifter can't harm a human unless that human is attempting a lethal attack. If that shifter had been in a pack, he wouldn't have lived long enough to be captured by the police. If he wasn't with a pack, he would have been rogue and any alpha would take a hunting party out to deal with him."

"That's murder," she argued.

"No, it's the rule of our world. A shifter who can't manage his or her animal can't live in the human world." Cole put his mug down. "Additionally, any shifter worth his or her salt could not be captured by normal human law enforcement, which means the captured shifter trusted someone to allow them to take him in. What happened?"

She'd been processing what he told her, and realized there were so many things the jackals had withheld about shifters. Clearly, they weren't a good source.

Convincing Brantley of that would be a battle.

She said, "When I saw the video of the accused shifter's interrogation, it hit me hard. I just did not believe he committed the crime. He'd never met the woman and, at the time of the crime, he'd been with his pack on a retreat in another state."

Now Cole looked angry. "He had an alibi and they still accused him?"

"Yes. I think law enforcement was feeling pressure everywhere because of constant rioting and killings. They wanted to show a strong front for the humans and let the shifters know they would not tolerate any shifter crimes. Things were crazy at the time." Like her dad introducing all kinds of over-the-top laws that thankfully didn't get passed. "Everyone was up in arms and wanted the death penalty."

"What about you?"

"I wanted someone to pay for that crime but not an innocent person, regardless of their being human or shifter. If they stopped at the first convenient shifter, that meant a killer remained loose."

"You're right," Cole said and she heard admiration in his voice.

Where had he been when everyone else had treated her like a pariah for taking the shifter's side?

She put her mug down softly and cupped her hands together. "The shifter, a twenty-two-year-old male, sat quietly in court as they railroaded him. The minute the trial ended, I was on the phone talking to his defense lawyer about getting an appeal. His court-appointed attorney said no and hung up on me when I tried to argue. At that point, I decided to take his case and—"

Cole pushed the chair barrier out of the way and covered her cold hands with his big one. His touch immediately stirred that energy in her, but in a way that warmed her soul.

He asked, "Why?"

She stopped fidgeting and said, "I wanted the real killer found."

"And?"

Letting out a long breath, she admitted, "I wanted the system to be built on honesty and truth. No one knew what the future would bring with shifters living openly among the human population. If we continued to convict those who did not commit a crime, we'd eventually end up in a civil war. Shifter governing groups, alphas and others, would never work with human authorities."

He gave her a solemn nod. "Thank you for being who you are, because this world would explode without the voice of reason from you and any others who agree with you."

His compliment soothed so many wounds she'd suffered over the years as she'd fought this battle, too often alone.

She had to finish so he'd know the truth. "It didn't end well. They put the shifter in a subterranean—"

"A hole. Just call it what it is." Cole pulled his hand back and wrapped it around his own mug.

Her body ached at the loss of physical connection.

Her energy slowed as if ... it was sad.

Now she was assigning emotions to an invisible energy?

In the silence that fell between them she felt horrible for allowing Brantley to send Colin—Cole—to a hole. She couldn't deny the truth in that label.

It was a death pit.

The place Cole had been headed to when he said he forgave her. That kept gnawing at her conscience.

He'd known who she was at that moment.

Now she didn't feel as if she deserved his forgiveness and moved ahead to get the words out that stuck in her throat. "The shifter couldn't change to his animal."

"That happens with some when they're put into an area that small, or if they're chained. The animal is confused and panics. The human goes mad and dies."

"He did," she admitted, fighting back tears. "They found him dead the next morning. They speculated he'd had a heart attack."

"That's not what happened." Cole cupped his mug, looking into the dark liquid.

"Tell me," she urged.

"No."

"Why not?"

Sighing, he put the cup down. "It won't change that shifter's death."

Her litigator side roared to life. "But I'd have evidence to show why those holding cells don't work for shifters."

"You had it," Cole snapped. "The body lying in the bottom of that hole should have been the strongest statement about shoving a being into that place without understanding their physiology."

The cold truth of his words smacked her in the face. Did he hold her responsible for shifters who died in the holes because she was with SCIS?

Should he?

"You were asking about how I'm different from the shifters you encounter," Cole said, clearly trying to change the subject, and probably for her benefit.

She grabbed at the new direction like a lifeline. "Yes."

"Most alphas of a pack, pride or whatever can draw power from their pack when they need more, but I told you I'm not part of a pack. Even with all that additional power supply they have, the average alpha is not a match for me or anyone in my unit."

"What kind of unit?"

"We have a highly skilled group who can work either together or independently."

"So you have no weakness?" she quipped, trying to lighten the air in the room.

He hesitated, admitting only, "Everyone has a weakness."

"But you won't share yours, will you?"

"No decent warrior would expose a weakness."

She considered all that he'd said. "What are you trying to say, Cole? What's the real reason you're here now? You could have just stayed gone and I'd have never known what happened to Colin."

"Now that I've been in your SCIS facility, I have a better idea how you operate. I don't want you or any of your people harmed, but you should know that you shouldn't trust those jackal shifters.

They're paid mercenaries. They'll kill their first born for the right price."

Her jaw dropped open. "You don't know that. You're generalizing."

"I do know. You haven't seen them in their natural habitat. They're bloodthirsty and hold no allegiance."

She rolled her eyes.

His eyes narrowed. "You have no idea what you're dealing with, Tess. I'm not discounting your knowledge but don't discount my experience."

Well, damn. He had her there.

When she said nothing, he continued, "My team is going to help find and stop the Black River pack, but this has turned personal. We're pretty sure they have one of our men. I'm going to find him, but I need you to stay out of my way."

Did he think he could dictate the way SCIS ran an investigation? Cole showed up out of the blue, broke into her home and thought she'd fold at the first sight of him?

Okay, yes, she did technically fold when he gifted her with one hell of an orgasm. She'd have to sort that out mentally later.

For now, she arched an eyebrow and challenged, "I thought you were a bunch of super shifters. How'd the Black River pack catch one of yours?"

"Our man's not well."

She didn't think shifters got sick, which would mean Cole's group should be even more bulletproof when it came to illness. That meant there was more to Cole's friend being unwell, but prying that information out of him would be harder than getting Cole to admit his weakness.

She crossed her arms. "Let me get this straight. You expect me to just ignore the bombing and that our transport was torched, plus two staff members killed? I can't walk into my office and brush all that off. This is *my* responsibility."

He stepped forward, a load of irritated male towering over her. "I'll make sure SCIS gets in on the final takedown, if possible. That's the best I can offer. I'm *asking* you to back off the Black River investigation until you receive word from your intelligence agency on something you can act upon."

Was he truly serious? "I have people I answer to and citizens who will be screaming over the food bank bombing, plus Colin escaping, so let me make something clear to you. I will continue investigating this bombing and the Jugo Loco distribution flowing through the southeast. You haven't shown me any credentials. You tell me you're part of some ancient group and your people are the key to shifter law enforcement. I'm not seeing it. What would you do if someone came to you with all that and told you to stand down, because they were a bigger deal than you and your people?"

"I hear what you're saying, Tess, and I can't show you paperwork to prove things that humans refuse to accept any other way, but I've been doing this for the best part of the last seven years. You'll just have to trust me."

He sounded tired, but she hadn't been sleeping so well herself. If he wanted her trust, he had to bring more to the table.

She scoffed, "Really? Trust you? Do you expect me to be so willing to accept anything you say that easily again?"

Cole leaned against the counter with those guns crossed, looked up at the ceiling, then lowered his head to her. "That was probably not the best argument on my part, but I am telling you the truth."

"Not all the truth. Not enough to allow me the ability to make an educated decision."

"Tess, be reasonable."

After all she'd been through, that was the wrong argument to use on her. "Oh, now I'm not *reasonable*? You know what? I'm done. I'm glad you're alive and that I no longer have to wonder what happened to you, but I need to think through all this. It's time for you to go. But know this. If you interfere with any SCIS investigation or harm our trackers, expect to pay a price."

Cole sighed so hard it came out a growl.

He picked up his cup and put it in the sink.

That was different. She used to find his coffee cups all over the house when he was working and in school.

That memory pushed through her frustration.

What was she going to do about Cole?

The confusion she'd waded through back in college after he left was nothing compared to right now. Her heart and mind argued between locking him in with her so he'd stay and telling him there was no way they could be together.

When she thought about how close she'd come to losing him

yesterday, her heart started winning the battle.

But she could not make a snap decision tonight.

She followed him to the door, paying too much attention to his profile and perfect butt.

Memories of hooking her hands on his naked hips and sliding her fingers down over those taut muscles of his backside sprang into her mind. She'd wrap one arm around his waist and use the other hand to caress his dick.

Her mouth turned dry as the desert.

Lost in memory lane, she failed to stop when he turned quickly, grabbing her shoulders.

She stared up, caught red-handed in a moment of lust.

"Where's your mind at, Tess-*alla*?"

Damn him. He used to say that and stretch her name out when he caught her ogling him naked.

That was his way of saying she could have him for the asking.

Her bruised heart still ached when he said things like that. She replied, "I was thinking you could use some time in the gym."

"You are such a sweet liar." He leaned down and kissed her again, taking it slower this time as he swept his lips over hers.

What did she do? Part her lips and let him in.

The energy zinging around calmed into a frazzled hum, as though even *it* was unsure where this was going.

She'd blame her capitulation on that.

One kiss and she lost what common sense she had when it came to this man. Was it his fault she felt pulled to him like steel to a magnet?

She should be backing away, not digging her nails into his shoulders. Hadn't she just ordered him to leave?

Her body caved without a sound of protest.

She held on as her world turned into a tornado of want. One touch blinded her mind to all reason.

Cole's mouth kept going, relentless and hungry. With each time he paused to kiss her gently, he pulled her soul closer to his. She could feel her resolve cracking and flaking away.

What if he disappeared again?

She'd felt rejected and not worthy of love the last time.

But he hadn't abandoned her without a thought.

That one kernel of hope kept wiggling its way into her heart.

Damn him. She'd missed him, missed everything about the two of them, for so long. Oh, she'd tried to banish his memory by dating other people from time to time, but she never felt this intensity with anyone else.

If anything, what she felt now was stronger.

She hugged him hard and forced a groan from his lips. Someone should lock her away. She had to be mental to want to throw caution to the wind and tell him how much she cared for him. The words were dangling close to her lips.

He was breathing hard when he lifted his head and dropped his forehead to hers. In the most forlorn voice she'd ever heard, he said, "I missed you."

Tears burned the corner of her eyes. "But you're still going to leave."

He chuckled. "You told me to."

"Oh, I guess I did."

"It's not your fault, baby. I have to go for now. I've got to deal with whoever grabbed my friend and killed Sonic. I can't be seen with you or it will put you at risk, but I want ..."

"What?" She held her breath, waiting on him to tell her he wanted her more than anything else.

"I want you safe." He held her head to his. "If anything happens to me, I'll make sure someone gets word to you. I won't leave you wondering again."

That's not what she wanted to hear.

Thinking about Cole in danger dropped hot embers in her stomach. She hated the panic seizing her body. "Come into SCIS and work with us."

"I can't, Tess, especially after what happened at the food bank and with your transport truck. They'd all judge you unfairly for not treating me as a criminal, and I have to be free to do my duty."

Duty meant he'd race toward danger, even against dangerous shifters.

Maybe she shouldn't wait until she processed all of this. Who knew what would happen tomorrow? "Cole, what about us?"

He straightened and studied her for a moment before shaking off a thought. "It's complicated. Even if we could get past everything else, I'm still a shifter."

She couldn't form a word in response.

This was the moment to say his being a shifter didn't matter to her. But it did. She hated herself a little for not being able to give him an inch, but she'd been hit with all this tonight and needed time. Allowing her emotions to drive her words would be worse later if she couldn't stand behind them.

Her father would turn his back on her if she brought a shifter into her life. He was the only family she had left.

But Cole had always been a part of her, even when he was gone.

She'd break her father's heart if she crossed that line. Tess was all he had left, too, after her mother died.

Everything she'd ever wanted stood right in front of her and she hated her hesitation.

They were doomed lovers.

Cole leaned down and kissed her hair then whispered, "Please stay away from the Black River pack. There's more than shifters involved and humans aren't equipped to fight them. Neither are the jackal shifters in SCIS."

She wouldn't agree or argue with him.

Shaking his head at some internal thought, he added, "I would be careful around Brantley, too."

"Why?"

"That transport trip was never headed to where you thought and those jackals will not lift a finger to operate on their own. They were following someone's instructions."

"They could have been paid by the Black River pack," she suggested, reaching for straws. She had issues with Brantley, but she couldn't let her feelings for Cole affect how she dealt with Brantley.

"It wasn't the Black River pack. My people got there first. Then a helicopter with an SCIS logo showed up as we were leaving."

"What?" No one had told her that.

"Exactly." He cursed. "I know that hardheaded look and how you'll need to verify it, but don't push back if someone blows you off. Just hold onto that information until we can get more to you. And please try to stay safe. Don't accept everything you're being told at face value. There *is* a mole in your operation. I don't have time or the authority to share enough to prove it to you, but I would not lie to you about something so important to your safety."

Unable to speak, she nodded.

"I replaced your firing pin while you were in the bathroom." He turned to leave, paused, drew a long breath, then turned back.

He leaned close, cupping her head as he kissed her once more. Then he whispered, "You are my only weakness."

In the next second, he'd slipped out the door and closed it behind him.

She stood there, unsure what to do for two heartbeats, then grabbed the door to call him back. She looked first toward the elevator thirty feet away, then toward the stairs, which were even further, but the hallway was empty.

No one could have vanished that quickly.

Correction. No human could have.

Cole expected her to sit back and do nothing? To let him fight this battle alone?

Silly shifter.

She had access to her own extensive network of information.

By tomorrow night, she'd know everything available on Cole Cavanaugh. The next time they met, she wanted to be on equal footing. Now that she knew what had happened to him, she would come to terms with it and ... with how they could move forward.

A new worry gripped her.

Could she redirect Brantley from hunting for Colin?

If she did and Brantley figured it out, she'd end up worse than a shifter convicted of a crime.

The government had no mercy for anyone who interfered with shifter investigations, especially if they were convicted of aiding and abetting a criminal shifter.

The easy penalty was one hundred years in prison.

The other option was death.

CHAPTER 19

Cole hadn't been gone from Tess five minutes when Justin and Rory fell into step on either side of him.

Rory kept his voice down when he said, "What's going on, Cole?"

Damn. Leave it to the curious cat in their group to figure out what Cole had been hiding. Cole said, "What do you mean?"

Justin leaned forward to look at Rory. "Are we talking about this?"

"Yes."

"What is it we're talking about?" Cole hedged, hoping he was wrong.

"Is that woman your mate?" Justin asked.

"No."

"See? I told you his head is up his ass," Justin said, leaning over to talk to Rory.

Cole gave Justin a quelling look, which had no influence on him whatsoever. These men had been through some hairy times on missions with Cole. They both knew he would step in front of a mortar blast six feet away and take the hit for them.

Rory eased his gaze over to Cole. "You're too young to be suffering the curse, but so is Sammy. Just tell us so we can help."

Cole should be angry, but he actually felt relief at no longer having to hide it from the people closest to him. He also couldn't accomplish what he needed to with the time he had left ... at least not without their help.

Giving in, he said, "There's something I want to tell you, but you can't share it with anyone." Just to make sure they knew what he meant, he said, "That includes the Guardian."

As expected, Justin said, "You know we got your back. If you say it stays between us, then it does."

Rory remained silent, a contemplative look on his face. He had always been the thoughtful one who gave balance to Justin, who never hesitated to go all in on whatever crazy plan Cole came up with to defeat an enemy.

Cole told Justin, "I appreciate your support, but to be honest, I'd rather not tell you two something that would put you in a bad position with the Guardian."

Before Justin could jump back in, Rory said in his quiet voice, "We can hold your confidence no matter what it is. What's up?"

That was the extent of what had to be said.

Cole trusted these two with his life, which he didn't expect to have for much longer. "My mating curse *has* started."

"Shit, that's what we guessed, but I was sure you were going to tell us we were wrong," Justin said. "Has to be some way to fix this."

Cole knew that would be their next thought, so he explained about meeting Tess in college and planning to ask her to marry him the night he was taken to the Guardian.

"Shit, man, that sucks," Justin said, frowning.

"Yes, it did and still does, but it wasn't anyone's fault."

Cole could admit that out loud now when he couldn't before. He'd been angry with everyone, including Gray Wolf, for the first two years. The difficult relationship with his animal was as much Cole's fault for not wanting to be a shifter as Gray Wolf's for being an impossible beast to manage.

With enough time, the pain had turned into a dull ache in his chest as if a part of him had died.

Rory had listened quietly, but now asked, "So, is Tess ... the one? Is she a Gallize female?"

"I would love for her to be, but she only fits one of the markers we were given." Cole had thought on that a long time. Gallize females originally descended from five women, each pregnant with female babies who had received the blessing of power from the Gallizenae druidess. He'd wanted to tell Tess more of the Gallize history, but he'd already pushed limits with what he'd shared.

"Which marker does Tess have?"

"She was born during a true blue moon month, but so were a lot of human children." Many people considered a second full moon in the same month at any time a blue moon, but originally, a blue moon was considered as a second full moon over the period of all four seasons. Gallize women were birthed during the thirteenth moon in one year.

"What about the marker about being second born?" Justin asked. "She got an older sibling?"

"No. She's an only child," Cole answered. He'd been told to watch for at least two of four markers, the other two indicators being a woman with mismatched eye color and someone who connected with a shifter telepathically.

Gallize shifters normally only spoke mind-to-mind in animal form with some exceptions. The way Cole understood it, if a Gallize shifter bonded with a Gallize mate, they could also enjoy telepathic communication while the shifter was in animal form even though she was in human form.

Those women were harder to find than a popsicle in hell. When the female guardian of Gallize women had vanished, she had not left a guardian heir.

Evidently the eagle guardians normally had at least one child to whom they passed the torch, which made sense for preservation of the Gallize warriors.

Cole's guardian had no mate or offspring though.

A team member had asked their shifter guardian about that once and received an icy look that could freeze a fire.

No one else asked after that.

Seemed that it would be simpler to match up male and female guardians, but that apparently wasn't the way it worked for them. Who was Cole to question any of this when he had his own problems?

"What color are your woman's eyes?" Justin asked, clearly still trying to make Tess fit the profile.

"Blue." That wasn't true, because blue sounded too simple. Her eyes were the color of deep water that could pull you under.

"You sure her eyes match?" Justin would not stop. He hated to lose at any challenge, which was why Sammy hadn't told him about Katelyn.

If Cole asked for help finding a mate, this crazy grizzly would go to the end of the world and return with one.

But Cole didn't want any mate.

He would never be able to bond with anyone except Tess.

Rory walked along silently, his gaze staring off in the distance, which meant he was in thought. He glanced at Cole. "The Guardian says it's not impossible to bond with a human."

Cole had considered that and every other possibility for a long time. He said, "Even if I would try that, which I won't, her father hates shifters. He's Senator Janver."

Rory groaned. "That's ... bad."

Justin said, "Ah, shit." Then he asked, "Why wouldn't you try with her if not for that?"

"Same reason Sammy didn't want to bond with his human woman." Cole explained, "I would never risk opening up my power to Tess when there's a good chance it would kill her."

"The last one that tried survived."

Cole countered, "Others died, which is why no one tries it." Yes, he'd done his research on that as well.

All it took for Cole was hearing that one woman had died.

Justin kept at it. "If Katelyn hadn't run off, Sammy might have convinced her to become a shifter. She could bond with him if he changed her into a bear. Then they'd have bear babies for sure."

Rory snarled, "That is not what we do."

Justin stopped.

When Cole and Rory turned back to him, Justin said, "We won't survive if we don't bond with a mate of *some* kind. Are you telling me you wouldn't at least ask a woman who loves you if she'd consider changing into a shifter?"

Cole and Rory both said, "No!"

"You're a pair of meatheads." Justin strode past them, but he didn't make it far, because he reached the bar where they had agreed to meet up.

That was *if* they'd waited there for Cole as directed.

Watching Justin disappear into the bar, Cole said, "So you understand why I'm not telling the Guardian any of this?"

"He doesn't know about your mating curse?"

"He does," Cole admitted. "He called me on it. That's not why I asked you two not to talk to him. I need help wrapping everything up before ... the time comes for me to do what is right. The

Guardian would pull me back if he thought I was too focused on protecting Tess instead of watching out for Gray Wolf and myself. I need some room to move and react at a moment's notice. He knows I'll come in when it's time, but I won't hold it against you if you call the Guardian before I turn myself in. I feel like I know when I'm in control, but ... that could change."

Rory listened intently and finally nodded. "You would do it for me."

"I would, but Justin isn't going to be easy to convince."

"True, but he's always done the right thing when the time came to act." Breathing out a rough breath, Rory asked, "Is there anything the Guardian can do for you?"

"No. Nothing has ever been normal about me being a shifter, starting with my changing too early. Just so you know, once I find Sammy, I want to see Tess one last time, then I'm going to the Guardian."

Rory put a hand on Cole's shoulder and looked him in the eyes. "The Guardian is allowing you to be out here hunting Sammy while you deal with the mating curse, which is unlike him, so I take that to mean we all have some autonomy. We're here to help find Sammy and to help you. How far along is the curse?"

"Claws come out sometimes. Gray Wolf was almost impossible to control up until three days ago, but something happened after he broke loose at SCIS and battled two jackal shifters. I have no idea. Maybe that release calmed him."

Or maybe being close to Tess calmed him.

Cole wished it was that simple, but it wasn't. If he stayed around Tess, eventually Gray Wolf would snap.

Rory muttered, "Good wolf. The only good jackal shifter is a dead one."

Cole would hate losing a future with these men. "I promise you I won't put anyone at risk, but if ... the unexpected happens and the curse progresses faster than I realize, you have to do your duty."

"Justin will balk."

"I know. That's why I'm telling you. Do whatever it takes. I don't want to die with the blood of an innocent on my hands."

Patting his shoulder, Rory said, "I understand. Now, let's get a beer and soothe Justin's fragile psyche."

Cole laughed at the idea of soothing someone who turned into a monster grizzly bear with jaws that opened wide enough to snap off a human head.

As they walked into the bar, Rory said, "Speaking of Katelyn, the Guardian says he'll have news soon about a meeting."

"We need to find her," Cole muttered. "Wait, did he call while I was up with Tess?"

"Yep."

"What'd you tell the Guardian about where I was?"

"Not me. Justin took the call and told him you were interviewing potential mates."

"I'm gonna kill that bear."

"You'll hurt his feelings."

Cole laughed, but the sound died in his throat. He'd lost his human life to being a shifter. Now he'd lose his shifter life and brothers-in-soul from the mating curse.

He never had a chance at a future, but he now wanted to make sure Tess was safe before he was gone again.

That wouldn't happen as long as Brantley was in the picture.

CHAPTER 20

Friday morning, Tess stood behind her desk at the downtown Spartanburg offices for SCIS, checking quickly through her messages. Nothing from Scarlett Sullivan, a consultant shifter who tracked and provided intel. No one in SCIS knew her animal. Not even the jackals on staff could figure it out. They scowled that her scent was off, whatever that meant.

Brantley took issue with Scarlett and didn't hide his irritation.

Scarlett rarely showed up at SCIS in person, preferring to send in her reports and speak occasionally by phone.

Tess believed it was because Brantley considered Scarlett part of the security department and under his thumb.

As for Tess, she'd been trying to build a professional relationship with Scarlett, the one shifter who said what she meant and didn't make Tess uncomfortable the way the jackals did.

Now Tess could add Cole to that list. Her worldview had broadened in the last two days.

Regardless, Scarlett trusted no one and hadn't checked in today when Tess was hoping to have heard back about the side project. She'd asked Scarlett to track down the alpha who was involved in the shifter battle that triggered her mother's heart attack. Tess had been putting out quiet feelers to her law contacts, seeking out a judge who might entertain her motion to have the court files unsealed. She'd been too off her game after her mother's death— and too close to the case for reasonable analysis—but now, she had questions.

Brantley walked in without knocking.

Tess held her temper, but she did not acknowledge his entrance while she finished working through her notes.

Rude attitude deserved a rude response.

She and Brantley were headed for a confrontation, but that would have to wait for the right time. Rumor was, someone high in the government had used his or her influence to push Brantley's resume through and influenced him ending up as Tess's partner.

But he was not lead on the Black River Pack investigation in the southeast, which clearly was a bigger deal for him than she'd realized. Her background with shifters had given her a step up on him.

And now Cole had her looking at Brantley even closer.

Tess kissed no one's butt at a job, but as a woman in SCIS, which was a dangerous field of operation, she had to go the extra mile every day to prove her capability.

Once she had a solid two years here, she'd put in to work with the national headquarters over all the SCIS operations, which would eventually lead to the director's position where she could really make a difference.

When her visitor exhaled a long sigh, she dropped into her chair, looked up innocently and said, "Anything new on the blast at the food bank?"

Brantley's face darkened with annoyance, but he pulled back a chair facing her and sat. "Body parts of one person have been recovered but no identity yet."

That would be Sonic. Cole's snitch friend had been blown to pieces.

Tess couldn't very well tell Brantley she had information on the identity of the body without exposing the fact that she'd seen their escapee last night.

She asked, "Do we know if the body parts belong to a human or shifter?"

"Lab report on a recovered limb indicates the person was human. They're still running tests."

Maintaining a hardnosed professional tone for Brantley's benefit, Tess asked, "Has there been any sign of Colin O'Donnell? I reviewed the traffic cam from the food bank explosion. O'Donnell ran out a second before the bomb detonated and he was carrying that homeless woman, but he never looked at the camera."

She knew that was because of Cole being a trained operative.

Tess pointed out, "He could have been saving that woman since I doubt she had any serious role in all of this. Probably an innocent caught in the wrong place at the wrong time." That was close to what had happened. Her chest had ached at watching Cole almost die in the video.

He had tried to protect the homeless woman.

Brantley snorted with disgust. "Probably more like O'Donnell intended to use her for a human shield."

Don't kick Brantley.

At least they had no positive ID for Colin-Cole other than the SCIS staff members who put the mask on him after he'd shifted back from his wolf. How much could they have seen while nervously hurrying to install the mask?

Tess might not be objective after having been with Cole last night, but Brantley was just as subjective with his opinions.

She thought of a way to keep Brantley busy today. "You should interview that homeless woman for more information."

Brantley waved off that suggestion. "You heard that initial interview with her. We'd get more out of a hamster."

"Not necessarily," Tess argued. "I just read a report from one of our people who found someone at the local shelter who knew the woman and could speak her broken language. Evidently she has no teeth and speaks Spanish. That's probably why it sounded like gibberish."

"So?"

Lifting the report, Tess scanned it and said, "One of the nurses who spoke Spanish said the homeless woman claimed an angel swooped in, picked her up and flew her away from the devil's wrath." Looking at Brantley, Tess added, "We could get more out of her with that translator."

"She's in the wind. Someone checked her out and no one can find paperwork on who did it or where she went." He shared that with a smug look.

"When, exactly, were you going to share that information?" Tess asked, glad she already knew what had happened to the woman.

"Didn't seem important since, as you said, she probably didn't play any role in the event."

She'd love to tell Brantley the escaped shifter was not with the

Black River pack, but he'd love that. She had no proof other than talking to Cole, which she could never mention.

More than that, Cole trusted her to protect what he'd shared. She couldn't betray that trust unless she discovered he'd lied to her.

She knew in her heart he hadn't.

Plus, when she began putting the pieces of her conversation with Cole together, she figured out why he didn't want to be seen with her or for SCIS to be involved in tracking Colin.

She believed Cole was making himself a target to draw out the Black River wolf pack.

The note on Sonic's chest had been addressed specifically to Cole.

The next time she saw Cole, she might shake his head loose for taking these risks.

If she ever saw him again.

Unwilling to entertain that dismal thought any longer, she asked, "So nothing new on O'Donnell?"

"I stopped by the lab on the way here and the only thing they have determined is that his blood doesn't match a specific shifter species of wolf or anything else."

Tess had an idea why.

Cole had described his kind as an apex predator.

She knew there was more to it than that, but she'd have to wait until he was willing to trust her with more.

The deeper she got into this investigation, the further she moved from the center where she belonged. She couldn't do a thorough job with her bias toward Cole, because she was withholding important information.

But Brantley was pushing just as hard to pin the bombing on Colin O'Donnell and prove he was a Black River pack member based on puny, circumstantial evidence.

Cole claimed there was a mole in her division of SCIS and she believed him, so for now she was sharing little.

Brantley scrolled on his phone as he spoke. "Our people continued tracking the missing paper trail on O'Donnell and actually got something. His identity disappears in records around the age of twenty-two when he entered this country. He dropped off the radar, which is suspicious in itself. No one disappears completely. Plus, we can't find a photo anywhere of this guy. Even if a person goes into an agency such as the CIA, someone can confirm or deny his existence through our agency channels, especially if that person is found committing a crime."

Cole didn't commit a crime at the food bank, Tess wanted to argue, but she had no way to prove who he was or what he'd done in the past seven years.

So why am I so ready to defend him?

Because while her mind was having a tough time with all of this, her heart had already made a decision and opened its gates.

Brantley was still reading from his phone notes. "On top of that, a year after O'Donnell disappeared, the Black River pack surfaced for the first time that we know of in the Middle East, then expanded to South America where they're now headquartered."

"You do realize this is all circumstantial, don't you, Brantley?"

"So? It's evidence. What's your point?"

"My point is that I don't want to get so focused on one potential tie to the Black River pack only to find out later O'Donnell isn't connected and we wasted a lot of effort on him."

Brantley didn't even blink. "It's not a waste. He's our prime target right now."

Showing a clear concern for the case so he didn't turn this around down the road, Tess said, "It's a shame we didn't get a photo of O'Donnell while he was here, which is understandable since our people would have been in jeopardy. The staff was right to worry more about installing the mask the minute O'Donnell shifted back to human form than in taking pictures, but we could sure use a photo right now. I suppose we all thought we'd have plenty of time to observe him once he arrived at the SNR facility."

Someone had tried to kill Cole on the way to that prison.

Tess intended to find out who inside SCIS was involved.

If Cole was correct in his suspicions and the mole turned out to be Brantley, she wanted to know who his powerful contact in the government was before she put him in cuffs.

Brantley eyed Tess with a superior look when he casually mentioned, "An image of O'Donnell is not a problem. I brought in a sketch artist last night to create an image. She spent hours with both of the men who had attached the mask."

Oh, hell. Brantley had probably been rubbing his hands together just waiting to drop that little bomb.

Tess refused to show any physical reaction about the sketches, but her stomach threatened to revolt over the results.

She said, "Really? When did the artist finish?"

"About one this morning."

"Eight hours ago. Why haven't I received those drawings?"

"You haven't? I sent them to you an hour later." He scrolled on his phone, mumbling to himself. "Here it is. I'll send it again."

Her gut was screaming that he lied about sending them earlier. She tapped the keys on her laptop and opened her email, then downloaded the images. Damn.

The artist had captured Cole's image right down to his intense gaze, which seemed to stare at Tess, accusing her of taking the wrong side.

She would always stand on the side of the law.

But her legs were a bit shaky at the moment.

Moving on as if he were now running the meeting, Brantley said, "I sent the picture to contacts overseas and in South America immediately. Nothing has come back from our South American resources yet, but I did hear back from someone with US military who confirmed the man we're calling Colin O'Donnell might have been seen in military operations overseas."

Tess pondered what Brantley was sharing. Did he have more he was holding back? "Are you saying O'Donnell was in our military, but we have no record of his enlistment?"

"No, but you're assuming he was fighting for our side. They didn't indicate he was, so he might have been with our enemies. Could be a sleeper cell sent here. We just don't know yet."

Great. Cole was either part of a deadly wolf pack or a terrorist.

Putting a push of challenge in her voice, Tess said, "Since I seem to be the only one looking at all possibilities, I'll play devil's advocate. What if O'Donnell was in a Special Forces group with missions off the books?"

Brantley leveled her with a hard look that said he didn't care for her dig at him. He moved ahead. "I sent an inquiry through a ... close contact I have in the government, one of which is an associate of a person in the Pentagon who would know about anyone in our military. I've heard nothing on it. I'd say that's not realistic right now."

Who was Brantley's contact?

Cole had made a valid point when he told Tess that SCIS had no evidence he'd committed a crime, but escaping from that transport yesterday screwed his argument for innocence. She had a hard time caring that Cole had broken a law by escaping since he'd managed to stay alive.

Ready to wrap this up, Tess asked, "What about the Jugo Loco? Was there any evidence of it being in the food bank building?"

"Actually, yes," Brantley replied. "The explosion knocked a metal wall over piles of food supplies which protected some of the supplies from the fire. They found six jugs of standard tea that tested positive on site for Jugo Loco, but our people are doing a chemical analysis to be sure."

So Cole had been telling the truth on that as well.

Why do I keep questioning him?

When she thought about it, she kept mentally judging everything she learned about him and the food bank explosion to build a case in her mind for his innocence.

A case she could defend, if she ever had to do so.

Changing subjects, Brantley asked, "You got an update on the bear shifter responsible for the Nantahala Honeymoon Massacre?"

Tess had just looked at a new report on that case this morning. "Not really. Can your jackal shifter who fingered the bear's scent at the scene see if he can find anything around the food bank location? If the Black River wolf pack really did take in a bear, which is odd in itself, maybe he was involved in this distribution point."

"I'd love to do that if that particular jackal hadn't been killed transporting O'Donnell," he replied wryly.

Crap. Since Cole's people rescued him, Brantley and SCIS would add that charge to the ones hanging over Cole.

Regardless, the bear shifter suspected of killing the human couple had to be brought to justice.

Tess shoved a loose strand of hair over her ear. She'd worn it up in her all-business mode with her mother's wooden barrette. That hair accessory had been old when Tess was a child. Wearing it these days gave her comfort she couldn't explain, especially when trying to solve these cases.

She couldn't be wishy-washy when it came to capturing

dangerous shifters, but Cole had her questioning a lot of what she knew and how SCIS operated.

Now was a bad time for her heart and mind to be playing a tug of war with her emotions. She wanted to believe Cole had the same goal as she did.

If so, then he would also want to end the Black River pack reign of terror and bring a dangerous bear shifter to answer for his crimes.

Tess couldn't let her screwed-up feelings for Cole confuse her when it was time to act.

And her emotions were *very* screwed up.

In her mind, she knew a human and a shifter couldn't mix, at least not her and Cole. Not in her world with a father like Senator Janver.

And how could it possibly work for a woman who wanted to remain on the career path Tess had laid out?

Just like Cole had said, it was complicated.

Whoa. Was she trying to figure out how to be with Cole? As in *forever*? She paused, stunned to find herself considering the pros and cons of that decision.

"Tess. Did you hear me?" Brantley asked, lifting his voice.

Shaking off her mental debate, she cleared her throat to explain the brief delay. "Sorry. I was thinking about how that bear plays into all of this with a wolf pack that shouldn't be allowing a bear to join them."

"Who knows?" Brantley said, brushing off her comment. "They're animals. Don't try to use logic with something that is only half human. I was saying I brought in two new jackal trackers."

Warning bells dinged loudly in her head. "Why? We could hand that to Scarlett when she comes in."

"That shifter twit isn't consistent enough with checking in. I want two dedicated trackers focused on nothing but finding O'Donnell."

Brantley kept pushing Tess closer to a showdown by acting as if he had full authority. She'd let him think he was skating by for now just to keep him complacent. Once she had next week's congressional meeting behind her, she might just put her own tracker on Brantley to get some answers before she lowered the boom on him.

That day was coming, but only when she was ready to act.

She'd bide her time, but she didn't have unlimited patience, especially when it came to someone who thought they could pull the rug out from under her that easily.

Tess dismissed him by saying, "That's fine. I have other cases for Scarlett even though she's better suited to the O'Donnell case."

Brantley cocked his head with amusement. "Not better than my new trackers. They're bringing part of their pack with them."

"Excellent," Tess bluffed. "I expect results quickly."

He studied her intently as if he had picked up on something.

Tess had cheered his aggressive stance as she normally would on hunting an escapee. That normally appeased him.

She hoped Cole was as good as he said when it came to dealing with other shifters. Brantley often described jackal shifters as invincible when they worked as a pack.

If they were as cutthroat as Cole had said, SCIS had just put a pack of killers on his trail.

That meant Tess had put those killers on his trail since she was in charge of this operation. Not that Brantley's action was wrong, but she didn't trust his motivations as being for SCIS. It was as if he wanted to bag a major shifter and present it as his capture when they met with the congressional committee next week.

He would one day find out she was similar to a Doberman.

Those dogs would allow you all kinds of room around them until you crossed the line into their territory.

Then they'd silently take you down.

She would be a team player only with teammates who worked toward a common goal.

Ending the meeting, she told him, "Please remember to let me know when we have an ID on the body from the bombing and if *anything* new comes in on locating O'Donnell, no matter how insignificant." She made a point of holding his gaze just to let him know aggressive men who liked to hear themselves talk did not intimidate her. "Some Jugo Loco testing has produced markers that connect the batch to where it was created. We need to find out if we can trace connections from the food bank to an origination point."

Grinning, Brantley said, "I'll put someone on that right away ...

boss."

Tess tilted her head in a sign that this meeting was over. "Good. Let's recreate everything that happened inside and around the food bank forty-eight hours prior to the explosion."

She stood.

Brantley popped up, too. "Where are you headed?"

"To update the chief," she said, not even hiding the frustration in her voice. Someone was working against her and SCIS, but she wasn't about to broach that topic with her already irritated chief. Without solid evidence, he'd see it as trying to blame their problems on an unknown person. She'd point no fingers until she could put handcuffs on the perpetrator. She'd received a blunt text from the chief this morning. His job required that he oversee and report on major developments, and a copy of his reports went directly to the Congressional Committee on Nonhuman Affairs.

When Tess and Brantley faced that committee next week, they had to show the tax dollars spent on SCIS were making a difference so they could request more resources.

Brantley gave her a look of concern, which she didn't accept as real. "Want me to go instead?"

Oh, sure. Like she'd tell him to take her place so the chief would think she couldn't take the heat. Neither could she tell the chief that the transport arrangements had been orchestrated entirely by Brantley. That would sound like she was pushing off the blame on him even though she approved the transport.

Brantley deserved the blame, though. His jackals had gone off in the wrong direction, which gave the appearance that they'd been hijacked or working with the person undermining the SCIS operation.

That fiasco would be Brantley's to explain at the congressional meeting. She planned to pass off any questions on security to him, since he claimed that area outright.

She picked up a folder and walked past Brantley, who could let himself out since he treated her door as though it didn't exist. She never left anything in her office she didn't want to end up in the wrong hands in case he snooped.

Telling her assistant where she was headed, Tess took a deep breath and went to face the chief. He'd made it clear he hadn't wanted her at SCIS, but only because she was a senator's daughter, and thus a high profile person he didn't want harmed. Aside from that, the chief had always been professional and treated her fairly.

Or he had been until she'd had two jackal shifter casualties, a brand new transport vehicle blown up and lost Colin O'Donnell in the process.

Hell, she'd fire herself right now.

CHAPTER 21

"The Guardian wants to talk to you, Cole," Rory said, holding out the phone.

Cole put down his fork from his half-eaten breakfast and took the phone. He glanced around the diner where no one was paying attention to them, then said, "Yes, sir?"

"We have a firm line on Katelyn."

Finally, some good news. Great way to end this week. "That's great, sir."

"Possibly. What I have is a phone number you have to answer this evening, no set time, then go immediately to meet her."

"That's not a problem, sir."

"It wouldn't be, but you'll be given just enough time to reach her. If you miss that window, she won't meet with anyone again. If anyone follows you or goes near the meeting, she'll vanish."

Cole pointed out, "That means I can't take backup."

"I understand." The Guardian added, "I don't like sending you in alone, but as I was told when we got this lead, she won't meet with anyone except you. She said Sammy only mentioned his best friend and never gave a name. We all know he meant you."

Cole did not want to let Sammy down. "I'll do my best to convince her to help us. To help Sammy."

"This is a risky gamble, even for one of us. I'm going to guess that Sammy has been suffering the full force of the mating curse for close to three weeks. Once it starts, a Gallize has as short as three weeks and as long as five before the mind deteriorates to the point of ..."

"I understand." More than the Guardian could know, Cole was

keenly aware of the early mating curse stages and where it was headed. Based on what the Guardian was saying, Cole had a feeling his curse was progressing quickly, the same as Sammy's.

"That's not the only reason I'm calling. We can't allow SCIS to learn that Sammy is a Gallize. There are too many leaks coming out of that organization. I'm close to securing our position with my contact for national defense before we go public, but even when we do, it won't be all at once and only for those who need to know. I've given this a lot of thought."

The Guardian paused. Their boss always thought before he jumped.

Cole interjected, "I've been hesitating to say this, because it still doesn't ring true in my mind, but I think Sammy might have gone to the Black River pack voluntarily."

"You think he believed they could cure the curse?"

"Maybe."

"If that was possible, I would have brought the cure here for all of you, even if it started a war among shifters."

Cole believed him.

The Guardian continued. "I think there's only one way someone would have convinced Sammy that they could cure him and that would have required a powerful magic user who could overpower Sammy's ability to reason. It wouldn't really cure anything, just fill him with the belief it would. The one major side effect is that every time Sammy hallucinates, the curse symptoms probably get worse."

If Sammy was coerced by magic, it didn't change anything in the end game, but Cole appreciated any reason to believe his friend hadn't just walked into their camp.

The Guardian continued. "I was asked point blank by a congressman who sympathizes with shifters if any of our people were involved with the Black River pack."

Cole said, "What'd you tell him?"

"That none of my team would willingly aid that pack and that we're exhausting every resource to stop them."

A fair statement. Cole would have said the same.

"This congressman is key to blocking the vote on branding shifters," the Guardian continued.

"Branding is a dangerous idea," Cole warned. He and his

teammates had the Guardian's mark, but that was a mark of honor and protection. It was also voluntary.

The Guardian went on to say, "Yes, but Senator Janver is on the committee trying for the second time to get a bill through as a means of containing the threat. We have to find a link to the Black River pack and at least take down this arm of it until we can locate the head. When that happens and I have the agreement I want, I'm going to present the League of Gallize Shifters in a closed-door congressional meeting as the strongest arm of shifter law enforcement. If I do that and they accept, I want full autonomy when it comes to shifter justice."

Going public might put a target on the head of every man on Cole's team, but the alternative was humans thinking there was no viable police unit for dangerous shifters. That would perpetuate a return to the world of eight years ago, with humans killing shifters on sight and shifters attacking at any provocation.

Having the Gallize go public might save a future shifter from enduring what Cole had at SCIS. Assuming shifters encountered agents who were honest and not like Brantley.

If humans knew there was a force capable of controlling criminal shifters and that the same Gallize shifters would also protect shifter communities, then both sides would have to think twice before crossing the Gallize.

Everyone had to work together to survive.

That was the best hope for stopping legislation to brand every man, woman and child shifter.

Cole shivered at the thought. "What else, sir?"

"You have autonomy to make whatever deal is necessary to convince Katelyn to help us. I want all of you to know that I will do anything within my power to help you avoid the mating curse. Keep me informed on how the meeting with Katelyn goes."

"Yes, sir."

With the call ended, Cole turned to Rory and Justin. Their exceptional hearing made it easy to catch phone conversations when they were close. He still asked, "You heard what I said about Sammy going to the pack voluntarily?"

Rory gave him a chin lift acknowledgement.

Justin said, "Yeah, we heard that and those Black River bastards probably used magic on Sammy. What kind of magic would they have that could manipulate our bear?"

"I'm not sure," Cole admitted. "But I don't think they could have gotten that close to him if not for Sammy already having problems due to the mating curse."

Rory mused, "If they used magic to get him into the pack *and* to drink Jugo Loco ... then maybe that's how they convinced him to kill humans."

Cole had thought that, too, but hadn't wanted to give voice to the sick thought. "Maybe, but we need to find him to get real answers and we're running out of time." He reviewed the rest of the call with his team and said, "Let's put money on the street for a Jugo Loco buy."

Rory scoffed, "No one's going to do a deal with us."

"They'll do a deal with a local drug dealer. We just have to turn one we know into our puppet."

"I might have just the guy." Justin stood up with that determined look on his face. "How much are we buying?"

"Offer ten thousand dollars worth for a trial run with a guaranteed three hundred thousand if that buy goes well. Then say we'll increase based on the quality and delivery."

Rory cautioned, "We're going to have to put word out on the street and let them send someone to us. That means risking exposure."

"That's why we get the big bucks," Justin deadpanned.

"If SCIS hears, they'll be sticking their nose into it," Rory warned.

"I'll worry about them." Cole said. "You just get the deal struck." Confident words he had to back up.

"Ah, hell," Justin muttered. "Look what's out on an APB with orders to contact SCIS immediately."

Cole and Rory looked at the phone Justin turned to them. The display showed a sketched image of Cole.

Cole sighed. *Thanks, Tess.*

CHAPTER 22

"That's a bad idea, Dad," Tess argued with her father.

He cut into his steak, taking his time to answer. "Why? They're beasts. They have the advantage over humans. They can scent things you can't imagine."

Oh, yes, she could imagine, but she let her dad continue because interrupting him only delayed the inevitable. She'd found him the best fine-dining steak house in downtown Spartanburg, hoping a good meal on a rainy Friday night would open the door for them to communicate better.

Maybe dial back his prejudice against shifters.

Not happening.

Her father continued as if she hadn't studied shifters for years. "When these shifters change into an animal, bullets often have little effect on them. Why not require branding and do it right on their foreheads while they're in human form? That way a *real* human knows immediately if they're dealing with a dangerous animal."

Tess hid her horror at that idea. She could not see someone like Cole, or the jackals working at SCIS for that matter, allowing anyone to brand their foreheads.

Not in this lifetime.

That would start an all out war and she wouldn't blame them.

Her father belonged to the extremist's side when it came to shifter politics. He'd been in on early issues that arose once the shifters came out in the open.

Ironically, it had been a shifter who had outed the existence of people who changed shape into animals. Thinking of Cole, she amended that maybe not all of the shifters had been made public, but the bulk of their world had been exposed.

A jackal shifter had been at fault.

Cole would be saying, "I told you so." The jackal had paid a human videographer to do a secret documentary on a wolf pack. After being invited in to talk with pack leaders, the cameraman had taken video of things that he had no authorization to shoot.

He and the jackal shifter had enjoyed their fame for less than twenty-four hours. Unhappy shifters who took the law into their own hands had never been fingered.

That created a huge distrust between shifters and humans early on, which had never improved.

She did not straddle a fence when it came to her convictions. She was not a sympathizer for a shifter or a human who broke the law.

She'd spent years hearing her father's constant preaching against the unnatural beings, but the older she got, the more her convictions shifted to fit the conscience of the woman she saw in the mirror.

She didn't like calling anyone a beast.

It wasn't as if shifters had a choice in being born that way. She'd seen some act like rabid beasts, but others were as normal acting as her or her dad.

Then Cole had come along, talking about being a descendant of an ancient group.

If she believed what he'd told her, and he had yet to give her reason not to, Cole and his men had probably saved a lot of military and civilian lives.

Was no one taking that into account?

Not when Cole's people stay so well hidden that no one knows what they do.

Yep, there was that.

This sucked. Visits with her dad were strained as it was, but she felt guilty thinking about Cole while sitting across from her dad.

That was absurd.

She was a grown woman who could make her own decisions.

But she didn't want to lose another parent.

Her mother had keeled over with a heart attack in Richmond and didn't make it to the hospital.

If Tess gave her father a heart attack, she couldn't live with herself. Her father did not have a bad heart, but that fear dangled at the back of her mind.

"What's the matter, Tess?" Her dad had paused in eating his steak to give her a weighted look.

She tiptoed back to the subject they'd been quietly disagreeing on. The last thing either one wanted was to speak loud enough for a quote to end up in the news tomorrow.

Still, with all that was going on, she tried to get her father to look at this issue from her side. "I'm just saying that tension is running high right now and—"

"Right. And why is everyone tense?" her father asked, sounding like the prosecuting attorney he'd been early in his career. "Because that Black River wolf pack is pouring Jugo Loco into this country, turning shifters into maniacal killers, as if they weren't dangerous enough without it. Maybe if that young couple camping out in the Nantahala National Forest had known the person approaching them was a shifter, they could have used a weapon to protect themselves. But they thought it was just another human."

She hated that he made a valid point, but she still would not brand a shifter. That crossed the line to treating them as nothing more than wild animals.

He picked up a cut of steak and stopped right before putting it in his mouth. "That's another thing. We have some brilliant minds working on weapons for civilians. We should have something capable of dropping a shifter at ten yards pretty soon."

"What about the shifters who are good people living in enclaves and not harming anyone?"

Some shifters had been willing to move into areas set up as enclaves where they could raise their family safely, but others compared that setup to a Native American reservation. That group fought it with every breath.

Some days, there was no perfect answer.

Her dad said, "You may think the civil shifters are not an issue, but the minute they get their hands on that damned enhancing juice you have an uncontainable problem. The rare docile shifter turns into a killer."

Again, she'd argue that docile shifters weren't as rare as he thought.

He finished chewing a piece of steak and added, "Like that bombing the other night. That pack strapped a human into the seat of the truck and stuck a bomb between his legs. What kind of person does that?"

She sat back, shocked, but quickly recovered to demand, "How did you know that? I haven't told you anything about my investigation and the details are classified." Or they should be. The last thing she needed was to be accused of being the leak in her department.

Especially with her father's political fingers in anything related to shifter law enforcement.

Cole had said she had a mole in SCIS and now her father had specific information from the bombing.

Who on her team was undermining their efforts? She wished Cole had given her a phone number to call so she could press him for more details.

Her father harrumphed at being chastised. "Don't make a big deal out of me knowing about your investigation. I *need* to know these things to do a better job on my committee."

"Who told you? That information is *not* ready to be disseminated. Have you thought about the fact that someone may finger me for it getting out?"

"No. And as far as who told me, it's someone with a higher security clearance than you, so stop worrying about it, little girl."

She used to smile at his occasional use of that term of endearment from her childhood, but lately it sounded condescending.

Her mother would not tolerate him talking down to her and neither would Tess.

"I'm not a little girl any more, Dad."

He waved that off.

So much for calling him on his attitude. Tess chose the battles to fight and this one would end with them not speaking again. That had already happened once when her dad found out Tess was studying shifters and demanded she stop. They'd both been hurting and a lot of words were spoken that couldn't be taken back.

It had taken six months before they began talking again ... on the anniversary of her mother's death.

Thinking about her mother, Tess recalled what Cole had said about alphas enforcing the law among their own people. Based on what he said, someone should have come forward to deal with the shifter who tried to mug her mother and the ensuing battle that triggered her mother's heart attack.

That tragic day, her mother had tried to reach Tess. She'd wanted Tess to join her at a doctor's appointment and then have lunch. Tess would have loved that opportunity to keep track of her mother's heart condition and spend quality time with her.

But Tess had been hip-deep in the day from hell by that point, and the stress had brought her crazy energy to the surface. Still angry and hurting over Cole, she'd let her emotions get the best of her and had fried her own phone two hours earlier.

She never got the call from her mom.

As soon as Tess got out of school and had access to research resources, she'd started digging into her mother's case.

Right away, she ran into a wall when she found the file sealed. No judge so far had been willing to risk the political backlash of reopening it against the wishes of a senator as powerful as her father.

Swallowing the lump forming in her throat, Tess took the risk of bringing that day up with her dad. "I know you don't like talking about this, but ... I want to ask about what happened when Mom died."

He kept staring down but he was no longer eating. He put his fork and knife down then lifted his head. "It's a closed case. I don't want to discuss it and I forbid your pursuing it."

Don't yell at Dad. This was exactly why she'd been digging secretly. "I'm not a child. You will not forbid me anything. It would be nice if you made the quick call it would take to get the file opened for your *daughter.*"

Fury burned in his eyes. "Do not talk back to me."

"I'm not being disrespectful, Dad. You seem to forget that I'm grown and I make my own decisions. I only wanted to discuss what happened, but if that's too painful for you, I understand."

He eyed her the way he did a wily witness on the stand. "If you want to research it, read the media articles."

"That only mentions an alpha who got sanctioned for his involvement. Who was the alpha?"

"Leave. It. Be. And stay away from that alpha."

Ignoring the vehemence in his voice, she said, "Mom had a bad heart. I'm not out to blame anyone else or drag this out again when I carry just as much fault for not being with her that day. I *have* been going through old news articles I couldn't bring myself to read back then. In one very small, shifter-supported newspaper article, the alpha claimed he was trying to save her."

Her dad's voice dropped to an evil level. "Lies, all of it. That alpha lied. He knows. I know it. Everyone does. Stay away from *all* shifters."

Tess gave him a dry reply. "That's not going to happen. I work with them."

He gave her a dismissive look. "No, you don't. That's why I put Brant ... " He sat back and didn't even have the grace to look remorseful.

Brantley and her Dad were communicating?

She knew very clearly where to find the leak now. Brantley was sucking up to her dad, probably intending to use that connection to step over her. Her dad would help him, too, if it meant keeping Tess away from shifters.

A hundred questions raced through her mind about Brantley and her dad, all of them making her sick.

Seething, she struggled not to raise her voice. "What did you do, Dad?"

"What any father would do when his daughter doesn't have the sense to stay away from dangerous animals. I went to a lot of trouble to get Brantley in SCIS to make sure someone else interacted with the shifters. That's why he heads up the security and deals with those damn jackals. That includes *your* security."

She was so pissed her anger blinded her for seconds. "That's how you're getting confidential information. Are you the one he called to ask about the military background on one of our prisoners?"

"Cool your heels. That information is not going anywhere else. Yes, he called me because he's doing his job and trying to capture that escapee." He wiped his mouth on the napkin and dropped it on top of his plate. "Did you really think I'd let you take that position with SCIS where you're exposed to those *things* on a daily basis and not keep an eye out for your well being?"

She'd become almost a friend with Scarlett, and Cole was ... another topic. For her dad to call people she cared about *things* grated on her. Arguing with a master litigator never went well.

Instead she said, "Let's be clear on one thing. You didn't *let* me do anything. I've worked my butt off to get where I am."

His eyes turned into slits of anger. "Yes, you did, and you have a genius IQ. I don't understand why you'd squander your education and talent on nonhumans when you could do so much more for your own people."

"I *live* in this world now, Dad. Humans. Shifters. They're *all* my people, whether you want to acknowledge it or not. I'm about upholding the law. I won't bend it for a shifter or a human. I choose to see all sides and to do what I can to find a happy medium between nonhumans and humans. I want to be fair to everyone."

He scowled and waved off her comments again. His phone buzzed with a text. He thumbed it open and read for a moment, then shoved the phone back in his pocket. "Damn trouble makers. A shifter went crazy in a courthouse back home. Tell me again how those creatures are so misunderstood."

She'd never said that. "I have a very simple rule, Dad. If that shifter breaks the law, then he or she should be held accountable the same as a human."

"Whatever." He stood up and looked at her still sitting. "I've got to get back for a meeting on Sunday."

"On Sunday? What's so important?" She'd expected him to stay in Spartanburg until Sunday evening.

He quipped, "Just keeping the wheels greased."

She hated that statement. It usually meant he was doing something he wouldn't share with her.

Pinning her with a look that was almost apologetic, he said, "Why don't you come back with me tonight and we'll spend Saturday together at home? You can fly back here Sunday on my jet. Be nice to see you more than once in a while."

She wanted to say yes and have some quiet time with him at the family home in Virginia to bridge the gap that kept opening wider in their relationship, but she had too much going on. "Afraid not, Dad. Too many things going on here. I'm not off this weekend."

Sighing with exaggeration for her benefit, he said, "When *are* you coming home?"

"How about when you take me and what I do seriously." Okay, that had popped out without *any* review. She was too tired to be with anyone right now.

He leaned forward, managing to keep his face an unemotional mask but unable to hide his disappointment in her. "It would be nice to have a daughter in my life sometimes."

That was classic Senator Janver, master manipulator. She'd told him more than once not to do that to her.

The last four days in her life had been hell. Add that to years of swallowing her pride to do as her dad wished and it all came to a head in her mind.

Even so, she managed to reply in a respectable tone, to show him she was treating him as a peer.

"As your daughter, I deserve respect for my position in this world, just as I respect yours, Dad. You don't want a daughter. You want a robot that agrees with you and does as you say. That's not me. You of all people should realize Mother raised me better than that. She taught me to make my own decisions, which I've done everywhere and with everyone but you. Stay out of my career if you want us to have a relationship built on respect."

Nothing happened, then he laughed. "Do you really think I worked this hard to become as powerful as I am to have *anyone*, especially my *child*, criticize me? You should be thanking me for protecting you."

She started to smart back, "Where was all that protection when mom died?" But that would cut deep and she didn't want to hurt him. Instead she muttered, "I wish I had a sibling so I didn't feel so alone at times with all this." She looked up at him, "Then maybe you'd be happy with one of us."

"We did have ... " He cut off his sentence.

"Have what?"

He looked guilty as hell all of a sudden. "Why can't you just let things be without bringing up the past?"

She hadn't brought up anything about her mother, but maybe talking about having kids reminded him of losing her.

His voice softened when he said, "Whether you believe me or not, I am proud." Tossing down cash to cover the meal, he shook his head.

Guilt came knocking and she was ready to make peace until he added, "But some days I wonder where I went wrong with you."

Argh. She told him, "Maybe by thinking I should live according to your plan instead of my own."

He ignored her and leaned down to kiss her forehead. "Be careful going home." Then he walked out of the restaurant.

She sighed. Her father loved her, but they were as different as night and day. He'd have blown his stack if he'd known about Cole showing up again. Tough. She was not unhappy that he'd returned, even with the news that he was now a wolf shifter.

Her head was a war zone over what to do about Cole. She missed him every minute that she wasn't telling herself to stay away from him. But nothing good could come of them being with each other.

She finished her gin and water, put her coat on and left. The rain had been coming down in fits and starts, leaving everything shiny now that night had fallen. She'd taken a cab to meet her father for dinner and could call a car service for her ride home, but she was too keyed up to just go home and stare at the four walls.

Admit the truth.

She was too keyed up to go home *without* Cole there.

Some force had taken over her body and at the moment that force wanted her to go track him down.

"Stop giving invisible energy a mind. The name of that force is horny," she chastised herself.

Besides, how could she find Cole when a pack of jackal shifters hadn't? She hoped.

On the way out the front door, she paused to figure out where she was headed. It wasn't nine yet. She could go back to the office and put in a few more hours, maybe clear enough off her desk to consider taking a real weekend off.

That wouldn't happen.

Still, having quiet time to clear off her desk and think would be nice. Rain had cooled the temperature which had reached the eighties earlier in the day. She'd walked this area often, completely at ease since a satellite police station was a block away, which meant they patrolled these streets regularly.

She pulled out her phone to text her assistant to see if files Tess had been waiting on had arrived yet.

The back of her neck tingled with a feeling someone was watching her.

Tess paused and looked around.

People strolled along the sidewalks. Businesses were open with lights shining through the glass windows and traffic moved at a lazy pace. Just a rainy night in the city.

Stop being so jumpy.

Her father had her looking for goblins everywhere now. Her phone dinged with a text.

You up for a drink at Twilight John's?

Scarlett had finally surfaced.

Tess had been trying to build a bridge with someone from the shifter community for a long time and Scarlett was the only female shifter Tess had met. Scarlett wasn't easy to break the ice with, but Tess felt like a ship ready to crash through a few icebergs tonight.

Shaking off the strange feeling she had a moment ago, she turned toward the bar.

CHAPTER 23

Cole drove down a dark road with his windshield wipers flapping. He'd rather be fighting Friday night traffic in Spartanburg than driving out here in the boonies to be disappointed yet again.

Tracking down Katelyn was turning into an extreme scavenger hunt.

Giving up was not an option, but this was beginning to feel like the definition of a wild goose chase.

The phone call he'd received had been from a woman, but when he met her it was not Katelyn, but a friend. Cole had made a mad dash to meet that person in the twelve minutes allotted only to find out that was the first of a series of trips.

He'd met three women so far and all in public places. The first woman ran a wand over him and his rental car, evidently checking for a tracking device. Then she handed Cole a note with directions to the next stop.

With his current instructions in hand, he'd driven forty miles outside of the last significant town into deep backcountry.

A human might be concerned, but to Cole this was beautiful land for running free.

Run with mate.

Annnd there was Gray Wolf.

Cole had to make Gray Wolf understand. "Tess is not our mate."

Lie.

The wolf had him there.

Cole tried again. "She *is* the woman I would mate if I could.

But she's a human. Our power will kill her."

Strong mate.

Scratching his head, Cole said, "Yes, she's a strong woman, but still a human. Even if I took her as a mate, she isn't a shifter and I would never try to change her into one. I won't allow *us* to harm her."

Protect her.

Cole was willing to protect her with his life and he knew Gray Wolf would too, but they would never have that chance. He wasn't up for arguing. His wolf had always been obstinate, with a head of sold granite when he wanted his way, unless they had to fight an enemy.

In those moments, Gray Wolf and Cole had fought in harmony as the deadliest beast with teeth and claws.

Those times wouldn't return either.

When Gray Wolf settled back down, Cole sent a voice text update to Rory. The last woman Cole had met said she'd worked with Katelyn in an office more than six months ago. Another woman had known her when they waited tables, but neither woman said much before warning him to leave right away or miss her.

These women had to be tracking him from point to point to make sure he didn't have backup hanging around behind him.

Cole was on his way to meet a woman he'd spoken to for less than fifteen seconds. She claimed to have a halfway house for women in need. That sounded like a shelter for abused females. His gut churned at the thought of any man harming a woman.

Was Katelyn afraid Sammy would harm her?

Cole never had a chance to get any information over the phone from this last woman. She said she'd only speak in person to Cole, rattled off her address and that if he passed this test, she'd set up a way for him to speak to Katelyn.

Meeting in person worked fine for him.

Cole had an edge.

Being a shifter, he could pick up on physiological changes that happened if someone lied. He'd carefully question her and get what he needed.

He turned off the country road onto a dirt drive two hundred feet long, which ended in front of a brick two-story home surrounded by trees. Everything about it, from the walkway being clean of leaves, to the short grass of the small yard and flowers blooming in window boxes, spoke of someone who cared for the house and land.

Stepping out of his SUV, he paused when he caught the scent of a shifter who had been through here.

Shit. Had someone else come by looking for Katelyn?

Please tell me I'm not too late.

Hurrying up the steps to a wide porch with a comfortable looking wooden swing on one end, he took in everything as he knocked on the door.

When it opened, a woman in her thirties stood there. She could be attractive if she smiled. Her overalls showed none of her shape, only that she was slender. Curly red hair sprung all around her face.

He planted a smile on his face to disarm the woman, but that smile fell sharply on his next inhale.

Shifter. Maybe one of the big cats.

Gray Wolf surged, snarling to get at her.

Cole gritted his teeth against the struggle to keep Gray Wolf quiet. "Who are you?"

"You can't come up to my house and ask that, wolf. Told you on the phone my name is Isabella."

So she figured out he was a wolf? What was she? "Have you done something with Katelyn?"

"What do *you* want with her?"

This woman clearly knew Katelyn and the way she was questioning him convinced Cole she knew where Katelyn was hiding. He couldn't get a lie past her any faster than Isabella could get one past him. She was no young shifter he might be able to outmaneuver with words. She might look only thirty, but she exuded power. An alpha female.

She could be much older.

Decision time and the one thing he didn't have much of was time. Plus, if he stayed here too long there was a chance Gray Wolf would get his way. The wolf snarled and prodded him, waiting for a chance to break free.

Cole went with the truth. "I want to talk to Katelyn."

"About the bear shifter, I suppose." She inhaled, closing her eyes. When she opened them she said, "Is he like you?"

She knew about Sammy? "What do you mean?"

"You don't smell like any shifter I ever met. Your power is odd. No, not odd." She narrowed her eyes and studied him as if she'd just realized the size of the predator hiding inside him.

Her voice thinned to a whisper. "Magic."

How could she know that?

Non-Gallize shifters noticed a difference, but most weren't able to pinpoint just what it was. Dividing his attention between her and the wolf trying to claw its way out demanded all his control. He waited to see what else this woman would say.

Closing her eyes again, her lips moved but nothing came out. As she did, Cole noticed an odd change.

Cole had been clenching his hands, but the tension in his chest eased. Gray Wolf calmed down. He didn't know why, but he stretched his fingers, glad for the respite.

She put her hand to her head and blinked. When she looked up at him, she no longer appeared wary.

Now she was sad. "I'm sorry."

He was afraid to ask, but he had no choice. "Sorry for what?"

"You're sick. Dying."

A shifter couldn't know all that. He suffered a moment of disorientation and shook it off. "What *are* you?"

Her sympathy fled. "Rude, very rude. Go away, wolf. I have nothing for you." She started to close the door.

Shit. "Wait."

Opening it again, she crossed her slender arms and looked at him expectantly.

"I'm sorry. I just ..." Hell, he had no idea how to deal with this woman. He wanted to find out how she knew so much about him, but this trip was to help Sammy. "I came to talk to you about Katelyn. She's important to my friend, the bear shifter. The way I understand it, they're engaged."

"That happened before Katelyn knew he was a shifter."

"True. It was wrong on his part not to tell her right up front, even if I do understand why."

"Explain it to me."

Cole recognized when he was being given an olive branch he wouldn't be offered a second time. "Sammy would never treat a woman unfairly. He's very protective of any woman. He told me he was in love with Katelyn and wanted the time with her that he had left. That's all. He would never try to make her a shifter."

That must have surprised her. She angled her head with a look of deep concentration. "Is he sick like you?"

"Yes." No point in trying to hide the truth from this woman who knew way more than she should.

Isabella stared past Cole, but he didn't turn to see what she looked at, because her eyes were unfocused. When her gaze returned to him a few minutes later, she said, "Katelyn loves him. She says Sammy is honorable, but he's been acting strangely. What's the cause of his illness?"

Cole had to draw the line somewhere.

Only Gallize shifters faced the mating curse—that he knew of—which meant he'd be exposing all of them by saying too much. "I'm not at liberty to say. If I could I would tell you, but I would be breaking my word to people who depend on me. I only want to talk to Katelyn to see if I can answer her questions and help her past her panic over learning the man she wants to marry turns into a bear. If she doesn't want anything to do with Sammy, I'll accept that, but my people want her to know we'll protect her at all costs to allow them this time together." He swallowed against his next words. "Sammy doesn't have long."

As he said all that, he realized something that didn't fit in all of this. "How does Katelyn know you? I mean *if* she knows you, I don't understand why she panicked at finding out Sammy was a shifter."

A slow smile lifted the corners of Isabella's mouth. "She didn't know I was a shifter either. I met her two years ago at a festival. We bumped into each other and when she turned to apologize for not paying attention, she put her hand on my arm. The minute she touched me, I saw her life at a point in the future when she would be running from a bear. Visions aren't literal, so I had no idea if the bear was trying to kill her or not. When we finished talking, I gave her a card and told her to contact me if she ever had a question no one else could answer."

This woman was the only hope of talking to Katelyn.

He knew that as well as he knew his wolf.

Cole straightened up. Why was his wolf quiet? Not that he

didn't appreciate a moment of peace for this meeting, but that was unusual, especially standing this close to another shifter he didn't know.

"Your wolf knows there is no threat here," she said.

"Are you a mind reader?"

"No. Your face said it all. You were in a silent battle the minute you walked up. Your wolf was unsettled. Katelyn is Sammy's cure, isn't she?"

"Possibly."

"Lie. You know she is. I've never encountered a shifter who had to mate to remain stable. I've heard of some that had to be put down, but they weren't stable from adolescence. It had nothing to do with being mated. I'm not sure what you are, but now I understand my vision of the bear chasing Katelyn."

"Will you help me contact Katelyn? I give you my word I will not try to force her to do anything. I just want to talk to her and maybe fill in any blanks you haven't been able to in spite of being clairvoyant and a shifter." He wondered if she'd clarify what she was.

"Nice try, wolf. I have my secrets too. I'll have Katelyn meet you tomorrow morning."

He wanted to argue, but he'd met his match with this woman. If he was the kind of person who would harm her, which he wasn't, he doubted torture would provide any more than she willingly gave up right now.

"I'll give you a number in case she wants to talk sooner."

"She won't," Isabella declared. "I'll have her here Saturday morning at ten. She knows she's safe with me. If anyone besides you comes near this property, I'll know it and she'll be in the wind. You'll not get a second chance."

"I won't risk that happening."

"I didn't think so, but you're special, which means someone will want you. Watch your back."

He felt that warning in his bones, but he knew the Black River pack was after him. "I'll call you if anything changes."

"Nothing will change. You'll be here. Don't call. I won't answer. I don't like the phone and only answered because I knew it was for Katelyn."

Isabella had to be a witch or a mage as well as a shifter. "If

Katelyn decides to see Sammy and I convince her that she'll be safe with me, will you allow her to leave?"

"I have no control over Katelyn. She will do as she pleases. I only watch over her because, once she called me, I put her under my protection."

"You're not going to tell me if you're connected to any of the Power Baron houses, are you?"

"Most likely not, but you never know," she answered cryptically.

"I'll be back tomorrow then. Thank you for talking to me and helping me meet Katelyn." The weight of failing Sammy lifted considerably as Cole turned to leave. He'd made it halfway down the steps when Isabella called out, "One more thing."

Turning half around, he said, "Yes?"

"You can be cured, too. You have to learn to trust your wolf and set him free."

Gray Wolf rumbled, *Truth.*

Worst advice ever.

Cole had lived with this beast for too many years to make the mistake of turning him loose now when, with every day that passed, Gray Wolf shoved Cole further and further into the background.

To be polite, Cole nodded. "I'll keep that in mind."

She withdrew and pushed the door shut, but he could swear he heard a muffled, "Foolish wolf."

CHAPTER 24

After sending back an acknowledgment to Scarlett, Tess trekked three blocks down to Twilight John's. She made one more turn to her right and entered the quiet pub, glad to be out of the drizzle. Shaking off any lingering water drops, she checked for the shifter.

Scarlett Sullivan sat at the bar, oblivious to her admiration club, which included every male in the place. Shiny brunette hair had been braided into thin strands and half of those braids twisted up with the other half falling loose around her shoulders.

Were all shifter females as attractive?

Tess knew this one only minimally and even that had taken some work. Scarlett didn't care for meetings and snarled at the jackals on staff. Maybe Cole did have a point about those shifters. Tess would ask Scarlett, but this woman kept everything close to the vest.

Their semi-relationship had started as professional and might never go any further, but Tess intended to keep trying to find common ground with her so that they could actually work as a team.

Tess would never truly understand shifters if she stayed in an echo chamber of her own people.

Cole would be an excellent resource.

She hadn't figured out how to move forward—or not—with him yet, though.

Better to keep building the bridge with this female shifter one step at a time and hopefully not lose any ground.

Scarlett dressed in jeans and boots that broadcast badass, but the lacy top she wore was all female. She dolled up with minimal makeup, but the mascara ramped up her exotic appeal.

Tess envied the long black lashes surrounding Scarlett's hunter-green eyes. More than once, Tess had wondered if Scarlett was a feline, but she'd never asked.

During her years of studying shifters, she hadn't nailed down protocol for asking about a person's animal. The jackal shifters didn't care much what you asked them, but neither did they seem to care what any human thought.

Scarlett turned as soon as Tess walked toward the bar and said, "You did show up."

"Why wouldn't I? You invited me. I texted back," Tess said, dropping her coat and purse in the empty chair next to the barstool she chose.

"You humans are hard to figure out. Some would accept out of fear of insulting me, but you're not like that. I see you more as someone who would accept out of curiosity. You want to know things. Everything."

Tess did not want to sound defensive, because Scarlett would often toss in a jab just to get a reaction. This shifter tested everyone and didn't care who she pissed off.

Tess shrugged. "Did you ever consider that I might want to get to know you better and that's all?"

"Nope. Not even for a minute."

"Well, you're wrong. That's why I agreed to come here."

Scarlett gave her a long look. "Hmm. Trying to throw me a curve, huh?" She called over to the bartender. "Boodles with a splash of water and lime for my associate." She turned back to Tess. "Did I get it right?"

"Yes. How'd you know?"

Scarlett tapped her nose that had a small, gold hoop ring in one nostril. "You have a tiny drop on your scarf. My guess is you had only one at dinner."

Tess took in the amber color in the shifter's glass. "So you're a bourbon fan, but I'm thinking that's not top shelf."

"Oh, got a tongue that cuts like a knife. Yes, on bourbon and on not top shelf. How'd you know?"

"My second degree was on the study of shifters and while I consider it limited in many ways, I did glean a few things. You can't get drunk on alcohol so many shifters find spending an exorbitant amount of money on something you're going to just pee out later to be a waste."

From the lift of Scarlett's eyebrows, Tess knew she'd gained a point by showing she paid attention to their world. She quipped, "What? Did you think I was making a commentary on your level of income or lack of expensive taste?"

Scrunching her pretty face into a funny expression, Scarlett said, "To be honest, that's exactly what I thought. People don't surprise me often. I'm going to have to work a little harder around you."

Tess took that as a compliment and felt sure this shifter didn't hand out many.

"Now that you're here and we've got posturing out of the way," Scarlett said with a sly grin, "you've got a problem in SCIS with leaks."

Damn her father and Brantley. But she didn't want to admit knowing about those two. "I agree. Got any ideas who is behind them?"

"Not yet, but I will soon, especially if it's a shifter. I won't work with a team I can't trust."

Tess bristled at that.

"Keep your shorts on, human. I can smell your anger. I didn't accuse you of anything." Scarlett leaned an elbow on the bar.

Note to self. Must do a better job of not showing reactions around shifters. Tess said, "Good. I don't accuse anyone without proof and ask for that in return."

"I'm on the same page with you there. But the mage intern sent down to snoop? I'm not so sure about him."

Tess wanted to keep the conversation light and chatty, but she had no idea who Scarlett was talking about. "Mage intern?"

Scarlett gifted her with a sly smile. "Wondered if you'd act like you knew. That's what most of those people would do."

"I don't play games. Who is he?"

"I don't have an ID yet, only that we've been infiltrated by the Power Barons."

That was interesting and frightening. Maybe Brantley wasn't sharing *anything* he knew and was only reporting on Tess to her father, which was more than just irritating. It could end up being dangerous. "You think this mage intern is behind the leaks?"

"Most likely. As soon as I nail down who he is, I'll be able to track him everywhere he goes."

"Would you be able to detect him if you were inside our SCIS facility?"

"No. If that were the case, I'd have figured it out the last time I slipped inside for a secret visit."

Tess didn't even comment on that and let Scarlett keep talking. "He's covering his scent trail with magic."

"What do you think is going on?" Tess asked.

"Well, I'm here first for the shifters. I'm their sole voice in what happens. You're here for the humans and he's most likely inserted on behalf of the Power Barons, which means he has little to no interest in protecting humans or shifters."

The Power Barons had never been photographed, one of their requirements for working with governments, and met with only a select few. Tess doubted even her father had met any of them or he'd have ranted on that for hours.

She corrected Scarlett on one issue. "I have never said I was only interested in human protection."

Smiling as if she held the answer to the origin of the universe, Scarlett snickered. "It's not a rule or law. It's in your DNA to watch out for your people. It's in my DNA to do the same. That's how we're wired."

Tess couldn't dispute the logic in that since she had yet to be forced to make a decision based on a person being a human or shifter, but she felt in her heart that she would choose according to what was right.

Just to throw this out for conversation, Tess said, "As I understand it, one Power Baron mage has voted twice in favor of shifter rulings."

"See, that's it. Why would he do that? That bunch only came out because they wanted to have access to all intel across the board, not because they give two shits about harmony between humans and nonhumans. I don't trust any of them voting or their intentions. They don't have a dog in this race."

Tess considered that. "Do you trust my intentions?"

Scarlett pondered on that moment. "Yes, for now, until you give me reason not to." Leaning back, looking relaxed, but always ready to pounce, she added, "I picked up a rumor that the intern was at the food bank building four hours before it got bombed. I haven't been able to confirm it but the information came from a good source."

Hold everything. That was ... very interesting.

But rather than jump on that and make Scarlett pull back, Tess switched the direction on her. "That brings up something that I can't sort out. I keep trying to figure out whether someone was trying to kill SWAT and SCIS first responders with a bomb, which would have happened if any of them had arrived even one minute sooner."

"I don't think that was the intention at all. I think they wanted you to capture that wolf you let escape."

Being fingered for what happened to Cole kicked Tess off balance. Before she thought, she said, "How could anyone have known he was going to be there? He said—" She caught herself before she shared what Cole had told her.

Scarlett's focus sharpened. "He said what?"

Checking herself to watch her words, Tess replied, "The prisoner claimed he had nothing to do with the Black River pack. He lost someone in the bomb who was strapped inside a truck and wearing the bomb as ankle cuffs."

"Interesting," the shifter mused.

Tess had a sinking feeling the thing Scarlett found interesting would not work in her favor. She finished her gin as her phone buzzed with a text from her assistant. The files she'd been expecting had arrived. "I've got to get back to work."

"Workaholic," Scarlett accused in a teasing tone.

"Some of us have ambitious goals." She smiled, pulling her coat and purse off the chair.

Playing with a straw from the stock of them on the bar, Scarlett said, "We all work, but in different ways. You go push paper and I'll poke around."

"Be careful," Tess said.

Giving her an eye roll, Scarlett pointed to herself. "Shifter here."

"True, but I'm sure there are all levels of shifters." Tess wondered if Scarlett knew about Cole's team. "By the way, anything on that alpha I asked you to check into?"

"I have a lead on him. Once I find him, I have to explain that you're the daughter of the woman who had a heart attack in Richmond where he got into a dustup with that jackal. If he agrees to talk, you'll know as soon as I do."

Tess felt a true friendship beginning. "Thank you. I'll repay the favor any time."

When Tess turned toward the door, Scarlett said, "Cougar."

Turning back, Tess frowned. "What?"

"You wanted to know what my animal was the last time we met. You were polite about it and didn't ask, just like this time. Mine is a cougar." The shifter winked in a sassy way and added, "I'm gonna own it for real if I can find me some young thang when I get old."

Tess laughed. "Thanks. I did want to know."

"If *you* had an animal, I bet it would be some form of cat."

That sounded like a second compliment from Scarlett. Tess smiled, unsure how to respond without screwing up the moment.

Scarlett added, "Just don't let curiosity get your tail in trouble."

"I'll keep that in mind." Tess stepped back out into a light drizzle and lifted the hood on her coat to cover her head. She didn't like getting wet but with only five blocks to go, this wasn't enough to warrant the small umbrella in her coat pocket.

When she reached the corner to get back on the main thoroughfare, she waited for the light to change so she could cross the street.

Sirens wailed, coming in from her right as the rain started coming down harder.

A police car screamed up with lights flashing and slowed just enough to be sure no one ran through the traffic light. Tess had stepped back to avoid being sloshed by water pooling near the curb. She sensed a vehicle stopping on her right, but like everyone else, her attention was on the two police cars racing toward some crisis or chasing someone.

Out of her peripheral vision, a door on a van to her left slid open and two men dressed all in black jumped out.

Her mind registered the threat at the same moment she lunged away to run and reached for the gun in her purse.

It turned into one of those bad dreams where it seemed like her body moved slower than swimming through mud and the attackers shot around her at hyper speed.

The first one cupped his hand over her mouth, stifling her scream even though the sirens drowned her out. He wrapped an arm around her chest, jerking her back. She yanked back and forth, but there was no breaking his hold. The second guy grabbed her legs even though she kicked as fast and hard as she could. She caught his chin with one shove and he snarled at her.

It took mere seconds for them to contain her and shove her into the van.

Scarlett wouldn't get caught like this, dammit.

Tess had a moment of fantasizing she was a powerful shifter capable of ripping through these guys, but they'd handled her so easily she had a sick feeling *they* were shifters.

The van pulled away slowly, turning right, which was in the opposite direction the police cars were headed. The one in the back with her stuffed a rag in her mouth and pulled a black hood over her head.

Panic settled into her chest, paralyzing her lungs. Every breath became harder to pull through the cloth. She had to calm down or she'd hyperventilate with no help from these guys.

One of them said, "Don't jerk around if you don't want to get hurt, human."

Definitely shifters.

Another voice said, "We get paid to deliver you alive. If you stay calm, you'll arrive without many bruises. Fight us and you might break one of those fragile little human bones."

Someone released a high-pitched cackle that made her skin crawl.

She'd heard that before around SCIS. Jackals.

They zip-cuffed her wrists and ankles, pushing her down on her back.

In less than a minute, her life had changed.

Her heart pounded at a crazy rate.

What did shifters want with her? Or were these mercs working for a human? Cole had said they'd do anything for the right price.

They hadn't tried to rough her up or molest her, but that didn't mean the person paying for this wouldn't. She'd never felt so helpless in her life.

Her father would go crazy at losing her.

He would assume the worst, that it was a shifter. Life would repeat itself if they grabbed the first available shifter and threw him in prison. No one would track these guys down.

Cole would.

He'd have to know where she was to do that.

These guys had likely set up the car wreck for the emergency vehicles to come by at that moment.

She strained quietly but they had her tied up tight.

This was the whole reason Tess had altered her life. She'd wanted to make sure the guilty were brought to justice, but she was beginning to think Cole might be right about jackals in general selling out their own.

If she didn't survive this, would the jackals find some poor soul to hand over for murder?

Someone who would die in a pit?

She couldn't think about that. If someone had sent these guys to bring her in alive, just maybe she'd have a chance to escape.

Optimistic even if it was unrealistic.

She would never stop fighting to survive.

The van had driven long enough to be outside the metropolitan area of the city. The further it went, the more she lost confidence that she'd walk away from this.

They were being careful, not driving too fast and stopping at what she assumed were traffic lights. Soon she'd be too far for anyone to hear her.

If she kicked the wall, would someone walking by think that was the sound of a captive fighting to get out?

Probably not. Most people kept to themselves. No one would help her. No one would know she was locked inside the van passing by.

She'd always been someone who didn't give up, no matter what, but she'd never been kidnapped.

Despair pooled in her chest and chilled her skin. Tears drizzled down her cheeks.

She didn't want to die.

Didn't want to leave her father to bury her.

Didn't want to miss seeing Cole again.

Fuck this bunch. A tear slid over her nose, ruining her defiance. She choked back a sob and focused on surviving.

Tess might not be Scarlett, but if she was going to die, she'd go down fighting.

CHAPTER 25

From the opposite side of the road, Cole shadowed the van as he moved with stealth along the dark sidewalk. He moved fast through the downpour. He thanked the heavy rain for covering his actions in this stretch.

He'd just gotten back to Spartanburg when Justin sent an emergency text. He and Rory had been watching Tess.

She'd been grabbed.

Cole left his vehicle with them and tracked her van, which was thankfully trying to leave quietly and unnoticed.

When he saw his opportunity, Cole called up his Gallize power, forcing the surge of energy into his right fist as the van slowed to make a turn.

He shot out of the dark, aiming for the driver's side.

At the last second, the jackal shifter driving the van turned toward him. His senses kicked in too late.

Cole dove forward, smashing the driver's window and slamming the jackal's head across both seats.

The shock reverberated all the way to Cole's neck.

A gun flashed up.

Cole snatched it away as the gun boomed, practically blowing out his eardrums. *Fuck*, that hurt. He ripped the door open and snapped the jackal's neck, then yanked him out of the way.

When he turned to dive into the rear area, he crashed into another jackal shifter in human form.

Fists slammed his head, chest and side. Cole couldn't get past the console to get equal footing in the back.

Tess gave a strangled cry, then shut down.

He couldn't divide his attention to check on her yet.

A third kidnapper had escaped out the rear door and was speeding away into the darkness, disappearing into the heavy rain. Cole needed this last shifter alive for interrogation.

That meant he had to stay in human form. Gray Wolf would rip the jackal to pieces for harming Tess.

Cole agreed with the wolf, but he couldn't allow it.

Fighting turned into a blur of vicious hits. Jackals lived for battle. The bloodier, the better.

Cole beat the kidnapper back with rapid hits, waiting for an opening.

He got it and slammed his pumped-up right fist into the jackal's throat, crushing his windpipe. The guy fell back, choking. When the kidnapper reached for his throat, Cole saw part of a tattoo on the jackal's left wrist. A known group of vicious mercs who handled snatch and kill orders.

The jackal's eyes turned wild.

Yeah, you lose, asshole.

The jackal shifter looked over at Tess curled up on the van floor.

Snarling, the shifter's face and jaw elongated as he rolled toward her. He was going to bite her.

Cole had a half second to land with all his weight on the jackal's half-changed head with both heavy boots.

Skull bones crunched. Blood splattered in an arch.

That piece of shit would have infected her.

When Cole could think past how close Tess had just come to being turned into a jackal, he cursed under his breath. Damn jackals. The fighters refused to die without taking someone down with them, even a child, as long as someone else suffered.

His hands were shaking.

Facing a swarm of terrorists coming at him with automatic weapons hadn't scared him as much as almost losing Tess. She would lose her mind if she'd been turned into a jackal shifter.

Any shifter.

Her whimpering shook Cole from his adrenaline-swamped state.

Rain splashed against the open rear door. That runner would be harder to track the farther away he got in this downpour.

For a half second, Cole considered chasing him but he wouldn't leave Tess alone.

She was too still.

He shoved the mangled body aside and dropped to his knees next to her. He touched her shoulder.

She jerked away with a muffled scream.

"Shhh ... it's me, Cole."

She quieted long enough for him to cut the ties at her wrist and ankles, then snatch the hood off and jerk the rag from her mouth.

She launched herself into his arms, shaking and rambling. "They grabbed me ... it was fast ... they were jackals, but I don't know who ... what ..."

He held her and stroked her hair. "You're okay." Finally, his chest eased from the fear he would be too late or that the jackals had more than he'd estimated inside the van. He cupped her head, holding her to him.

Even Gray Wolf calmed down.

Their mate was safe.

Only with us, Gray Wolf huffed.

Cole was too exhausted from expending that much energy at one time, particularly calling up his Gallize magic, to argue with his wolf.

Gray Wolf functioned on instinct alone. His rules were simple. Protect what was his and kill at will when challenged.

Touching another shifter's mate was a death challenge.

Cole had a similar philosophy, but he had to balance shifter laws with human laws.

Stupid laws.

Not the first time Cole had heard that opinion from his wolf.

When Tess calmed enough to pull back a little, her gaze went to the front before he could turn her away.

"Don't look, baby."

She gagged and shoved her head into his shoulder. "His head is ... backwards."

"I know. Let's get out of here."

"We have to call the police."

"No, that's the last thing we need to do."

"Cole, they tried to kidnap me and they're ... dead."

"I know, but if we call in law enforcement, the police will go after shifters. These weren't local shifters. Remember what I told you about jackals? This particular group is rumored to enjoy the protection of someone with significant power and influence."

"A Power Baron?" Tess sounded dumbfounded at that possibility, but while she knew about Power Barons, she didn't really know the preternatural world as Cole did.

"Could be or it might just be a lone mage. These jackals are paid to kidnap, kill or both. I promise you this has to do with your investigation on the Black River pack, but proving that is going to be tough. My people will deal with this and find what they can—"

"But—"

"You have to believe me on this, Tess. Your people will have nothing on record for these guys. No government will. Even the jackal shifters working with SCIS are not in this league. Even if SCIS could bring these guys in, which they can't, the Black River pack would send an assassin who would get to them. This is going to be a bloodbath before it gets better. Let my people process all of this and I'll share what they find out. Fair enough?"

She took a long time answering. So long he was starting to think she'd say no, which wouldn't matter since he had plans for her that did not include going anywhere near SCIS.

Tess asked, "If I agree, will you tell me who your people are?"

He couldn't do that, not even for her. "Don't ask me to betray people who have fought alongside me. They're the reason I even knew where you were tonight. If not for them keeping an eye on you for me, you'd be gone and ... no one would have been able to find you. This is bad stuff."

She stared at him with eyes wide in shock.

Even though she worked around shifters, this was a lot to take in and he doubted she'd ever been around this type of merc.

Leaning in, he kissed her forehead and saw headlights on an SUV pull up with a BEAR IT BABY tag on the front.

Justin's ride.

Helping Tess up, Cole walked her out the back of the van, keeping his body between her and the smashed head. He held his hand up for Justin to wait in the vehicle.

Cole was already putting his own life in jeopardy, but he would not put theirs at risk.

A low rumble announced the approach of his personal SUV,

which pulled up on the other side of the street along the curb. Leaving it running, a figure all in black with his head covered got out and crossed to the van.

That'd be Rory.

Cole said, "Thanks," on his way to the car and Rory lifted a glove-covered hand in response.

He put Tess in the passenger side, glad to feel heat pouring through the still-running car. Pulling out, he drove past the van where Rory had the engine cranked. They'd take the van to where they could process it properly. Cole would have to find time in the next few hours to send them what he knew.

He could smell the anxiety wafting off Tess even if he hadn't noticed her shivering.

Full-blown shock was setting in.

He'd driven ten miles before she looked around. "Where are we going? This isn't the city. My apartment is back the other way."

"We're not going there."

"Why?"

"Because one of the kidnappers escaped. The minute he informs his contact that he lost you, they'll send a backup team. Those jackals will send however many they need to get a job done, no matter the body count."

"That's insane. How much money can someone pay for that?"

"A lot, but that's not the reason. In the paranormal underworld, it's all about reputation. They can afford to take a financial loss on a job, but not to undermine their street cred. That would cost them ten or twenty jobs."

Cole had somewhere to take her that wouldn't cause the team to blow a gasket over him exposing their safe zones. He'd been taking more breaks from the team over the past few weeks, getting away to where he could shift without putting anyone in danger. He'd run his wolf hard and fast.

Gray Wolf didn't wear out easily, but it took the edge off his wolf's desire to kill any living thing that hit his radar as even a potential enemy.

Right now his wolf had settled down until he was barely noticeable. When was the last time the wolf had remained present and attentive, but quiet?

To be honest, other than when he'd been near Tess, Cole

couldn't pick a time Gray Wolf had behaved this way and he doubted it was due to the mating curse.

It was obvious that having Tess close was influencing his beast.

If only that would last, Cole would curl up at her feet and stay there for as long as she'd let him.

Tess moved a little then curled up on the seat and gave into the crash that came after a shit load of adrenaline shot through a body.

He drove quietly, merging onto the interstate and enjoying the absolute silence inside and out of his body. His wolf would eventually wear on him until Cole gave up more and more control.

If he believed the wolf had a goal of killing him, Cole would hate his animal, but they'd managed to rock along for years without much trouble. His wolf had taken so long to get under control, Cole hadn't realized that wasn't normal until a non-Gallize wolf shifter told Cole that he and his wolf were almost like one. A partnership where they shared a body.

Not Gray Wolf.

The only reason that wolf didn't burst out of Cole's body at will had to do with the magic that Cole had as a Gallize shifter. On the other hand, his wolf was a beast because it was a Gallize animal.

The shifters who inherited their animal genetically had their problems, but Cole doubted any of them would trade with him once they got a look at Gray Wolf on a rampage.

Blood and guts would fly.

Time passed faster than he'd expected as he traveled south of Spartanburg. The next thing Cole knew, he had exited the interstate and driven twelve miles into the country. He took a left onto an unmarked dirt road. The surface was packed firmly enough that the recent rain had created only a few mud holes, which his SUV handled easily.

He rounded a curve and found the dirt driveway through large hardwoods. At the end of it, the woods opened up to a one-story summer home. Just a frame house with a basement a couple had built thirty or forty years ago. They'd passed away and their three grown kids turned the property over to a rental company so they wouldn't have to sell it. They used it during the summer, but Cole had it for another eighteen days.

He'd rented it two years back for the woods and stream running through it, where he fished. When his team was sent to South

Carolina to shut down the Black River pack, he'd rented it again with hopes of spending a few days here, maybe even with Sammy, before ... time ran out for both of them.

Once he parked and turned off the engine, he circled the truck and slowly opened the passenger door so she didn't fall out.

Tess jerked and sat up. "*Get away!*"

He stood still to let her get her bearings. "It's me."

"Oh, damn, I'm sorry." She raked a handful of black hair off her face, looking like a beautiful urchin.

"Don't apologize for anything. You've been through hell tonight. You're allowed some room to snap at me." He smiled and when she lifted her gaze she gave him a crooked smile in return.

She'd be okay once he got her inside and in something clean. He offered his hand. "Ready?"

Struggling to unfold, she twisted around and shoved her feet out and reached for his hand.

Smothering a curse, he pulled her up and scooped her into his arms.

Giving him a wry look, she said, "Do I look like some freaking damsel in distress?"

He chuckled. There was the Tess he knew from years back. "If I let you walk barefoot to the house, you'll cut your foot on something. I'm too tired to bandage you up tonight."

"Oh, I get it. This is all about you."

"Right."

She shook her head, then laid it on his shoulder.

His protective instincts had been in overdrive since he found out she'd met her father for dinner and had left on foot. Seeing her wiped out and vulnerable only doubled his need to care for her.

Up on the small porch, he put her down and opened the door, leading her inside where he flipped on a lamp for light. Taking a look around the small structure, he nodded and said, "Give me a minute and I'll show you where everything is when I get back. I need to get my bag out of the truck."

She looked at him like he was an idiot. "Did someone leave this place unlocked?"

"Yes. Me."

Same look this time, only darker. "Aren't you worried about a serial killer waiting in here?

"I would have smelled a human or a shifter the second I opened the door. No one has been here since I left."

Using his shifter speed, he got the bag from the car and returned in thirty seconds.

Tess was giving him yet another look, one filled with questions she was reluctant to ask.

He'd prepared himself for the what-kind-of-freak-are-you reaction. Not that he'd try to convince her he was just Cole in spite of being a shifter, but a small part of him wanted her to be happy to be around him right now.

The nine days he'd spent here before meeting up with the team had been the hardest he'd spent alone. Every day was another step toward the mating curse oblivion. Every day he saw his future slide further out of his grasp.

"What were they going to do to me?" she asked, throwing him way off.

"The kidnappers?"

She nodded, standing there with her shoulders tense but still upright. He didn't want to rush her to do anything, but he wanted her wrapped up in a thick blanket ... in his arms.

Protect mate. Gray Wolf had roused, but wasn't trying to rip out of Cole.

I will if you go back to sleep, Cole said silently.

Tess needed an answer, but Cole wasn't about to give her more fodder for nightmares. "My guess is the kidnappers wanted you for ransom money. Even if that group isn't working for the Black River pack, they find high-profile targets to fund operations in different countries that way." Huge lie. Those jackals did not give up a live body unless a lot of parts were missing, but he felt justified in sugar coating it when her shoulders relaxed and she nodded.

"I need ... I —" She couldn't finish her sentence.

He gave up standing back and moved in, wrapping his arms around her and pulling her in close, whispering. "Anything you need is yours."

She swallowed hard and moved her head, letting him know she understood, but seeing the fallout in her face from tonight's attack ripped him up.

He would find who had done this and they would pay. Not

tonight, but soon.

She wasn't bonded to him, couldn't be unless she accepted the mating bond, but he'd taken her as his mate the day he decided to marry her. He just hadn't realized back then all that he knew now. If she had died tonight, he'd have had no way to stop Gray Wolf from breaking free to avenge their mate.

If he was telling the truth, Cole had to admit that he would have been right there with his wolf.

The Guardian would have put him down immediately, as was his duty, but not until Cole had completed his *own* duty to Tess.

He stroked Tess up and down her back. She would never know he'd chosen her as his mate all those years ago, but she didn't need to know as long as he kept her safe.

We keep her safe.

Yes, Gray Wolf.

When she moved to leave, Cole opened his arms.

She looked around, searching. "I'm going to take a shower. I have to..." She took a deep breath, trembled once and said, "Get their nasty hand prints off me."

He gave her arm a squeeze and pointed down the short hall. "Go through that door and you'll find a bathroom on your left." Bending down, he pulled out one of his long-sleeved T-shirts that would cover enough for her to be comfortable. "Take this. There's shampoo and soap in the shower. The drawers are stocked with extra toothbrushes and ... things a woman would want."

She lost her smile. "You need lots of extra toothbrushes?"

He inhaled without thinking why, but realized she was jealous. Big character flaw, but that made him happy. He thought she'd never want to be near him again when she found out he was a shifter, but jealousy ... that was special.

"The extra amenities are supplied by the rental company. I've never used any so use what you need. No one will care."

Blush spread across her cheeks. "That was stupid of me."

Standing, he put his hand on her soft neck. "I like it when you get all possessive. It's sexy as hell."

She dipped her chin, but not before he saw the twinkle in her eyes.

Holy hell. What was he thinking to flirt with her now when both of their bodies wanted release after the kidnapping?

He should not be playing with her right now, not on the heels of what she'd been through. Her emotions were in a free fall and it was his job to do the right thing.

How was he going to spend tonight and not touch her?

He had no idea, but touch her he couldn't. She'd regret it in the morning when she started thinking about being with a shifter.

No way was he going to see the accusation and disappointment in her eyes.

She reached up to touch her hair, still disheveled from her attack. "My barrette. I lost it."

He stopped her panic. "It's in the car. I remember seeing it when you got in, but it must have fallen all the way out when you went to sleep."

"Oh, thank goodness."

"A barrette?" he asked, finding her concern a bit funny considering all that had happened.

"I know. Sounds ridiculous, but it belonged to my mother. She wore it all the time and I just ... like to have a piece of her with me."

Oh, man. Not funny at all. "Don't worry. I'll find it while you shower. I know we have it."

"Thank you."

His voice came out gruffer than he planned. "Get going and I'll fix you some tea." He never drank the stuff but he always heard women drank tea when they were upset.

Walking away, she called back over her shoulder, "Only if you put a shot of whiskey in it."

That's my woman. He smiled and turned to the small galley kitchen.

By the time Tess returned with damp hair falling around her shoulders and wearing the long-sleeve T-shirt he'd given her, he had a nice hot toddy of tea with whiskey, honey and even lemon for her. The best rental company ever had stocked lemon juice packets with the honey.

The whiskey was his. He couldn't get loaded, not being a shifter, but he liked the taste.

She plopped down on one end of the sofa looking drained.

Having this moment with her struck Cole hard. He'd never let himself dream about being with Tess again. Not like this. He'd anticipated her disappointment and anger over and over until he forced himself to let it go.

To let her go.

Or so he'd thought.

He'd only managed to tuck her memory away to save and now ... he wanted her more than ever. His heart was slowly crushing under the weight of accepting that he'd never have anyone and definitely not Senator Janver's daughter.

She looked up at him expectantly.

Brushing away his sadness, he walked over and placed the mug on the table next to where she'd curled up on the gently worn sofa. Reaching around the other end, he found a blanket and laid it over her.

"Thanks." She sounded small even though she was trying to be strong.

Cole settled next to her and draped his arm around her shoulders. *She's mine for now.*

Gray Wolf huffed softly, but didn't interfere.

In fact, Cole couldn't describe the calm he felt and the way Gray Wolf was at ease. It was something he and Gray Wolf had never experienced, something that felt whole and solid.

None of that made sense. Cole was at the point of taking any good moments when they came along. He wouldn't question this one, just accept and enjoy.

Tess sipped on her toddy, making a contented sound that Cole took to mean he'd chosen well.

"You're pretty," Cole said, brushing his hand over her hair, which was starting to dry in the warm room.

"I'm a mess."

"A beautiful mess," he teased. He liked her with no makeup. She'd always been one who needed her full armor to start the day. Had to be completely put together.

Too perfect sometimes.

Her armor had fallen away and left her emotionally bare. She trusted him to see her this way and he loved it.

Why couldn't he have this?

Sammy had probably thought the same thing as he slowly deteriorated. Like Sammy, Cole didn't need a lot in life to be happy. Having Tess next to him, snuggled against his side, was plenty. He closed his eyes, holding on to the feeling. Just touching her was heaven.

It didn't take long for that incredible mind of hers to start clicking again. She took another drink, set the mug down and said, "I need to know what's going on and who you are. I need to know the truth."

Cole considered how little he could tell her and weighed that against how much time he had left with her.

He heard the challenge in her voice to meet her halfway and knew he had to make the right decision. Everything she wanted to know had emotional land mines ... for both of them.

CHAPTER 26

Twisting her shoulders to look Cole in the face, Tess waited to see just how much he trusted her. Light from the kitchen cast a gentle glow on his carved features. If she could stay in this cozy cabin, wrapped in his arms forever, she'd do it. But life would get in the way again.

She'd seen two sides of him tonight. The fierce warrior who dove into a van of killers and the man now holding her tenderly.

But she needed to know who he really was *now* after having been a shifter for seven years.

She understood that he worked with a highly skilled group of shifters.

After seeing the results of his ability tonight, she believed Cole's claim that he was one of the apex predators.

Thankfully, he was on the good side of the law.

She'd struggled for days trying to decide how to move forward, but after having that conversation with her dad, she realized the truth. Her dad trusted no one, not even her, and she couldn't live that way. The world was changing and she intended to change with it.

She trusted Cole. At his core, he was still the same man as the one she'd trusted without question when they were in college.

He'd come to her after escaping the transport truck and bared his soul when he could have remained hidden.

He'd faced being put in a hole that had sent other shifters into madness and had still forgiven her.

He'd jumped into a pack of vicious jackals tonight in his human form and faced death to save her.

Her Cole had not changed, only his physical makeup.

In fact, the more she thought on it, the more she was becoming comfortable with what he was, because above all, he was an honorable man.

But she'd asked for the truth of who he was and what was going on. What was his hesitation? "Cole?"

"I'm not avoiding answering, Tess, just trying to figure out how to do right by you, my duty and my team."

"What's worrying you?" Now that she was away from SCIS and alone with Cole, Tess sensed an underlying sadness she didn't understand. She'd missed it the other night in her apartment because she'd been reeling from the shock, and okay, then from a monster orgasm. But she felt it now, though she couldn't explain how.

The ever-present energy hummed in her and seemed content for the moment, but she had this weird sense that the energy inside her was the reason she was able to pick up on something that was off with Cole.

"I've had to make gut decisions since learning I was a shifter, which is what I'm going to do now. I'm going to tell you as much as I can, but please know that I'm going to trust you with information that can't be shared at SCIS under any circumstances. Can I have your word that you'll not share it?"

Tess chewed on that a bit then said, "I accept that condition."

"Thank you, because I do want to tell you more. You need it to stay safe. I've already told you that your agency has a leak, a bad one. It's more than that, though, and we're pretty sure the Power Barons have a hand in all this. One or more might be behind the Black River pack."

Scarlett's words came to mind, but Tess wasn't entirely sold that a mage intern was wandering around SCIS. It took time just to be cleared for a position with the agency.

She argued, "The Power Barons can't interfere in our agency. That would be like the Department of Education interfering with Homeland Security. We're not at all related. The Power Barons have an agreement based on doing their part."

Cole huffed a sound that was a cross between a wry chuckle and a scoff. "That sounds good on paper and allowing no interference between agencies works in an ideal world, but it's the perfect backdrop for a mole. That mole might get my friend killed before I find him."

"The sick shifter you mentioned?"

"Yes. He's a close friend, someone who taught me that I had full responsibility for whatever my animal did. He would have submitted to our leader to be put down before harming an innocent human or another shifter."

"Put down? That's ... that's ... "

"The way our world works," Cole finished for her. "We live with a dangerous animal inside of us, especially my group. If a shifter is out of control, he or she might kill a lot of humans before someone stops them. If one of my group is out of control, few things *can* stop us."

"What could stop you?" Tess asked in all earnestness. She wanted to know how bulletproof Cole was, not that she thought he'd lose control.

He shifted, moving against her until he seemed comfortable. She loved having his body next to hers and so did her energy. Her body wouldn't say no to Cole's, but right now they were quietly in tune with each other.

"The only thing that will stop one of ours would be an equivalent shifter, our leader, or maybe a .50-caliber machine gun fired continuously into us until it ripped a body completely apart."

"Gruesome," she murmured. "So how did your friend get captured?"

"That's a tricky one. We think he might have gone willingly, but the only way that would have happened was if magic were involved. If they used it to manipulate him."

"We're back to the Power Barons again?" Tess prompted.

"Yes. I explained that our animal has to be called up, which requires magic."

Tess had struggled to accept that magic really existed, but when the Power Barons became known and cut a deal with governments in different countries, most realistic people had to accept it. Religious groups didn't and considered the Power Barons the devil's spawn.

Based on what little she knew, and what she thought Cole was insinuating, they might have it right.

She waited Cole out. He might never talk about this again and she wanted everything she could squeeze out of him.

He said, "My shifter group has a powerful enemy who goes back many centuries to the beginning of both of our kinds. We suspect that enemy is now aligned with the Power Barons, but we have no proof yet."

She put a hand on his arm and he stilled. The sizzling energy between them ignited.

"Tess?"

"Mmm?"

"The line between talking and not is a fine one. I love your touch. I crave it, but I can't give you answers while your hands are on my bare skin."

Talk about a heady feeling.

He claimed to be an apex predator, among the most dangerous, and she had that kind of power with her touch.

Squeezing his rock-hard bicep a little, she moved her hand back and smiled like the vixen living inside her. "Sorry."

"No you're not." He gave a real chuckle this time and kissed her head. "What did you want?"

If she answered that honestly, all talking would end. She said, "You mentioned the beginning of your kind. Can you tell me about that?"

His chest lifted and lowered over several slow breaths. "I'm sworn to protect my kind. The only people we can tell are our mates, which is why I'm going to tell you."

"I'm a mate?"

"No, but you're the closest I'll ever come to having one. I wanted so much for the two of us, but ... no point in rehashing that. But I believe my leader would approve of my decision to tell you more. I trust you. He trusts me."

She couldn't push that word out of her mind. Mate.

But he'd just agreed to tell her what she was dying to know. "I trust you, too. I'm ready and I will always hold your confidence."

"Back in the fifth century, during the time of Breton, nine virgin druidesses known as the Gallizenae lived on the Isle de Sein. It was offshore from Finistère in western Brittany. Some claimed they called sailors into the dangerous rocks of the pass between them and the mainland. Others believe they watched over those on ships. These women were capable of changing their forms to anything from an animal to a bird."

Tess listened calmly, but what a tale.

Cole continued in that soothing, deep voice of his. "One of the nine virgin druidesses, known as Vercane, was sad that she would never have a child, so she decided to have many. Vercane snuck away from the Isle of Sein clothed as one of the female workers from the village on the island who went home every few days to see their husbands, since no men were allowed on this island. When Vercane reached the mainland, she shifted into a bird, took flight and found a small pool of water fed by a waterfall. She shifted back to her human form and entered the water naked, calling all the drops of water to touch her body and be infused with her power. She bestowed the first male and female eagles who drank from the pond with the ability to take human form. They were the first Guardians. She charged those two with the duty of protecting her unique *children*. She wanted only pregnant women who were pure of heart to receive her gifts."

"So Vercane wanted perfect mothers?"

"No, only those who came to the pond with a heart open to receive her gift. She didn't want anyone to misuse it. Next, she blessed the pool so that the first five women to drink who were pregnant with boys would become mothers of future male shifters—the Gallize—who would take different animal forms. She then blessed the first five women to imbibe who were pregnant with girls to birth future mates of the Gallize shifters. Those females would receive powers from Vercane."

Tess felt her heart jump in her chest. Call her insane, but what if the energy she'd fought all her life had a purpose? "What kind of powers?"

"Not a lot of specifics on that were passed down since our guardian deals specifically with the males. Females had a different guardian who evidently dropped the ball two hundred years ago when she disappeared, so there's no one to follow those families and watch for the females, or to continue the history."

"Do you think someone killed their guardian?"

"There's been a lot of speculation over the years, but no one has figured it out."

"Well, that sucks. The females have no protector."

"Not unless they meet a Gallize shifter who becomes their

mate."

She smiled at his fierce tone but didn't want him to stop. "What else can you tell me about the women?"

"In the past, some of those females had the gift of foresight. Some had unusual strength. Some had telekinetic powers. Some had telepathic ability. I have no idea just what gifts they'd have, but each woman supposedly has a unique makeup."

Her analytical mind was in overdrive. "You said your animal had to be called up. Do the women require something similar? Do they have animals?"

"The female Gallize are different from the male shifters. Women always mature earlier."

"True," she teased.

He teased her back with a groan. "Like I said, this is information that has been passed down for many years so I'm not entirely sure about all of it. As I understand it, the female Gallize come into their powers slowly. When they're ready to take ownership, they open their heart to the powers. They aren't thought to be shifters, but since their guardian was lost with no one to guide future generations, it's certainly possible a Gallize female might be born of a shifter and human union. Without their guardian around to intervene like mine did when the time came, my guardian thinks the Gallize females must be able to gain their full powers another way."

"Like how?"

"If a Gallize shifter found one such woman and mated with her, accepting the mating bond would open the gates to the energy inside both of them."

Energy? Like hers?

Project much, Tess?

She was grabbing at the first answer she could find to explain her weird energy. But she was on a fact-hunting mission, too. "Is that the only trait of a Gallize female? I mean, how would your group of shifters recognize a woman like that as a mate? Or do you just automatically find each other."

"No, that would be too easy. For us to take a mate, it's no different than a human finding that perfect person. You find that person who you know you can spend forever with." Cole sounded wistful. He cleared his throat and said, "There are specific traits that identify a Gallize female. From what I understand, they normally possess at least two of those traits in addition to their unusual power or gift."

"What are some of the traits?" Okay, that sounded anxious. Call her foolish, but she'd be lying if she said she wasn't hoping to have two of them.

"The women have mismatched eye colors."

Nope, not her.

Cole went on. "They have all been born in what is known as a true blue moon month from way back, which is a year, or basically four seasons, with a thirteenth full moon. Scholars began noting it in the sixteenth century, but those who were Gallize paid attention to it much earlier."

"How many of those type years are there in recent history?"

"Are you trying to figure out if you were born during one?"

Busted. "Yes. I know it sounds silly, but you remember the way I screwed up watches?"

"Yes."

"I've stopped other electronics. Is there any chance I might have enough energy to be one?" There. She got it off her chest and wanted to know one way or another.

Cole's breathing slowed and his voice quieted. "You *were* born during a blue moon month, but you would be special even if you weren't."

That was the man she'd wanted forever. "Thank you. Now what's the third trait?" She held her breath.

"This one is key, because I've never heard of a mate who didn't have this marker. A Gallize woman is the second-born child in a family."

Her hopes crashed, falling as low as Cole sounded.

So much for energy making her special.

She squeezed her eyes to stop a tear from escaping. Had she really been thinking she was a Gallize female? Her parents had been married for four years when they had her, their only child.

To lighten the air, she joked, "Guess that leaves me out."

Cole didn't reply.

She arched around to look at him and caught the tail end of devastation in his gaze. Clearly, she hadn't been the only one wishing for a match.

What about other traits? Would it matter based on what he'd just told her? No.

He said, "Ready for another toddy?"

She recalled how he'd do a redirect to avoid being asked something he didn't want to answer.

Shaking her head and turning around to lean back against his solid chest, she said, "Nope. You promised to talk. That's what we're doing. Where did your enemies come from?"

"A woman who was turned away from the pond."

"Why?"

"There have always been guardians over our kind. They live for a long time."

"What's a long time?"

"Our current guardian is over three-hundred-years old."

That didn't even compute in her mind.

She started to ask how that was possible when Cole told her, "I know some things sound fantastical, but you now live in a world with shifters. Just remember that."

"Okay, back to your enemy." She still had to process three hundred years.

He continued, "The woman the first guardian turned away was a dark witch known as Cadellus whose heart was blacker than a tar pit, or so the story goes. She argued her male child's right to the pond, but the eagle guardian still refused her from where he perched on a limb overhanging the water. In the end, she had to leave without drinking any of the water."

"So what has she got to do with your enemies?"

"She became the mother of the Cadells."

"Never heard of them."

He explained, "You won't unless they tell you or an informed Gallize does. Cadellus lost her son in childbirth and blamed the Gallize. She swore she'd rid the world of male Gallize offspring, leaving the females to mate with males she created. She made a deal with a demon who then killed the mother of a Gallize male and ate her heart while it pulsed. He received some of the Gallize power, but he could not shift into an animal as he and Cadellus had hoped."

"Ugh, what woman would do that to a mother?"

"You'd be surprised at what the Cadells are capable of. The

demon took the bodies of three different males who practiced magic, impregnating Cadellus each time. She birthed three different bloodlines of children who lived to a great age, breeding their own sons and daughters. Those that bred with humans were not as powerful as the original three, but those men who found a Gallize female to breed with, voluntarily or not, received powerful children who are known today as Cadells. The men still force themselves on women or steal a Gallize mate to keep or kill, which is devastating to a male shifter or female who is bonded."

"What happened to Cadellus?"

"Basically, she rocked along, happily sending her prodigies after Gallize shifters, until one of her descendants killed a child born of the Greek god Atlas and his human mistress. Cadellus was given an option of killing all of her descendants to end her lineage or live eternity in a cave which she can leave only during a total lunar eclipse."

"Is anything easy in your world?" Tess mumbled, amazed at how much she didn't know about all shifter history. That Cadellus woman deserved what she got, though. "So your people and these Cadells are waging a secret war none of us know about?"

"Pretty much. It's been secret until now."

"Are the Cadells involved with the Black River pack?"

"We think there's a possibility. Hard to tell until we know more."

"I'm hearing hesitation in your voice, Cole. What aren't you telling me?"

He sighed. "I saw someone at SCIS I believe is a Cadell, but I don't want to identify him and risk you confronting him without me present."

"Don't you think I need to know?"

"Not until I can get it confirmed. At that point, you won't have to deal with him. We will."

"That's not a good plan," she argued. "I could do the wrong thing just because I didn't know."

Cole said, "You aren't going to let this go, are you?"

"No. I can't. It's too important. I had questions earlier and no way to reach you."

"You'll be able to reach me twenty-four-seven after tonight."

Tess shook her head. "Tell me. Who do you think the Cadell is at SCIS?"

"First I want your promise to continue acting normal around him." Then he muttered, "If I ever let you out of here."

She was not staying in a cabin forever, so he was definitely letting her out. "I promise."

"I think Brantley is a Cadell."

Okay, she hadn't expected that. She was thinking a lower level staff. "Brantley? But he's so ... "

"Human?"

"Yes."

"He hides his trail with magic, but I saw something unnatural in his eyes. It was killing me to leave you around him when I was trucked away."

She had a lot to digest later, but hearing about that truck, she said, "It was killing me to watch the truck drive off."

Cole snuggled her closer to him and just held her for a bit until she returned to the Black River pack. "I hate to say this, but do you think they've killed your friend Sammy?"

"I doubt it."

"Why?"

Cole had started rubbing his fingers slowly up and down her arm, which was covered by his soft T-shirt sleeve. She didn't think he even realized it as he continued answering questions she knew he'd never told another who was not a Gallize.

He said, "We believe they used magic to convince him to join the pack."

"What enticement do they have for a shifter like one of you?"

"Sammy may not live much longer."

"Why?"

"He's suffering from what we call the mating curse, for lack of a better reason."

Tess crossed her arms, thinking. "He can't divorce his mate?"

Cole laughed softly. "That's not what I mean, but that's a no on divorce. Our shifters mate once, and only once, for a lifetime. Upon losing her child, Cadellus cast the curse on Gallize shifters. Many believed it was only a myth until it actually happened to one of ours."

"Why question that when it's not stranger than the rest of the story?"

"Because many generations back, couples chose mates much earlier in life. The myth indicated that Gallize males had to bond with a mate by ten years after meeting their animal, or face the curse of their animal turning against them. Basically, the animal took over and left the shifter's humanity in the dust."

She couldn't move. The fear of Cole being cursed spread through her body. The current of energy she lived with hummed a little stronger, but then it slowed, feeling content.

"Tess, I'm fine."

"You've been a shifter for seven years, but ..." She couldn't finish that thought. Cole said he'd never have another mate besides her, but she wasn't a Gallize.

"Our people are doing extensive research to determine if there really is a curse or if it's a genetic issue."

"Huh. Okay." But it wasn't okay. "What about Sammy? Why would he go to the Black River pack for help with the curse?"

"Sammy is in love with a human he won't bond with, so he may have been manipulated with magic to believe the Black River pack has a cure, which is bogus. They don't."

"Why doesn't he want to bond with her if he loves her?" Now Tess was getting riled up on the woman's behalf.

"She's not a Gallize female. Sammy would know if she was. Being a human, when she opened herself to accept the bond, the power would most likely kill her on contact. Sammy loves her too much to risk that."

Damn it all. Now Tess was heartbroken for Sammy and worried even more about Cole. "Why didn't Sammy pick a Gallize woman?"

"For the same reason humans can't just pick a spouse based on a shopping list of perfect traits. All the magic in the world doesn't equal the feeling of falling in love. The heart wants what the heart wants."

Her energy spun up with a noticeable buzz.

Was Cole talking about her and him?

She was not the mate for Cole, but how she wished her freaky body fit the Gallize criteria. She'd been trying to convince herself that she couldn't be with Cole when the truth was that she couldn't face being without him.

Almost afraid to talk in the stillness, she asked, "What will happen to Sammy if you find him and he's still having issues?"

"That's why we have a Guardian who is more powerful than any of our shifters. If a Gallize loses control of his animal, the Guardian will do his duty to end the shifter's life."

"That's horrible."

"Trust me when I say by that point, it's an act of mercy for the shifter. None of us want to leave a raging animal lose to kill innocent people."

She had a hard time agreeing, because she kept picturing that happening to Cole.

Could he mate with another woman?

Why did that send her stomach into turmoil? She couldn't be with him. Tess did not want him with anyone else. She also didn't want Cole to face that curse.

Maybe it didn't exist.

She had a bad feeling it did. She asked, "So you're hunting Sammy to deliver him to your guardian?"

"Not exactly. Sammy has one more option, but the woman he loves would have to ask him for it and he'd have to believe she wanted it."

"What's that?"

"To change her into a shifter, because that would give her the best chance at surviving the bonding."

Tess tensed.

"Relax. I would never ask that of any woman, Tess, and neither would Sammy. Now you see the dilemma he's in. He kept it secret that he was seeing someone special, because she was human. He knew he screwed up by not telling her he was a shifter first. He fell in love, asked her to marry him, which she accepted, *then* told her he was a shifter. She panicked and ran."

"Where is she?"

"I hope to know soon. We have a lead on her and if it pans out I'll be able to talk to her in person."

Tess worried her lip between her teeth. "Are your people going to force this woman to come in to be with Sammy?"

"Hell, no. None of our shifters would do such a thing. Even as bad a shape as Sammy was in, he wouldn't go after her. He was afraid he'd frighten her more. I just want to talk to her to find out if I can answer questions and maybe get her to talk to Sammy on the phone if we can find him. I want to see if she feels a bond toward Sammy. If she does, then maybe she is as worried about him as he has to be about her. If she wants nothing to do with any of us, we'll protect her for Sammy until he can ... or if he isn't able to in the future."

That sounded ominous. Tess asked, "Why would she need protecting?"

"If the Black River pack has plans to use Sammy, they would want his fiancée to use as leverage to make him do horrible things. If his bear wasn't out of control yet, that would do it. He'd snap and everyone would face death by teeth and claws."

"I don't see a good ending on any of this, Cole."

"There isn't one other than if his fiancée is willing to allow Sammy to spend his last days with her. To have Sammy back and give him that, would be ... would make losing him easier."

The awful sound she heard in her head was the crack of her heart breaking for Sammy and his woman.

"That's all I can share—"

"Oh, come on, Cole. It's me. I'm not going to screw you over and blab what you tell me, so no holding back."

His deep voice rumbled with a chuckle. "If you were a shifter, you'd be a tiger. A tigress."

That was the second time someone had said that to Tess. Her heart thudded at what he was saying. Did he wish she was a shifter? She couldn't do that.

Cole's face fell. "I was teasing. What's wrong?"

"Nothing."

"Lie."

She lifted her eyebrows. "So you can tell a lie from the truth?"

"Pretty much, but it has to do with physiological change."

"What about the jackal shifters? Can they tell?"

"They should be able to tell if you're lying, too, but you can't trust anything they tell you. I'm not being prejudiced against a different shifter group. I'm just telling you how it works in our world. So what were you upset about?"

Her mind had gone back to SCIS and wondering how much the jackal shifters had figured out with the unaware humans.

Cole nudged her shoulder.

"I'm just thinking," she groused. "I wasn't upset, but when you said if I was a shifter I'd be a tiger, it made me wonder if you're disappointed I'm not ... like you."

Moving slowly, Cole turned her to face him. His eyes were solemn and his voice held a longing that hurt to hear. "I would never wish this on you or anyone. It's my destiny, but not something for you. I wish ... I wish we didn't have this between us, but you're perfect the way you are and I'll hurt anyone who tries to change you."

She knew by the way he said *change* that he meant if someone tried to turn her into a shifter.

Her emotions went on a roller coaster ride. She was happy to know he didn't wish for her to be a shifter, but did that mean he didn't want to be with her as a human? What about him finding a mate?

The selfish bitch inside Tess, who loved Cole, raised her ugly head and said, *"Mine."*

Then there was a third hurdle.

If Tess met him halfway and tried to make this work to have time and figure a way they could stay together, what would she tell her dad?

It would be a catastrophic nightmare.

"Where'd you go, Tess?"

Into Fantasy Land, the only place where they ended up together.

Lying to Cole was out of the question now. Not when they were in the same room anyway.

This was a man who'd gone up against three mercenary jackal shifters who had kidnapped her. She didn't want to think about how much more risk he'd be in if she said what she was thinking.

"You all sound like a bunch of badass men." She glanced back at him.

He winked. "We are, but we're marshmallows around our women."

Returning to face forward, she smiled, glowing under his attention. "Confidence is clearly not an issue."

"Not when we know we're the most powerful beast in a fight, but the enemies we have aren't the garden variety. They even the odds with magic and now synthetic drugs."

"You said you were overseas. Are you back here for good?"

"Pretty much. We had to come back to the US because the

Black River Wolf Pack criminal operations had turned into a cancer that was spreading too quickly."

"Why is that?" she asked. "SCIS was formed last year to get a handle on the problem, but it seems the more we do the worse it gets."

"You can't win a war if some of your people are helping the other side." He held up a finger in front of her face to stave off her objections. "The jackals were brought over from Asia and Africa. From what my people have determined, the decent ones who want to live in harmony and help their neighbors stayed in their home country. The Black River wolf pack located the ones who wanted to leave home and trained them to fight. A jackal we captured in a bloody wolf shifter territorial battle admitted the final step in being accepted by the Black River pack was to kill any shifter not a wolf in front of the pack."

"Just murder someone? Sounds like some of our really bad human gangs."

"It is, but worse."

She dropped her head back. "I have years of studying behind me and feel like there's so much more for me to learn."

"You can't know all the dark side and politics of shifters without a tour guide."

Sitting up, she asked, "Are you offering to be my guide?"

"Not on your life. I don't want to ever come between you and your father. Nor do I want you anywhere around my world."

Just like that, her heart fell to her feet.

He'd never consider having her around his shifter life even if she could figure out her end. She shouldn't feel hurt, but if she was willing to take a step forward, why couldn't he?

Maybe because he doesn't know I'm willing to take that step. Would telling him make a difference?

The day was catching up with her and she needed a clear brain to figure out anything else.

She pulled out of his arms and stood, stifling a yawn as she turned to face him. "I need a bed."

Heat deepened the blue of his eyes.

A sizzle of vibration whipped through her, pooling down south. She didn't dare look at herself and draw attention to the tips of her hard nipples pressing against his shirt.

She stood there, unsure what to do next, but she wanted the same thing he wanted if she was reading his gaze right.

Glancing away, he said, "The bedroom attached to the bathroom should be warm now."

She looked around. "Where are you going to sleep, and don't say out here because I would be stiff sleeping on this thing." She dipped her head to look down around the bottom. "Unless it's a fold out."

"No fold out. I don't sleep a lot. I'll find somewhere if I get tired."

Turning back to him, she debated on putting words to her thoughts.

What the hell?

Would this moment ever happen again?

Probably not.

She gave him her best smoldering look and hoped he didn't think she was having a brain seizure. "Are you saying you won't sleep with me?"

His surprise was so sudden and honest she laughed and asked, "Is that such an awful idea?"

"Hell no, I just didn't think you'd want, you know, me in there."

"Oh, but I do."

His eyes were full of calculations in progress. After a few seconds he said, "Go ahead. I'll come in a bit later."

Damn. That didn't sound like a man excited about being in bed with her.

I deserve that subtle rejection.

Cole had changed, a lot, since she last saw him.

He didn't realize she'd changed a bit herself, but she guessed he hadn't noticed.

She didn't have to be a shifter to sense that he had no intention of coming near her unless he was stepping into danger to protect her.

CHAPTER 27

Cole let out the breath that had backed up in his lungs until Tess left the living room.

He leaned back, then dropped his head back against the couch. In one corner of the peeling ceiling, a spider was busy perfecting its web for the unsuspecting tiny moth flitting around up there. The moth kept bouncing up and down against the ceiling as if it expected an attic door to open for escape.

Then the moth fluttered toward the corner as if drawn by some invisible light.

Wings hit the sticky web and panic set in. Fragile wings beat harder. The moth twisted back and forth until it had trapped itself good.

The spider raced out from where it had been hiding and put the final screws in the moth, wrapping it up like a web mummy.

While Cole admired the spider's skill of spinning a damn good trap, he sympathized with the moth facing its end.

One minute a creature was moving along, thinking its life was perfect, then out of nowhere it slammed into a death sentence with no way out.

Cole had experienced that same panic the first time he found out he was a shifter. He'd thought that was the end of his life, because his wolf scared the devil out of him. It wanted to fight everything and he was forced to observe the vicious attacks with no idea how to stop them.

But Sammy had shifted into his massive bear the first time Cole worked with him, and had shown Gray Wolf that he wasn't the only one with jaws and claws.

Cole had gained control slowly, in small steps. It took months and months of getting his ass kicked until he'd had enough, before he finally started paying attention to the Gallize shifters trying to teach him, the human, how to be a shifter.

That's when Sammy decided to spend day and night with Cole for two months of misery.

Gray Wolf didn't like the grizzly sleeping in the same room.

Early on, Cole would wake up in wolf form with a giant grizzly towering over him. Cole's wolf was a beast, but Sammy's grizzly was a monster that stood over ten feet tall and sounded like someone had released it from the depths of hell.

Gray Wolf learned respect and Cole finally got a grip on his control.

Later, Cole found out that Sammy had come in to keep the Guardian from putting Cole down. Everyone had run out of patience with Cole and his out-of-control wolf, especially since Cole had been doing little to help.

But Sammy believed every shifter deserved a chance.

Now with Sammy suffering from the mating curse and possibly under the magical control of the Black River pack, Cole felt useless.

This was his chance to save his friend and he was failing.

At the rate the mating curse was moving through Cole's body, Cole hoped he had ten days, but worried it would probably be less, before he'd have to submit to the Guardian. There was no exact time period to depend upon because there had been so few incidents over past centuries, and many had not attributed the problems to the mating curse.

The Gallize lacked information their shifters desperately needed to survive.

The only person who could stop Cole's downfall had just walked out of the room.

Tess was never going to be his mate.

Our mate, Gray Wolfe snarled.

Quiet down or we'll be sleeping outside to keep her safe.

Gray Wolfe lunged, giving Cole a pain in his side, but Cole ordered him to stand down or not see her again.

Gray Wolf quieted and pulled back deep inside. That's how much the wolf wanted her as their mate.

Cole now understood exactly what the Guardian had been saying. That Gray Wolf had likely come to life sooner than he should've back in college, because Cole had chosen a mate. His wolf had wanted to be part of the bonding.

Maybe down the road if Cole had been given enough time to let Tess get used to the idea, and understand that he might not live more than a few years, she would have considered marrying. Cole would have taken that and been a happy man until his time ran out, but he didn't have that option now. Also, he didn't want to burden her with his impending death.

She could do nothing about it and that knowledge wouldn't change the outcome, only put a dark blanket over the time they had left together.

He'd take whatever she would give him for now.

Like the change in her scent he picked up on when she'd hinted about him spending a night with her.

In plain words, she wanted to have sex.

Part of that was the reaction to almost dying, and he had no doubt that she'd thought she was going to die tonight.

Another part of her flirting might just be curiosity.

Give her more credit than that, asshole.

Okay, no way would she treat him that way. Likely, she just needed someone to make her feel safe. Once she got to sleep, he'd sit in the wooden chair by the window where she'd find him if she woke up.

He had to go meet with Katelyn tomorrow and he still had to find Sammy.

How was he going to do that and keep Tess away from SCIS and any other threat?

The Guardian was allowing Cole room to work right now because the Guardian understood that Cole had chosen a mate years ago.

Saving Sammy came before saving himself.

Katelyn had told Isabella she loved Sammy. Tomorrow Cole would find out if she would come in with him to be available for when they found Sammy. Then they'd see what happened once the two were together again.

Cole's plan was simple.

Sammy had a chance to survive and Cole would make it happen

if that was possible.

CHAPTER 28

Brantley stood on the roof of a ten-story building in downtown Spartanburg, enveloped in a misty night. The drizzle had cleared, but a storm wouldn't have stopped him.

Opening his arms, he said, "Mother Cadellus, I call upon you to help your child."

She couldn't come in person except during a full lunar eclipse, but he didn't need her actual body, just to speak to her.

A mouse ran out from the door he'd left open when he stepped onto the roof.

The small creature scurried up to him and stood on its hind legs. Slowly it grew three feet tall. Once the mouse's eyes changed to solid, empty black, like Mother Cadellus, the mouse said in a husky female voice, "I am here, Bastien."

He loved hearing his birth name on her lips. "I have found the Gallize known as Cole Cavanaugh who took my brother's life." Brantley had been raised with another Cadell who'd died last year while attacking Cole's black ops team. His brother foolishly thought to impress Mother Cadellus but lost his life instead.

It took Brantley a while to narrow down where the Gallize, known as Cavanaugh was located. Once he learned that the shifter had returned to this country, it was simply a matter of asking Mother Cadellus to call upon her minion creatures to give Brantley and the Black River pack aid. Ironically, her minions had followed Sonic, which eventually led Brantley to Cavanaugh. Then Sonic spilled even more during motivational therapy.

"Did you kill the shifter?"

That miserable Cavanaugh had survived the food bank

explosion only because Brantley had allowed him ten seconds. He'd wanted Cavanaugh to feel bone-deep fear before being captured. Even better that the wolf shifter had been stupid enough to try to save the old woman and thus suffered massive injuries.

"No, but I have good news," Brantley hurried to reply. He'd intended for his jackals to deliver Cavanaugh to a secret location in the mountains. Even if the shifter ended up with an arm pulled off, he'd have shifted and healed enough to survive the trip.

That was fine. Brantley had a solid plan in hand this time.

"What could be better than the death of a Gallize male?"

He smiled, "Finding his mate and allowing him to bond before I kill him." If those bloody jackals he'd hired to capture Tess had been successful, Brantley would be informing Mother Cadellus about her new daughter-in-law-to-be.

This time, Brantley would handle things himself.

Admiration churned in the mouse's dark eyes. "Well done, my child. How is our new alliance with the Power Baron mage?"

"Not bad. I don't trust him, but then I trust only Cadells."

"As it should be."

"Definitely," Brantley replied, enjoying this moment to shine. "He has agreed to help the Black River pack as long as he remains anonymous."

"Power Barons believe staying in the shadows will keep them safe. Such fools." The mouse smiled.

"He is enjoying anonymity for the moment by having me as liaison between him and the Black River pack. He did provide me with a boost to my kinetic power, as we agreed. Only time will tell if he is truly an ally."

"Wise decision to wait and see, my son. What is your plan now?"

"To set a trap for the Gallize wolf. If he has bonded with his mate, he will hand his life over to protect her. If he has not bonded yet, then she will watch him die and I will take her as mine."

The huge mouse chortled with pleasure.

Brantley had made Mother Cadellus proud, but she would truly be happy when he took Tess to meet her.

Mother Cadellus would bond them as one.

CHAPTER 29

Big hands clutched Tess's neck and squeezed.

She couldn't see. Everything was black. She fought, struggling to breathe. Somehow she screamed and screamed.

Her arms were pinned alongside her body. A heavy weight held her down. He was going to kill her now.

No. Jaws opened wide with long fangs to attack.

He wanted to change her into a ... she started sobbing.

"Come on, baby, wake up."

Soft words kept pouring into her ear. She blinked her eyes open to find she was wrapped up with her face against Cole's chest.

How humiliating. She forced out, "I did it again?"

"If you apologize to me one more time, I might have to punish you."

"Promises, promises," she grumbled.

His chest moved with laughter, but his voice sounded tired. His hand continued stroking her back up and down, soothing her.

This was nightmare number three.

No one was getting any sleep, especially not Cole. Dragging in another ragged breath, she said, "If you'd just climb into bed like I suggested, I'll probably sleep because I'll feel you close."

"You might be right."

He was capitulating? She didn't react or make a big deal out of it for fear he'd change his mind.

When she eased over to make room, he followed her.

She immediately rolled away from him and he spooned her back like old times. Blood pumped fast through her, which she could blame on the nightmares, but that wasn't the reason.

Her energy had changed. It slowed and hummed in a rhythmic beat. She felt two heartbeats.

Cole's heart and hers were in sync.

When she shivered in surprise, he must have thought she was cold and wrapped her snug within his mighty arms. He had some serious guns. She'd been crazy about him before, but those arms were sexy as hell.

He also had a serious boner tucked up nice and warm against her.

She sure as hell wasn't mentioning that.

Cole would probably leave the house.

"Sorry," he said, moving like he was uncomfortable. "Just ... ignore it."

Now she wanted to laugh at the absurdity of ignoring *that*, but she mumbled something that could be construed as her saying no problem and lay there wide-awake.

She tried to be still. Really. It was a monumental effort when her body had a serious desire to inch backward.

"Tess."

"Um hmm?"

"Go back to sleep."

That was not happening. Having him close had sounded like a solid idea after three crazy nightmares, but that energy she'd been fighting cranked into high gear.

Her female parts were buzzing, too.

She wanted him.

"Cole?"

"What?"

He sounded surly. She sighed. "Are you or maybe I'm, uh, I'm just wondering if, uh, crap ..."

"What the hell?"

At least he was laughing now. She scowled at him. "I don't want to say something to piss you off."

"You can't, baby."

"That's not the way I remember it."

He didn't reply and she started wondering if she'd lost him with that comment.

When he did respond it was in that sexy nighttime voice she loved. "I never minded fighting. You never backed down, always willing to go toe-to-toe with me and I'd forget what we fought over because you were so damned sexy when you got your back up. I knew we'd have lots of make-up sex."

She fell back in love a little more with him when he gave her that sweet memory. She smiled and snuggled back against him.

He jerked and pushed his lower part back. "Holy hell, Tess. You trying to kill me?"

That was funny. "Sorry."

"No, you're not."

"Okay, maybe I'm not. You going to punish me?" she taunted in the same voice she'd used once on a camping trip that had turned kinky.

A deep, painful groan climbed out of Cole. "Stop saying stuff like that. I'm ... I'm uncomfortable as it is."

Uncomfortable? Was that all?

She wasn't trying hard enough.

"What were you trying to ask me?" he asked, putting a little bit more distance between his chest and her back.

She was having second thoughts about what she had wanted to say. Would she sound weird? On the other hand, what could be much weirder than being captured by three jackal shifters?

Good point.

Licking her lips to stall, she said, "Do you remember touching my arm at the SCIS compound when I thought you were Colin?"

"Yes."

"I've been, well, for lack of a better word, I've been buzzing since then."

"What? What do you mean? Explain it."

This is when she was glad no lights were on to show her full humiliation. "Remember the night you showed up at my place after you escaped?"

"Yes."

Here goes nothing. "I was having trouble dealing with feeling aroused. When I went to shower, I started thinking about Colin and everything ached. I think it's because you were there. I was thinking about taking care of myself and—"

He flipped her on her back so fast she yelped.

When she looked up into his gaze, those beautiful golden-brown eyes were too bright to be normal. "Cole? Are you okay?"

He closed his eyes. "Tell me what you were going to do."

The night in the shower was nothing like the energy rocketing through her now. Her skin felt on fire and needing more fuel. She wanted Cole to touch her everywhere, but he wasn't even looking at her.

He wanted to know what she'd been about to do when he showed his face that night?

She'd give him something to think about.

In a sultry voice, she said, "I was going to start out with massaging my breasts. My nipples were hard and they've ached so much. I ran the rough cloth over my tits, teasing them, but that only made my need worse. I brushed the cloth between my legs and dropped it. My skin felt too alive to touch, but I used one finger between my legs, playing there. Oh, it hurt so good, because it wasn't enough. I scraped a fingernail gently back and forth in my wet heat, over and over, rubbing that one spot until I wanted to scream."

She shivered, needing to get out of this pain she was causing herself.

Cole inhaled deeply and opened his eyes on a shuddering exhale. "You are so fucking hot. You're making me crazy. I want to taste you and push deep inside you so bad."

That sounded like a winning plan right now. She lifted her hips and rubbed against his oh-so-ready erection.

Cole's hands were pressed into the bed on each side of her. His arms shook and she knew damn well the strain he was suffering had nothing to do with those arms being tired.

She cupped his face, turning it down to look at her again. "Why are you holding back?"

Drawing a ragged breath, he said, "You'll regret it tomorrow and I can't face that look on your face."

"When did you ever think I needed someone to make my decisions?"

Muscles in his jaw twitched. His eyes were now far too bright to be human. He said, "This can't work for us, Tess, and you know it. Your father hates us. You're a part of SCIS. I don't want to pull you deeper into this world. I'm trying to keep you safe, baby."

She leaned up and kissed his chin. "Who keeps you safe?"

Dipping down, he kissed her lips in a slow roll, taking his time as if he savored every time he touched her.

She broke the kiss and asked, "What is it going to take to tear down the wall you've got between us? I want you, Cole. I'm a big girl. I understand what you've told me and I'm wide-eyed about this. I'm not afraid and I'm not going to regret anything except not having this moment together."

His eyes were a normal blue again, but filled with sadness she wanted to take away. Everything about him said yes, but he still held back.

He said, "I have no tomorrow to offer you. To take what you offer tonight and leave you again would be worse than the first time. I can't live with myself if I hurt you again, and I will, because there is no scenario where we end up together. I would give anything for that, but it won't happen."

They were at a standoff unless she could ease his mind. "I'm okay with whatever tomorrow brings. I'm willing to let tomorrow take care of itself. I would have given everything I possessed to have seen you one more time before you left. I have that chance now and I'm just as determined not to lose even one minute of this night. Don't take this from me. Love me tonight and I promise you I'll cherish it."

She'd pleaded her case and left everything on the table.

If he still said no, she'd have to accept it.

CHAPTER 30

I'm going to burn no matter where I go after I die.

Cole was stuck between two lives. One was the man who had loved Tess so freely at one time and the other a cursed shifter headed for his death.

Was he selfish to give in?

"Stop it," Tess said.

What had he been doing? "Stop what?"

"Ripping yourself apart with trying to make up your mind. It's real simple. Do you or don't you want me?"

"Ridiculous question. I want you twenty-four-seven."

Her whole face relaxed at that. Why couldn't he make her happy all the time?

"Five."

"Five what, Tess?"

"Four."

What the hell was going on?"

"Three." She had that determined look on her face.

"Two." Now she had an evil smile lighting her eyes.

"What are you counting down to, Tess?"

"One. Okay, had your chance."

Now he got it. "I hear you. I'm getting up." And he climbed over her to get off the bed. He turned to leave when he heard her moan.

Slowly turning around, he saw her shirt pushed up.

His shirt and he liked it on her.

She grasped a breast in each hand and started working those puppies.

His dick hurt, like really hurt. Blue balls kind of hurting.

She drew her legs up. When one of her hands moved south, he was done.

Cole dove on the bed and yanked her legs out straight.

She jerked her head up and stared at him. He watched her eyes while his hands inched up her thighs. Now her legs were shaking.

But she wasn't afraid.

Not his Tess.

His fingers went on autopilot. They knew this body. His eyes stayed on hers, not wanting to miss the least reaction.

His arms were around the outside of her legs as he pushed his fingers slowly to her bottom where he inched his thumbs around to slowly massage the inside of her legs.

She made a strangled sound, but didn't break eye contact.

He eased her legs into a bent position, spreading her thighs carefully inside his arms. He leaned and kissed her on the core of her heat.

On the heels of a keening noise, she mumbled some threat if he stopped.

Damn but he loved her.

He put his hands back under her sweet bum and lifted so he had her right where he could put his tongue to the best use.

Trembling started in her legs and traveled up her body.

He didn't stop no matter how much she begged him, "Now, do it now. Now!"

She was wet and sweet.

He'd waited a lifetime, never expecting to have this woman in his hands again.

Cole took her up and down that tightrope of tension until he knew she couldn't take any more. With one hard flick of his tongue, she came off the bed, calling his name.

When she shuddered back to the bed, he made another swipe across her damp heat and she came again.

"Cole," she whispered.

He had to stretch up over her body to get close to her lips. "What, baby?"

"You better not be done," she warned, struggling to catch her breath.

"Tell me what you want and it's yours."

She reached down and had his dick out of his shorts before he could stop her. "This. I want to feel it inside me."

"Tess," he warned.

"Thought you said I could have anything I wanted."

"I'm not as ... human as I was."

She looked down at what she had a damned snug grip on, then glanced back at him. "And you think I'm passing *that* up?"

Only Tess would have that reaction. "

"Or are you afraid the condom won't fit?" she asked, running her hand slowly down his length and back up as he now shook. "Tell you what, we'll sew two together, because I know you have condoms."

Gritting his teeth to keep from drenching her hand on the next swipe, he said, "I need to be able to reach the nightstand.

She opened her hand. "You have ten seconds."

He started to lean over. "Takes more than ten seconds to—"

"Nine."

"Tess, dammit."

"Eight." She was laughing so hard she could barely speak. "Seven."

He put a condom on faster than he'd disarmed a bomb with seconds left to go.

"Four."

Sitting back on his knees, he crossed his arms to see what she'd do.

"Two ... One." She sat up and pushed him back.

He let her, thoroughly entertained by the Tess of years past. The one who made him laugh, curse, shout and love her every minute they were together.

Now she kneeled with her legs on each side of his hips. She lifted up and fed him into her an inch ... then stopped.

He clenched his teeth, wanting to shove inside of her. "There's plenty more, baby."

"Oh, I know." She smiled as if torturing him was her new favorite pastime. Then she sank down another inch.

His fingers gripped the sheets. "Come on, baby."

"You mean like this?" She leaned down and bit his nipple as she took a little more of him.

His heart pounded his chest. He wanted to give her this lead, but he might not survive it.

She reached around and massaged his balls.

Every muscle in his body tightened with the struggle to hold back. He would not end this show on one stroke. Not happening.

Squeezing gently, she said, "Are you ready?"

Was she kidding? He grunted out, "Born ready."

Straightening up, she slid all the way home on him.

"Oh, fuck yes."

Joining with her felt so incredible, he might be the first shifter to die of a heart attack.

She started moving up and down. He grabbed her hips to help her when he shoved up to meet her.

She dropped forward and grabbed his shoulders, keeping her rhythm. He met her over and over again. He felt the heat building between them and moved his hands. One cupped a breast and tweaked her tight nipple as he stroked fingers on the other hand between them.

Her body tensed.

He kept hammering up into her.

She arched and dug her fingernails into his arms, letting go with a wild banshee cry.

Hallelujah, he was right behind her. Stars blazed through his gaze and the burning need for this woman uncoiled in a sharp whip of ecstasy.

He could hear both heartbeats thumping together.

Why, why, why couldn't he have this forever?

CHAPTER 31

Buzzing woke Tess. She sat up, or tried to. A heavy arm was draped over her middle. Her hair fell around her face like a mistreated mop head and the shirt she'd worn last night was gone.

The room looked like a disaster.

She grinned. A really, really good disaster.

Something buzzed again. Not her this time, thankfully. Come to think of it, the energy was so low she hardly noticed it.

"Cole. Where's your phone?"

He muttered something dark.

Laughing, she popped his sexy, naked butt, which she could look at all day long. "Get up. The phone. It might be important and I want coffee."

Rolling over on his side and giving her a heart-stopping smile, he said, "So it's all about you?"

She loved that rough morning voice. "I thought you'd figured that out by now."

More phone buzzing.

Growling, he rolled off the bed and stood up, scratching his hair that looked like he'd been hit with heavy voltage. All of that was adorable, but not as sexy as his morning woody.

Oh, yes, she remembered that very well.

Without looking at her, he warned, "Stop ogling me or I'll never find that miserable phone."

"Sounds like it's coming from your cargo pants over in that corner." She pointed.

"Ah." He retrieved the phone and walked into the bathroom, closing the door.

She'd let him do that. He needed to talk to his people and she'd pushed as far as she could last night. He thought she'd regret making love with him.

Not in a million years.

After a few minutes, the toilet flushed, water ran in the sink, then he came back out with wet hair he'd managed to tame. But he had the start of a beard shadow and every rock-hard muscle was on display.

Basically, a sex god.

Her sex god.

"I just got this thing under control," he said, eyeing his dick that was busy coming back up to attention.

"Why waste it?" she chided him.

His long sigh should have warned her. He said, "I have to leave for a bit."

Her face fell. "You're not leaving me here."

"Just until we can figure out who's behind the attack last night."

Well that ruined her morning. "No. Hell, no. I need to get to my office and find out if anything new has come up overnight."

"This is not an argument you're going to win, Tess."

She jumped up, grabbing the sheet to wrap around her body. She had no problem being naked with him, but she couldn't argue decisively in the buff. "I thought I made it clear last night that I am not the little woman who needs someone to make my decisions."

"That not what I'm saying," he snapped, pissed off.

She was unprepared to litigate this yet. "I'm taking a shower. Don't you dare leave while I'm gone or you will regret that."

Not allowing him another word, she stormed into the shower.

He'd see it her way once she could get her thoughts straight. Just like she planned to show him how with a little patience on his part, they had forever to figure out their relationship.

CHAPTER 32

Cole was ready for battle.

Standing with his legs apart and arms crossed, he waited in the middle of the small living room for Tornado Tess to come out and wreck his mind.

She stepped from the bedroom wearing her pants from last night and another of his T-shirts. No makeup and hair pulled up in one of those magical buns women created with nothing but a clip, showcasing her high cheeks and smooth skin.

In this case, the clip was her mother's barrette he'd found. That had to be worth some brownie points.

She cocked up her chin. "Now, we can have a conversation."

"You mean now that you've got your armor in place you're ready to do battle?"

"What armor?"

Shaking his head, he got down to business. "You can't go back to Spartanburg today."

"You expect me to just wait here and do nothing?"

"No. I'm not expecting anything. I'm asking you to work with me on this." He unfolded his arms and walked over to her and held out a plain looking mobile phone. "This is a burner phone. It can't be traced. You can call in and find out what's going on at work. I'd appreciate it if you did not tell anyone where you are."

She twisted her mouth and chewed on one side. That was the best sign he could get, because it meant she was considering a counterproposal.

He wanted to end negotiations before she had time to think it all through. "I'll be back in three, maybe four hours. That's all I'm asking. If you need to go to work after that, I'll figure something out, but it's Saturday. Surely you can beg off one day, even a weekend."

More logic for her to work through.

Time to close the deal. Cole said, "If you tell anyone where you are, you'll get me hauled in to face extreme discipline."

Her fear hit him so hard he hated that he'd shaded the truth a bit on that one.

She shook her head. "What are you talking about?"

"Please don't ask me to tell you more than I have."

Her face softened. There was the compassion he'd hoped for because he hadn't shaded the truth too much.

"Just a short time, okay?" Cole asked, trying to get her agreement.

She crossed her arms. "Here's my offer."

Had he really thought he was going to convince this woman to stay out of the way or actually get cooperation? "What?"

"You take me to my apartment where I have excellent security."

"I got past them," he pointed out, reminding her it was dangerous to underestimate shifters.

"But that's because you and your team have superpowers, right? If I'm not available for my office to courier files to, they will become very suspicious. I've agreed to keep your secrets, but to do that I need you to work with me. Also, if my father comes into town again he'll want me to either meet him or to come see me."

He could come up with a half dozen ways others could get into the building, but that wasn't what had him thinking twice. This home was well hidden in the woods, but he kept assuming he'd be back no matter what.

If the Black River pack got their claws on him, she'd be more vulnerable out here alone if they had any way to figure out where she'd gone.

Miss Smarty Pants was staring him down with a look that said she had won her case. She only waited on him to admit the obvious.

Brilliant and gorgeous.

He made it look as if he'd thought on her offer and said, "I admit, you make a valid argument."

No litigator had smiled so brightly. "We just have to coordinate our day. How long are you going to be gone after you drop me off?"

"Four hours should be maximum."

"Then I expect to see you or hear from you in four hours. Not a minute longer."

His hardheaded negotiator would not stop until she'd won every concession. "Agreed."

She stood there looking ... worried.

She was concerned about him.

Gray Wolf had been banging around but not being annoying yet. His wolf liked that their mate cared.

Hell, I do too, Cole silently admitted. *I'm just as fucked up as you are to even be here with her.*

Me good.

Of course, Gray Wolf didn't think he was psychotic.

Needing to get rolling, but wanting to make sure she was safe, Cole walked over to his duffel bag and pulled out one of three guns. He had more in his SUV. Sometimes a bullet saved ripping into the enemy with his claws.

"I know you have a weapon at home, but can you shoot?"

She surprised him when she said, "Yes."

"Really?"

"Don't piss me off or I'll show you," she groused. "I grew up a politician's daughter. Security everywhere, but once I went out on my own I told my father I didn't want to bump into security the rest of my life. He said he wouldn't assign anyone if I proved I could defend myself. I took an intense self-defense class, then spent three months training and brought my father to the gun range to watch me shoot targets at twenty-five yards. Nailed them."

She just got hotter and hotter.

Cole wanted no chance someone would get to her. "Just remember, if you have to use it, no double-tap like for a human. Empty the magazine."

She said, "Got it. I need clothes. I can't walk into my building like this."

"We'll hit a Wal-Mart on the way and get you enough to enter your apartment looking decent." Personally, he preferred her looking indecent.

"That works." She handed the gun back to him.

He loaded her into his SUV and took one last look at the cabin he might not see again. An hour later, Tess wore new sneakers, jeans and a button-down shirt, looking more like the young woman he'd met in college.

When they reached her apartment, he had her inform the security she had a stalker. No one was to be allowed entrance as her guest other than her father and Cole. Packages were to be left at the front and delivered by security.

Her apartment was no different than he'd seen the other day, beyond clothes being picked up.

Letting her go when the time came would be the hardest thing he'd ever done. She stood in her doorway and lifted up on her tiptoes to kiss him. "I love you, Cole."

Cole's heart paused, then thumped hard. Those were the words he'd wanted to hear seven years ago.

She said, "I know you love me and that you think we can't figure this out, but we can at least try."

He wouldn't be around that long. "We'll talk."

That was the most he could commit to without lying to her. He cupped her face and kissed her back then said, "Go inside, baby. Be safe. I need to know you're safe no matter what."

She sniffled, but not a tear fell. Not his tough girl.

She nodded. "I'll be fine as long as you're the one who comes back for me. No one else. If any foolish shifter tries to get to me, I'm a good shot, and they won't like which part has to heal."

His woman. He loved her and it hurt not to say so, but that would make his final parting even worse. "Take that burner phone with you and answer it even if you're in the shower. If not, this building will be under siege from an army of shifters like me. I'll be back soon."

She gave him one last look and turned to walk inside.

He grabbed her arm and gently turned her around.

"What?" she asked, her heart in her eyes.

He kissed her with the desperation of a man afraid he'd never see her again, then whispered, "I have never stopped loving you and never will."

Her lips parted but not a word escaped.

He eased her inside the apartment and closed the door, reminding her at the last moment to lock up.

With her eyes shiny from unshed tears, she smiled and shut the door. He waited to hear the locks being set before he was on his way.

Cole called Rory on his way back down. "Tess is set. I gave her the burner phone and you have the number if you need to reach her. I'll be back as soon as I see Katelyn. I need to hurry to be on time."

"We got your back and your woman covered."

Cole didn't correct him. "Thanks."

He did a quick time check.

Katelyn said she'd meet with him for ten minutes. He had to get there ahead of that schedule to make sure she didn't show up early, get cold feet, and take off.

CHAPTER 33

Tess took the damn burner phone into the shower with her, wishing she had Cole in her hands instead. She understood the need to be extra careful and did not want her father to get wind of what had happened yesterday.

He'd show up and wouldn't leave until she returned home with him.

But that wasn't her home. It hadn't been since her mother died.

Her father loved her in his own distorted and demanding way, but she couldn't live her life for him.

She couldn't avoid being honest with him and have any kind of real relationship that would last. She'd allowed him to get away with too many things since her mother's death. It was time he showed her the respect she deserved or they wouldn't be able to move past a semi-polite relationship.

But what if her dad wouldn't come around? She had to consider that possibility. Dammit. Just when Tess felt like she had a handle on how to deal with her father, her conscience began layering on one pile of guilt after another, warning her that he might never speak to her again.

And that he could die unexpectedly, just like her mother, if he and Tess couldn't figure this out.

She didn't understand nearly as much as she'd thought about the shifter world, but Cole could explain it as they took some time to get to know each other again. The way she saw it, she had three years to come up with a final plan so he never faced that witch's mating curse.

Evil witch.

She opened her computer and ran through emails to see if anything significant had happened at work.

No. Not unless Brantley had broken the case wide open and was holding a party to celebrate his next step up over the top of her.

But what if he was this Cadell person Cole had talked about?

What if he *wasn't*, and Tess was prejudging him on no evidence?

Tired from so many mental battles, she kept moving through her messages.

An email she didn't recognize popped up. She clicked on it and read:

Ms. Janver -

I understand you want to speak with the alpha who was present when your mother died. Below is a number for you to call.

Tess looked for any other notation besides the phone number, but there was none.

Looked like Scarlett had come through.

She snatched up the burner phone and dialed.

A long night of robust sex had supercharged her. She was a woman on a mission to get answers. Even her energy was churning at a low hum, acting content.

The phone rang twice then she heard, "Is this Ms. Janver?"

No hesitating now. She said, "Yes, it is. Who is this?"

"Please hold for a moment."

The sound of the phone being handed off followed. "Hello, Ms. Janver. I am Alejandro, the alpha of a small pride in eastern Tennessee. I understand you have questions for me." He had the cultured voice and soft accent of a man from Spain.

Her request had been answered. "Thank you for contacting me, Alejandro. I would have contacted you sooner, but I only recently figured out how to find you."

"I will assume your father doesn't know, as he spent a lot of money to make sure you never spoke to me."

Shock stole her voice.

"Ms. Janver?"

"Sorry, I was trying to figure out why my father would do that. As I understand it from reports I've read, you were never convicted of any wrongdoing."

"That's because I didn't commit any crime."

She had no way to smooth that over. "Would you tell me what happened the day my mother died?"

"Do you question the court records?"

"To be honest, I don't have them. They're sealed and I haven't found a judge willing to issue the order to open them. I know from media articles that there was another shifter present who got away."

"He was much worse than a rogue shifter. He belonged to the Black River wolf pack."

Her heart hit her feet. Her father had never shared that. She managed to keep her voice even. "I didn't know that. Did you two have a quarrel?"

"Not exactly. We didn't know each other before that day. I was on my way to a meeting in Richmond when I heard a woman in distress. I went to investigate and found a wolf shifter threatening to change from his human form and attack her if she didn't take him to an ATM and empty her account."

Tess clutched her throat, envisioning her poor mother in terror. Where had her daughter been? Drowning in her despair over being a freak who couldn't keep the man she loved. She'd been so angry at the world that day, her mobile phone had fried in her unshielded hand.

She hadn't cared. Just threw it against a wall.

She didn't hear the message from her mother until the day after her mother's funeral when she'd had the phone replaced.

From that moment on, she'd pushed herself to rejoin the world, care about something other than her broken heart, and to wear gloves when she couldn't get around it.

Clearing her suddenly thick throat, Tess said, "What happened next?"

"I intervened, intending to send him on his way and help your mother reach her destination safely. But the wolf shifted, right there in public, and attacked. I'm strong, but I had to release my animal to match his power or he'd have killed us both before any law enforcement showed up. I shifted and almost lost, but in the end I stopped him."

"How?"

"I ripped his throat out." Alejandro had said that with the

simplicity of ordering a meal. "I'm sorry your mother had to witness the brutal battle, but I had no option and was trying to protect her at that moment. I shifted back to human form and went to her. She was still alive. I held her hand and waited for the EMTs to arrive."

"She was alive?"

"Yes. We spoke briefly."

Tess was strangling the phone. "What did she say?"

"This is the reason I contacted you. Your mother said to please tell you and her husband she loved you very much. She also said you must never blame yourself for her death or she will not be at peace. I tried to tell her she would survive, but she just smiled and said, 'Tell Tess to follow her heart.' The emergency team showed up at that second and we were separated."

The world twisted and turned out of shape. Tess hurt thinking about her mother. It *always* hurt, but his words were a gift. She would have preferred to be the one holding her mother, but she was thankful this man had been there and for the words.

The year her mother died, shifters were automatically taken into custody if they shifted in public. No questions asked, just hauled off. There had been some allowances since then, but changing into an animal in public was still a bad idea for anyone who wanted to remain free.

"Did they arrest you, Alejandro?"

"Yes."

"You went willingly?"

"Yes. If I had not, my pride would have suffered."

Tess asked, "Where were you held?"

"In a death pit, but I am older and survived."

Just as she'd thought. She sympathized with shifters who considered the subterranean holding facilities nothing more than a death pit. She'd never get over allowing Cole to be sent there. After all that had transpired, she would be working for changes.

"Why did you do it?" she asked.

"Do what?"

"Shift and fight the wolf when you knew how humans would treat you?"

"Because your mother needed my help," he said as if he couldn't understand Tess questioning his action. "First, I'm an alpha. As such, we protect. But above that, I had a sister who was a submissive. Three Black River wolf shifters attacked her when she was eighteen. No one lifted a finger to help. No one would help me find the pack responsible. If I ever do, I will deal with their punishment personally. She never recovered. She jumped from a cliff over a thousand feet high in her human form, which crushed her body beyond her animal's ability to shift and save her. She was too humiliated as an alpha's sister to come to me. That is my fault for not seeing what was under my nose. Since then, I have never failed another woman, human or otherwise."

Tess cupped her mouth to keep a noise inside that shouldn't be allowed out. A tear spilled down her face. When she could talk, she said, "I'm so very sorry. Thank you for being there for my mother."

"Thank you."

There were very, very bad shifters like the Black River pack and there were very, very good ones like this man and Cole.

She thanked him for speaking to her and assured him her father would not lift a finger against him. Then she told him of the position she had at SCIS and gave Alejandro her contact information. "If you ever need my help, please don't hesitate to call me."

She put the phone down, thinking of the many things her mother had taught her. Her mother had once told Tess to choose her own way in life and not to let her father or anyone else stand in her way. Her mother loved her father, every irritating part of him, but she was a woman who had *chosen* him. She'd known just how overbearing he could be but never allowed him to prevent her from doing as she pleased.

When her mother fussed at her father, he'd grunt and make a comment about stubborn women. Two steps away, he'd smile when he looked back at his wife. He loved her so much that he never recovered from her death, which he blamed on shifters.

The story Tess had gotten was that her mother had been caught in the middle of two shifters fighting over territory, oblivious of humans present. Witnesses said her mother backed up, grabbed her chest and crumpled to the ground.

Of course, that had not been the whole story.

No one talked about how Alejandro had jumped in to be her

mother's savior, only that two crazed shifters had tried to kill a human. That had been front-page news for weeks and set the negotiations between shifters and humans back for months at the time.

That story hadn't been the truth.

With his media contacts, her father could have had a hand in spinning it, because he wanted every shifter to pay for his wife's death.

Now she understood why her father had used his influence to keep her hands off the court records. He hadn't wanted to give his only daughter reason to feel sympathetic toward that alpha, someone her father would never recognize as a real person.

Tess covered her face with her hands. "How am I going to keep Cole and my father, too?"

She dashed through the shower, feeling more normal in her own clothes and at ease in a pair of jeans and a pullover.

When she was dressed and ready to face the world, Tess checked her office voice mail. No one other than an IT person with authorization could pick up her messages without a code. She had told her father to call her office and leave a message there rather than on her cell phone. With so many things going on when she was on her mobile, she sometimes skipped his calls and later forgot to return them. Then he would be pissy for weeks.

There were a couple of messages from Brantley demanding to know where she was and claiming she was supposed to meet him Saturday morning. Not true.

Was he creating bogus situations to make her look bad at work? Probably.

Then she heard a chilling message in an odd tone as if it spoken through a filter –

"You cost me three good jackals last night. We have your father. We know shifters are watching your apartment. Your father is of no use to me. He can't do what you can. This time, you're going to make it easy. I will give you one chance to meet without any trouble. If you do, I'll exchange you for your father. If anyone follows you, we'll know. If you contact anyone, we'll know. I have a very simple way for you to leave the building without drawing the attention of the shifters keeping surveillance on you."

This guy knew about Cole's friends?

She paused the message so she wouldn't miss anything, because her mind was about to explode.

They had her father.

Full-blown panic hit. Her breathing sounded like a horse run into the ground.

Grabbing a paper bag in the kitchen, she breathed into it and got a grip. No time for this crap.

She hit the play button.

"It's your job to get away from those Gallize shifters, Janver. I want to be very clear. If someone follows you, even if you're unaware of it, then I will give you one more chance, but only one."

Great. Maybe she'd have time to find Cole.

"But know this, if you don't come to me the first time, your father will be missing both hands when you see him. He doesn't really need them to be a senator, so I consider that mercy. Call the number I give you at the end for final instructions and remember, we know everything that goes on."

She listened for the number, clicked the message off and raced for the bathroom where she threw up until her stomach cramped. Sliding to the floor, she gasped for air, still clinging to the mobile phone Cole had wisely put in a thick, protective cover for her.

When she could breathe again, she lifted the phone and called her father. No answer, but that was not unusual when he was in a meeting. She called his assistant next who answered, "Hello, this is the office of Senator Janver."

"Pete, this is Tess. I need to speak with my father."

"He's out of pocket for everyone until tomorrow."

She wanted to scream over her dad and his 'keeping the wheels of justice greased' special meetings. "It's an emergency, Pete."

"Oh, I'll find him at once. Are you at a number he has?"

"Just find out where he is and I'll call him."

Tess counted seconds dragging by on her watch until Pete came back on. "The Senator said for you to call this number." Pete rattled off the digits quickly.

"Thank you." Tess hung up and dialed.

A man answered and spoke before she could. "Now that you've confirmed we have him, get moving."

She held the phone until the dial tone returned.

Cole was going to be so hurt that she broke her word, but she could not let this faceless man torture her father.

Struggling to her feet, she splashed water on her face and stared hard at the woman in the mirror. This was not the time to fold. "I'm going to make them regret ever screwing with me."

Not that she had any superpowers for backing up those words, but they made her feel better.

She twisted her neck back and forth, breathed deeply to calm down, then started planning before she made the call for instructions.

CHAPTER 34

Cole smelled the smoke before he turned down Isabella's drive. A tendril of dark gray lifted through an opening in the trees.

Oh, shit.

When he parked in the yard, he stared at her home, smashed and burned as if some giant had hit a fist in the middle and torched it.

Getting out, he ran for the house.

"Here," a voice croaked.

Cole whipped to his left and squinted at a pile of rags in the grass. He hurried over and Isabella appeared in the material. He didn't want to ask how she'd done that.

Lifting her carefully, he asked, "Where can I take you?"

Any supernatural being would not go to a human hospital.

"My people will show up soon." She gripped Cole's shirt. "You have to find Katelyn."

Shit. "What happened to her?"

Isabella heaved a deep breath that seemed to steady her. "She was living here in the basement."

Don't curse at the witch, if that's what she is. Cole couldn't believe how close he'd come to meeting Katelyn yesterday.

Isabella said, "Don't be angry, wolf. Katelyn needed time to make up her mind to talk to you and I needed time to convince her."

When Cole realized this woman had been trying to help him, he let go of his anger.

The witch-shifter said, "Katelyn was ready to go back to Sammy. She really loves the shifter and just panicked, like you thought. If that Cadell hadn't shown up, she'd have met with you."

"Cadell? How do you know that's who came here?"

"He was in league with the Power Barons. I recognized a magic signature when he used power a Cadell shouldn't possess."

Cole couldn't hide his surprise that she even knew what a Cadell was, which was why he said, "Are you *sure* you know what Cadells are?"

She gave him a look that made him feel as if he'd lost most of his IQ points. "Yes, I'm sure. I'm half Cadell. My sire was one and my mother was a shifter. This Cadell bastard was only interested in Katelyn because Cadells keep trying to build a powerful mix from both bloodlines."

"I know, but Katelyn was only human."

"They will either force him to change her into a bear and bond with her, or they'll use her to manipulate him into doing what they want."

"His bear will go mad either way."

"That could be, but when magic is involved anything can happen."

"Why aren't you in the middle of the Cadell community?"

She made a raspy cough. "When I was born, I didn't make the cut as a Cadell. Their *mother* wants strong males of her blood, not women. She thinks we're only good for breeding if they capture one of you. She has no idea what I'm capable of and I don't plan to enlighten her. Basically, I was tossed aside and my mother was handed around to his friends until she died. I hate Cadells. So do you, Gallize."

Cole nodded. "Thank you for that truth."

"You're welcome. Now find Katelyn."

"I'll do my best. How did they know to come here for her?"

"Probably followed you, wolf."

"Not a chance. I'm trained to elude any tail."

"I'm not talking about human tricks. You know Mother Cadellus uses creatures as her minions, right?"

"I thought she used nightingales."

"That was back in the first couple of centuries. When the world expanded, she adapted, even from a cave." Appearing thoughtful, Isabella said, "She had something like a bird or animal track you. Whatever it was, you wouldn't have noticed it."

Right then, Cole decided if he lived he was going to make

friends with this woman and find out what she knew about those bastards.

He said, "Do you have any idea where they were taking Katelyn?"

"My guess would be to Sammy, but that doesn't mean they'll deliver her alive."

Shit. He could hear vehicles coming in the distance. "Who are your people so I don't let an enemy near you?"

Isabella patted his arm. "I'll survive. The Cadell got what he wanted. My people will be turning in the drive right ... about ... now."

Two vehicles tore down the drive, then cars parked and doors slammed.

Voices called out, "Izzy!"

Three women ran up to them, all of them looking ready to turn Cole into a toad or a stump.

Lifting her shaking hand, Isabella said, "He's in my circle." That's all it took to back off the crazy glares. They surrounded Isabella, fussing.

Cole started to stand, but Isabella yanked him down. Her eyes stared straight up and were glazed over.

Everyone went deathly still, including Cole.

Isabella said, "Your woman. Go to her. She needs you."

The bottom fell out of Cole's stomach. "What are you talking about? What's wrong with Tess?"

Isabella shook her head and looked at him. "I don't know, but go to her now. And make her your mate before it's too late."

Cole had stepped away in a hurry to leave. He swung back. "I can't."

"You have to open the bond."

"Thank you. I'll find Katelyn. Take care of yourself. If I can, I'll be back."

"You'll be back, wolf."

That sounded like a threat.

Cole jumped into his SUV and spun wheels cutting around all cars to get out of there. Before he rattled Tess, he called Rory. "Is Tess okay?"

Rory said, "Everything looks quiet ... wait a minute."

Three words hit Cole in the gut. "What. Tell me."

"An ambulance just rushed up to the entrance of her building, but I've been monitoring the police band. Call Tess."

Cole snapped the phone closed and hit the speed dial for the burner phone he'd given Tess.

After eight unanswered rings, he knew the truth.

He shoved the accelerator to the floor and called Rory.

Rory picked up his phone with the calm he had when they were under mortar fire. "We got problems. One of the EMTs is definitely a shifter. I saw his eyes."

Cole said, "Follow that ambulance and keep me on speaker."

"Already on it." The sound of Rory's car squealing away to chase the ambulance came next. Then Rory shouted, "The ambulance is driving crazy."

Cole could hear the tires screeching as Rory took a corner.

"Shit!" Tires screamed loudly.

Cole was losing his mind. "What?"

"They ran a red light and a tractor trailer pulled across right behind them. I have their tag. I'll get a—"

The next sound was a gun blast, cursing, then the snarl of a pissed jaguar.

Rory had shifted.

Then loud animal howls and growling.

Then banging around ...

Then nothing.

Cole's skin turned to ice.

Whoever had come for Tess had gotten Rory, too.

If Cole called Justin, the Guardian or any other Gallize, they'd all come to his aid. But he couldn't do that until he found Rory and Tess, if they were together.

Once that happened, Cole would call in everyone he could muster to get them back.

His heart was trying to explode.

He had to get a grip and think. First he'd find Tess, because he had ensured he could do that by sticking a tracking device in her hair barrette.

That would work if she'd still had her hair twisted up when she was snatched.

CHAPTER 35

Tess opened her eyes and blinked. She was lying on her side and pushed up on an elbow. Slowly the inside of an enormous room came into view. Concrete floor and steel walls. Four chairs were casually tossed around a table, but no sign of a guard.

A dark hallway stretched away from her at the opposite end of a room over fifty feet long and twenty feet high.

No windows. The air was moderately cool.

Was she underground?

She'd been in her apartment and ... the phone message.

Oh, Cole would lose his mind if he found out she'd voluntarily left the apartment on a stretcher. She'd walked into a kidnapping, but what had been her other option?

To have her father's hands cut off?

She didn't even know where he was. The minute the ambulance pulled away, she opened her mouth to demand to see her father and felt a prick on her arm. At least she didn't feel badly drugged.

Moving to sit up, her leg yanked to a stop.

Twisting, she found her leg chained to a thick metal plate anchored with bolts as thick as her wrist.

Once she managed to get up, she had six feet of chain.

And an unconscious man was piled two steps away on her left.

"Hey you," Tess called, her words echoing. She had no reason to think this guy was a friend even if he also had leg jewelry.

"Wake up," she said, stepping closer. When she could reach him, she used the toe of her shoe to nudge the body.

He'd been turned away from her and now flopped to his back, groaning. He had a wound in his shoulder.

Crap. She dropped down next to him and opened his shirt to find blood oozing from a hole. Lifting his shoulder, she could see the exit wound. Bullet.

Lowering him back down, she went into action yanking up the end of her T-shirt and biting a spot to get a rip started.

That was not as easy as it looked on television. When she had a sort of patch, she pressed it against the wound.

"Ow," he grumbled.

She eased up on the wound and explained, "You've been shot. You're bleeding."

His face was paler than his arms, which were a tea color. Sleek brown hair fell over his forehead. He had a face carved for modeling, right down to the perfect eyebrows and mouth. His body was cut up with muscle, too.

None of that interested Tess one bit.

Her patient opened his eyes, which were an interesting gold-brown color.

She only had eyes for one man, who topped all others from his body to the endless blue of his gaze. Cole.

Her energy hadn't increased at all, clearly in agreement with her.

Her new friend closed his eyes.

"You need to wake up," Tess said, not really sure if that mattered. Her specialties were shifters and legalities. Beyond pressing on a wound like this, her medical expertise extended to a box of Band-Aids.

Golden eyes opened again. "Oh, hell, you're Tess."

"How do you know me?"

"I was watching your apartment while Cole was out of pocket."

"You're a friend of his?"

He moved his bad shoulder and grimaced. "Yes."

"Are you a wolf, too?"

He slashed those eyes at her and the gold deepened, making him appear not quite human. "No, I'm not."

Shifter etiquette required not asking, but she wasn't in a social mood. "What are you?"

One of those attractive eyebrows lifted. "Impertinent little thing."

"Yes. I tend to get that way when I've been kidnapped. What's your name?"

"Rory." Moving his arms, he worked his body to a sitting position.

She warned, "You should be careful or you'll bleed out."

"I appreciate your concern, but I'm not bleeding out. I'm just not healing as fast without shifting."

"Why aren't you shifting into a ... ?" She let that half question hang in the air.

"Persistent, too," he muttered. "I can't do what I need to do in my animal form right now. Why don't we forget about me and figure out how to get you out of here."

"You mean us, right?" she corrected.

"Okay, sure. Us. Once you're safe, I'm coming back to have a chat with the kidnappers."

She knew without asking that the chat would involve claws and teeth.

The sound of someone approaching, and not trying to be quiet about it, drew Rory's attention. She followed his gaze to look toward the dark hole that had to be a tunnel to this spot.

One of the jackal shifters from SCIS appeared and kept walking toward her. She tried to recall his name. Something like Leonard.

Tess stood up. "What the hell is going on?"

Leonard never slowed and slapped Tess sideways. Her head spun. She shouted and hit the ground.

"Touch her again and die, jackal."

The thud of bodies being hit hard echoed in the room.

Flipping around, Tess shook off the stars she saw and took in the fight.

The jackal pulled a three-foot-long, half-inch-thick pipe from a holder on his back, then cracked it across Rory's head, knocking him down.

Tess yelled, "You bastard. He's chained."

"Don't, Tess," Rory called out, rubbing his head.

The jackal kicked Rory over on his back, catching Rory's wounded shoulder.

Hissing at the pain, Rory tried to lunge, but he was no match for that miserable coward Leonard who beat a wounded man chained to the ground.

Leonard's pipe weapon had been sharpened on one end into a

tip. Now Tess noticed sharp metal thorns sticking off the outside of the pipe every two inches.

The jackal lifted his pipe and shoved it down through Rory's abdomen.

Tess fought to keep from throwing up. Every muscle in her body clenched at the brutal attack.

Rory howled in a sound that made her think of a large jungle cat that had been wounded. He gripped the titanium rod and jerked up, then sucked a breath in and stopped, doubled over.

"There you go, you fucking cat," Leonard chided. "Give me any more trouble before my superiors arrive and the next one goes through your balls. They have plans for you."

She waited as Leonard walked out, disappearing in the dark tunnel. Once his footfalls silenced, she rushed to Rory. "Oh, shit. What can I do?"

"Nothing," he gritted out.

"We have to do something or you'll die."

He gave a mirthless laugh. "No, they won't kill me yet. This is titanium. It won't allow me to heal while it's in my body. If it stays in long enough, I'd die, but that would be wasting a Ga... shifter. I could rip it out, but I'd need to shift immediately to heal all the new damage I'd cause."

"That sounds awful, but if you can handle the pain, then do it. I'll help."

"No. I can't heal fast enough to be of any help to you."

"I'll watch over you. Just fix yourself. You can leave me and go for help."

Rory finally took a long look at her. "I can see why Cole chose you. You'd make an excellent mate for him."

That was flattering, but Rory was still bleeding out of two wounds now.

He said, "Tess, I'm not going to die. I won't lie. Hurts like a ... son of a gun. But I need you to stay safe as you can until my people show up. Don't antagonize that jackal. They follow orders, but only to a point."

"Will your people find us?"

"Eventually. I'm just hoping they find us here, before Leonard's boss shows up with whatever plans he has or they move us. Or they separate us. None of those are good scenarios."

Rory didn't sound like he was trying to unnerve her but only trying to prepare her for potential situations. She appreciated his simple honesty. No trying to convince her all would be well, when it clearly didn't look possible at the moment.

She was going to have to finally accept that jackals who had traveled to this country to work as mercs could possibly have criminal intent. It went against all she believed in to consign one group with a predetermined evaluation, but from now on she would at least be on her guard.

She shoved loose hair off her face, no doubt still looking like hell, but she couldn't feel in control with her hair in her eyes. "I hear what you're saying and I won't antagonize him. I'm sorry if he did this to you because I yelled at him."

Rory unleashed a smile and she could see women falling all over themselves to catch this one. He said, "You didn't cause this. He had already planned to pin me with this pipe before he walked in."

Tess sat down next to him, trying not to think about how bizarre her life was at the moment.

She was in love with a wolf shifter.

She'd been captured by jackal shifters and locked in the basement of some building.

And she was sitting here carrying on a conversation with a man who might be a jungle cat shifter and had a three-foot pipe driven through his stomach.

Got it.

She murmured, "I have no idea why I'm here."

"I'll make an educated guess," Rory offered.

"Go for it."

"They plan to use you as bait to bring Cole in, then use you as motivation to make him do what they demand."

Tess had actually considered that but was hoping they wanted ransom money instead. "But what do they want?"

"We'd like to know, but I'm guessing they might think you and Cole were bonded. If so, it seems as if they'd have plans for both of you, but not to be together. If they know you aren't bonded, then there are many possibilities, none of which I want to go into."

She could push him, but she'd rather not think about how awful this could all get and focus on not letting any of those possibilities happen.

Rory pulled in a shallow breath and flinched, then grunted. He said, "It would help to know more about this group so we could get a step ahead of the Black River pack."

Her ears perked at the mention of that pack. "Is this the same group that has Sammy?"

"Probably. I'm pretty sure Sammy is being set up to take the fall for the couple murdered on their honeymoon."

"Sammy? *He's* the bear shifter SCIS has been hunting?"

"Yes, but Sammy has never harmed a human. He put his life in danger many times to save them."

"What about the mating curse? Would that make him lose control and kill someone?"

Rory gave her a long look as if surprised she knew about the curse, then explained, "It would if Sammy reached full loss of control. When that happens, the animal takes over and remains in that form until he does something self-destructive or is taken down, which usually happens first."

Silence trickled along between them for a moment.

Turning to her, Rory asked, "Do you love Cole?"

"What? Why do you ask?"

"Just ... answer," he ground out, clearly in pain.

Unwilling to make this moment any more difficult on Rory than it was, she gave him the truth. "Yes, I do. I don't care that he's a shifter. He's my Cole."

"Good. Then you can ... " He stopped talking and lifted a finger to keep her quiet.

A high-pitched noise deep in the tunnel shattered the quiet.

Rory went into what sounded like a combat tone. "Be quiet and don't react to anything."

Tess couldn't move a muscle out of pure terror.

CHAPTER 36

Cole followed the tracking signal being sent from the barrette Tess hopefully still wore until the transmission stopped. He ended up thirty miles outside of Spartanburg at a brick building that had once been a manufacturing plant.

At that point, he followed the scent that was driving him close to madness with worry. Tess's unique scent mixed with sheer terror.

Inside the building, Cole wasted no more than seconds taking out a jackal guarding the stairs.

That's how he found Tess in this underground room.

Bastards had chained her to the ground.

Gray Wolf roared inside, just as furious as Cole at seeing their mate chained.

One glance at Rory and Cole knew his friend had been staked with titanium. The ones who did this would all die.

Not slowing a step, Cole first reached Tess, who lunged up at him. He grabbed her in a hug, trying to quell her shaking. "Are you hurt?"

"No, but Rory is. He needs to shift." She started rambling at a rapid pace. "You have to get out. They're using me for bait. They have people coming."

"It's okay, baby."

"You have to go before they catch you."

"Screw them," Cole said. "I'm getting you both out of here with me. Can you stand?"

"Yes."

She smelled terrified, but her voice held the conviction that made her a woman deserving of all the admiration he felt for her.

When she let go of him to stand on her own, Cole backed up and held his hand out, feeding power down to both of his fists. He reached down and grabbed the thick chain. He channeled his extra Gallize power his into his limbs.

Stretching out the chain, he focused all his energy on the links, which heated as he pulled the chain in opposite directions.

The center link began squealing.

A crack started in the metal and kept opening up until there was a half-inch space.

He dropped the chain, heaving a couple hard breaths. That drained his energy, but with a little luck he'd have all three of them out of there before any other shifters showed up.

Looking at the ankle cuff, he said, "I don't have time for that right now, baby."

"How did you ... I mean ... that was insane," Tess mumbled.

He kissed her quickly. "I'll explain later. Can you walk with that?"

She snapped out of her moment of shock. "I'm good. What about Rory?"

Cole dropped down next to Rory. "Be ready. This is going to fucking hurt."

"Your bedside manner sucks. How'd you find us?"

"I put a tracker on her barrette."

Tess said, "No way."

Rory frowned. "You trusted her to wear that barrette? Are you kidding—"

Cole grabbed the stake and pulled, ripping flesh and muscle as he did. He could feel it. Bile ran up his throat at what he'd had to do for his friend.

Muscles in Rory's face and neck were taut when he stretched his head back and bit down, muffling a howl.

Cole told Tess, "Take off Rory's shirt."

She dropped down and started unbuttoning while Cole removed his boots and socks.

Rory fumbled, roughly unzipping his jeans, which Cole yanked off.

Tess stood with Rory's shirt in hand.

When his friend was down to nothing but cotton boxers that

would disintegrate easily, Cole said, "Shift. I've got your back."

Rory normally shifted slowly, allowing his animal time to acclimate, or so he said.

Not this time.

Pain must have driven him into an explosive change. One minute a man lay there and, in the next, the largest jaguar Cole was sure Tess had ever seen snarled and huffed under his breath.

"You're okay," Cole said, encouraging Rory to stay quiet.

Rory shook the chain off one leg now that his human foot was no longer there to prevent it sliding off. He turned his gaping maw to Tess whose eyes doubled in size. The jaguar had holes in his chest that didn't line up and were both leaking blood.

Then Rory keeled over, whining as his massive body landed next to the wall where he and Tess had been chained. Shit, Rory weighed too much and was too big in animal form for Cole to carry him out over his shoulder.

How was he going to get Rory and Tess out of here?

The roar of a grizzly raised the hair on Cole's head.

He turned, sick at what he scented coming toward him.

A ten-foot-tall grizzly standing upright on his hind legs slowly emerged from the dark tunnel.

He'd found Sammy.

Cole searched the bear's eyes for a sign of his friend. Sammy's normally warm brown gaze turned a bright amber color when he shifted.

There was too much white around the color of those too-yellow eyes.

No one was home.

Cole's worst nightmare had come to life.

He was going to have to fight Sammy

Cole had only one way to protect Rory and Tess. He told Tess, "Stay with Rory. Don't touch him. I trust his jaguar, but he's in a lot of pain. And don't leave this corner."

"What are you going to do?"

The bear stopped in the middle of the room and roared a challenge.

Gray Wolf snarled, ready to answer that challenge.

Cole grunted at the effort of keeping his wolf in hand. He told Tess, "I wish you didn't have to see this, but that's Sammy and he may have snapped. If so, the mating curse, magic, drugs or all the above has him and I'm the only one who can stop him."

He hoped he could back up those words.

It didn't matter. Cole had no choice. He told Tess, "Back up as far as you can."

She did as he said, standing against the wall next to Rory's jaguar that was panting hard for every breath.

Cole called up the change and not a second too late. His wolf was going mad over the need to attack the bear.

Shifting fast was never fun and even more painful with his wolf rushing to the surface. The minute Gray Wolf stood on all four paws, Cole warned him, *Don't shut me out if you want to protect our mate.*

We fight.

Yes. We fight to win. Cole hoped there was a sliver of sanity in Gray Wolf. He couldn't spare a look at Tess. Didn't want to see the gaze of disbelief on her face. If he died here, he wanted his last vision to be one to take to the grave.

Now, Cole had to convince himself he could defeat a bear twice his size who he'd battled many times before in training that had turned bloody.

Cole had never bested Sammy.

Sammy's bear unleashed a loud roar and dropped down on all fours, fangs on display.

Gray Wolf slowly moved to one side, circling the bear that turned with him.

Now able to speak to the shifters mind to mind, Cole first told Rory, *I know you're hurting and need to stay animal to heal, but Tess will need you in human form. She might try to help unless you can talk to her.*

Rory answered, *I can do it.*

As Cole got Sammy turned so that the bear's back was to Tess and Rory, Cole caught a glimpse of the jaguar crawling over to pile himself in front of Tess. Then Rory shifted to human, lying naked on his side with his back to Tess and pain etched in his face.

Cole could never thank his friend enough.

Tess had grabbed Rory's shirt and was wrapping his wounded shoulder.

Sammy stopped moving and snarled at Gray Wolf.

Wait, Cole told Gray Wolf. The only answer he got was Gray Wolf dropping his head down and the deep rumble of fury vibrating in his throat.

Cole tried reaching Sammy telepathically. *It's me, Cole. I'm here to help you.*

Sammy's words were garbled. *No help. Mate ... everyone die.*

No, Sammy, Cole said, as his huge wolf continued circling the bear, taking a step in and back. *I found Katelyn. She loves you and wants to talk to you. She wants you back.*

Cole hoped he was being honest by making that leap based on what Isabella had said.

Six-inch claws extended from Sammy's massive paws. He argued, *No mate. I have no mate.*

Cole pleaded, *Yes, you can have a mate. She loves you.*

Lifting his head, Sammy bellowed a noise to the heavens that sounded as if it had been ripped from his soul.

No dying animal could howl that awful.

When the monstrous bear head lowered back down to look at Gray Wolf continuing to prowl around him, Sammy said, *You killed her.*

Cole had his first real fear that Katelyn had been harmed. *No, Sammy, I would never hurt your mate. I found her for you.*

Sammy shook his head. *Dead. She's dead. I saw. Her body ripped by wolf.*

Fuck. If the Cadell had killed Katelyn, there was no hope for Sammy.

Cole had always thought he'd save Sammy and go with him to meet the Guardian when the time came.

He'd never planned on killing his best friend.

Gray Wolf roared right back at the grizzly.

Pitting two Gallize shifters against each other was a bad match even if everyone fought fair, but Sammy had lost his sole connection to humanity when he lost his mate.

CHAPTER 37

Tess did her best to help poor Rory, who had to be in agony. She might not be a shifter, but she'd studied enough to know that he would have been better off staying in his animal form to heal faster.

Her heart had climbed up her throat and threatened to choke her every time Cole's wolf or the bear snarled.

She whispered, "Shift back, Rory."

"I can't. I told Cole I'd be human so I could help you."

"When did you tell him that?"

"We can speak mind to mind in animal form, but I can't speak to Gray Wolf in my human form."

She kept her eyes on the humongous wolf that had once been Cole. Gray Wolf was just that. A stunning, silver-gray wolf that stood head high at her shoulder. He kept circling the bear, making threatening sounds, but neither had attacked yet.

Keeping her eyes on them, she asked, "Are Cole and Sammy talking?"

Rory was taking shallow breaths. "I'm sure Cole is trying to talk Sammy down off the ledge, but that bear is gone."

"I thought Cole had found Sammy's fiancée and she could save him."

"She'd have to be here now and ready to take him as a mate. Sammy might be lost to all of us."

The grizzly, Sammy, charged.

Gray Wolf backed up on his haunches and launched up at the ferocious bear.

They met in a clash of claws and teeth.

Tess breathed through her mouth to keep from passing out from the heavy odor of fresh blood. Her entire body shook from fear for Cole and Gray Wolf.

She wasn't squeamish, but she'd never been around this much carnage.

The shirt she'd wrapped around Rory had soaked through. He might bleed out if he couldn't shift back.

Rory gritted his teeth. "I need to help him."

"Sammy?"

Shaking his head, he said, "If Cole can't reach him no one can. They're best friends."

Tess wasn't sure her heart could take any more pain on Cole's behalf.

Rory said, "There's no one inside those yellow bear eyes. I need to help Cole fight him. I can't lose both of them."

She didn't want to lose Cole either. "Is there anything we can do?" She flinched at a vicious swipe Sammy's bear made.

"I can't help unless I shift again and I'd still need time to recover." He paused then said, "You're the only one who could make a difference in all of this."

She flinched when the bear snapped at Gray Wolf's hind leg, but the big wolf leapt away before those jaws ripped into him. "What do you mean, Rory? Tell me, because Cole's wolf is bleeding everywhere."

"You can't do anything until Cole shifts back into human form."

She had to lean close to Rory because his back was to her. She urged him, "Tell me so I can be ready."

"If you were his mate, Cole would be stronger. He's going to kill me for telling you, but neither of us may live long enough for the argument at this rate."

"He doesn't want me as his mate." She wanted to scream at Cole that he should pick a mate even if he didn't want it to be her. She wanted him to live even if it meant without her. "I don't want to watch Cole die."

Rory chuffed out a noise. "Then save him if you get the chance."

"What do you mean?"

The wolf ripped the grizzly's ankles, probably tearing at his

Achilles. Did bears have those?

"*Look out!*" Rory shouted as Sammy brought a claw down over the wolf's back.

Gray Wolf yelped and rolled away but then he was back on all fours with blood streaking his fur. His muzzle had been gashed and he limped.

Sammy's grizzly seemed to lose his direction, wandering around in a circle.

She looked at Rory. "Tell me how to save Cole."

"I shouldn't, but ... Cole is deep into the mating curse."

"No. He said he didn't want a mate and he had three years to go."

"Were those his exact words or did you just think he didn't want to mate?"

Tess realized Cole had talked around the topic without actually lying.

Sammy the bear chuffed one breath after another, each coming out in a pitiful rattle. A gaping hole had been slashed under his front legs. He'd backed into a corner, leaning against a wall. Gray Wolf stood in the middle of the room, still ready to fight.

Rory spoke softly. "Cole told you he didn't want a mate, because your dad would never accept it and Cole won't be the reason you lose another parent."

She stared at the wolf, sick that Cole would accept death over disrupting her world.

Didn't Cole know she had no world without him?

"I told him I love him," she said, more pissed than arguing. "Isn't that enough to become a mate?"

The bear started rocking back and forth as if he was getting revved up. He lifted up on his hind legs, showing more jagged rips in his massive chest, and walked out of the corner slowly.

Rory replied, "Admitting love is good, but only one step. In a mating ritual, both parties have to accept the mating bond. It's forever and Cole doesn't want to put that burden on you or risk that you won't survive his power, which is possible."

"What if I'm willing to accept the bond? Can I just yell it out to him?"

"You could reach him if he was in control, but it won't do any good with him in animal form right now. Gray Wolf is in power with Cole fighting to maintain control. Don't interfere and distract Gray Wolf. If that happens, Sammy will kill him. Then us."

CHAPTER 38

Cole felt every cut and gash that Gray Wolf suffered.

He was losing blood faster than Gray Wolf could regenerate.

The only reason his wolf still remained upright was because as vicious a fighter as Sammy's bear was, Cole's friend was no longer in his right mind.

His Sammy was gone.

Just admitting that punched his heart.

The grizzly fought out of pure rage and instinct. He was bleeding from three lethal wounds, too. Every cut on that bear stabbed Cole.

He'd failed to save Katelyn.

He'd failed to save Sammy. If not for trying to survive long enough to save Tess and Rory, Cole would quit fighting and wait for the end with Sammy. They could go together. Cole's soul screamed at losing all that mattered to him in this world.

The grizzly roared and came at Gray Wolf with jaws open.

Gray Wolf was ready to leap up and meet the grizzly in midair.

Cole told his wolf, *Don't jump. We'll lose. Go low.*

Would Gray Wolf listen?

Cole had no idea. At this point, he was riding shotgun in this fight and hoping if they managed to survive Sammy, that Cole could keep Gray Wolf from turning on Rory and Tess.

The wolf might not hurt Tess, but Rory would just be another threat to their mate.

As Sammy's giant bear pounded forward, weaving with each step, Gray Wolf jumped to the right and ran around.

That was not what Cole said to do.

Gray Wolf dove at Sammy, grabbing the ankle he hadn't ravaged yet and yanking back.

Sammy's bear howled in pain and struggled, turning around.

Then tilted back.

Oh, shit.

Move, Cole shouted to the wolf, which sidestepped just in time before Sammy fell on his back so hard the room shook. Bone in the bear's head cracked against the hard floor.

Before Cole could stop him, Gray Wolf had his jaws locked on the grizzly's exposed throat.

No, Gray Wolf.

Kill him, the wolf argued.

Don't do it. The bear is my friend.

Bad friend.

Sick friend, Cole argued. *Let me talk to him.*

The wolf kept his jaws in place but eased up, not making a move to rip through.

Sammy, can you hear me? Cole asked.

The voice that came into Cole's head sounded like it was from very far away, but more like the Sammy he knew. *Cole. They used magic on me. Made the curse worse. Can't control my bear. He wants to kill you.*

I know, Sammy.

Don't give in. He won't let me come back. Tell the Guardian I'm sorry. They gave me Jugo Loco and set my bear to kill that couple. I tried to stop it, but ... my bear had been starved for two days and wanted blood.

Pain bled through Sammy's words.

Cole hurt more than he thought possible. The only other time he'd hurt this much had been when he lost Tess at nineteen.

Cole said, *I'm sorry I didn't get Katelyn here in time, but I swear I didn't kill her.*

I know. Wolf didn't smell like you.

So a wolf had killed her. Cole told Gray Wolf, *Let Sammy live.*

The wolf snarled a dark sound, his jaws still locked in place.

If Cole didn't get control of his wolf, he wouldn't make it back to human form again. One last time, Cole drew on what magic he had available and powered his words.

Let the bear live, Gray Wolf. Do it now.

Gray Wolf's chest rumbled with each breath, but he finally unlocked his jaws and backed up three steps.

I'll miss ... you ... Cole. Good man. The best.

Cole could hardly send his words in reply. *You deserve peace, Sammy. I'll be here with you to the end.*

No, Sammy argued. *Shift back. Do it ... don't let ... the wolf win. Don't give in.*

Then Gray Wolf snarled, turning his head to the tunnel.

That fucking Brantley walked in.

Cole had been wondering if their kidnappers were nearby watching. They'd unleashed Sammy, expecting Sammy to kill Cole probably.

It would be like a Cadell to enjoy seeing one Gallize kill another one, then come in just in time to keep one of them alive.

That bastard Brantley was Cole's the minute he pointed Gray Wolf to attack, but a new scent had caught Gray Wolf's attention.

Cole had smelled that shifter scent before ... the night of the explosion. Glowing yellow eyes shined through from the tunnel, then a black wolf that stood eye level with Gray Wolf stepped up beside Brantley.

A fucking Black River pack wolf.

This had to be the shifter who had left Sonic sitting with a bomb between his legs.

As fresh as the blood had been on Sonic, this shifter had probably been the one to cut the snitch's throat.

Gray Wolf sniffed.

The black wolf stank of magic.

Cole started talking to Gray Wolf. *We have to be careful. This one is not like us.*

Gray Wolf howled and snarled his challenge.

That did not encourage Cole.

His wolf continued to pull away from him. Cole barely had a grasp on Gray Wolf, but he had to hold on so he could protect Rory and Tess.

Cole directed his wolf to walk around the feet of the grizzly still sprawled on the floor and wheezing.

Time to prepare for another battle.

Moving so quickly it surprised even Cole, the black wolf dropped back on his haunches and leaped on Sammy, ripping his throat viciously.

Sammy's head fell to the side.

Gray Wolf howled a mournful sound. Rory released a cry from the heart of his jaguar.

The black wolf looked past Cole and took a step toward Tess and Rory.

Cole roared to protect their mate.

Gray Wolf took over.

CHAPTER 39

Tess froze with her hand pressed on Rory's wound. He tensed.

Brantley. She would kill him if she could just get her hands on his neck.

Right now, she was more concerned with Gray Wolf and the black wolf that had just killed Sammy.

She couldn't imagine the pain Cole suffered. He'd been clearly trying to save his friend.

That miserable black wolf had stolen Sammy's last minutes.

The smell of blood bathed the air.

Yellow eyes didn't seem normal to Tess to begin with, but the black wolf's eyes glowed. He looked deranged.

And Brantley was behind this bloodbath.

Rory whispered, "If I have to shift, stay back as far as you can from all of us."

The building suddenly shook, as if a giant had wrenched it back and forth. What was that?

When the black wolf started toward her and Rory, trembling in her body spread throughout to her arms and legs, but she was not going to back away. Cole was exhausted and Rory would still be injured even in cat form.

She was so damn useless as a human.

She hated this.

Gray Wolf lunged at the black wolf and they turned into a blistering rush of snarling, clawing, biting beasts ripping into each other.

How much more damage could Gray Wolf take?

Within seconds, so much blood covered the fur on both wolves, she couldn't tell who was winning. She hoped her heart was stronger than her mother's, because it was in overdrive. She could see how this had been too much for her sweet mother.

Again, the building shuddered.

Rory cursed, "Don't know what's going on, but we need to get out of here soon."

"Are you shifting?"

"Not yet. Not unless Cole says he needs me to or if that black wolf heads this way again."

Cole's wolf yelped and flipped in the air, landing hard on his side. He shoved to his feet and weaved where he stood.

Tess said, "No." She couldn't watch Cole die. Tears poured down her face. The energy in her chest was spinning wildly, but it was of no use. At its worst, the energy had only killed a computer. Not any help here.

She begged, "Please, Rory, tell me how to reach Cole and connect this mating thing."

Rory's biceps pulsed when he fisted his hands. "I can't help unless I can talk to Cole, but he trusts me not to change unless he loses this fight or if I have to shift to protect you."

That would only happen if the black wolf killed Gray Wolf.

The next moment happened in a blur, but Tess knew she'd see it in slow motion over and over forever.

Going on attack, the black wolf went for Gray Wolf who kept his head down. The black wolf in turn clamped down on Gray Wolf's front leg.

Bone cracked loud enough to be heard.

The battle should have been done, but Gray Wolf came alive and twisted his neck under the head of the other wolf. Gray Wolf's huge jaws clamped down on the black wolf's throat.

They wrangled back and forth, but the black wolf gave up his hold on the crushed leg to put everything into getting his throat free.

Gray Wolf's eyes had an unholy look in them as he held on, shaking his head back and forth until he tore away muscle and veins, exposing the black wolf's throat, which was now bleeding profusely.

A thundering sound approached from the same dark hall that had vomited the black wolf.

Brantley ran to a wall on the left where he put his back to it and held his hands up in front of him.

Rory sat up and made an inhuman roar.

Gray Wolf took a step and fell on his side.

Even Brantley looked afraid.

CHAPTER 40

Tess jumped up as six beefed-up men flooded the room. With one look at Sammy's body, the men released a series of howls, growls and moans, sounding like a mix of animals.

Rory said to her, "These are our people. Stay down behind me or you put Cole in danger."

Those were the only words that could have stopped her from going to Gray Wolf, who was still on his side, panting. He could heal in wolf form, right?

Right behind the men, an unnaturally huge eagle came gliding through the tunnel. Gold eyes flashed with wrath.

Energy sparked where Brantley still held his hands up as if warding off an invisible threat.

Rory said, "What kind of power is that miserable piece of shit wielding?"

"Are you talking about Brantley? What's he doing?" Tess asked, now squatting behind Rory.

"He's producing a telekinetic field of power. Magic."

When the eagle landed and its powerful claws touched the ground, the majestic bird was as tall as Tess in her stocking feet.

Energy swirled around the giant bird.

In the next moment, the eagle had changed to a man dressed in a suit, and so smoothly it was as if there had been no actual shift from bird to human body.

Tess could feel the weight of this man's presence.

Okay, she'd seen it all now. "Cole needs me."

Rory lifted a bloody hand. "No. That's the Guardian. Our boss. Don't move yet."

"Cole could be dying."

"You risk killing him for sure if you get in the way when magic is involved."

Then their guardian needed to get busy doing whatever he planned to do. She could see the stuttering rise and fall of Gray Wolf's chest getting slower and slower. Blood oozed from too many cuts to count.

Why wasn't Cole's animal healing faster?

The Guardian took a look at the dead bear and his badly bleeding wolf, then at Brantley. He said, "I'm sorry we were too late for you, Sammy."

With that, the Guardian swung a vicious look at Brantley. "Your name is not Brantley. It's ... ah, Bastien. I knew of you as a child. You have made a grave error by touching one of mine."

Brantley had never looked frightened the entire time he worked with Tess, ordering people around like her ruled the earth, but he was scared now. "Your wolf killed our wolf. It was a justifiable fight."

"A Black River abomination is not worthy of a life," the Guardian said. "You made a careless mistake by setting a bomb for Cole."

"No, I made a mistake by allowing him ten seconds to suffer before he died. His fault. He walked right into my hands by coming after the wolf pack."

"So now you're a minion for the Black River pack?"

"Like hell." Brantley talked bold, but his fear was showing through. "Here's the deal. I was only told to take down Cavanaugh."

"You lie. You may have originally wanted only Cole, but you were also told to take his mate."

Tess stared at Brantley, sick about all the time she'd spent around him.

Brantley said, "If Cavanaugh lives, then keep him and your other animals out of our business. You don't want to cross my leader."

"Oh, but I do," the Guardian said in an accommodating tone. "Why don't you call Mother Cadellus here now?"

When Cole's boss smiled, hair stood on Tess's arms because of the threat in those eagle eyes in a human face.

The Guardian said in a taunting tone, "Ah, that's right. She's stuck in a cave in another country, but she didn't give you this level of power to hold a kinetic wall. Who have you been associating with? A Power Baron? What's his name?"

When Brantley didn't answer, the Guardian gave a soft nod. "He put a spell on you in case you were caught so you couldn't expose him. That's too bad. Your usefulness is dwindling by the second."

Brantley was clearly running out of options. As he kept his hands up to maintain his invisible shield, he started negotiating. "Look, let's be reasonable. We have her father. Let me go and I'll free him."

"That's a generous offer on your part."

Brantley smiled, the slimy bastard.

Tess ground her back teeth, needing to unload all her frustration on him. This worthless excuse for a human, or whatever he was, had terrified her father and bloodied Cole.

Gray Wolf was still bleeding heavily. Tess hoped that meant the Guardian had super powers or believed in Cole's.

The Guardian told Brantley, "Yes, quite an offer, but my people have killed the jackals you left in charge. Her father is safe. I have a message for you to deliver."

Tess thanked whoever had created the Guardian for saving her dad.

But was he going to just release that pig? She had a nice prison cell waiting for Brantley.

A subterranean cell.

"What's your message?" Brantley asked, but the color had flushed from his face.

The Guardian walked forward and shoved a hand right through Brantley's invisible shield. It cracked and exploded out in clear pieces, which floated in the air.

Brantley stared, open-mouthed.

The Guardian grabbed him by the neck with one hand and lifted him off the floor. Speaking calmly, the Guardian said, "Your Cadell kin will find this as my message."

When the Guardian squeezed, Brantley's eyes bulged, his tongue enlarged and protruded as he strangled to death.

Dropping his slack body to the floor, the Guardian crossed the room and went down on one knee next to Cole's wolf. Without looking away from the wolf, he said, "You may send the woman now, Rory."

Tess didn't wait for Rory to speak.

She leaped over him as one of the men guarding the room crossed over to Rory and squatted down, speaking low to him about his injuries.

When she reached Gray Wolf, Tess fell down next to his outstretched legs and stared into the blue eyes this wolf shared with Cole.

She said, "Hey, baby."

"He doesn't know you," the Guardian explained gently, but that just pissed her off.

She pushed up to face the Guardian. "Yes, he does! You don't know what you're talking about. He's the man I plan to marry so don't go telling me he doesn't know me."

All the low talking quieted.

Until now, these men had been casting glances at Gray Wolf, but making no move to go near him. It was like a collective intake of air as everyone swung their attention to the Guardian and waited to hear what he would say.

Or maybe they were waiting to see if he struck her down.

The Guardian studied her in such a bird-like way it was disconcerting. "You would marry Cole even though he is a shifter?"

"Well, duh. I'm saying it with him lying here as a wolf." She glanced down as Gray Wolf made a pained sound on the next breath. "Do something, dammit. He's dying."

"I'm sorry. It was his choice."

"What?" She looked up to face the Guardian straight on. "No, that's *not* his choice. He would want to stay with me. If you're the all-powerful Guardian, then tell Cole to change back so he can speak to us. He's not healing as a wolf. He needs medical attention."

In the silence that followed, Tess took in the other men who were looking away as if uncomfortable.

Twisting around in the other direction, she said, "Rory?"

"What our Guardian is trying to tell you is that Cole has been suffering with the mating curse, like Sammy was, but Cole managed to keep how badly affected he was from most of us until now. I think fighting Sammy snapped the wolf's connection to Cole's humanity and accelerated the influence of the curse."

Rory took a shuddered breath and in a voice thick with emotion, he said, "We've lost him."

"*No!*" She could have saved him with bonding as his mate. This was worse than the first time she lost him.

It was too much. She couldn't let him go.

Tess yelled at the Guardian, "You will do something! Fix this!"

He repeated, "I can't, child. Cole has taken it past the point any of us could intervene, even me. You are the only one who could have saved him. It was up to him to ask you to be his mate, but he was protecting you by not placing the burden on you to save him. All my shifters know that a mating bond must be freely given and accepted."

Her eyes burned with tears. She pleaded, "He's not a burden. He's the one person I need so I can breathe. I can't lose him."

Shifting his gaze to Cole, the Guardian said, "I've never seen one of mine this far gone who came back to his humanity. It's unfortunate, but the wolf has definitely taken full control."

"Fuck all of you," Tess said. "I am *not* losing him."

Another intake of breaths sounded around the room.

She lowered herself to lie down close to Gray Wolf's head so she could stare into his eyes.

They were definitely not human eyes.

Gray Wolf snarled, but there was no power behind it.

Reaching out, she put her hands on each side of his muzzle and got the wolf's full attention.

"Listen to me, Gray Wolf. I will not give up Cole. Not to you or anyone else. You will give him back to me. If you do, I will be the best mate you two could ever want. I. Am. Cole's. Mate. And he is mine. Give him back or ... take me with you."

Energy hummed in her chest like a turbine on high.

Tingling started up her arms. She held her breath, but the wolf did not change back to human.

She tightened her grip just enough to get the wolf to focus, because his breathing kept growing weaker. She couldn't use her hands to wipe the tears and sniffled her way through her words.

"Cole Cavanaugh and Gray Wolf, I love you both. I will love

you and be your mate for eternity. If you go, my heart goes with you. Do you take me as your mate? Will you be here for me or leave me to face the world alone?"

The tingling intensified.

Gray Wolf shut his eyes.

She couldn't catch her breath. No.

When the wolf blinked, Cole's human eyes stared back at her. Those gorgeous blue eyes held the same worried look as the day he'd told her he would never come between her and her father.

Drawing in a deep breath, she said, "How many times do I have to tell you to stop making my decisions for me? I'll handle my father if that's what you're worried about. I'm strong enough to accept your power and, if I'm not, then ... we go together. Now, are you going to accept my offer, or leave me to explain to these scary shifters that I wasn't good enough to be your mate?"

Gray Wolf's eyes close again.

Oh, no, that's not what she wanted her last words to him to be. "Cole, *please?*"

Energy pulsed through her arms and a bright light glowed over her and Gray Wolf ... who changed into Cole, her beautiful naked man even though he was beat to hell and bleeding profusely.

He gave her a weak smile and said, "I accept you ... as my mate ... forever."

The room erupted into a blast of cheers. She was laughing and crying.

Then Cole closed his eyes and his chest stopped moving.

She screamed, "No!"

CHAPTER 41

Three days later

Tess finished unpacking groceries and slammed the last cabinet, muttering to her empty kitchen the whole time. "He knew for weeks that he was suffering from that damned mating curse. Did he come looking for me? No. Did he tell me when he found me? No. Did he tell me when I told him I loved him? No."

She shoved the empty cloth bag into a cabinet. "Men are stupid. They need to be taught how to discuss their feelings and curses and other crap."

Two arms snaked around her waist from behind and she went still, holding her breath. When she exhaled, she said, "Please be real."

"Hello, beautiful."

Her heart thudded back to life at the sound of his hoarse words. She said, "You pissed me off."

He hugged her and snuggled against her neck. "I'm sorry I scared you. How long was I out?"

"Three days, six hours and something like twelve minutes." She hadn't looked at her watch since the groceries were delivered, but she'd counted minutes the entire time Cole slept in her apartment.

"How did you get the Guardian to bring me here? Not that I'm complaining, just surprised."

"Oh, he planned to take you wherever giant eagles live, but I put my foot down and reminded him that I was your mate and the only one who'd believed you could survive."

"I shouldn't have survived. I remember waking for a second and thinking I was dead, then the Guardian telling me the curse had been broken. It's all blurry. I don't understand. It should have been impossible."

"Nothing is impossible if you believe enough, and I did," she answered quietly, waiting to tell him everything that had happened until he'd had a little time to be awake. She'd been standing at the door to her bedroom when Cole's eyes had opened and the Guardian had spoken those words about the mating curse.

She'd wanted to push the Guardian away so she could look into Cole's eyes again, but Cole had passed out.

He clearly thought the Guardian had saved him.

She'd tell him the truth soon, but she wanted to just feel him, alive and breathing, next to her right now. The last three days had been a roller coaster through insanity, and she never wanted to get on that ride again.

First Cole had been dying, then he changed back to human form and she'd been relieved, only to have him black out from blood loss. She'd thought he had died after all, but the Guardian had put his hands on Cole's chest and declared him alive ... and beginning to heal. Cole changed one more time on the way to her apartment. His men and their guardian hadn't batted an eye.

At this point, she didn't care if he changed into a giraffe. She'd find a place to live with tall ceilings where he wouldn't have to bend over. He and Gray Wolf were hers.

She was a little nervous, but also excited about getting a chance to go into the woods with Cole and see Gray Wolf again soon.

But she never, *ever* wanted to see him with blood dripping from his fangs and wounds.

Once Cole's black ops shifter friends had him settled in her apartment, the Guardian explained that Cole's healing was accelerating from two shifts into his wolf. Evidently, as long as Cole was on the mend, and his wolf was calm, he wouldn't shift again until he woke up. The Guardian explained that Tess had a calming influence on Gray Wolf now that she'd mated with Cole, which would also help him heal.

The only worry she'd had at that point was her father, but he'd shown up at her apartment right behind them, delivered by the Guardian's men. The senator had been badly shaken, but he was alive and unharmed. She'd hugged him and cried, happy to have him back.

Instead of issuing orders and trying to take over the situation as he normally would, he'd stayed unusually quiet, subdued even, until the Guardian had turned as if to leave.

Her father had stepped over and shown her the man she'd grown up admiring when he thanked Cole's boss for saving his life. The Guardian gave him a gracious reply before leaving. After giving Tess another hug and gaining her promise to come home so they could talk, her father had left with two of Cole's friends who had been instructed to accompany the senator home.

That moment with The Guardian was a start, but her father could do more and possibly would, now that he knew first hand, and undeniably, that not all shifters were bad. At least the door had been opened for future conversations.

Remembering something she had to tell Cole, Tess first said, "I'm sorry about Sammy. I know you were close. I'm just so sad about him and Katelyn."

Cole squeezed her and said nothing at first. After a quiet moment and in a voice laden with hurt, he said, "I am, too, but Sammy was ready to join Katelyn. He was suffering more every day. I refused to believe he was gone already, but he was, even before I saw him the last time. The Guardian tried to tell me, but I think I had to see for myself to accept that we couldn't bring him back. I miss him so much it hurts, but I'm glad he's at peace. I hope he and Katelyn are together."

Her eyes misted. She'd thought of Sammy many times over the past three days, hurting for him, for Cole, and the rest of his team. Swallowing the lump in her throat, she said, "The Guardian said once you were better, he would call all of you together to say goodbye to Sammy."

She could feel Cole nod against the side of her neck, as though unable to speak.

She gripped the powerful arm wrapped around her middle. "I don't want to delay anything, but I'd like a little time together before we have to walk out the door and face everything."

"I want that, too. I'm honestly surprised the Guardian doesn't have us *both* in one of his facilities," Cole said, snuggling his head against hers and giving her a kiss on the temple. The sound she made should be bottled and labeled *happiness*.

"That wasn't happening and your boss knew it," she explained.

"When he said you would heal on your own, I made it clear that I wanted you at home—with me—and he agreed."

Looking back on her confrontation with the Guardian, she realized how he'd allowed her to get away with ordering him around.

Rory and the other guys had stared at her as if she were a mouse swatting at a tiger.

But the Guardian had given her a smile and said, "Do you know what you are?"

"A pissed-off mate at the moment?" she'd replied, ready to get Cole out of there.

"You saved him. That required an extraordinary power. You must be a Gallize female."

"But ... Cole told me about their traits. I don't fit the criteria."

"That is perplexing and we'll have to review it again with you, but I don't make a habit of arguing with success."

The men had cheered again but this time just for her.

She'd been in tears and not caring who saw her cry.

When the room had quieted, the Guardian said, "You have earned the right to decide for your mate." That's when he arranged to have Cole brought to her place and left a contingent of shifters guarding them.

Cole brought her back to the present by nuzzling her neck, getting his tongue involved. She flashed hot all over and her energy that had been buzzing happily kicked up a notch, but satisfying that hungry energy needed to wait a little longer.

There was too much to talk about.

She had to make him understand, so he'd knock off this stupid martyr complex he had going when it came to her. She patted his arm. "I think the Guardian knew better than to cross me on this."

Cole groaned, but it was all for show. Admiration flowed through his voice. "The Guardian respects power. I bet he loved you being all bossy and figured you're not going away as long as I'm alive, which better be true." Cole kissed her neck again and sighed. "He even said something similar about believing in the impossible last week when I told him there was no way for us to be together."

She smiled over the compliment and over Cole thinking his Guardian was allowing her to stay around out of the goodness of his heart. She didn't think a man like him made decisions that way. "The Guardian did say when you were feeling better to bring me to his bat cave so we could join forces to work on stopping the Black River wolf pack."

"Bat cave?"

"Eh, he might have said his penthouse."

Cole pulled her tighter. "You're too adorable, even when you were ranting about me when I came into the kitchen. I really am sorry I scared you, baby."

She swallowed the emotion choking her and said, "I'm not pissed about you scaring me, because you sleeping for three days is not anything close to watching you fight two massive animals to the death. But I'm *furious* that you would risk dying rather than give me the chance to decide about being your mate."

His sigh brushed over her hair and he dropped his chin on her head. He tucked her closer to him and she went willingly. He said, "I don't want to see you lose your father over a shifter after you lost your mother that way, or face conflict over being with someone like me."

One day, she would teach this man to stop trying to give her a perfect world. All she wanted was one full of love. "My mother didn't die because of a shifter. In fact, before I was kidnapped, I spoke to the alpha of a pride. He was there the day my mother died. He was trying to protect her. When the jackal tried to mug my mother, that alpha intervened and ended up arrested because of shifting. The shifting and the battle wasn't his fault. I think my mother would have been just as terrified and still had a heart attack even if a human had mugged her. But that alpha was with her while she was still alive and passed along a message from her that I should follow my heart. That's what I'm doing right now."

"Your father will never accept ... me."

"That's his choice, just like it's mine to choose who I want to spend my life with. I was terrified when they kidnapped him and unbelievably relieved when your boss and your team saved my father. I love him and he loves me, but our relationship has been little more than polite for a long time. That's going to change. At the moment, I'm pissed at him, though, because he's been interfering with my job and not respecting my choices. When you're healed, I'm going to find out who referred Brantley to my father, because I found out that my father got Brantley his position with SCIS."

"We'll find out, and it'll be taken care of," Cole said, sounding like a man about to lead a charge.

She spun in his arms. "See? There you go again. You're fine with my dad not dictating my life, but you better understand that you and your bunch of Gallize shifters are not going to make my decisions, either."

"Tess—"

"*I* saved you for *me,* Cole. *My* power bonded with yours." She hadn't planned to spit it out like that, but her emotions were running unchecked.

Cole stared at her. "I ... thought I dreamed about us bonding."

"You don't feel the bond?" For the first time, she feared having done it wrong.

He stood there, a mix of emotions flickering in his eyes. "Yes, but I thought, hell I don't know. I thought the Guardian had done something to heal me and that was the reason for this incredible peace I feel. Even Gray Wolf is truly calm." He lifted his hands to grasp her arms. "We really did bond ...?"

"Yes. As you lay there dying, my energy went into overdrive and I begged Gray Wolf to give you back to me," she whispered. "I promised to be a good mate to both of you. Forever."

Pure shock rode across his face, then a smile that she would remember for the rest of her life. He picked her up, kissing her as he swung her around.

She was laughing and crying. "Put me down you brute. You'll hurt yourself."

"Holding you could never hurt me." He pulled her back down in front of him. "You're sure my power didn't harm you in any way?"

She put a hand on his chest. "No, and for your information, your guardian said *I'm* a Gallize too, so you're not the only hot shit here these days," she bragged, not the least bit bashful about it. But as she thought again about how close she'd come to losing Cole, she couldn't hold the smart-ass tone. Her voice broke, coming out a whisper. "That's why I was able to save you when no one else could, not even the Guardian."

Cole's jaw dropped open. "But you don't have two of the traits, just the blue-moon birthday month."

"When your guardian said he didn't understand either because the Gallize women are always second born, I came home and did some digging to see if there was anything else I didn't know. My parents lost their first child. She only lived a week. I'm sure it was devastating so I don't think they could handle talking about her. Then when my mom died, my dad would not talk about anything from the past. That has to change for us to move forward. His stubborn determination to have his own way may have put me in real danger because of Brantley and that may actually shock him enough to open a new door for us. I'm going to find a way to work through all this with him, but I'm in your secret club now."

Cole just stared at her in awe. "You're really a Gallize."

The wonder in his voice snuggled up next to her ego and gave it a warm hug. She'd never felt more special than now.

He ran a hand over his head, trying to take it all in. "Oh, shit, that means ... that means I can tell you everything."

"Damn straight."

That earned her a smoldering kiss. She hoped he was healing fast, because he was revving up her energy and she had plans for that body.

He pulled her close to him in a hug that let her know she was his and said in a humble tone, "Thank you for saving me. I thought our bonding was me fantasizing, but I remember hearing your voice like an echo deep in a cave. Slowly, Gray Wolf receded, then I started hearing you clearly when you said you wanted to be my mate forever. That's the moment I thought I had died and gone wherever lucky shifters went in the afterlife, because I felt the power and love of opening up to join with you as my mate." He kissed her head. "You broke the mating curse for me. That's not something any other power on Earth could do."

She experienced a rush of pride at truly being his equal.

He smiled at her. "That means there is nothing more powerful than your love, but mine's just as strong for you."

She burst into tears.

Cole hugged her to him, whispering words of love and running his hands over her. "I'm so sorry, baby."

Tess stopped crying, sniffled hard once and said, "You should be. Keeping that mating curse from me was a total dick thing to do."

His chest moved with his laughter. "My woman is never one to sugarcoat it."

"The men in my life had better learn that, too." She pushed back so she could face Cole. "Are you feeling better?"

He gave her a wicked look. "Want me to show you how good I feel?"

Tess's wild energy had calmed to a feeling of just being very alive, but that threatened to rev it right back up again. He had better get ready for a mate who wanted his body all day and night. But first she had something else to say. "I want to go to Virginia next week and talk to my father."

Disappointment crossed Cole's face briefly, then he said, "Of course, and I'll support whatever you decide."

She frowned. Did he think she was going alone? She arched an eyebrow at him. "Good, because you're going to be right there with me when I announce our engagement."

His lips parted. He closed his gaping mouth then asked, "Are you sure you want to do that?"

"Listen up, shifter, I'm one hundred percent your mate, but I'm also human. You're marrying me."

Cole's eyes were suspiciously shiny. "I was planning to ask you the night I left seven years ago. From the moment I bought a ring that afternoon, I'd started feeling strange. I didn't realize I had taken you as my mate at that point. By the time I got to your place, I couldn't stand being in my body. I thought I was sick and left to get my shit together. That's when everything spun out of control."

Her chest clenched at being reminded of how much they'd both been through to reach this point. "You better be able to find that ring. That's the one I intend to wear."

His blue eyes sparked with love. "It's the only thing I kept from my original life. But ... we're going to go out to dinner and let me ask you like I planned."

"Okay." Why did she sound like a little girl?

Maybe because her dreams were coming true?

"Do you plan to tell your dad I'm a shifter, because he'll find out eventually?"

"I already told him when they brought him here after the Guardian rescued him. I told him I couldn't go home with him while the man I loved was in my bedroom healing from his battle with another shifter. It might be a little surprising to find out it's you, but we'll explain what happened during your missing years. He's about to get a new education in shifters from his daughter."

"I'll go anywhere with you, but I don't want you being caught between—"

She put her finger on his lips. "My dad is healthy as an ox. His heart is fine. I'm not living my life based on what-ifs. My mom constantly told me to not do things just to please him. She would have thanked the shifter who intervened the day she died if she'd lived long enough to do it."

"I always liked your mother. She was her own woman."

Tess gave him a watery smile. "She liked you, too. She was a fair and open-minded person. She'd be cheering me right now and would love having you, a wolf shifter, as her son-in-law. I will expect no less of my father if he wants a relationship with me. It may not be smooth sailing for a while, but I'm good with that as long as I have you."

Cole kissed her with enough heat to burn her panties off. "I'm yours forever, baby."

"And I'm your mate forever, wolf."

The End.

Thank you for reading my new shifter series. I hope you enjoyed it and would appreciate a review wherever you buy your books.

Coming up next is **MATING A GRIZZLY, Justin's story**. All the books are stand alones, so you can read them in any order. If you'd like to be notified of each future releases and special deals I offer my readers, just sign up for my newsletter at www.**AuthorDiannaLove**.com and/or join my PRIVATE READER COMMUNITY Group on Facebook. I DO NOT share anyone's information. I hate to have mine shared. All I do is send you occasional news, extra content and exclusive material from time to time.

January 2018

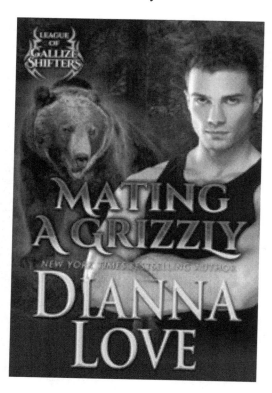

Raves about Dianna's other series:

Belador urban fantasy:

"When it comes to urban fantasy, Dianna Love is a master." Always Reviewing.

"There is so much action in this book I feel like I've burned calories just reading it." D Antonio

"There are SO many things in this series that I want to learn more about; there's no way I could list them all." Lily, Romance Junkies Reviews

Slye Temp romantic thrillers:

*"...suspense, thrills, excitement, danger and a super romantic couple...**Dianna Love** writes romance suspense so well, as I consider her one of the best at creating believability and hooking us in from the start all the way to the exciting climax."* ~~ Barb, The Reading Cafe

"Dianna never disappoints! ... would have give it a 10 if they would let!!! Very enjoyable read, can't wait for the next one :-)." ~~ Amy, Goodreads

"...one of those books that you wish would go on forever." ~~Billie Jo, Romance Junkies

Red Moon young adult sci-fi/fantasy series by Micah Caida (pen name of collaborators Dianna Love & Mary Buckham):

"Time Trap is amazingly original and unexpected...I loved

every second of reading it!"~~ Alexandra F, 15, who has read *The Book Thief, The Hunger Games,* and *Anna Karenina.*

"I was totally captivated by every scene in the first book...The imagination of Micah Caida takes the reader on an exhilarating journey...TIME TRAP is originality at its best." ~~Amelia Richard (adult), SingleTitles.com

"Reading this book is like riding on a roller coaster, getting to the top and not knowing when the next drop is."~~ Alex B, 12 years old and has also read all of *Rick Riordan's* books, the *Hunger Games,* the *Chronicles of Nick,* and the *Rangers Apprentice* series.

More By Dianna:

Dianna also writes the Belador urban fantasy series and the Slye Temp romantic thriller series (completed for those who want to binge read!). Keep watch for more Belador books and her new League of Gallize Shifters coming out soon.

Book 1: Blood Trinity
Book 2: Alterant
Book 3: The Curse
Book 4: Rise Of The Gryphon
Book 5: Demon Storm
Book 6: Witchlock
Book 7: Rogue Belador
Book 8: Dragon King Of Treoir
Book 9: Belador Cosaint
Book 10: Treoir Dragon Hoard (2018)
Tristan's Escape: A Belador Novella

*To keep up with all of Dianna's releases: sign up for her newsletter at http://authordiannalove.com/connect

The complete Slye Temp romantic suspense series

Prequel: Last Chance To Run (free e-book for limited time)
Book 1: Nowhere Safe
Book 2: Honeymoon To Die For
Book 3: Kiss The Enemy
Book 4: Deceptive Treasures
Book 5: Stolen Vengeance
Book 6: Fatal Promise

For Young Adult Fans – the explosive sci-fi/fantasy Red Moon trilogy by *USA Today* bestseller Micah Caida (collaboration of *New York Times* Bestseller Dianna Love and *USA Today* bestseller Mary Buckham).

Book 1: Time Trap (e-book free for limited time)
Book 2: Time Return
Book 3: Time Lock

To buy books and read more excerpts, go to
http://www.MicahCaida.com

Author's Bio

New York Times bestseller Dianna Love once dangled over a hundred feet in the air to create unusual marketing projects for Fortune 500 companies. She now writes high-octane romantic thrillers, young adult and urban fantasy. Fans of the bestselling Belador urban fantasy series will be thrilled to know more books are coming after Belador Cosaint plus Dianna is launching a new paranormal romance series – League of Gallize Shifters. Her sexy Slye Temp romantic thriller series wrapped up with Gage and Sabrina's book–Fatal Promise–but Dianna has plans for HAMR BROTHERHOOD, a spinoff romantic suspense series coming soon. Look for her books in print, e-book and audio (most series). On the rare occasions Dianna is out of her writing cave, she tours the country on her BMW motorcycle searching for new story locations. Dianna lives in the Atlanta, GA area with her husband, who is a motorcycle instructor, and with a tank full of unruly saltwater critters.

Visit her website at Dianna Love or Join her Dianna Love Reader Community (group page) on Facebook and get in on the fun!

A word from Dianna...

Thank you for reading *Gray Wolf Mate*. I've been so excited to get this book on paper. It's a new series with fun world building – I hope you enjoyed it.

As always, my amazing husband is the wall at my back that keeps me moving forward. Karl still surprises me to this day, a romantic at heart and I love him for it.

A special thank you to Jennifer Cazares and Sherry Arnold for being very early super readers who put fresh eyes on the pages after they've been through a gauntlet of readers and editing. Thank you for always stepping up to read whenever I need it and sometimes on short notice (sorry! :->).

I always mention Cassondra, who has been with me through too many books to count. She has a sharp eye for details and does a great job of helping with continuity. Her husband, Steve, has jumped in to read and give a new perspective on pages any time we needed it. He sees the most amazing things. I'm still smiling over the last note from Judy Carney after doing an early edit read. I love that she enjoys my stories so much. No story goes out without Joyce Ann McLaughlin reading through and catching her own special edits. I do hope to have this series in audio (soon, please be patient with me since it's a huge investment) and when that happens Joyce Ann graciously steps up to be my audio editor.

Here's cyber hug to Kimber Mirabella and Sharon Livingston Griffiths, who find time to read the early pages, too. They also bring a joy into my world with their messages of encouragement. A special shout out to Candace Fox who does a bazillion things to help me online with guest visits on our Reader Community Facebook page and supporting my books all over the place. Thanks also to all of my awesome early review team who have been with me for a long time – you just keep amazing me. I really appreciate the wonderful ideas Leiha Mann comes up with to help me connect with readers. Thanks for supporting me from my first book!

Sending a special hug to Xiamara Parathenopaeus, of S Squared Productions for all the wonderful art and promotional creations.

The very talented Kim Killion has once again created a cover I love, and Jennifer Litteken thankfully accepts my "help Mr.

Wizard" call when I need formatting.

I have a special place in my heart for Karen Marie Moning for more her sincere friendship and the wonderful time Karl and I spent with her this year.

Sending more love to my peeps on the Dianna Love Reader Group on Facebook. You rock big time.

Dianna